D0729895

COLOR FROM A LIGHT WITHIN

A Novel Based on the Life of El Greco

Other books by the same author:

THE PALACE GUARD
PUTNAM'S GUIDE TO THE ART CENTERS OF EUROPE

COLOR
FROM A LIGHT
WITHIN   *A Novel*

Based on the Life of El Greco

by DONALD BRAIDER

G. P. Putnam's Sons, New York

Southern Baptist
FELIX GOODSON
LIBRARY
Walnut Ridge,

Copyright © 1967 by Donald Braider

This book, or parts thereof, must not be reproduced in any form without permission. Published simultaneously in the Dominion of Canada by Longmans Canada Limited, Toronto.

Library of Congress Catalog Card Number: 66-20265

PRINTED IN THE UNITED STATES OF AMERICA

23,455

F
B731c

12-30-67 B.T 6.95

For Katharine and Baekeland Roll, with my dearest love.
And for the memory of Jackson Pollock and Franz Kline.

I should like here to acknowledge gratefully the friendly assistance and guidance so generously offered me by one of the most distinguished of El Greco scholars, Professor Harold E. Wethey of the University of Michigan, and by Mrs. Wethey. They are, of course, in no way responsible for errors that may appear. But without their help, the errors would doubtless be far more numerous.

"Out of your proof you speak: we, poor unfledged,
Have never wing'd from view o' the nest, nor know not
What air's from home. Haply this life is best,
If quiet life be best; sweeter to you
That have a sharper known; well corresponding
With your stiff age: but unto us it is
A cell of ignorance; travelling a-bed;
A prison for a debtor, that dares not
To stride a limit."

—CYMBELINE

PART I:

Crete (1541–1560)

FELIX GOODSON LIBRARY

One

MASS was being chanted in the Metropolitan Church of Candia. Worshipers, dressed in their best Sunday black, knelt in prayer as the familiar polyphonic intonations echoed sonorously. Except for the hundred little ovals of candlelight that illuminated the altar, all was obscurity within the church. It was a gray November morning in 1546. Little could be discerned, save for the movements of the celebrants.

Suddenly, the rays of the autumnal sun pierced the banks of low-hanging cloud and shone dazzlingly through the narrow windows of the nave, catching the twin icon paintings of St. Catherine and St. Titus, patrons of Crete, that adorned the simple iconostasis. The gold of the frames and the silver and encrusted jewels of the panels' surfaces flashed brilliantly.

The abruptness of the sun's appearance startled the small boy who sat near the front of the church with his parents and his older brother. He looked up from his prayers, whose strange-sounding words, in any case, he understood not at all. By now, nearly two hours after the long Eastern ritual had begun, he was bored; it was the only feeling he had ever associated with God and His Earthly servitors. As his eyes rose, he saw the paired icons blazing in the white fall sunlight. He stared. Never before in the whole of his five years had he seen anything so wonderful. As it happened, until this moment he had never even noticed these little pictures so venerated by adult parishioners. The images were beautiful, he thought, so very beautiful. He gazed at them in the burst of light, transfixed, and in this moment realized that he would never be the same again, that in some manner as yet unclear to him, he had been transfigured.

The sunlight failed as suddenly as it had revealed itself. Through-out the remaining hour of the mass, Domenikos found it impossible to avert his eyes from the iconostasis; the sun might illuminate it once again. He found it difficult even to blink, fearing that some quality, some detail of the pictures, might thus escape his notice. He regarded them, and yet recognized that he wasn't looking at them at all. It was as if he were seeing through them, but seeing *what?* That he couldn't have said. Whether in the icons or in himself, he had discovered something sublime.

It was only when his father touched his shoulder as the benediction concluded the service, the gesture causing him to start with surprise and disappointment, that at last Domenikos was made to look away, numbed by the unfamiliar emotion. He appreciated that something magnificent and stunning had happened to him, for in its aftermath he was trembling.

The little family left the white-walled church and emerged into the pale gray brightness of the daylight, into the Mediterranean air which caused the leaving congregation to cough, so briskly did it contrast with the incense-laden stuffiness of the interior. While mother, father, and brother chattered, Domenikos Theotokopoulos accompanied them homeward in complete silence, something he had never previously done after mass; as a rule, he babbled, coherently or not, simply out of relief. But now he was still; in his eyes he retained with a precious exactitude the vision he had had of the two saints caught in the sudden sunlight.

His mother knew the boy too well. "What's the matter with you, Menegos?"

The little boy refused to say a word. He shook his head slowly, still reluctant to disturb the brilliant image held, more and more tenuously as the minutes passed, in his memory's eye.

"Are you all right, boy?" inquired his father, but very casually, because he had noticed nothing amiss.

And once again, Domenikos merely revolved his small, dark, shocky head.

"Speak up," the man commanded, his tone sharp but not unkind.

"Nothing, papa," the child mumbled softly.

It was a soft spring day in the year 1552. The breeze that came through the opened window was beckoning and sweet, filled with sunlight and the odor of early blossoms.

Everyone entitled to an opinion agreed that Domenikos was a

gifted pupil, eager with relevant responses, capable in his understanding, able quickly to relate information acquired in one area of knowledge to experience encountered in another. He, however, thought himself no more than a normal boy of eleven. All he wanted to do at this moment was go out into the country that he loved so much, to walk, to run, to leap, or simply to lie down beneath a tree and let the soft March air play over his long, thin face.

Instead, he found himself in a large, familiar room of the Monastery of St. Catherine, half-listening to brother Constantine, who would, he imagined, soon begin yet another class in drawing. It wasn't that he had anything against drawing; indeed, he had long found it his favorite class. Domenikos had never forgotten that instant, six years before, when he had first been moved by pictures. Moreover, he was considered by Brother Constantine to be very good at drawing—his best pupil, in fact. He and his classmates had been learning to sketch and draw for a long time, for two school years. They had been taught first how to use charcoal and then had switched to ink, discovering as they progressed how to achieve total precision in their work.

But it was spring now, the first real spring day, and Domenikos felt he could afford the little luxury of inattention at so glorious a time. Furthermore, he had no reason to suppose that this was going to be anything but just another class in drawing. He supposed it was the rules that bored him, for they prevented him from attempting to sketch the things and people he observed. Learning to draw precisely, though a simple matter for him, was far from easy for his fellows. So he had been compelled to wait, with growing impatience, as they attempted to attain his level of proficiency. Domenikos was not smug about his talent. It was a condition over which he had no control.

Brother Constantine was standing in the arched doorway of the bright room. He brushed back the cowl of his habit to disclose a narrow, ascetic face and deep-set eyes—hunted eyes, Domenikos often thought them. His cheeks, his mouth, his chin were concealed by a black beard and moustache that were streaked with gray. He smiled, and even in this expression, ostensibly of mild amusement, there was a trace of anguish, or sorrow, as if it evoked a remembrance of some sad experience. "Who will volunteer," he began in his high-pitched, quite unpleasant voice, "to go to the poultry house for me?"

Before the fourth word had escaped the monk's lips, Domenikos had sprung up from his hard bench and was making for the door.

"And find me three eggs?" Brother Constantine concluded.

The boy nearly slipped on the terra-cotta floor, so abruptly did he bring himself to a halt before the tall figure of his master. He looked up in perplexity. "Eggs, brother?"

"Eggs, Dominikos. Three eggs." He raised three skeletal fingers, the nails grimy. "And I implore you not to spend the whole day at it."

"But what would we want with eggs, brother?"

"We're going to paint with them. We're going to make tempera colors with them."

"With eggs, brother?"

The boy giggled at the very preposterousness of the idea. His laughter was inevitably followed at once by that of the other pupils. "Do you really mean that we're going to make colors with eggs, brother?"

The monk grinned, exposing a jagged row of little, most imperfect teeth. With a wave of his long, thin hand, the pale wrist and forearm appearing as the dark sleeve fell back, he despatched Dominikos from the room.

The boy disappeared hastily in the direction of the base court, where the hens and other domestic beasts were more or less confined. (Some occasionally escaped and entered the classrooms, even the chapel.) He was delighted to have his wish for escape realized, to be in the open air on this lovely day. He paused and reflectively caressed the soft ears of a patient donkey. There was no need to hurry. In spite of this temptation to dally, he was intrigued by the prospect of learning by what strange process one converted eggs into color. He remained by the ass's head, indecisive.

His mother believed that Dominikos was too tall for his age. He wasn't, as a matter of fact, very tall; his height was exaggerated by his leanness, by his narrow bones, by his sharp, somewhat elongated features which were dominated by a long, slender nose and enormous, wide, black eyes that seemed never to lose their intensity. Nothing eluded his attention, when he was attentive. The color of his hair set him apart from most Cretans, for it was much lighter than was common on the island. And never was the slight oddity more marked than when, as now, he was wearing the dark cassock affected by lay pupils.

With sudden resolution, he proceeded to the poultry house. His delicate hands moved with efficient speed as he plucked the required eggs from the nests. The hens scolded noisily and scurried distractedly hither and thither across the broad courtyard, raising little puffs of dust with their claws and the frenzied flapping of their futile wings. Impulsively, he chased a hen all the way across the area, laughing riotously. Then he straightened himself, holding the eggs carefully with both hands, and made for the classroom, his curiosity prevailing against all other urges.

As soon as Domenikos returned, Brother Constantine began to demonstrate the method of mixing eggs with water and pigments to make tempera colors.

"It is very important," he said as he cracked a shell on the edge of a bowl, "that you employ an egg that is absolutely fresh. And you have to separate the yolk from the white very carefully." He accomplished this deftly, pouring the clear albumen into one container, the yellow into another. "Now, some painters I've heard of mix the two together, but in my experience this does not give you the density of colors that you require for some of the darker shades." Brother Constantine added a bit of water from a blue ceramic ewer. "You mix the yolk and the water together very, very slowly." His voice was patient. "Not quickly, definitely not quickly. You are not going to make a meal of it." He completed this operation, and then poured a small quantity of the unctuous mixture into a small shallow dish. To terminate the process, he took a pinch of what appeared to be pulverized earth, almost black when seen from Domenikos' distance. "Now, you must add your pigment. And always remember that it has to be a pure powder. If it is at all lumpy, grind it in a mortar. Otherwise, you will never succeed in making it blend properly with the yolk and water."

Brother Constantine hesitated and looked at the little cluster of pupils, his intense, dark, doleful eyes full of wonder, expressive of as much delight as a perpetually sorrowful temperament permitted him. It seemed that he had never ceased to marvel at what a perfect, if modest, miracle the good God had made it possible for him to perform. His face immediately straightened. "But once you have your color mixed properly, you have to use it quickly. If you do not, the egg yolk dries up and your paint will be wasted." He picked up a small rectangular panel, holding it with one hand and pointing to it with the other. "This piece of wood has been specially prepared with something called gesso, a thin coating of white plaster." He beckoned to the boys to come nearer to him. With a narrow brush, he painted a few short strokes on the smooth surface.

"What a wonderful dark blue," Domenikos exclaimed.

The monk glanced at him, his black eyes bright. "Ah, yes, it is a very fine color. But that is one of the first things you must pay attention to. With tempera, the colors become paler and more transparent as they dry. Watch."

And it was true. Domenikos observed, fascinated, as in a few moments the deep blue which Brother Constantine had so recently applied faded to a faint, translucent film, barely distinguishable from the white of the panel. "But how do you get the darker colors, brother, if they all fade that way?"

The responding gaze was patient. "It is quite simple, though it is a bit tedious. You just keep adding layers of paint until you have the strength you require." He then showed the boys how this was done. He painted over the brushstroke he had just made, so that they could not fail to see the difference that each additional layer made. At last, he turned to Domenikos.

"All right, now you try it." He smiled sadly. "But there is no point in your mixing the egg with water this time. We have plenty. No reason to waste another egg. So you pour some of this that I have made into a clean dish and add a different color of pigment to it."

The boy was enchanted. Indeed, he realized at once that this was a great moment, comparable only to that experience in the church. He did his best, however, to conceal his emotion. He poured a small quantity of the mixture into a dish, and with the tips of his narrow, soiled fingers, as he had seen Brother Constantine do, sprinkled some pigment—red it was, vermilion—into the shallow vessel. He began to blend this combination with a spatula. In his eagerness, he succeeded almost at once in beating the now-pasty formula into a froth. "No, no," said the brother, his tone gentle but full of anguish. "As usual, Domenikos, your ears have been in your eyes while I was talking a moment ago. You were not listening when I told you to mix it very slowly."

"I'm sorry, brother. I forgot myself. Is it ruined?"

"It is. You will have to start again."

"I thought——"

"Whatever you thought was mistaken. The point I've been trying to make," and here he addressed the whole group, "is that you are not proposing, or at least I trust that you are not, to make a meal of this. You are going to paint with it." His eyes gleamed with suppressed amusement. "Have you ever imagined it possible, Domenikos, to paint a picture with bubbles?"

However gently put, the question naturally provoked an explosion of laughter from the other boys. Domenikos could feel the hot blood of embarrassment and anger rush to his face. He was no fonder than anyone else of feeling himself the fool. Brother Constantine raised a hand in remonstrance. "It is not Christian, my children, to enjoy the mistakes of others."

The boys immediately repressed their laughter, but it was, Domenikos knew, difficult for them. And he knew too that they would tease him about it afterward. Later, when it was the turn of another pupil to err, he was himself sorely moved to laugh.

"Now, Domenikos," said Brother Constantine when the boy had finally concocted a satisfactory tempera, "I want you to paint a few strokes on the panel."

Domenikos was surprised by the slippery ease with which the color went on the surface. He painted a straight line, then a simple curve, then an S-shaped figure, and returned the brush to the dish of red tempera.

"No, my son. You will have to put the brush in clear water. If you don't, it will stiffen right away and have to be soaked in warm water before you can use it again."

The boy, his ears in his eyes again, didn't hear the brother, who found it necessary to repeat the instruction twice more before Domenikos complied, so dazed was he. At prayers that evening, in the plain white chapel, he expressed his most fervent thanks to God for having put color in his hands. The prolonged service of the mass passed quickly for him; his mind was concentrated on the image his eyes preserved—that of his hand dipping the little brush into the dish of vermilion tempera, and then applying it to the panel. He recalled nothing else that happened that day.

When the last sound of the office died in the throats of the monks and pupils, Domenikos began his homeward walk down the slope to Candia, his pace slower than usual, his eyes wide and apparently vacant, filled with the memory of this wonder. His hand trembled once again with the recollection of it. The feeling lost little of its sensual delight in remembrance. Then, abruptly, when he found himself about halfway to his father's house, the boy began to run. He was bursting with this overwhelming intelligence, and he felt he must communicate it at once to his parents.

With his wife Cleo and his son Manusos, Giorgio Theotokopoulos had just returned home, that same March evening, from prayers in the town. The little group was gathered at table as the servant girl noisily made preparations for supper in the adjacent kitchen. All awaited the arrival of Domenikos. This waiting had long been a custom. They had had to put up with it when Manusos had been a pupil, for the monastery was at a fair distance from the house, much farther than was the center of Candia.

Giorgio was a handsome man, not very tall, but squarish and tending now to be tubby, with thick, wiry hair that was going gray, as were the wide moustache and the trimmed, full beard. He was fifty, an age then thought advanced. But there was nothing ancient about the snapping black eyes, no hint of decrepitude in the vigorous, abrupt gestures that accompanied much of his conversation, his puffy, hairy hands pumping forcefully up and down or sweeping grandly from side to side. For Giorgio Theotokopoulos, everything was either yes or no, seldom maybe. He was, as well, a man with opinions on all subjects, many of his views not heavily reinforced by accurate information.

He habitually dressed in the black costume that was favored by Cretans, though it would have been more politic had he chosen to wear the brighter fashions so admired by the Venetians. He was nearly as proud of his island's heritage as he was of his family and his position. Of the latter, his pride was very great.

He had never successfully reconciled himself to this evening delay. He was impulsive and impatient. When he was hungry, he wanted to eat at once. When he was thirsty, he wanted his retsina to be served without delay. When he was happy, he wanted to celebrate. When he was angry, he expressed his feelings to the first person he encountered. When he was sad, he wept. When frustrated, he became petulant. His wife of thirty years thought these violent displays of temperament childish.

On occasions when Cleo taxed him with his impetuousness, Giorgio would ask the world that was present if he hadn't a perfect right. His success, his position, entitled him to be as he was, as he wished to be. He was as successful man, an important merchant of the town, with his own warehouses overlooking the small, fortified harbor of Candia. He had productive vineyards and olive groves at nearby Fodele, these managed by his older son, now in his twenties. His trade with Venice was sufficiently profitable to warrant the permanent installation there of his younger brother. And he was himself on good enough terms with the Venetian rulers of Crete to possess the socially important and fairly remunerative post of tax collector. He had a decent house, comfortable and in a desirable location. He contributed a tithe to his own Eastern Church and gave generously, if somewhat grudgingly, to the Roman Church that was supported by the Venetians. Had such a man, he would ask, no right to receive the attention of those who were dependent on him? Had he not, after all, achieved his position by aggressiveness? Timidity had no place in his life.

Giorgio was determined that both his sons should follow in the tradition which he and his brother Manusos (the one in Venice) had inherited from *their* father. Half of this ambition had already been realized. His older son, always a tractable and amiable child, worked hard and invariably followed paternal instructions to the letter. If young Manusos lacked brilliance, Giorgio felt he couldn't justifiably complain (though of course he did complain, often and loudly) because this son was obedience and filial duty personified, as he had himself been with respect to his own father.

On the other hand, he had severe misgivings about Domenikos. The boy had long been a puzzle to him, a problem, and he was not, as Cleo would point out now and then, very good at dealing with problems that didn't lend themselves to easy, immediate, and categorical solutions. The fact was, as Giorgio saw it, that the boy was soft. And it pleased the father to blame this presumed defect on his wife's side of the family. Two of her brothers had become monks and were now members of the great monastic community of Mount Athos, on the Greek mainland. Another was a priest and likely, they were told, to become a bishop, since he had remained celibate.

As he reflected, seated at the table, on the pale, fragile-seeming Domenikos, Giorgio had the feeling that his son might well be inclined in a similar direction. The lad appeared much too gentle for the rigors of this world.

Cleo was pouring him another glass of wine as his lips began to move. "These damned monks," he muttered sullenly. "Don't they have any respect for the supper hour of decent people? It must be nearly seven."

Ever tranquil, his wife responded soothingly. "You mustn't be so impatient, Giorgio. Menegos will be home any minute. It's a long walk. Just drink your wine and compose yourself."

He wasn't, for the moment, to be so easily put off. He raised his right hand as if he intended to bring it crashing down on the heavy table, something he often did. Then he let it fall limply into his lap, the image of frustration. He sighed raspingly. "He worries me, that boy."

Cleo looked at her husband, her small, sweet features full of concern. "What are you thinking of? He seems perfectly well to me."

"As I've told you before, I don't think he's got any iron in his soul."

He scowled. "Where's the Cretan in him? Answer me that. Where's the Greek in him?"

She smiled. "Oh, I think it's just that he's quieter than you or Manusos, Giorgio. He has all the will he needs. Believe me, you'd be surprised how willful Menegos can be at times."

Giorgio was plainly reluctant to agree. His expression turned suddenly grim, and she thought he would make another pass at the table with his fist, but he merely sighed once more, very profoundly. "I'll tell you one thing," he said, eyeing his wife with suspicion. "I'll not tolerate their trying to make a monk or a priest out of him up there."

He pointed in the general direction of the monastery.

Manusos, who had been sipping his wine in silence, half bored by the conversation whose purport was all too familiar, set down his glass and shook his head slowly. His face was, save for the absence of a beard, almost a mirror of his father's. He grinned. "Oh, I don't think there's very much danger of that, papa. The only thing Menegos cares about is drawing pictures."

Giorgio grunted scornfully. His opinion of his older son's acumen in such matters (in all matters, when it came to that) was not very high. "And what would you know about it?"

Manusos shook his head again, more abruptly, his expression mildly dogged. "But I *do* know. When I see him, papa, he talks to me. It's mostly gibberish, of course, but at least he tells me things."

"What does he talk about?" asked Cleo.

"Drawing pictures, just as I said."

Giorgio turned rather fiercely toward his wife. "You know what I think? I think there's some of *your* family's fanaticism in Menegos. He's going to become one of those icon-painting monks, or he wants to. And that's your family's heritage, not mine."

"I don't understand what you mean. If Menegos has a true calling, surely you can't mean that you'd think of standing in his way."

He grunted again, unhappily; he was beaten. "No, no, of course not. But how can I know whether he feels a call on his own or has been persuaded by those monks?"

"I don't suppose you *can* be certain. But it's not important, is it? What Menegos feels is what matters."

Giorgio was obdurate. "I'll not have them trying to put ideas into his head. I need him a lot more than the Church does. Let her have the peasant boys."

Cleo laughed. "But isn't that why you're sending him to the brothers in the first place, to have them put ideas into his head?"

He threw both hands into the air and brought them down explosively against his heavy thighs. "Oh, you know what I mean. You *know* I'm talking about the unimportant things they teach. All anyone needs to learn in a school is how to pray and how to count. Isn't that right, Manusos?"

The young man once more set down his glass and nodded his agreement, smiling a little sheepishly. "Well, I don't know, but it's all *I* learned."

Cleo protested. "Not a bit of it. You learned to read, didn't you?"

"Yes, mama," he responded, then added, almost smugly, "but I never do."

"And whose fault is that?" she demanded, surprised by the sharpness of her tone. "Menegos reads all the time." She hadn't intended this comparison and hoped that her older son had not taken it to be invidious.

The young man shrugged and declined comment. But there was an expression of modest triumph in Giorgio's face as he turned to her. "There. You see?"

"I see nothing. Manusos isn't interested in reading, Menegos is. That's all I see. He likes his work with you." She paused and smiled. "And I'm grateful for that. . . ."

"You ought to be," said her husband hotly. "That's how it will be possible for all this to go on after I die." He made a circular gesture with his hand as if to encompass, it seemed to Cleo, the entire known world.

But she had no intention of being deflected. "We were talking about Menegos, He—"

"Will do exactly what Manusos is doing, when the time comes."

Cleo didn't reply at once. She knew it was perfectly right that a son should obey his father. Didn't the Scriptures say so? "Yes," she said at last. "But won't you give some consideration to *his* desires?"

"None."

"Not even if you think him unsuited for the work he must do for you?"

"He can learn. Isn't that what they say up there?" He pointed again toward the monastery. "They say he's their best pupil. He can become my pupil and learn affairs just as well as he's learned Aristotle, or whatever. And I'll tell you another thing," said the man hotly. "If Menegos isn't here within one minute, I'll give him something to think about." He whacked the air with his hand, and grinned.

Domenikos, panting with excitement and from having run half the distance from the monastery, entered precisely on cue. His face was streaked with dust and perspiration. His features were strikingly similar to his mother's, though in caricature, his face longer and narrower, pinched now with emotion. His cassock was dirty and askew, his hands grimy and stained by the red pigment he had been using. His eyes, wide with pleasure, surveyed the scene about the table. He sensed in an instant that he had been the subject of conversation, and that all of it hadn't been to his credit.

He hastened now to his father's side and planted a sweaty kiss on Giorgio's woolly cheek, kissed his mother's unlined forehead, and exchanged a perfunctory embrace with his brother. He was about to seat himself beside Manusos when Cleo lifted her hand. "Go wash yourself, Menegos. You're transformed with dirt."

He nodded and quickly disappeared into the inner courtyard of his father's substantial house. Sounds of splashing water filled the air. The servant girl made her appearance with bowls of soup and a basket containing thick chunks of dark bread. The flagon of retsina was refilled. Domenikos, looking a bit more presentable, his hair darkened with water and smoothed down, reentered the room, wiping his hands on his filthy cassock. In silence he took his place by his brother and confronted the steaming bowl.

"And what made you late *this* evening?" his father inquired evenly. "What was it those brothers had you doing for them this time?"

The boy looked at Giorgio, then at his mother, his long, slim fingers clasping and unclasping themselves rapidly. "We made tempera colors," he began, almost breathless. "And then we put the colors on a panel."

The father made himself smile appreciatively. "That sounds logical," he observed drily.

"You make the colors by mixing them with eggs, papa. Don't you think that's strange?"

The man grunted. "I can think of a lot more important things to be done with eggs than that."

"Let him finish," said Cleo softly.

The boy looked from one parent to another, bewildered and offended that both should have failed to understand the magnitude of his announcement.

"Go on," said Giorgio dully.

"Well, that's all, really. We just made colors and then we painted with them."

"And *that's* why you're late? And *that's* what you're all out of breath about?" Giorgio's incredulity was honest. He looked at his wife. "Is this sensible? I ask you. Is this thoughtful? Is this contemplative, or even clever or calculating? Is this what an education is for?"

Domenikos was confused. What had they been saying in his absence? He must be, he recognized, extremely careful in what he said to his father, and how. The mood was full of anger; full, therefore, of danger as well.

Cleo ignored Giorgio and turned to her younger son. "Well, Menegos, at least I hope you were able to paint some nice pictures."

"Oh, no, mama, not today. It's much too soon. But we shall. Brother Constantine—"

"Which one is he?"

"The tall, thin one, papa. He's been very kind to me."

"Is he the one who's praying for your soul all the time?" Giorgio asked jeeringly.

Domenikos smiled gravely. "I think all the brothers do that, for all the pupils. Brother Constantine is the one who teaches us drawing. And now he's teaching us how to use paints. He must be a wonderful painter himself. The panels he's painted, or at least the ones I've seen, are perfect."

Giorgio stared at his son suspiciously, as if he were a stranger. "And how would you know about a thing like that? How many icon panels have you seen in your life?"

Domenikos nodded. "Not enough, papa. But I think I've seen every one in every church and chapel around Candia."

The father's eyes widened. "Oh?"

"Yes, every one of them . . . or almost."

The man frowned. "Now, why in God's name would a boy of eleven want to do a thing like that?"

"Well, in the beginning, I looked at them because I thought they were beautiful." He smiled brightly. "But of course, that's all changed now. And I'm going to have to look at them all again."

"You no longer think them beautiful?"

"No, papa. I have to look at them again because I've decided that I'm going to be a painter of icons."

Domenikos studied his father's face as the words sank home. He hadn't intended to say so much just now. But then, unexpectedly, the desire had simply forced the words out. Giorgio stared at him in hostile silence. Without a sound, he rose from his bench and departed.

The silence, weighing heavily on the boy's emotions, continued. Cleo at last cleared her throat.

"You want to be a monk, Menegos?"

"I don't think so, mama. Perhaps, but I don't think so."

"But I thought all icon painters were monks. They certainly are here in Crete."

"I thought so too, until today. But Brother Constantine told me that quite a few laymen paint icons, and most of *them* are working in Venice or Constantinople."

"And that's what you want, to go away?"

"Oh, no." The boy hesitated, his tone increasing in intensity. "I don't know, mama. It's all too soon."

"And yet you're certain that this is what you want."

"Yes, mama."

"If I may ask it, how long have you known this?"

Domenikos was long in answering. He wanted to give an honest reply because it was a very important question. "Well, it's been in my mind for a long time. I don't know how long. But I suppose I wasn't certain until this afternoon, when I had a brush in my hand and actually put some color on a panel."

Cleo considered this for a moment. "I think," she finally said, very softly, "that we'd better put off this discussion until later."

Cleo recognized that the argument had merely been postponed. Sooner or later, it would have to take place. If Giorgio could just look at the boy objectively for a little time, see him in this new and odd light he had just thrown on himself, she felt certain (or so she told herself) that he *would* understand the boy, would see that he was different, and different not simply from his brother but from any other child she had ever known.

Not for an instant did she believe this opinion to be purely the expression of maternal pride. To the contrary, she supposed she would have been much happier were Domenikos as easy to deal with, as comprehensible to her, as her other son. But to know he was different, you had only to look at him, to be with him for a little while, to watch him in his strange silences (which were, she thought, far too many and too prolonged to be healthy in a creature of his age and vitality), to listen to him when he *did* talk, to take notice of his intensity of feeling. What it all meant, what it implied for his future, she could not guess, but in no way did this perplexity shake her confidence in the accuracy of her judgment. He was in some fashion exceptional. And for his part, Domenikos was wise enough to follow his mother's counsel, saying no more to his father about his desire to paint.

Constantly reminded of it by Cleo, Giorgio also managed to keep silent. It was no less difficult for him than for Domenikos. It wasn't in his nature to suppress his feelings. Nor was he a mite more persuaded, as he observed his younger son with greater interest and concern, that his wife's plea for patience and time had been wisely founded. Better, he thought, to make it plain to the boy right now that his future lay in Crete, in trade, and that any far-fetched dream of painting icons in a distant city or of hiding within the secure walls of a monastery for the rest of his life was no more likely of realization than was the possibility of Giorgio himself taking a vow of poverty.

In no way had he altered his position; in no way was he planning to alter it. He felt that he must discuss the situation with someone in a position to give him an informed opinion, even though it wasn't his way. Not many weeks after Domenikos had announced his appalling intentions, Giorgio arranged a meeting with Brother Constantine.

It was a warm Sunday in April, just after mass. Claiming some urgent business matter that he must talk over with a colleague, Giorgio walked slowly, perspiring greatly, up the long, gentle hill to the monastery. As he stood before the white gates and looked into the exterior courtyard, a sort of atrium, brilliant in the scorching midday sunshine, he recalled with very little nostalgia his own years here as a pupil.

Brother Constantine was awaiting him in his classroom. Here and there, on shelves, in niches and on brackets, were mounted models to be copied, or examples of boys' work—drawings, sketches, icons in the beginning stages. All the subjects were religious, all based on the traditional styles so long established: the figures rigid in their stylized postures, the details of each piece so ritualistic in their adherence to the divine prescriptions and proscriptions of the past that only by imputation did this art have any claim to reality, to realism. Yet these little panels were, in the Eastern rite, of immense significance. No home whose inhabitants worshiped at an Eastern altar was without its own icon; many, especially those of the better established, possessed a reliquary as well. (Giorgio's was in the form of a Greek-cross church, in which was contained a sacred relic of St. Catherine herself, protectress of Crete.)

As he approached the aging monk, Giorgio observed the gaunt features of this person whom his son so adored. Why, for God's sake, he was barely half a man, poor devil; he looked as if he hadn't eaten a decent meal in years. If his was the most direct route to paradise, Giorgio wanted no part of it, and none for Domenikos either. He understood, however, that he must evince no disrespect for this agent of the charmed hereafter. He remembered too vividly the boyhood occasions when his mockery had been rewarded with a sound beating. He had carefully rehearsed a courteous opening for this interview. But it was Brother Constantine who spoke first.

"You are Domenikos' father?"

Giorgio nodded, smiling damply, wiping his face with a kerchief. "For better or worse, brother, that's who I am."

The monk extended his arms in welcome. "I am glad to meet the man who could produce such a boy."

"Thank you, brother."

"He is brilliant, my son, brilliant."

Giorgio stared at the floor. "So my wife tells me. But what does this mean? That he can't join my older son and me in the affairs we have here? Is that what you'd tell me?"

In the monk's expression the visitor thought he discerned an element of disdain. For no apparent reason, he felt that this cadaverous figure imagined he had Giorgio at a disadvantage. No trader relished thinking himself in such a position.

"You have it in your mind," the monk said calmly, "that in some way I'm attempting to interfere with your plans?"

Giorgio shook his head stubbornly. "I have nothing in my mind, brother. I'm just asking a question."

Brother Constantine laughed softly. "Questions are occasionally statements. Yours seemed so to me. And statements are either to be accepted or rejected. If I do you an injustice, forgive me."

"It was a question, I promise you."

The monk's smile, though fading, remained in vestige. "Then my answer must be that I'm doing for Domenikos only what I do for all the pupils I teach. I show him how to apply paints to a panel. Some of the boys detest it; most of them do, I suspect. Others seem to enjoy it. Some are good at it, others frightful. It happens that your son is the most gifted pupil I have ever taught. The time is not terribly far off when he will be able to teach *me*. That is the fact. Oh, I have had many boys with admirable talent. Domenikos is the first who seems touched with genius. I believe he will serve God well as a painter of icons, and in this way he will be a true ornament to our Church, our faith. But I have never breathed this opinion of mine to him. I have never attempted by word or intimation to persuade him. I suppose I should have, but I have not."

The monk's calm induced in Giorgio a desire to explode with rage, but he resisted it, contenting himself with another benign question. "But can't he serve God nearly as well in my vineyards and warehouses?"

The frail brother acknowledged this possibility with the slightest inclination of his graying head. "Oh, yes. But aren't we taught that each of us best serves God by doing best what we know best and love best?"

Giorgio at last dared to be mildly impolite. "And how would you know, brother, whether my Menegos isn't just as well suited for commerce as he is for art or even God?"

Brother Constantine was not a bit ruffled by the hostility of tone. He had, in fact, been surprised by his visitor's forbearance, having learned from others of his legendary volatility. "Just so, just so. Only your Domenikos can know that; he and God, of course."

Never wholly at ease when discussing matters of faith, Giorgio felt especially uncomfortable when, as now, they came up in discussion with one officially connected with the Church. He flailed the air helplessly with his arms. He sighed peevishly. He protested. "Do you mean to tell me that I have no rights to my son's help during my old age? I thought that was every father's right."

The brother regarded him solemnly. "You imagine your rights to Domenikos greater than God's?"

So gently had the monk interposed this question that all the rage accumulating in Giorgio's heart was abruptly dissipated. He looked at his adversary in supplication. "What's he really like, this boy? I'm beginning to think I don't know him at all."

With a delicate downward inclination of his hand, Brother Constantine invited Giorgio to seat himself on one of the hard benches. Meekly he complied. "He's an exceptional child, your son. He has intelligence. He has grace of body and grace of speech. He has, I think, a profound and beautiful soul." He paused for effect. "He is also *very* stubborn."

The father of this prodigy found himself grinning proudly, recalling his own misgivings, his fear that Domenikos had no iron in his composition. But when a man of the cloth told you that your son was stubborn, you had to believe him. "That much I know already," he responded, lying but not without a pang of shame.

"It is not necessarily a bad quality," the monk went on. "Our Church owes a great deal, perhaps everything, to men and women who were obstinate. Our Lord Himself was a very stubborn man."

"I confess, brother, that I'd never thought of Our Lord in that way."

Brother Constantine walked deliberately to the window that overlooked a rugged Cretan landscape in which undulating ridges, mostly covered with scrub, interrupted now and then by groves and vineyards, stretched southward to the summit of Mount Ida.

"He is curious," he said at last. "I mean, he is inquisitive." He turned to face Giorgio, his slender figure in its dark habit silhouetted against the window. "And that concerns me. Curiosity can be both a virtue and a vice. In Domenikos it has both these aspects, I think. What disturbs me, for him, is that he never seems content with the answers I am able to give him, or find for him. He is full of doubt." He hesitated, looking back through the window. His high, thin voice was more remote as he continued. "If he *were* to choose to become a monk, he would have a very difficult time learning to accept authority without question. I have no doubt that he would manage it in the end, because, as I said, he has a beautiful soul. But I am not certain that the experience would not break his spirit. I would not like to see that. Nor, I suspect, would God."

"What I mean is that at times he is inclined to ask the wrong questions, the wrong kind of questions." Brother Constantine walked to a corner of the large room and picked up a small panel that depicted St. George slaying the dragon. He brought it to Giorgio and offered it for his inspection. "This is Domenikos' favorite subject just now."

Giorgio crossed himself before accepting the panel. He considered it with reverence. Though he was as devout as any other townsman, and as superstitious, and though he regarded all icons with the veneration due them, he had often confessed to himself that he had never found them very appealing in themselves. He stared briefly at the little picture, then looked back to the monk. He had felt nothing; in fact, he had seen nothing either. "I see," he remarked indifferently.

"Yes, well, the reason I show it to you is that yesterday, your Domenikos asked me why the sky in this picture does not resemble the real sky."

to marry; only bishops must be unmarried. Should the wafer representing the Host be made of leavened or unleavened flour? Should the service of confirmation be reserved to bishops, as Rome held, or could it be performed by priests as well, as practiced in the East? These were some of the "major" differences. Of such, with considerable complications introduced by personal and political ambitions, came the Great Schism of 1054.

Nor was it left at that. When it became clear that the two orthodoxies were thereafter to follow separate paths, ingenious ecclesiastical lawyers discovered other "significant" causes for the split: The priests of the Roman Church shaved their beards. They wore hats while saying the offices. They gave their benedictions with five fingers instead of three. They buried bishops with their hands unclasped.

For their part, the Romans deplored what they described as sorcery, witchcraft, astrology, and general superstition that attended the practices of their Eastern brothers. The vending of amulets was common in the atria of Eastern churches. The churches themselves were desecrated; in some cases, it was said, impecunious heads of households installed their starving broods within the naves of churches. Their livestock grazed in graveyards. Astonishingly, it was alleged that when attending mass women were known to have flashed their eyes alluringly at men in the congregation. Merchants tore pages from liturgical manuscripts in order to sell the illuminated miniatures to art lovers.

On the central issue of the schism, Venetian bishops were more in sympathy than out with their Cretan subjects. Both, for different reasons, actively resented the authority of the Pope. This topic seemed as lively in 1560 with the Venetian clergy as it had been among the Easterners 500 years before. The issue was simple enough: Why should the Bishop of Rome automatically be Pope? The Latins held his ascendancy to be directly traceable to St. Peter, Rome's first bishop, the Rock of Christ's Church. The Eastern prelates maintained that the bishops of Antioch, Constantinople, Jerusalem, and Alexandria had equal claims to the papacy. From the outset, the question had been more political than theological, and questions of power were to be resolved only by power.

The only severe inhibition imposed on the Eastern-rite worshipers of Crete was a limitation on the size of their churches. This was not, in fact, an expression of religious discrimination at all; it was intended to prevent more than a large handful of islanders from con-

Giorgio returned his gaze to the panel, and noted that indeed the sky was represented by a series of rippling lines, suggestive, certainly, of no cloud formation that *he* had seen. He nodded. "And what did you say to him, brother?"

"I told him that the picture was inspired directly by God, which is true. I told him that therefore we mortals have no right to question God's wisdom in these things."

Intimidated, Giorgio flushed. "And what did Menegos say to that?"

"He said, 'Do you mean, brother, that God doesn't see the sky in the same way we do?' I said, 'I mean that you are not to bother your head about things like that. That is the reason why we copy icons with so much care, because, originally, they came to us from God. They are the work of God, the word of God in images, and they are neither to be altered nor questioned by man.' "

Giorgio was at once dismayed and elated by the force of the monk's tone. The authority was unmistakable. The content, however, eluded his comprehension. "I hope he said no more to you about it after that, brother."

"Not then, no. But there are bound to be other occasions. Domenikos is like that."

"I'll have a word with him."

Brother Constantine sighed and shook his head doubtfully. "Well, you can try, and that would be good of you. It would be good for Domenikos too, hearing it from his father. But I fear that you will find he has a question for each of your answers. He is very logical, and very hard to put off."

Giorgio, believing that he could now see light where he previously had seen only darkness, looked at the brother who towered above him. He returned the panel. Brother Constantine pressed it to his bosom and stared vaguely toward the benches at the rear of the room.

"Then, if I understand you, you think that he's very ill suited to becoming a monk."

The brother's eyes focused on his guest. "Oh, I can scarcely tell you that. But I can say that if he continues along the path he now seems to be following, he would be a very unhappy one." He paused and held the little icon at arm's length, smiling proudly. "He has it in him to be a great hagiographer, though. And what a fine thing that would be."

It was all Giorgio could do not to laugh. It appeared that the strong position was his. "Then by all means let him paint to his heart's content, brother. And I'll gladly pay for any extra materials he may need."

Giorgio knew that while a few pupils from St. Catherine's such as Michele Damaskinos, had left Crete to make a living by painting icons for the laity, most hagiographers were monks. If Domenikos were unable, because of his temperament, to become a monk, it seemed to his father that the boy wouldn't, in all likelihood, seriously consider such a career outside the Church. More important to Giorgio, it seemed improbable that Domenikos would ever willingly leave his native island.

Two

During the first half of the sixteenth century, the political, social, economic, and religious structure of Crete reflected in very large measure the curious relations between the native inhabitants and their masters from Venice, who had assumed control shortly after the Crusaders, in 1205, had overcome and sacked Constantinople.

Like the parents of willful and spirited children, the Venetians sought to govern their stubborn, insular subjects with alternative doses of kindness and cruelty, the carrot and the stick. They were never wholly successful in maintaining their ascendancy, nor did they wholly fail. In the main the Cretans did as they were told, but they did it sullenly and occasionally with menace. Not always, moreover, did they do it well. Even a man so utterly dependent on Venetian friendship as Giorgio Theotokopoulos was for his prosperity and social position could and frequently did openly express his contempt. And he was permitted his scorn; he was permitted as well to continue his observation of the Eastern Church ritual, a faith that was shared by practically all the islanders.

Venice believed she could afford to be generous in this respect because, in this epoch when so much of western Europe was rocked by conflict, she remained a bastion of comparative enlightenment, a product of the humanist revolution in thought and worship that was to be called the Renaissance. Besides, the great doges of the Republic who presided over the extensive, if now dwindling, empire in the eastern Mediterranean were primarily concerned with the mainte-

nance of their immense and vital commerce with the lands of A Minor. They would therefore tolerate, to the annoyance of the Po important differences of religious opinion, so long as these differer in no way affected the security of Venice's maritime trade rou Crete represented a major protective link in the commercial er prise. Thus, loyalty to the Church of Rome among the islanders than was unswerving and practical loyalty to the Most Serene Rep lic of Venice, the political and economic entity to be ad and obeyed.

The Serenissima didn't ignore the precepts of Rome on the sub of doctrine. She did, however, understand better than did most ernments that power made its own possibilities as well as its own sponsibilities. The doges were successful in their insistence tha bishops designated for service in their territories be themselves l Venetians; Venice came first, Rome second in all disputes. They no less demanding of total acceptance of Venice's authority in clesiastical matters than in politics or commerce.

Because, whenever there was doubt, they acted in the interes Venice rather than Rome; the bishops of Crete dealt softly with separated brethren of the Eastern faith. The schism, after all, taken place a long time ago. Besides, the issues that divided the great churches were questions of practice more than of doctrin dogma. What, for example, could be less consequential than the w ing of a creed? The phrases propounded by the Roman Church cluded the *Filioque,* which established it as an article of faith tha Holy Spirit proceeded from the Father and the Son, were a difference of opinion, since both churches were agreed that the Spirit itself existed.

There had also been the matter of icons, which had been reso more or less to everyone's satisfaction, two and a half centuries b 1054, the year that produced the Great Schism with Mi Cerularius, the Bishop of Constantinople. The first Counci Nicaea had agreed that icons were to be worshipped no longer, th they might continue to be objects of "veneration." Eastern bis had been delighted by this decree; in their frenzy of enthusiasm devotion, pilgrims had been licking the paint off some of the hallowed images.

Other difficulties were comparably inconsequential: Should pr marry? The Latin Curia was emphatic in its insistence on cle celibacy, while the Eastern hierarchy defended the rights of pr

gregating in the same place at the same time for purposes of planning a revolt.

Revolts were perpetually in the air, like pollen in spring. No master, however benevolent his intentions, could have hoped to be made welcome on an island whose civilization antedated his own by thousands of years. No opportunity was overlooked for reminding the occupying power that his presence was unpopular. As Giorgio put it, "We Cretans have no need of churches to plot rebellions in. We can manage that just as well in the open air."

Over the centuries of Venetian occupation, there had been many attempts to overthrow this authority. All had failed and had resulted only in the most brutal and shameless reprisals, massacres of women and children. It had by now almost reached the point where Crete, in the view of the hard-bitten Venetian mercenaries, was no longer worth sacking. Periodic uprisings persisted, and they were as firmly repressed as ever.

The indifference of Venice to her subjects' faith was hardly matched in tolerance by the regard of Cretans toward the Church and bishops of Rome. The real issues may have been slight, but the antagonisms, inspired so long ago by the schism, remained sharp, propounded by the local clergy and unwittingly emphasized by the Venetian primate's love of luxury and pomp. The rumors of scandal that dogged the Latin Church in northern Europe were no less frequently heard in Candia, nor were they either more or less accurate. The irony was that, on the whole, they applied but little to Roman Catholicism as it was observed in Crete.

The families of Venetian administrators maintained a standard of living hardly less sumptuous than that of the hierarchy. To an insular population whose livelihood derived mostly from work provided by Venetian trade (in the fields or in the warehouses and galleys of Candia), such opulence was in itself responsible for much of the resentment so firmly rooted in the Cretan soul. Only a few exceptions, such as Giorgio, could successfully (and with good conscience) walk on either side of the fence. He managed this by treating his fellow Cretans with exemplary generosity and his Venetian masters with exemplary deference—to their faces, at any rate.

Internal strife was not the only important threat to Venice's hold on Crete and her other major possessions. The Ottoman Empire, following its capture of Constantinople in 1453, had been systematically snapping up Venetian holdings. This process, though slow, appeared each year to be increasingly inexorable, and its significance to the future of the Venetian economy was emphasized by the discovery of the New World. Genoa, better situated to exploit this burgeoning commerce, seemed close to supplanting the Serenissima as the great mercantile state of Italy. And Spain was becoming more powerful than either.

People were saying (Cretans repeated it with glee) that Venice was slipping. Many islanders would have welcomed an Ottoman conquest of their island, for the Moslems were reputed—not without justice—to be far kinder, wiser, and more reasonable masters than the Venetians. The Ottoman invasion of Crete, however, lay well in the future.

The presence of Venice permeated all aspects of Cretan life. It obsessed Giorgio. His preoccupation with the niceties of his dealings with the republic's officials, with her shipowners and captains, was all but complete. If anything, it made him a more militant advocate of independence. What could be a greater argument, emotions aside, than the creaking bureaucracy developed by Venice over the centuries? "They always send us their idiots," he complained. And who could know better than he the depths to which the conqueror would stoop when he thought his position menaced? To those who occasionally accused him of playing a double game, Giorgio would respond heatedly that someone had to deal with the devils. Who could be more judicious than he?

If he had any feelings of guilt or remorse, he concealed them from his family. Only on the subject of perpetuating his rather squalid bit of preferment and his successful business did he reveal his true sentiments. The position was precarious, he thought. It just wouldn't do, alas, for his son Manusos to take over the daily diplomacy required to maintain good relations with the Venetians. Were he to lose his patronage, the family could be ruined overnight. Giorgio was tactful enough to withhold these apprehensions from Manusos, but he stated them with plaintive frequency to Cleo: "Only Menegos, when he's old enough, will have the intelligence to take my place here."

No matter how often his wife attempted to soften his resolve, Giorgio remained adamant. Domenikos might continue to play with his paints (and he invariably termed it "play"), but when he attained manhood, the youth must join him. Cleo's only success in coping with her husband's and son's mutually hostile determinations was in assuring that they not be a matter for daily harangue at table, still their only regular meeting point.

So the years passed in a state of truce, albeit an uneasy one. Neither

Giorgio nor Domenikos appeared inclined to yield an inch in his conversations with Cleo, but neither insisted on imposing this obduracy, for the time being, on the other.

Everything about temperas and their application had remained for the boy to learn after his initial encounter with them. In the seven years following that first shattering afternoon in 1552, Brother Constantine instructed him in the combination of primary colors to compose other tones.

And then there was the copying; the models were invariably icon panels from the monastery or from other places of Eastern worship in Candia and its environs. Although he never lost patience, the monk was meticulous and exacting in his demands on the pupils, proving himself profoundly dissatisfied if any detail was different from that of the original. The less able were made to use stencils to improve their accuracy; and accuracy was the sole criterion, though Brother Constantine referred to it as "fidelity." "Remember," he would say, "that this is God's work we are doing. We do not tamper with God's work." And at such moments he would glance at Domenikos. "We do not attempt to improve on God's work, either." Thus, slowly, painstakingly, the youth became at first a good and eventually a brilliant copyist.

At the same time, though under the direction of another monk, Domenikos learned the application of pigments to wet plaster, the process of making frescoes. It was a technique, however, that proved not at all to his taste. The fastidious Domenikos preferred the less messy methods of tempera.

During this period, he became an adolescent, and then a man, his long features filling out, his body stretching; but he remained slender. To his mother's mild dismay, his hair grew darker, though it was still of a lighter shade than was usual for Crete, and that, at any rate, gratified her.

Other changes were more profound. The need to maintain silence with his father had altered Domenikos far more than could have been imagined from his impressive physical development. How he longed to talk with Giorgio; and how, for the same reason if from a wholly different viewpoint, Giorgio longed to talk with him. From a gay, open, fairly gregarious child, he had become brooding, introspective, seemingly beyond his mother's emotional reach.

Brother Constantine, too, was increasingly conscious of this change. Domenikos' natural and candid curiosity seemed gradually to have been replaced by a kind of querulousness. Though still inquisitive, he posed his questions now in more contentious tones. There was a note of defiance (and, the monk wondered, of disbelief?) in his voice, his face pinched, his body tense, his fists clenched. And the brother observed with sorrow that Domenikos, never a leader, appeared intentionally to avoid his fellows whenever possible, to isolate himself from them, preferring his own bleak company.

If he didn't understand it, Domenikos was aware of his desire for separateness. Especially in the summer, when the long days afforded him sufficient light after school hours, he would walk alone up into the hills to the site of the ancient Roman ruins, the Colonia Julia Nobilis. Here he made sketches of the wind-bent trees, the sparse, sharply angled clumps of scrub, the hills themselves that rolled almost endlessly in the direction of Mount Ida, the island's greatest natural landmark.

He attempted to draw the fragments of columns and entablatures that were scattered over the area of the old Roman community. These efforts he recognized at once to be childishly inept, for Domenikos knew nothing about perspective and proportion, matters that simply didn't enter into the creation of icons. The landscapes he drew ran straight up the precious leaves of paper that his father imported for him from Venice. They had no proper regard for the relative size in space of the objects he observed. And when he attempted to represent a church or a house, comparable problems marred his effort. He was unable to master without instruction the difficulties of planes and surfaces. His eye, which plainly perceived what was wrong with the finished work, couldn't direct his hand.

A comparable gap revealed itself between his own conception of life and that proposed by his Church. It seemed strange indeed that the readings of Plato and Aristotle, the neo-Platonists, the poets and the heroes of mythology, should have stirred no feelings of incongruity among his fellows. All proclaimed man not merely God's earthly image but His agent. Yet the Church seemed constantly to denigrate man, to reduce him to the status of cipher. To every question Domenikos posed to his instructors, the inevitable response was, "You ask that as if you were a Papist." The youth, however, had but the faintest idea of what it was to be a Papist. He had never set foot in a Roman church.

His frustration found no satisfactory escape. There was little point in raising major theological questions with Brother Constantine; although occasionally, driven by anger at his own clumsiness, theological or artistic, he was impelled to speak, always to his eventual chagrin.

In the late summer of 1559 there was such a moment. It was after an especially tedious session in which the pupils had been required to copy certain details of an icon depicting an exploit of St. Titus, Crete's first bishop and her patron. It was a theme they had often explored. As the others departed, Domenikos hung back. By now, he was at least wise enough to know that unorthodox questions, if put to Brother Constantine when his fellow students were in the room, would be treated with polite but total disdain.

Nearly nineteen now, Domenikos was taller than the monk. Brother Constantine, it seemed to the youth, had begun to shrink as he entered his declining years.

"What is it, my son?"

Domenikos shifted his feet, embarrassed to feel it once again necessary to ask what he had so often asked before. "I still don't see what prevents us from painting the things we see in nature, the things we see with our own eyes."

The monk sighed and closed his eyes. "Oh, not again, Domenikos. If you cannot accept it by now, I fear that you never will. I've told you: that is not for icon painters. That is the only answer."

"I suppose what you say is theologically so, brother. But what is the law that prevents me from going beyond what I've been able to learn from you, from painting what I see in nature?"

"Come," said the monk quietly, placing his hand on Domenikos' shoulder. His skin was translucent now, the thick veins making subcutaneous ridges of blue across the pale, wrinkled surface. "Let's go for a stroll in the cloister. I need the air, and so do you, I think."

In silence for a time, they moved together in the cool shadows of the white arcades. Domenikos was dazzled whenever he glanced toward the plain stone well in the center, so bright was the sunlight.

"You see," said the brother at last, his tone weary without losing its patience. "You are asking the wrong kind of question again. You are trying to question the will of God. In fact, in one way, you are questioning the very foundation of our Church."

"You can't mean that it's a sin or a crime to want to apply what I've learned to a use that's secular."

"Not if the use is virtuous, no."

"Then painting from nature isn't sinful."

"No." Brother Constantine chuckled. "If it were, we would long

ago have had to excommunicate men like Michele Damaskinos and
the other painters who, I am sorry to say, have perverted the icon as
we know it to suit secular tastes abroad. But they retain their spiritual intent. That is the essential."

Domenikos stared at the the old man, whose face, seen in profile,
now looked ravaged by fatigue and pain. "Then why do you keep putting me off? If it's not a vice, what's your objection?"

The brother considered briefly before replying. "Perhaps, for you,
as long as you remain a layman, it is *not* a sin. But the painting itself,
insofar as it is an expression of our Church, insofar as it is orthodox
in intent, must adhere to the rules. No eclecticism is permitted. You
confuse the Greek conception of man's role in life and his role as a
functionary of the Church. If you seriously propose to dedicate your
life to painting icons, you have to reconcile your mind and soul to the
fact that they must be painted as prescribed. They are the will of God,
as I keep telling you. If you doubt this, that *is* undoubtedly sinful, an
evil thing, call it what you like, and you must pray for forgiveness. We
must all pray that God forgives you for questioning His holy ordi-
nances."

"Then why is it, brother, that I never feel any sense of sin when I
look at the beautiful landscapes on a day like this, or at people or animals when they're moving, or at churches and houses, and I think that
because they were made by God, or inspired by God, we should be
able to paint them as we see them?"

"Because you see as a layman sees, not as a cleric." The
monk smiled sadly. "And perhaps because you have not yet a highly
developed sense of sin. Why should you? Or it may be that you are
misinformed. You believe what it pleases you to believe. That is ignorance, however, not innocence. And ignorance, Domenikos, *is* evil."

"Then I'm doomed, brother, for I can't control this desire."

"You are doomed, *if* you are doomed, only in the sense that you
are not permitted to paint in this way within the framework of the
Church, my son."

"I realize that. But how am I to learn?"

"Not from me. And I tell you this not only because it would seem
an evil thing for me to do, though that would surely be reason enough.
I say it because *I* know no other way of painting." He looked sternly
at Domenikos. "*I* have never wanted to paint another way. It is in no
way relevant to my commitment to art in God's name. What
you propose for yourself is art in man's name. And there is probably

nothing wrong with that so long as you do not confuse it in your mind with anything that resembles an act of faith."

"No doubt you're right, brother. But I can't help myself. I can't stop questioning. How does one learn to control the mind?"

"How does one learn to contol the body? By discipline."

"I don't think it's the same thing at all."

"Then you will just have to pray. I shall pray for you."

Domenikos nodded. "I'm ashamed to confess, brother, that I'm not sure I hope your prayers are answered, in this connection, I mean."

"The serpent of thought has made you bite into the fruit of doubt." The youth's smile was rueful. "I fear you're right."

Another silence followed. They had almost reached the door of Brother Constantine's classroom before the monk spoke again. "When February comes, Domenikos, I shall be able to teach you no more. You will have to leave the monastery."

Shocked, Domenikos stared at his old master and saw that there were tears in his eyes. "But why, brother?"

"Long ago I had taught you all I knew. You were aware of that, of course, and it was then I should have urged you to go. But your other teachers, though they were just as upset about your doubts as I, thought you might yet find a vocation in the Church." He hesitated, then continued sadly. "It is my duty to tell them what I warned your father of some years ago. You will never be a religious. Your spirit is too arrogant, Domenikos. Your spiritual feelings are confused by your intellect. You have great brilliance, even genius, both in your mind and in your hands. God put it there, and you should be grateful for it."

"I am, brother."

"Not sufficiently, however, to be willing to do His work on earth."

Even at such a moment, Domenikos found it impossible wholly to suppress his annoyance. "Are you telling me that it's the dictum of the church that God's work can only be done by the religious?"

The old monk smiled. "I seem to recall that your father asked me the same question. I shall answer you by saying that only *you* can know the entire truth about yourself—you and God, of course. When the term ends I think we here will have taken you as far as we are able. It may disturb the other pupils to hear you expressing your constant doubts, posing your wrong-headed questions; your refusal to accept, as it is presented to you, the truth as it has been revealed to us by Scripture is a disruptive force, or potentially so. Your fellow pupils do not understand that you are not a heretic—"

The youth raised a protesting hand. "Heretic? They think me a heretic?"

"That surprises you?"

"I'm a believer, brother."

" 'Oh, Lord, I believe. Help Thou my unbelief.' Oh yes, Domenikos, *that* is how you believe."

"I believe in revelation."

"And you maintain that logic and belief are mutually exclusive."

"In our Church, yes, as least as far as doctrine is concerned. I have always believed that we could arrive at a better understanding of God, of our faith in Him and in Our Lord, by thinking, by reasoning, by reading, by examining our minds."

The monk shook his head. "That may be the scholar's way, the way of Mount Athos. But it is not for pupils. I wish you well, Domenikos. There is no other boy I have taught who has given me the joy and sense of accomplishment that you have. And there is none, either, who has brought me the pain and anguish. I suppose they must go together. Whatever you do with your life, my son, you must do by yourself. You are far too independent, too cut off from others, from what they want or believe or think. I dearly hope it proves a happy existence, a rich one for you, even a noble one. Because I am sure you will always be lonely."

Without another word, Brother Constantine disappeared into his classroom and quietly shut the door behind him, leaving Domenikos with a confused sense of what had transpired. He was to be sent from this place in February, when the present term ended. He looked about the bright cloister and could feel in advance the pain he would know when the moment of departure came. Virtually all the delight of his life was in some intimate way associated with this monastery.

He was much perplexed by the monk's allegation that he might be a menace to this community. Was he, in fact, a heretic? Until this exchange, Domenikos had failed to relate his tendency to question God's wisdom in matters of hagiography with his questioning of aspects of doctrine. Did he question doctrine? Certainly he did, at least to the degree of doubting its legitimate application to art. Was there more? Was he, as Brother Constantine said, too independent in all things? He gazed once more about the cloister, shielding his eyes from the sun.

"Oh, God," he muttered bitterly. "I'm alone."

And abruptly he was elated. If he *was* doomed, if he was destined, like Ishmael, to be a wanderer all his life, then let it be so. He would be what he had always understood he would be; until this moment, the knowledge had been unrevealed. There was ferocity in his joy—and pain.

Three

One evening, shortly after his conversation with Brother Constantine, Domenikos was drawn aside by his brother. They walked to the interior courtyard. Just beyond the well, they stood at the wall overlooking Candia. They had a fine view of the harbor. A large fleet of Venetian ships had that day been towed in from the breakwater. Some were now at anchor; others were tied up at the quays.

Brightly dressed seamen crowded the narrow passages between the moorings and the warehouses, the inns and shops that lined the waterfront. A few were dancing to the accompaniment of lutes and pipes and whistles. Others stood apart, watching in the gathering twilight. A few drank from straw-covered flagons. All seemed to be having a fine time, their first evening ashore.

By now several inches shorter than his younger brother, Manusos was constructed along the same heavy lines as Giorgio, though as yet there was no puffiness about him. His shock of black hair projected slightly beyond his broad forehead, giving him an air of jauntiness wholly in keeping with his free and easy nature. It was a quality Domenikos had always admired, even envied, so alien was it to his own character. Nothing seemed to alarm or dismay or disappoint or dishearten Manusos. In most instances, as he himself so frequently said, this meant that he accepted with complete equanimity, and generally at their face value, Giorgio's injunctions on all things.

They stood silently for a time, watching the sailors. Domenikos envied them as well. This was a part of Manusos' life, not of his. He had, indeed, no idea of how one went about deliberately having a good time. How did one plan such moments? An evening breeze, descending the hillside behind the houses, softened the shrill sounds that climbed from the quays, blew them out toward the shadowy breakwater and the blackness of the sea.

In this lull, Manusos looked into his brother's pale, drawn face. He smiled. "Do you ever amuse yourself, Menegos?"

Domenikos grinned. "Of course."

"How?"

The younger brother shrugged. "I go for walks in the country. I sketch. I read. I think."

Manusos nudged him and winked. "But you're always alone, aren't you? Or aren't you?"

Domenikos flushed. "Oh, yes. I'm always alone."

His words made him wince; he recalled what now seemed Brother Constantine's curse.

"And you enjoy that, being by yourself?"

"Oh, yes."

Manusos grunted, incredulous, and sounded like his father. This made Domenikos laugh.

"What's funny?"

His brother explained, adding, "But then, you're really alike in a lot of things, you and papa."

"And different in a lot of things too." Manusos paused. "I know how to have a good time for myself. All papa knows is how to work and worry. I sometimes wonder if he knew how to have a good time when he was young."

"I suppose so." Domenikos looked with new interest at his brother, "How *do* you have fun, Manusos?"

"You can't imagine?"

"Would I ask if I could?"

Manusos pointed to the town spread out beneath them and smiled. Then, abruptly, he tugged his brother's sleeve. "Come on. I'll show you."

A ripple of excitement, at once terrifying and delicious, ran from Domenikos' shoulders to his toes. Half with reluctance, half with anticipation, he allowed himself to be led from the courtyard through the now-deserted dining room and into the darkening street. Manusos was walking purposefully ahead, his massive head down, his short, powerful arms pumping briskly back and forth, his hands clenched. It had rained a little earlier, a quick Mediterranean squall; the footing, as they descended the hill, was a treacherous combination of mud and smooth stones. Manusos slipped, and would have fallen had Domenikos not darted forward to grasp his arm.

"Thanks." Manusos stopped and shook himself, like a dog emerging from the water. They continued walking, side by side now. "You know, Menegos," he said wonderingly, "I keep forgetting how young you are. You're so big. But you're really still a baby, aren't you?"

Domenikos was indignant. "I'm nearly nineteen, for God's sake."

"But you've done nothing, seen nothing."

The reply was soft. "Oh, no, Manusos. I know what I want."

"To be a painter? Papa won't permit it. You know that. It's hopeless. You might as well forget it."

"He'll have to permit it," Domenikos mumbled, his tone grim, his long jaw firmly set.

Manusos shrugged. "Well, for your sake, I hope so. But you know how determined he is." He sniffed huffily. "He doesn't think much of me. He thinks I'm stupid."

"That isn't so."

"You know damned well it is."

"He's never said so to me."

"Not in so many words, perhaps. He doesn't have to, does he? See how he looks at me whenever I try to tell him something. He thinks I've no brains at all." He hesitated. "But I can do most things just as well as he can."

"I believe you."

Manusos suddenly burst out laughing. He took Domenikos by the arm and drew him down the hill at a more rapid pace. "Oh, the devil with it, eh? That's no talk for a nice evening. What does it matter? Let's have some fun."

They had by now reached the level of the more settled districts of Candia. Manusos slowed his step. It was nearly dark. The houses that flanked the narrow, squalid streets of this quarter were occupied by stevedores and warehousemen, small tradesmen and artisans. Most windows were dark, though an occasional oil lamp could be discerned. Despite the comforting presence of his more knowledgeable brother, Domenikos felt vaguely alarmed; he had seldom wandered the alleys of his native town during this hour between the dog and the wolf.

They traversed the darkened main square, aware of the surrounding buildings only because of their angular silhouettes against a sky still faintly luminous. Then they were on the quays. The paired lights of the opening in the breakwater reflected their orange glow in the corrugations of the harbor's surface. Each of the ships riding at anchor was denoted by a single, small light at the masthead, utterly disembodied, swaying gently in the little swell.

No longer were the sailors amusing themselves on the quayside. Domenikos stopped, struck by the silence and the gloom.

"Come," said Manusos peremptorily and drew him away once more.

They approached a doorway over which a flickering lamp offered uncertain welcome. Without hesitation, Manusos pushed open the door. The interior, dimly lit, was brilliant by comparison with the blackness of the quay. In a large, low-ceilinged room, a group of ships' officers were drinking and singing by a smoky light of lamps and candles. Some had girls on their laps; other merely observed the scene with disinterest and drank in silence.

A large, dark woman with snaggled teeth sauntered up to Manusos and took his hand in both of hers. "It's good to see you," she said, her Greek thickly affected by an Italian accent.

He acknowledged the greeting with a smiling nod. "This is my little brother, Menegos." He turned to Domenikos. "Claretta is the proprietress here."

She grinned at him and winked broadly. "Little? Where's your big brother, then?" She laughed raucously, her breath exuding stale wine. "If you're like this one," she went on, her voice carrying effortlessly over the noise of singing and clanking goblets, "if you're like him, I know just what you want."

Domenikos smiled feebly, alarmed. But he permitted himself to be propelled toward the single empty table in the room. A pretty, slim, dark-haired girl immediately came over to them.

"Wine, *cara*," Manusos said to her in Italian. She nodded, smiling, and disappeared. "All the girls here are from Venice," he said. He looked at Domenikos, whose face was pale, a fact to be perceived even in the warm, smoky glow of the room. "You're scared, Menegos?" He patted his brother's wrist comfortingly. "You're going to become a man tonight." He extended his short arms grandly, in the manner of Giorgio. "Pick any girl you like."

"The one who served us, I think," Domenikos mumbled, embarrassed and excited. Without warning, all the boyhood whispering behind the doors of the monastery came into focus. He looked timidly at his brother. "You know, Manusos, I have no idea what to do."

"Don't worry. She'll show you." He laughed darkly.

Domenikos began to tremble as he saw the pretty girl return with a pewter ewer and a pair of goblets. She started to leave, and he was both relieved and regretful. But Manusos signaled with his hand. He pointed to his brother. "He likes you."

She stopped, looked over her shoulder, then whirled, moving with quick little steps toward Domenikos. She placed her small, almost childish hand on his perspiring forehead. "*I* like *you, caro*," she said, seating herself on his lap. "How do you call yourself?"

"Menegos," he said, barely above a whisper.
She kissed his cheek. "I am Serafina."

Serafina poured wine into a goblet and held it to his lips, laughing lightly as a little of the heavy red fluid trickled over the edges of his mouth and down his long, smooth chin. She bent over and licked it away with her darting tongue, her warm breath moist against his cheek.

"Thank you," he muttered nervously.

"Why, I believe you did that on purpose, Menegos." She put the wine to his lips once more. "Now drink, like a good boy. We must go and put the devil in his place." She wiggled provocatively in his lap, causing him nearly to spit out the mouthful of retsina in his embarrassment. "I can feel him stirring nicely already."

As soon as he had emptied the goblet, Serafina stood up and took his hand, leading him out of the crowded room. As they reached the door, Domenikos turned and glanced back at Manusos, who was watching them amusedly. The brother winked and waved them on. Domenikos looked to the girl, who was waiting for him at the foot of a narrow staircase.

"Come along, Menegos *caro*. Come along now. We have to hurry."

He followed her upward into the relative darkness of the first floor, which was illuminated by a single candle that sizzled fitfully. Shouts of laughter and little cries resounded in the bare corridor. All but one of the doors were closed, giving a poor semblance of privacy to the pairs of occupants behind them.

From the single vacant room a pale light offered spectral welcome. Serafina paused in the doorway and deftly pulled the bright red gown over her head, turning her slender, naked body toward him briefly so that the angled light cast deep shadows of her fine breasts on the wall of the corridor, her white skin contrasting dramatically with the black triangle of her groin.

It was a Saturday afternoon. Domenikos was taking a desultory stroll along the quays, revisiting (unconsciously, perhaps) the scene of his recent moral undoing. There were few ships moored at the wharves now, and none at all anchored in the harbor; little activity to distract his eye from its inward focus. Even the yawping gulls had grown torpid in the heat of the day. They swooped lazily now and again across the still, intensely blue water, but were mostly poised listlessly on the battlements and ramparts of the quays or in the rigging of the ships.

His thoughts were disturbed. He could scarcely pretend that he had not enjoyed his interlude with Serafina, nor could he deny the accuracy of Manusos' summary of this incident: "Now you know. Imagination is no substitute for experience." He supposed the judgment reasonable, as far as it went. But there *were* things that could only be imagined. And occasionally, he believed, the thing imagined was more vivid than the thing experienced.

There had been something so tawdry about his coming together with Serafina. He had hoped for a situation more romantic, a triumph of affection rather than a mere assuaging of the flesh. As soon as they were finished (as soon as *he* was finished), she had quickly dressed herself, helped him on with his breeches, and waited for him at the foot of the stairs only long enough to collect her fee. In fact, it was Manusos who paid; Domenikos had had no money with him. She had given him a quick farewell kiss and gone back to serving wine, her eyes gleaming no longer for him but rather at the prospect of finding another client before the night was over.

Domenikos knew, nevertheless, that he would return to Serafina. The animal so suddenly born in him would not be denied. But the process lacked elegance.

He reached an intersection, and mindlessly turned in the direction of the main square with the principal buildings of the Venetian administration. There, directly before him, was the Cathedral of St. Titus, a Roman church. Without considering his action, he approached this fine, classical façade with its sculptural adornments and its Corinthian pilasters, typical of the architectural style imported by Venetian culture-mongers. The great bronze doors stood open invitingly in the breathless heat. He entered without reflective purpose, as much, it seemed, in search of shelter from the sun as from curiosity.

As soon as he was standing within the narthex, just beyond the main portal, the chill welcomed him. For an instant, all was darkness. Gradually, his eyes became accustomed to the cool, lofty, vaulted entrance. He walked into the nave and was surprised by the cheerful, open arrangement of this church, so much brighter than the one he attended.

All was color and air and sunlight, the light transmitted through windows taller and broader than those with which he was familiar. Patterns and tones flashed on the slender columns supporting the high, coffered ceiling. Small chapels lined both sides of the nave, each with its gilded altar and alabaster statuary. But as he walked down the center aisle it was the brilliant, elaborate high altar that held his full attention. The retable was in the form of a large triptych, heavily framed in gold. The subjects were scenes from the life of Christ—the Annunciation, the Baptism, and in the center, the Crucifixion.

He was staggered. Never before had he seen work accomplished outside the hagiographic tradition of the Byzantine. Here was a revelation more electrifying, more galvanizing than the discovery of the little panels in the Metropolitan Church so many years before. The saints, the Archangel of the Annunciation, the Virgin, Our Lord Himself, all were portrayed in poses that were natural to the human body. There was no stylization, no ritualism. They had a quality no painter of icons would have dared to attempt. The youth laughed to himself; in any case, none would have had the vaguest idea of how even to begin.

It wasn't simply the postures that stunned him. The flesh of these figures was flesh. The clothing was draped realistically. And in the backgrounds of each painting there was a landscape with trees and houses and sky and hills. And the colors—oh, God, the colors; such depth and richness of tones, such light, such a sweep of conception.

Motionless, Domenikos stood before the triptych, absorbing every detail, every nuance. Suddenly he felt a tap on the shoulder. He spun around to find a wizened little priest, a head shorter then he, peering up at him, amused.

"You're standing in the sanctuary, you know. I'm afraid you're not supposed to be here."

Domenikos flushed and began to back away, on the point of muttering an apology. But the priest restrained him. "Oh, I think it's all right this time." He turned to face the altarpiece. "It's magnificent, isn't it? It's one of the treasures of all Crete." He nodded. "It's by a pupil of the great Tiziano, you know."

Domenikos bobbed his head enthusiastically. "It *is* magnificent, father."

"Tiziano Vecellio is Venice's greatest painter. We were very fortunate to get this. It's a gift from the archbishop."

"I'm ashamed to confess that I've never heard of Tiziano Vecellio, father. Is he still alive?"

The old priest laughed huskily. "Oh, yes. I'm sure he must be. If *he* had died, we would have heard of it."

"And he's in Venice, you say?"

"He's in Venice." The cleric sighed nostalgically. "He has a great house. Some say he's almost as rich as the Doge himself."

Domenikos grew more excited as he looked down at the priest. "Does he take pupils, father?"

The old man gave an elaborate Italian shrug. "Ah, as to that, I really couldn't tell you." He looked with curiosity at Domenikos. "But you're not Italian, are you? You speak the language well, but you're a Candiot, aren't you?"

"I am, father."

"And they let you enter our cathedral? I find that astonishing."

Domenikos grinned. "I'm afraid *they* don't know I'm here. In fact, I didn't expect to be here myself. I just wandered in. Your doors were open. . . ." He pointed to the triptych. "But this . . ."

"Yes?"

"Is it wrong for me to be here? I mean wrong from your church's standpoint?"

The priest appeared surprised by the question. "Have you the intention of profaning the cathedral?"

"Naturally not."

"Then we shall say nothing to anyone if you decide to come again."

"I may come again?"

"Of course. Come as often as you like. As you say, our doors are open, open to all God's children. You *are* one of His children, aren't you?"

"I suppose I am, father, but my people don't seem to see it in the same light as you do."

"Well," the priest began, with as little condescension in his tone as he could manage, "we regard these differences as quite unimportant, we Venetians. The Romans don't view them as we do. Man's soul is our only concern. The Romans are lawyers. They enjoy splitting hairs." He smiled. "What is your name, my son?" Then as soon as he put the question, he lifted a hand. "No, you don't need to tell me. I don't have to know. It was merely a matter of interest. We have very few Candiot visitors, you understand—to my regret. We're not really the ogres some try to make us out." He laughed. "You know, there's comparatively little fornication in our choir stalls."

Domenikos blushed. "My name is Domenikos Theotokopoulos, father."

"You're Giorgio's son?"

"I am."

"Well, Domenikos, you're very welcome. I know your father, in a business way, you might say." He laughed again, lightly. "I confess that I'm surprised to learn that a son of his should be interested in our paintings."

The youth grinned. "It surprises him too, father. He doesn't understand it at all."

"Ah, well, we can't always comprehend these things. It's God's will." He made to leave, then turned back. "I'm called Father Vincenzo. I shall always be glad to see you, Domenikos. But the next time," he added apologetically, "I hope you'll stay out of the sanctuary."

It would be inaccurate to suggest that Domenikos' conversion to the Latin faith was the result of his enthusiasm for the paintings in the cathedral. There were, he learned, several others, mostly Venetian, though none seemed comparable in quality to the great triptych. Nor was he seduced by the remarkably relaxed and generous outlook of Father Vincenzo. These were certainly important elements, for they were evidence of a sort of faith that he realized he had been seeking for some time, elements that revealed a recognition of man as more than the toy of a whimsical and frequently angry God. Domenikos had read Aristotle carefully, and it required no great feat of intellect to relate the philosophy of the Greek master to the tenets, as Father Vincenzo expressed them, of the Latin Church.

The priest met frequently with Domenikos, after dark, during the months of autumn and winter. He instructed the youth in the mysteries, the articles of faith, and the ritual of the Roman communion. He gave him volumes by the Fathers of the Church. And he eventually saw to it (quite improperly) that Domenikos was admitted, in secret, as a communicant not long after Christmas. However, the Church of Rome had grown fat by making exceptions to its own immutable rules.

His conversion and his increasing exposure to Venetian art had convinced Domenikos that he must go to Venice to study with Titian, whose influence was everywhere to be seen in Candia's Latin churches and monasteries. Father Vincenzo's information about the great Adriatic city, and about the master (inflated by the safety of distance) grew more and more detailed. The youth realized, however, that departure would be impossible without his father's consent and very substantial material assistance. This never seemed less likely than in February of 1560, just after Domenikos had said farewell to the monastery of St. Catherine. For it was understood, by Giorgio at any rate, that his younger son would at last join the family concern.

It was a period of crisis. Domenikos recognized that he must act now or lose all hope. Yet he floundered; sure of his will, of himself, unsure of the method he should apply. He was disturbed to discover that he would make use of any means that appeared to offer the possibility of success, would conceal his conversion, which after all was central to the person he had become.

Domenikos perceived with shock the profundity of his hypocrisy. There was irony in the realization that he was, in his fashion, quite as willful as his father—and probably much more devious. So complete had been the closure of communication between himself and his parents that as he considered his approach to them now, it seemed likely that their understanding of him was predicated on a boy of eleven. Could he make them comprehend the extent of his change, the nature of his ambition, without wholly disillusioning them? To gain his end, he would use all his wiles. But he trembled; success seemed so improbable.

He took care to select an evening when Manusos was not dining at home. The servant girl had cleared away the dinner things, and Giorgio was about to leave the table. He had just pushed back his bench when Domenikos spoke.

"There's something I have to say to you, papa, if you have the time."

The youth's pulse seemed all but to stop as he watched his father halt midway in his motion. He gazed down the table at him, his expression half annoyed, half curious. He sat down and carefully composed his stubby, hairy hands before him.

Domenikos breathed deeply, paused, then blurted it out. "I want to go to Venice to study painting with Titian."

The silence that followed was at last broken by Cleo, her face contracted with concern and anxiety.

"You're sure about this, Menegos?"

"Absolutely sure, mama. I've learned all I can here. Brother Constantine, as you know, has no more to teach me." He smiled sadly. "The other brothers have rejected me too. If I'm to learn more about painting, I have to go to Venice, and Titian is said to be the greatest master there."

Silence again. Domenikos waited for Giorgio to make some comment, but he remained still.

"You see," he continued hastily, "I want to paint in a different way, papa, not as it's done here."

Giorgio seemed to have found, deep within him, a small island of calm to which he now sought refuge. His voice was preternaturally soft and controlled. "I am not sure that I understand what you are trying to say. What is it about the Cretan way of painting that isn't good enough for you?"

"Oh, it's good enough for its purpose, papa. But I want to go beyond the restrictions that are imposed on icon painters. There are other ways of painting, and those are what I want to learn."

Giorgio grunted. "I've seen some of them too. The Venetian's houses, and even their churches, are full of them. How can you think of worshiping in front of them? What have they to do with God?"

Domenikos broke in anxiously. "Most of them have nothing to do with God in our terms, papa. They have to do with man. They look like people doing the things the people do, in settings that look real, that look like life."

"I still don't understand. What religious purpose does it serve? What has it to do with God?"

The youth was amused to hear from his father's lips a question that had been asked by Brother Constantine. He restrained the urge to grin. "In the Latin Church, these pictures are perfectly acceptable. That's all I can tell you."

His father glanced at him, at first with suspicion, then with contempt. "A lot you know about the Latin Church. I deal with the priests every day. They're a pack of scoundrels, merchants in priests' clothing, the lot of them."

Domenikos resisted with difficulty the temptation to observe that he did know quite a lot about the Latin Church. "I've seen the paintings in the cathedral, papa, and the ones in the churches and in the Franciscan monasteries. They seem perfectly suitable to me, given the differences between the two faiths."

"And what would you know about the Latin faith?"

"A great deal. I've talked with their priests."

"Why?"

"Because, when I saw the pictures, I was interested. A church that produces art like that is interesting to me."

"And that's as far as it went?"

"That's as far as it went."

The words of the lie fell so easily from his lips that Domenikos was more surprised than ashamed. He had known he would lie; he had not known it would be so simple.

His father grunted once again. "I hope so."

"You'll let me go, papa?"

Giorgio finally released the growing pressure on his temper. He raised his heavy right fist and brought it down on the table. "Yes, by God. Yes."

The youth didn't hear. "But you must, papa. You must."

His father began to laugh, richly enjoying the astonishment his reply had produced. At last, the fact of his assent sank in. Domenikos stared at him. Giorgio lifted a hand. "Oh, I admit, Menegos, that I've been prickly about this. You've not been exactly pleasant about it yourself. But I really have thought about it in a different light since I learned that you were leaving St. Catherine's. I need you with me. I'm not going to pretend that I don't. Manusos is a fine fellow, but he hasn't your intelligence. On the other hand, I've thought of what your mother says. If she's right, who am I to fly in the face of nature? It seems that God has intended you to be a painter. I can't see why, but shall I try to fly in His face too?" He raised a thick finger and aimed it at his son. "But let me tell you one thing, Menegos. This had better be the right decision. You'd better prove that you deserve it, that you're the greatest painter alive. Because you have it in you to be the greatest merchant alive. I will not stand for your being second-rate at anything."

"No reason to fear, papa."

Giorgio leaned forward, relaxing at last. "Tell me something. What is it that makes you so sure about this?"

"It's difficult to explain. I don't know how a man feels when he knows he has a vocation for the priesthood—"

The father interrupted. "But that's got nothing to do with this."

"I know, papa. I was trying to think of something similar, something that might help you understand how I feel." He laughed, embarrassed, and still so elated that the words tumbled out carelessly. "Something that might help *me* understand, too. I mean that a man who's certain his calling is to the Church, he gets this certainty not from rational convictions. . . . We all have more or less the same religious convictions, after all. There's nothing basically different about his *beliefs*. It's his feeling about God, about what he wants to do with respect to God, that's different—"

"Different, different." Giorgio's explosion of impatience alarmed Domenikos. Would he change his mind? "What does 'different' mean? I hear you and your mother say it, but I've heard no satisfactory explanation."

The youth put his head between his hands, resting his black-sleeved elbows on the table. He had rarely felt so inarticulate. "Well, in my case, it's that I feel the one thing I can do best in my life and with my

life is to paint. I can feel it in my hands." Here he extended his arms
to their full length, inclining them toward his father, his slender fingers
splayed out as if in supplication. "I really don't have any control
over them. Painting is all they'll let me do."

Giorgio grinned. "And you damned well don't *want* to have any
control over them either, do you?"

Domenikos nodded. "You may be right. Ever since I first put a bit
of tempera on a panel, it's been the only thought in my mind. Nothing has happened to change it. Painting is all I've ever wanted to do."

Giorgio sighed and turned to his wife. "Why me? Why should such
an unreasonable, such an irresponsible idea occur to a son of mine?"

She smiled. "Perhaps, as you like to tell me, it's something to do
with my side of the family."

He stiffened with proud indignation. "Why should it be your side
of the family all the time? You think there's no quality, no intellectual-
ity, on my side?"

She extended her hands to him. "I married you."

He snorted. "You married me, my love, because your father ordered
you to."

She laughed gaily. "You imagine that I would have married you if
I thought you without quality? You think my father or anyone else
could have forced me to do something so important against my will?"

Her eyes were as fierce as his own had been a moment earlier. He
flushed with pleasure and reached out to take her fingers. He shook
his head, smacking his forehead with the flat of his palm. "No, by God,
that's true enough. The devil himself couldn't force you to do something against your will."

Her amiability returned at once. "You can *persuade* me to do almost anything, Giorgio."

Their eyes met and held. This sudden intimacy embarrassed Domenikos, for in it he perceived far more than a devotion he thought
proper to one's parents. At last Giorgio looked away. He raised his
face and stared for a long moment at his son, his expression at once
melancholy and contented, as if he felt himself both fortunate and be-
leaguered. He turned back to Cleo. "I didn't oppose you, did I?"

"No."

"I knew you'd have your way in the end. I thought I'd try something different. Instead of saying no, I'd say yes." He chuckled. "It
didn't matter, though, did it? I never had a chance, did I?"

"Never."

"And you?" He looked back to Domenikos.

The youth, in a flood of tears, was barely able to make out his father's features. "I'm not so strong-willed as mama."

"Oh, I think you are, Menegos. It takes great strength to want the same thing when you're nineteen that you wanted when you were eleven. I *used* to think you had no will."

Domenikos blushed. "It's not a matter of will, papa. It's even stronger than that."

Giorgio waved this aside. "You know our saying: 'If a stone falls on an egg, too bad for the egg. If an egg falls on a stone, too bad for the egg.' " He smiled sadly. "Too bad for papa."

The head of the family studied the pair who had defeated him without a struggle. He nodded at his son. "So it's your plan to leave us alone." There was no trace of self-pity in his tone, but it was plain to Domenikos that this arrow was aimed straight at his conscience. Giorgio might accord his consent, but he wasn't granting his approval.

"There's Manusos, papa."

The father's disdain was etched in his face. "Oh, I'll admit that he's a good son, a lot more respectful of me than you are. He's impulsive and clumsy, like me, but he hasn't my wit."

"He's a good man," said Cleo. "He has a good, kindly heart."

Domenikos wondered how his mother would feel if she knew of Manusos' introducing him to the brothel. But then, of course, there was the matter of his own conversion. Motivations were, on all sides, open to question.

Giorgio sighed again. "Well, then, it's settled." He smiled at his son. "We're going to miss you. My God, how we'll miss you, Menegos." He began to weep softly, wiping his great nose repeatedly with the back of his hand. "But go, and go with my blessing." He paused. "And with my help." He grew more animated now, leaning forward and pointing his finger at Domenikos. The old Giorgio had returned as rapidly as he had vanished. "You can't manage this kind of expedition without a lot of money, you know. And you can't do it without making arrangements ahead of time. Of course, you'll stay with your Uncle Manusos in Venice. I'll see to that. I'll have a letter to him on the next ship. And I'll provide you with enough money to live there as a son of mine should."

Domenikos struggled to his feet, his face streaked with dampness, and moved around the table, first to embrace Cleo, then his father. Giorgio took the youthful face between his powerful hands, holding the chin firmly, and looked into the immense dark eyes. "I'm not sure that you're right in this, Menegos. But I've made up my mind that your mother is right, that you should have a chance at it. If anything goes wrong, or if you change your mind about it, it's easier to come home if you've not had to run away, isn't it?"

Domenikos nodded and grinned through his tears. "I suppose, but there's no danger of that, papa."

Giorgio released him and bobbed his head. "I think you're sincere. If you try as hard as I think you will, there's no danger, as you say." He laughed. "I'm not sure what *I* want to happen, Menegos. I want you home. But I don't want you home thinking of yourself as a failure. I don't think you'd be of any use to me in that frame of mind."

Domenikos laughed. "If I have to come home—"

"You won't. I know that."

He slept badly that night. Thrilled, he would have been restless for that reason alone. But to this was added the painful remembrance of his deceit. He had lied about his conversion, and this in spite of the fact that Father Vincenzo had urged him to tell the truth.

But how could he? It wasn't possible for him to imperil the trip to Venice. He could hardly tell them of it before his departure. And yet, for all that this deception appeared to flow so logically from the situation, Domenikos rued it bitterly. It was the first major lie of his life.

PART II:

Venice (1560–1570)

Four

DOMENIKOS Theotokopoulos was reborn the morning of May 7, 1560. The heavy mist that enveloped the barque was beginning to lift. A Venetian galley had taken her in tow and was drawing her slowly toward the Arsenale, which occupied the seaward tip of the city's largest island. There, Domenikos had learned, a representative of the Magistrate would inspect the cargo, the crew, and the few passengers aboard before permitting the ship to be towed to her mooring by the Molo.

As the craft glided through the still water of the lagoon, the only sound was of the galley's oarsmen as they rowed in cadence to the cries of the hoarse-voiced coxswain. The sun, barely above the horizon, appeared as an orange ball through the dense mist. Domenikos stood at the bow with the other passengers, his eyes seeking the channel ahead, scarcely able to contain his excitement.

He was sure he would have no trouble making out the chief landmarks of Venice. Had he not studied, in the library of the Catholic archbishop in Candia, Jacopo de Barbari's wonderful plan of the city? Admittedly it had been drawn from the presses in 1500, but his father and others even more familiar with this capital had assured him that there had been few major changes since that time; a number of new churches, a *scuola,* an *ospedale,* some houses and *palazzi* here and there, but nothing that would alter the general accuracy of the old chart.

Suddenly the oarsmen ceased to row, and all was silence. The barque rocked idly in the calm water. After what seemed a long time another galley, much more gaudily fitted out than the somber black scow that had her in tow, could be seen approaching through the mist. Domenikos moved to the starboard side as the oarsmen, mostly black-amoors, shipped their blades, drawing their gilded craft to the side of the ship. A middle-aged official, plump and smiling, scrambled up over the side, casually returning the captain's salute. He was sump-tuously and colorfully attired, more richly than any man the youth had ever seen.

Domenikos returned to the little cluster of passengers and watched as the Venetian, chattering cheerfully and constantly, made a cur-sory examination of the documents and cargo manifests the captain handed him. He then exchanged brief, familiar greetings with each officer and member of the crew, all of whom he plainly recognized. And now he approached the passengers, smiling and nodding as he spoke with each. When it was Domenikos' turn, the official, who seemed almost grossly fat when seen at closer range, smiled brightly and offered a limp, moist hand.

"Ah, signore," he began in a travesty of Greek. "And with whom have I the pleasure?"

The youth returned the smile and bowed. "I am called Domenikos Theotokopoulos, signore," he responded in his excellent Italian.

"Oh, I'm grateful to note that you have our language," said the of-ficial, nodding. "Not everyone in Venice speaks Greek, you know." He paused then, apparently musing. "Theotokopoulos? You are per-haps a connection of Manusos Theotokopoulos, the merchant of the Rio dei Greci?"

Domenikos grinned. "He's my uncle, signore."

"Ah, yes." The portly man hadn't stopped smiling, but he now contrived to increase the intensity of his expression. "Ah, yes, we know him very well in Venice, very well." The smile relaxed slightly. "And what, if I may ask, has brought you to our beautiful city?"

"I'm to study painting. It's my hope to study with Maestro Tiziano Vecellio."

The face of the official revealed astonishment, then awe, then in-credulity, these emotions crossing his features in a fraction of a sec-ond, each nevertheless clearly defined. "To study with Maestro Tiziano," he exclaimed. "Ah, now that would be a privilege indeed." Once again, a bit more firmly this time, the official took his hand. "Well, well, I can promise you that you'll be very welcome in Venice, signore. We're all very proud of our Tiziano Vecellio."

The man turned sharply away and moved back to the captain. They shook hands. Accepting the discreet assistance of two powerful deckhands, he climbed over the railing and disappeared down the side of the barque. Orders sounded, and the official galley moved off. Soon the craft that was towing Domenikos' ship began once more to draw her forward, this time in the direction of the Molo.

The mist, grown patchy in the breeze that had risen with the day and the sun, parted for an instant to give Domenikos a brief glimpse of the green domes of San Marco, the tall shaft of the Campanile, and, in the foreground, on the Molo itself, the elegant façade (so cruelly described by Vasari as "Gothic") of the Palazzo Ducale, all structures that he was able to recognize from Barbari's plan. But what a difference. In reality, color was everything. The old woodcut couldn't convey the glittering spires and domes, the particolored walls of the Doge's Palace, the pale blue sky, the thin sunlight of the Venetian morning, cloudless now that the mist had mostly lifted.

Nor could Barbari have suggested the muddy waters of the canals, the hints of bright tones to be discerned in the furled sails of the many ships moored before the Molo and the Riva degli Schiavoni. Nor indeed could any picture convey the impression of motion, of vitality. To a country boy (and Domenikos was forced to acknowledge, if only to himself, that this was what he was), the bustle of Venice was astounding, even a little alarming. There was nothing like it in Candia. Could all this movement really be to some useful end?

As the galley drew the barque up to the stone curbing of the Molo's quay, a fair crowd was gathered about the foot of the gangway. Domenikos searched their faces, seeking his uncle, whom he had last seen long ago. Nearest at hand were flocks of grubby small boys begging crew and passengers to throw them coins or sweets. Comparably grimy men of all ages and colors, with ill-kempt beards and torn clothing, offered to unload the cargo; some were quarreling with the children, for the men were begging as well. Beyond, at a distance, were what appeared to be merchants with their clerks, the former dressed in garish silks that no self-respecting Greek or Cretan would have dreamed of wearing, the latter in black tunics and tight-fitting breeches favored in Candia. Among none of these faces was Domenikos able to make out that of his uncle. And his self-confidence, which had been reinforced by the excitement attending the landing, began to fail. He felt helpless and, unexpectedly, homesick.

He lifted his great, bright, black eyes from the edge of the quay to the Palazzo Ducale just behind it, feasting them briefly on the splendor of its intricate, elegant design. Then he lowered his gaze to the white stone arcade at ground level. And there, leaning casually against a column, his yellow-stockinged legs crossed, was his Uncle Manusos, unmistakable in his resemblance to Giorgio, looking as if he had no connection whatever with the scene of confusion being played out at the foot of the gangway. Yet, as Domenikos stared at the man, he realized that his uncle was looking directly at him, smiling sardonically.

Physically, at any rate, Manusos Theotokopoulos resembled his older brother; and there were similarities too in his powerful gestures, his capacity for enthusiasm, his tendency to assume an attitude or position and thereafter to cling to it until compelled by circumstance to yield. Yet these likenesses, like perceptions made in a distorting mirror, were deceptive. For Manusos' interests and outlook were different from Giorgio's, his arrogance and pride resting on a different kind of foundation.

He was concerned to see that his family was secure, that he could live as well as was required; but this was not his obsession, nor was the trade with Crete that made life here possible. He had, since his arrival in Venice many years before, become almost wholly Italianized. He was preoccupied more with the appearance of success and prosperity; and thus he should, as Giorgio had so often said of him, be grateful that in his case the appearance and the reality had gone hand in hand.

Manusos was ambitious, politically as well as socially. And to the degree that it was possible for an alien, albeit one who could call himself a citizen, he had achieved a high position in the Greek community of the city; this numbered several thousand souls. His success, however, wasn't impressive enough for Manusos. More than anything else in life, he would have liked to be at least the unquestioned leader of the Venetian Greeks, to be head of their Council of Forty. At most, he dreamed of being elected to the Consiglio, the council that advised the Doge. He realized that this greater ambition was impossible to attain (one had to be noble, a true patrician), yet he desired it none the less passionately for this knowledge.

Manusos had managed to make himself widely known in Venice, had made it a point to recognize by name every member of the Greek community, even most of the children. He cultivated as many of the native Venetians as he came in contact with in his affairs. Because of his ambition, he was, in a curious Italian fashion, extremely cautious in expressing his opinions. "As soon as a man knows what you really think," he would rationalize with his wife, "you cease to be of interest to him. If you agree with him, there's no reason for him to go on trying to convince you. And if you disagree with him, you become his enemy."

While this policy had undoubtedly served him well in a commercial way (by not alienating powerful Venetians who controlled all trade), his tendency to shilly-shally over significant issues had made him important enemies among the outspoken Greeks. He had a fatalist's understanding of the effects of his folly, realized that it threatened even his attainable ambition; but he was unable to help himself. Such folly was an essential part of his nature. So too was conspicuous generosity; no favor was too great to ask of him, and if he failed to grant it, or to see that it was granted, it was never for want of his having tried. It would have been difficult to determine where ambition left off and vanity took over as motivations for his behavior.

What had damaged Manusos most severely in the eyes of his fellow Greeks had been his refusal to take a strong stand when the Consiglio had decided to close down all the Eastern-rite churches of the city, of which at one time there had been eight. Manusos had temporized in a way they considered shameful, arguing that if his coreligionists were patient, all in the end would be well. And in the end—now—all was proving, if not well, at least better. Manusos took full credit for this amelioration, but his presumption impressed few of his acquaintances.

As befitted a man who enjoyed what he termed "visibility," Manusos dressed in the gaudy style of the native Venetian, affected the brilliant silks and satins, and was contemptuous of the attire worn by the Greeks. In other ways too he was more Venetian than the Venetians, bubbling over with enthusiasm for all the virtues he noted in his adopted city, expressing fury at any effort to detract from what he conceived as Venice's greatness, her invincibility, her culture. No native could have been prouder than he of the Republic's past glories and present riches.

When all on deck and on the quay below was in readiness, the passengers were permitted to descend the gangway. For the first time Domenikos set foot on the soil (the cobbles) of Venice. Manusos, who had strolled leisurely from the arcade to the side of the ship, embraced the youth warmly, loudly expressing his greetings. He took Domenikos by the arm as he went to arrange for the transportation of his effects to his house in the Rio dei Greci. Then, elbowing his way through the crowd, uttering terrible imprecations at the beggars who approached them, he drew his nephew free and guided him toward the Piazzetta.

They paused briefly between the columns that supported the celebrated Venetian winged lion and the warrior St. Theodore. Manusos, a few inches shorter than Domenikos, looked up at him, smiling triumphantly. "Well," he said in Greek, "and how do you like our magnificent Venice?"

Domenikos laughed, and responded in Italian. "It's a little soon for me to say. I've hardly seen it. It's so busy. It confuses me."

"Busy?" Manusos was surprised. "Why, this is nothing. It's still early in the morning. Wait until noon. Then you'll see how busy it can be. Or better still, wait until the Feast of San Marco, or the Feast of Bucintoro on Ascension Day. Then you'll see something that I promise you will blind your eyes. Venice is the most beautiful and greatest city the world has ever seen, my boy."

As they moved up the Piazzetta toward the Piazza, Manusos chattered incessantly, his tones reminiscent of his namesake, Domenikos' older brother. He pointed with pride to the wonders to be seen. The youth wasn't listening with complete attention, however, so absorbed was he in all there was for his eyes to take in, for his ears to hear, for his nose to smell. The odor that permeated the ever-warming atmosphere seemed a particularly noxious blending of dead and dying fish, of raw sewage, of the ordure that citizens habitually jettisoned into the canals, and of the food that was prepared and vended in the streets and squares. Not even offensive odors, however, could take any of the loveliness away from the architectural masterpieces of the Piazzetta and Piazza, nor did it detract from the color and vivacity of the populace that swarmed everywhere.

Then they were standing in the great Piazza. Pedestrians darted frantically across the great square in all directions, scattering, as they passed, the innumerable pigeons like dry leaves in a driving wind. Here and there, little groups were conversing, segregated by sex, gesticulating broadly, their hands flying abruptly about, their feet stamping furiously on the pavement, their heads bobbing to and fro.

And what a variety of people they were, of every size and color, in every sort of dress. In his own usual black, Domenikos felt conspicuous. It was all very exotic. What he found especially diverting was the differences of race here represented. Apart from his limited exposure to the sailors whose ships called at Candia, his information had been restricted—until now—to the Biblical pronouncement on the descendents of Ham. Black he had imagined to be black. But here were all gradations even of white, and others ranging from the palest Chinese to the darkest Nubians who had come from Africa as slaves in Venetian galleys. If there were slaves in Crete, it was the poor natives.

And the boldness of the prostitutes astounded him. In Candia, they were strictly creatures of the night. In Venice no such distinction was made. The practice was highly organized and rigidly governed by the Consiglio. In pairs the women patrolled the Piazza, their tight bodices forcing their breasts upward and outward, their mocking cries dense with coarse images. Nor was it women alone who openly solicited. Foppish young men importuned Domenikos and his uncle, offering ways of passing an hour that were quite lost on a country boy, though he was quick to appreciate their impropriety. He was priggishly indignant about the calm with which Manusos brushed aside such outrageous proposals, hardly interrupting his chatter to reject them.

So preoccupied was Domenikos with the animation of the square that they were halfway across it before he looked back at the immense Campanile that rose precipitously from one corner. The base was prefaced by the delicate Loggetta of dolomite marble, a recent addition by Sansovino. The remainder of the tower's fabric was of warm-toned brick. As he was staring at it, the great bells began to chime, a wild sound that thrilled and startled him. Others in the Piazza, however, appeared to take no notice, except perhaps that for a little time their conversations were made superfluous. But the pigeons went mad, swooping about the square in vast clouds with each profound stroke.

Manusos tugged at his nephew's cape and beckoned him to follow. Domenikos turned obediently, but as he did, he found himself confronted by the Church of San Marco. It was surely a wonder of the world. From the ship he had been able to see only its five copper domes, gone green with weathering. Here was its principal façade, a fantasy so extravagant, so eclectic in its sources that it was not to be believed. He was unable to move, nor could he have said, as he remained rooted to the pavement, whether he was more struck by the mosaics (of which there were none, so far as he knew, in Crete) or by the huge bronze horses standing about the central portal. His eyes, in their wonder, seized first on details. The entirety of the vision was too overwhelming to be immediately comprehended.

As if out of respect for Domenikos' awe, the bells fell silent. Manusos, who had assumed that his nephew was still at his heels, had continued walking and was now at the far side of the square, standing beneath the Orologio with its odd Moorish figures. The uncle returned and once again plucked at the youth's cape.

"Come, Menegos."

Domenikos could only shake his head. "It's so wonderful, uncle."

Manusos nodded. "Oh, yes, it's magnificent. There's nothing like it anywhere else in the world." He paused. "But do you want to know what I think? I really don't like it very much."

The nephew was amazed. "You don't?"

The man flushed. "No. Well, you understand what I mean, don't you? It's excessive, too garish, too old-fashioned."

Domenikos glanced at his uncle's bright attire, and with an effort resisted a smile. "I see exactly what you mean. But old-fashioned? No, I don't see that. Is everything to be scorned simply because it's old?"

"Of course not, but you should see this one inside."

"I'd like to."

"That's not what I'm talking about. I mean about its being old-fashioned. It doesn't compare with the churches that Sansovino and Palladio are building today. Why," he went on, pointing toward the Piazzetta, "it's not nearly so fine as the Libreria." He faced the opposite side of the square. "Even the Procuratie is better, and it's quite old, too."

Domenikos shook his head. "I think San Marco is superb."

"Well, come along anyhow, Menegos. You must be hungry, and your Aunt Marica is waiting to meet you."

Until his uncle mentioned it, Domenikos had been unaware of hunger. Now he nodded and turned back to the church for a final look. "My God, my God."

"*Their* God, you mean," said Manusos, chuckling at his pleasantry. "It's a Latin church. Actually, it's not a church at all. It's the Doge's private chapel. But come, Menegos, you'll have all the time you need for sightseeing, and even if *you're* not hungry, I am."

With reluctance, Domenikos accompanied his uncle.

"I must tell you," the man said as they walked, "that I do think those four horses are nice." They were about to leave the square.

"Nice, uncle? They're magnificent."

Manusos shrugged. "If you say so. They were brought here from Constantinople hundreds of years ago." He laughed. "Now *there* was a piece of Venetian genius for you. The Doge persuaded the

Crusaders to put the whole Eastern empire out of commission for him."

Domenikos snorted. "That, I presume, would be the sack of twelve hundred and four. You'll remember that it was that incident that gave Venice control of Crete."

The uncle was indifferent. "Something like that, I imagine. I'm not very good at dates. But it doesn't matter, does it? It was bound to happen that Crete was conquered by some power. Better Venice than Naples, eh?"

Domenikos smiled wryly. "Perhaps. I don't know the Neapolitans."

"Exactly, and I do."

Domenikos made no reply. There was no point in arguing about a matter that neither was in a position to resolve. They were walking through streets that were, for Venice, quite narrow (though in Candia they would have seemed wide), all faced with houses of some elegance. Vendors were everywhere; they accosted the pair by leaping suddenly into their path. Manusos pushed them away, cursing them in crude, guttural Italian.

"This is nothing," he repeated. "Wait until you visit the Mercecia on the other side of the Piazza. Of course, you'll only go there to buy things, so you'll have no cause for complaint. You'll have to mind your purse, though. They'll cut it from you before you know what's happened."

Here and there they passed dark, dank, narrow alleys covered with filth, flanked by grim houses teeming with dirty, screaming children. Domenikos was appalled. "I had no idea there was such poverty anywhere, uncle. We have nothing like it in Crete."

Manusos' laughter was, the youth thought, forced. "This is a big city, Menegos. In all big cities, real cities, you find poor people. Lazy, most of them are. They'd rather beg than work, rather steal than beg. And if they get arrested, what happens? And most of them are arrested at one time or another. Then what happens? They're sent to prison, and the citizens, you and I, the self-respecting people, have to pay to feed them and put clothes on their backs. They're scum." He put his finger to his temple. "But they're not stupid, are they?"

"Wouldn't it be cheaper, then, to find work for them?"

Manusos grew sad. "That's not so easy as you make it sound. There just isn't enough work for everyone, except when Venice is at war."

Domenikos laughed. "Isn't that practically all the time?"

"No, I mean when we're preparing for a great battle. That's when the Arsenale is busiest. Fifteen thousand men can find work there then."

"If there's no work, I don't understand why you're so scornful of the poor. How else are they to live?"

Domenikos had intended no show of disrespect, but it was plain that Manusos took it so. His silence was sullen as they walked. They crossed a number of little humpbacked bridges. At last, when they had reached another, the man brightened. He pointed to a church on the opposite side of the narrow canal. "Now *that's* what I meant when I was talking about modern churches. That's our new church."

"San Giorgio dei Greci?"

"Correct. It's not completely decorated yet, but we're using it just the same. It's the one church the Consiglio will let us have now, you know."

"I've heard the story, uncle, but I'm sure there's much about it I don't know."

Manusos appeared disinclined to discuss this sore subject. "Our own Master Michele Damaskinos has been doing some of the frescoes. Do you know him?"

"No, uncle. He left Candia when I was a small boy. I know of him, of course, and his father is a friend of papa's."

"He's an excellent painter, and a great friend of mine."

The youth studied the building in silence. "I must say it doesn't look to me very much like a Greek church. The style is completely Venetian."

"But this *is* Venice, Menegos. We're all Venetians here, no matter what religion we profess."

"Oh, I know that. But does it mean that we have to renounce all our old traditions? Does everything in Venice have to look like everything else?"

Even as he was saying this, Domenikos felt a powerful twinge of guilt. Why should he goad his uncle, especially on a point about which he himself had feelings so confused and ambivalent? If he loved the coziness of the Greek churches, he admired the spaciousness of the Latin ones—and the spaciousness of the Latin faith even more. They paused halfway across the bridge and looked at the church once again. From this side, at least, it *was* purely Venetian in plan, with a gable typical of the Roman Catholic churches to be seen even in

Candia. Only the dome evoked Byzantium, and this feature, after all, was a detail borrowed by the West many centuries before.

"It's a good church, Menegos. I'll say no more than that. You may be the expert on art and architecture, but for the present you'll have to accept me as the authority on Venetian life. If you insist on being a militant Cretan while you're here, you'll get nowhere with the Venetians. And they're the people you need to know if you mean to get ahead, and I'm sure you do. If you fail to make a good impression on them, you'll find yourself standing still, like those horses on San Marco, with nothing to do and no place to go but back to Candia."

There was no more to be said. Domenikos nodded, and followed his uncle into the street of the Rio dei Greci. The man paused before the door of a house that was perhaps a hundred feet beyond the church. "Here we are, Menegos," he said with pride. "This is my house."

The exterior of Manusos' house was sober, of plain stone, the windows tall and broad, without architectural adornment. Domenikos noticed that none of the shutters on the ground floor had as yet been opened to admit the hot light of the morning. By eight o'clock in Candia, everyone was up and about his daily tasks. But Venice was, after all, another world. He shrugged, and followed Manusos into the cool, darkened hallway.

The beamed ceiling of the white-walled dining room seemed very high in the half light that emanated from the entrance hall and through the slits of the shutters. Domenikos saw that it was furnished with a heavy oak table and with chairs; he bumped into a chair as he entered. Only when his uncle had thrown open the blinds was the rest of the decoration revealed; a large cupboard for the pottery stood against the distant wall, beside a door leading to the kitchen and scullery. A tapestry with colorful geometric patterns hung opposite a large fireplace. Next to it were a pair of icons of St. George and St. Catherine, both of which he guessed to be of Cretan origin. In the center of the table was a pewter bowl containing a small bouquet of flowers.

"Sit down, Menegos. I'll see that you get something to eat right away, and then I'll fetch your aunt."

Domenikos obeyed. And shortly after his uncle left, a pretty, dark-haired servant girl, who reminded him, happily but somewhat uncomfortably, of Serafina, entered with a small tray on which were bread and cheese, a pitcher of wine, and a Venetian glass goblet. She placed the tray on the table in front of him.

"Thank you very much, signorina," he said, stammering. The sudden recollection of Serafina had embarrassed him.

The girl put her hand to her mouth as if she were about to be sick and rushed from the room, closing the door sharply. As soon as she was gone, he heard a shrill scream of laughter. It dawned on him that he shouldn't have addressed a servant as signorina. He blushed, and then he shrugged.

Soon after he had begun to eat the bread (which, though whiter than that obtainable in Candia, seemed to him much less tasty), his uncle returned, preceded into the room by his wife. She was a woman who in no way resembled Cleo. She had a strong face, with black eyes and a ready smile that disclosed even white teeth. Her black hair was streaked with gray, combed harshly back to reveal a wide, high forehead.

Domenikos stood up as they entered. He noticed on his Aunt Marica's left hand a flash of zircon and amethyst rings as she extended her short, fleshy arms to embrace his waist. At this moment, his mouth was stuffed with bread and cheese, and without the benefit of wine to wash it down, Domenikos almost choked in his effort to respond audibly to this warm greeting.

Marica laughed wholeheartedly as she stood back from him. "My God, Menegos. You are really a big fellow. Your father said so."

He tried to reply, gulping desperately at the damp clot of food in his mouth.

"No, no," she protested. "Finish your meal. Just sit down there and finish eating. That's right." She sat beside him. As the servant girl returned with trays for Marica and Manusos, he avoided her amused glance. "How are your bowels?" Marica laid a hand on his bicep and squeezed. She was strong. "No, don't try to answer. The reason I ask is that I was constipated for a whole week last year after I got back from Ragusa. Do you know Ragusa? No? Well, I was born there. That's right, Menegos, just nod your head. Now tell me all about your family. How's your dear mother? Has she put on any weight? No? I don't see how she manages it. Thin as a stake, poor thing. And Giorgio, is he well? Good. I can imagine that he's no thinner. Is your brother married yet? No? That's too bad. You mark my words. He's going to wait too long. A man ought to marry before he's twenty-five. Your Manusos must be thirty. That's what I keep saying to my Anastos. 'You've got to get married.' Of course, he's only six-teen. He's studying at our monastery school. But I always say that it's never too soon to begin thinking the right kind of thought. I have no daughters, thank God. Can you imagine trying to find husbands for them?" Marica saddened suddenly, tears filling her eyes. "We had two other sons, though. You knew that? Of course. One came before Anastos. The second came after him. We lost them both, may God have mercy on them." She solemnly crossed herself, then dabbed her eyes with a white silk kerchief. "Well," she said, smiling again, "that's the will of God all over. We have to learn to love whatever fortune he provides for us."

By now Domenikos had contrived to swallow the bread and cheese, washing it down with a large gulp of the strong, sour red wine. He wiped his mouth with the back of his hand, and smiled apologetically. "Forgive me, aunt. I was starved, I'm afraid, and took too big a mouthful."

"But of course you were starved, poor boy. It's nothing. You have to eat, don't you?"

Manusos had seated himself on the opposite side of the table and regarded his wife and nephew with amusement. "What would you like to do first, Menegos?"

"Why," said Marica, "he wants to go to his room and have a rest and arrange his things, don't you?"

"Oh, no," Domenikos protested. "I'm not a bit tired, aunt. If it's all right with you, I'd like to see something more of Venice. I've waited so long for this. And I especially want to see the house of Maestro Tiziano." He paused and grinned. "And I want to pray, of course. I want to thank God for my safe arrival."

Marica crossed herself again, nodding. There was a brief silence of embarrassment, however, or so the youth thought, after which Manu-sos ostentatiously cleared his throat. "Well, now, Menegos, of course you can see as much of the city as you like, and I've already shown you where you can pray. But as I wrote your father before you left Candia, I'm afraid that you're going to have trouble finding a place in Titian's studio."

Domenikos nodded. "I read your letter, uncle, and I want to thank you for all you've done, for receiving me. But you must know some-one who can help me. Papa says you know every important man in Venice." Domenikos felt ashamed for thus preying on his uncle's vanity, but as he had done on another occasion, he again assured himself that the end justified the means.

Manusos smiled smugly and acknowledged his nephew's flattery as if it were a statement of irrefutable fact. He bowed with false humility. "Well, perhaps not *every* important man, Menegos, but most of them. The point I'm trying to make is that Tiziano Vecellio is in a class by himself. You might almost say that in Venice he's one of the nobility."

Marica seized on this thread of the conversation and tugged for attention. "You have to see him. The way he travels through the streets. You'd swear he's a prince. Of course, he *is* a Count Palatine. *That* title was given to him by the Emperor Charles himself, may God have mercy on his soul."

"Besides," said Manusos, "it's our opinion that you'd be a lot easier in your mind if you were studying with someone who speaks our language, like our friend Michele Damaskinos. I was speaking to you about him earlier. He's a first-class painter, as we know for ourselves, and I'm told he's a wonderful teacher, too. You know, he's had great success here as a *madonnere,* an icon painter."

"Your uncle has arranged for you to meet him," Marica added eagerly. "Oh, Menegos, I'm sure you're going to like him."

Domenikos was more than dismayed by these words. He must be polite, however. But on this issue he proposed to make himself clear from the outset. "I'd enjoy meeting him, uncle. I'm sure, as you say, that he's a fine painter and teacher. But you see, I want to study with Titian. That's why I came to Venice."

Manusos sighed. "Well, it will be very difficult."

"But I must try."

"You must try," the uncle echoed wearily.

Anxious not to disappoint him, Domenikos went on in tones that were brighter than his feelings. "But that doesn't mean that I don't want to meet Master Michele."

Manusos was gratified. "As soon as I knew that your ship was due this morning, I made an engagement with him for this afternoon."

Michele Damaskinos occupied a substantial house in the Rio dei Greci; it stood near the point where this canal emptied into the Canale di San Marco. In his thirties (though affecting a greater age), he had been in Venice for about a decade, and in this time had established himself as one of the city's most successful commercial hagiographers, his icons attracting not only numerous members of the Greek community but the native Italians as well. The latter, wishing to take no unnecessary religious risks, found in these little paintings, which they thought quaint in comparison to the rich art their own masters were creating, a quality of holiness, even divinity, though hardly the divinity attributed to them by disciples of the Eastern orthodoxy.

Italy denied any supernatural claims for the icons; but then, who really knew? The suspicion of the native Venetian for the Pope contributed heavily to Damaskinos' popularity. His icons sold in Venice as briskly as did reproductions of the Crucifixion in other parts of the peninsula. The man was, moreover, a skilled and cynical vendor of his own wares.

Damaskinos was tall, swarthy, and most fastidious in appearance, invariably dressing himself in black to demonstrate his kinship with the Greeks and to emphasize his difference from the Venetians. His manner was obsequious. When Manusos presented him, Domenikos felt at once that even were he a better craftsman than Titian, he couldn't have long endured this young master's tutelage.

Their host bowed them elaborately into his studio, or what he called his studio, for it was actually a display room for his work. Solemn little arrangements of icons lined the walls, each lit by a pair of candelabra to give the prospective client an impression of how each piece would appear in his own home. The odor of incense failed to suppress the more pungent one of rotten eggs and pigment so characteristic of freshly applied tempera.

"Come in, gentlemen, come in, please," he said to them in Greek. "Welcome."

Domenikos looked about him at the paintings on the walls, and realized that Master Michele had little to say to him as an artist. His work, while disclosing appreciable indebtedness to his experience in Venice, was fundamentally Cretan. The youth had no need of further training in techniques already taught him by Brother Constantine.

"This is my nephew," said Manusos.

"Ah, yes." Damaskinos stood back and made theatrical gestures and postures to suggest that he was studying this newcomer with interest. He even hummed a little tune. At last, he smiled gravely. "And tell me, how are things in our pathetic little Candia?"

Domenikos had difficulty in responding politely to this condescension. "The same as ever, master. We survive."

"Just so." The man seemed suddenly concerned. "So you think you'd like to be a painter."

The youth's temper flared and expressed itself before he was able to control it. "I already *am* a painter, master. I've come to Venice to learn to be a better one."

Manusos was scandalized. "Menegos," he protested.

Damaskinos tittered. "Oh, it's quite all right. It shows courage. It shows that he knows what he wants. I like that in a pupil of mine." He turned back to Domenikos. "I suppose you had the usual schooling at St. Catherine's, with old Brother Constantine."

"I was his pupil for nearly ten years."

"Did he speak of me?"

"Oh, yes, a great deal. You're a source of great pride to him." This was something of an exaggeration, but at least not an outright lie.

"Ah, well, I suppose I must be, though I know he always hoped I'd join the order." He rubbed his hands together. "But I decided otherwise, as you see." He smiled complacently. "But here we are speaking of *me*, when we ought to be discussing *your* future. What can I do for you?" he began wearily. "I daresay you'd like to come into my workshop. But before you answer, I must warn you that I'm a harsh taskmaster, much harsher than poor Brother Constantine. I'm not nearly so patient as he was." He laughed richly. "Of course, I'm only joking. Why, I have men who've been working with me for years. You can ask them what I'm like."

Domenikos looked at the floor. He was embarrassed because, far from intending to discourage him, Damaskinos was attempting to attract him. "I'm afraid, master, that that wasn't exactly what I had in mind."

"Ah?"

"I want to learn the style of Tiziano Vecellio. I want to paint as the Venetians do. That's why I've come."

There was a short pause while Damaskinos rearranged his attitudes. "Well," he said airily, "it's a fair enough way of painting, if you like it. In my own judgment it's too opulent. It has nothing to do with faith, has it? With our faith, I mean. It lacks taste and restraint and discrimination." He waved a limp hand. "Oh, you mustn't misunderstand me. I've nothing against Titian. I know him very well, in fact. He's a good friend of mine. It just happens that I don't share the King of Spain's high opinion of his art."

Domenikos pounced. "If you're a friend, perhaps you'd be good enough to give me a letter of introduction to him, master."

As if slapped, Damaskinos recoiled a few steps and eyed the youth carefully, hesitating a long time before replying. "If it were only a social introduction, my young friend, I'd be delighted. But I'm afraid it would be of no use for your purpose. Maestro Tiziano takes no more pupils. I know that for a fact. He's told me so himself. He'd not dream of having you around the studio even to sweep his floors and size his canvases. I'm very sorry." He flapped his arms lamely in a gesture of reluctant hopelessness. "But that's the way it is. There's nothing to be done."

Perplexed, Domenikos turned to his uncle, and perceived that Manusos was sharing his thought—that in fact Damaskinos, like everyone else in Venice, recognized Titian when he passed in the street but didn't know him to speak to. Manusos began to back away, his movements quick, angry, expressive of his humiliation. He gave the painter a curt bow. "We've already taken up too much of your time, master. Thank you for your trouble."

"No trouble at all," was the bland reply. "If there's ever anything else I can do, I trust you'll not hesitate to call on me. My house is your house. I wish you all success, young man, but I fear you have the prospect of nothing but disappointment in this ambition of yours."

Domenikos smiled grimly, bowed, and turned to follow his uncle down the dark staircase and into the brilliant, noisy street.

Five

A week passed. Manusos scurried from acquaintance to acquaintance in a vain quest for an introduction to Titian. Domenikos explored the city alone, visiting churches and the public portions of the Palazzo Ducale, the Libreria, and the Procuratie. He listened to Venice's voices and sounds, inhaled her fragrances and her stenches, observed scenes of violence—violence of joy, of anguish, of anger, of outrage —all played with a theatricality wholly unfamiliar to a Cretan. For Domenikos the panoply of daily life here was a spectacle so rich, so varied, so gaudy that he found it difficult to believe his uncle's assertion that on the great feast days the tempo could be more rapid, passions more heatedly exposed.

Venice appeared to be at once expressive of the Middle Ages and the Renaissance. Born in the period of the Lombard invasions of the eighth Christian century, rising to the height of her power during the Crusades, she now sought to conceal from her citizens the accelerating rate of her decline. This deception was accomplished, or at least attempted, by constructing ever more wonderful monuments to the principle of eternal greatness. Manusos' refusal to accept the fact of Venice's wane, perceptible even in Candia, was reflected in the attitudes of the Doge and his advisers. Except perhaps for Genoa, this condition was common to all Italian states and principalities, even those governed by the Pope.

The incredible defeat at Fornovo, in 1495, when Italian troops, unified for the first time since the epoch of ancient Rome, had failed to destroy an inferior, disease-ridden, booty-laden force under the inept leadership of the French Charles VIII, had presaged the ensuing thirty-odd years of foreign invasions which culminated with the emperor Charles V's terrible sweep southward in 1527. Thereafter, only Venice, because of her comparative isolation, managed to retain some outward evidences of power. Even the awesome Church of Rome found its authority questioned.

Physically, Venice showed no scars. She was still the Pearl of the Adriatic, a dream city floating off the coast, glittering with a hundred domes and spires, more of which were being added at the time of Domenikos' arrival in 1560. Most notable was the Church of San Giorgio Maggiore, on its island, which was rising under the direction of the day's most favored architect, Antonio Palladio, whose popularity was eclipsing that of the older Sansovino.

Intelligent and remarkably adaptable, Venetians succeeded in offsetting the declining trade revenues by increasing their banking activities. Thus, in a sense, Manusos and others were not totally mistaken in their optimism. The situation was grim, but it didn't as yet give this impression; and no one was inclined to peer too deeply into the future. For most Venetians, the salubrious present sufficed.

One wound, however, was obvious in 1560, and it refused to respond to cosmetic surgery—the state of religion. Rodrigo Borgia's nomination as Pope Alexander VI in 1492 and his subsequent malfeasance, rendered more distasteful than most papal reigns by the disgraceful behavior of his son Cesare, led to the defection of Martin Luther. This prelate provided the initial spark which would, in the following century, become the conflagration of the Reformation.

In areas where it counted heavily, there were matters of power and influence that cut more deeply than did the question of ethics. Recipient of the tithe, the Church had vast wealth at her disposal, the expenditure of which at the diocesan level was the prerogative of archbishops and bishops. Control over their appointment was a subject of surpassing interest and was considered (by kings and princes) to be but incidentally an ecclesiastical affair. Rulers insisted, more than once at sword's point, that the popes give them more discretion in episcopal selections. (The kings of Spain had absolute authority in the filling of these posts. Protestantism never thrived in Spain.)

To heal or at least to conceal these blemishes exposed by a succession of venal pontiffs and all-too-human kings, Pope Paul III convened the nineteenth Ecumenical Council in 1545. The site was the Italian mountain town of Trento. This council continued for the next eighteen years intermittently to discuss and seek resolution of the more serious problems. The Councils of Trent propounded the philosophy of what came to be called the Counter-Reformation, a churchwide movement to clarify doctrine and dogma and to purify the clergy.

This noble effort proved futile. It failed to destroy or even permanently to retard the spread of Protestantism and other heresies. Clarification of doctrine, however, showed itself an easier task. Purification of the clergy seemed unlikely until an entire generation of priests, monks, and nuns died off.

The standards established, as the newly organized Society of Jesus was to discover, were occasionally overzealous. In her passion to stamp out venality, debauchery, and heresy, the Church threatened her whole intellectual structure. Books were banned out of apparent caprice. Rational discussion was inhibited. Ridiculous rules were laid down for what painters and sculptors might create as religious art, what poets might write, what musicians might compose and play.

To most intelligent Venetian churchmen of 1560, the tone of the debates at nearby Trento was anathema, threatening the basis on which they predicated their comfortable and remunerative lives. The Holy Inquisition, following its successful revival in Spain in the previous century, was but grudgingly accepted in Venice. Its tribunals functioned timidly. Heresy in a city overrun with transients was hard to identify. It was, indeed, a popular Venetian view that the most dangerous heretics were those who actively supported the Inquisition. And in any case, mass arrests and persecutions were deemed un-Italian. A vengeful murder now and then was comprehensible in Venice; genocide was not.

It remained indisputable that the Church's principal intention was to widen and deepen comprehension, to intensify religious experience, to draw man closer to God. In this effort, the debates at Trent, though not yet terminated, had the effect of stimulating people everywhere to examine their beliefs and their souls.

Domenikos had heard oblique references to these great questions

from Father Vincenzo in Candia. But in Venice they were common-
places of general conversation. It was impossible to walk through the
Piazza without hearing at least one discussion concerned, and often
violently so, with an aspect of the Trent Council. If his understanding of the issues was as yet insubstantial, he could take solace from
the knowledge that he wasn't alone in his ignorance. Churchman and
layman alike wallowed in a quagmire of fact, illusion, prejudice, ru-
mor.

Domenikos' wanderings through Venice took him each day, late
or early, to the Biri Grande on the opposite side of the city's main island from the Rio dei Greci. Here, in the splendor befitting his position, resided Tiziano Vecellio. From the outside, the house seemed
not excessively imposing; two stories of pink brick rose above
ground-floor level, surmounted by a simple cornice and a flat roof.

The entrance in the Biri Grande, a recessed portico with a semicircular arch supported by Corinthian pilasters, disclosed (when the
door was opened) a tantalizing view of extensive gardens stretching
down to the lagoon and of the master's immense studios. Bounding
the property was a high brick wall.

Each day Domenikos paused across the street from this doorway
and waited a long, breathless moment, hoping to have a glimpse of
the great man. And each day he was disappointed. At length,
he would proceed to the parish church of San Canciano, a street or
two away from Titian's mansion. Seeking consolation and repose in
the bright coolness of a side chapel, he would burn a candle before
an altar to St. Francis, a saint whose simple virtues had been exhaus-
tively extolled by Father Vincenzo. He prayed for what seemed increasingly unlikely, the realization of his single hope.

It was noon. Domenikos was just leaving the church. Ten days had
passed since his meeting with Damaskinos. He was looking down at
the dusty marble steps as he emerged. Suddenly, the voice of his uncle
startled him. "What are *you* doing here, Menegos?"

There seemed no surprise in Manusos' face, only mild interest.

"I was praying, uncle."

"There?"

Domenikos realized at once that he shouldn't have spoken the
plain truth; its implications had occurred to him too late. He was
beginning to understand the Venetian tendency to say exclusively
what others wanted to hear, but only in this instant did he fully appreciate it.

"There," he answered dully.

They walked slowly toward the Rio dei Greci. "You belong? You're a communicant?"

"I am."

"For how long?"

"Only a few months."

"And how does your father feel about it?"

"I'm ashamed to confess that he doesn't know. I intended to tell him, but then I just couldn't. He'd not have let me come to Venice."

There was a short silence. "But of course, you're planning to tell him."

Domenikos sighed. "I mean to, but the proper moment hasn't presented itself."

"And when do you think the proper moment will come?"

Abashed, Domenikos looked down at the cobbles. "I don't know."

"If you were to write him of it now, Menegos, would he make you return home?"

"I don't know, uncle."

Manusos laughed harshly. "Oh, my boy, be honest. You know very well. He's a man of strong feelings. He'd have you back in Candia by the next ship."

"What would that prove, if I went back? After all, I've joined the Church, and I'm not going to change my mind again. It's too late for that."

"You're being childish. Why do you think something has to be proved? Your father will be angry. He'll do the first thing that occurs to him, which will be to bring you home, because it would be the last think *you'd* want. There are no complications."

"You're right."

Manusos appeared perplexed. "Why? Tell me that much. Why? What possessed you to make such a strange decision? Do you know what they're like, these damned Romans? No, I'm serious. Do you have any idea what they're like? No, you don't."

"I think I do, uncle."

"You know nothing."

This flat assertion so reminded Domenikos of his father that he turned abruptly to face his uncle. "I'm not a child."

"You've not told me why."

It was so complicated. Moreover, Domenikos felt he had no reason to apologize to anyone for his religious convictions. Yet to offer no explanation would appear disrespectful. And there remained the possibility that an irate uncle might communicate with Giorgio himself.

"It's their art," he said at last.

Manusos was momentarily puzzled. Then his face cleared. He laid a warm hand on his nephew's shoulder as they walked. "Oh," he said briskly. "You mean that if you're to have a chance of success in *their* world, you'll have to be one of them."

This notion had never occurred to Domenikos, but it was plain that his uncle, ever the opportunist, would accept such a reason as sufficient and justifiable. With a conscience less than easy, the youth nodded. "Something like that. Certainly, there's not much hope that many Greeks will want to buy the sort of painting I'm likely to do when I'm working on my own."

Once again Manusos patted his shoulder, more enthusiastically this time. "You really surprise me, Menegos. I had the feeling you weren't much better than a spoiled monk, all conscience and regret. You're right, of course. The only way for you to get ahead is to join them. I'd have done it myself except that I work mostly with Greeks." He paused, chuckling appreciatively. "That's very Italian of you. I'm proud of you."

"I guess I'm learning how things are done in Venice."

They walked in silence for a little while. It was just before they reached the bridge by the Church of San Giorgio dei Greci that Manusos spoke again. "I think you were right. And if I were you, I'd say nothing about it to Giorgio, not for the time being, not before you've established yourself here. And I think it would be wise if we said nothing about this to your aunt, Menegos. She would hardly appreciate it. She has what she calls her principles." He smiled sardonically. "You understand? She'd want to write your mother, and then . . ." He raised his hands to the level of his bearded chin and moved them sideways. "You'd be in trouble, yes?"

Domenikos nodded. "All right, uncle. God knows, I want no trouble now."

Thus, on the same day, he was trapped into living not one lie, which he had planned eventually to confess, but two; and to neither could he see a possibility of absolution.

Dinner had just ended. It was a few days later. The entire family, including young Anastos, Domenikos' cousin, was seated about the large dining table. Stocky like his father, the boy had inherited Marica's candid nature and her common sense.

As was usual, the conversation during the meal had been desultory, touching casually on many minor events of the day, all quite exasperating for Domenikos, whose anxiety increased daily as his failure to establish fruitful contact with Titian seemed ever more conclusive. Out of diffidence and perhaps from a reluctance to hear more bad news, he had refrained recently from introducing it at table. So he wasn't happy when his aunt brought it up with Manusos.

"I suppose you've made no progress with Menegos' little problem."

Her husband shook his head. "None," he responded curtly.

"Whom have you seen?" she asked.

The uncle slammed the flat of his hand loudly on the table, as Giorgio would have done. "Whom *haven't* I seen would be a question I could answer more easily. And in one way or another, they all tell me the same thing, just what Michele Damaskinos told us. Maestro Tiziano takes no more pupils, and that's the end of it. They say he's a rich man, which we all know. They say he's an old man, which we also know. And they say that he doesn't want the trouble of teaching any more. It's all very simple, except for Menegos."

Anastos ventured boldly into the conversation. "Have you seen our bishop, papa?"

Manusos stared, astonished, at his son. "Seen Gabriele Seviros? Now why in the name of God should I think of disturbing *him* about a thing like this?"

"Because he knows Maestro Tiziano."

There was a prolonged pause while Manusos, Marica, and Domenikos regarded the boy with interest.

"And how have you come by this information?" his father finally inquired skeptically.

"There's a portrait of him by Tiziano hanging in the monastery. I'm surprised you never noticed it, papa."

Marica clapped her hands with delight, then pressed them to her lips and blew a kiss to her son. "There, you see?" She tapped her temple with a finger. "He has brains, this little one. He knows how to think."

Manusos ignored this observation. He was lost in thought. He gazed at the table, his hand on his forehead. Then he looked up, smiling hopefully. "You know," he said to Domenikos, "he might just be right."

"But of course he's right," snapped Marica indignantly.

Manusos continued to speak, unperturbed. "I'll try to see His Excellency tomorrow." He rose. "On second thought, it might be a better idea if you came with me, Menegos." He hesitated, frowning. "You won't lose your tongue or do anything foolish like that, will you?"

The youth grinned. "You needn't worry, uncle, not when it's so important to me."

His uncle walked to the door and turned to face the youth. "I don't think there's any point in getting our hopes up just yet, but I don't think there's yet reason for despair either. If the bishop can't help us, we'll keep trying until we find someone who can."

"Thank you, uncle. I'm very grateful to you."

Manusos dismissed these thanks with a brusque sweep of his hand. "There'll be time for gratitude when we've succeeded. And by God, we shall succeed." He opened the door to the entrance hall. "Now I'm going to the taverna." It was his customary evening exit line.

"I hope I don't have to tell you," said Manusos as they walked toward the residence of the Eastern Church's patriarch in Venice, "that you're to say nothing to His Excellency about your conversion."

Domenikos laughed. "Can you really think I'd do such a thing, uncle?"

"No, but it occurred to me."

"What if *he* should bring it up?"

"He won't. Why should he? You're my nephew, aren't you? He knows my faith. It's hardly probable that I'd bring a nonbeliever to ask a favor of a bishop."

Manusos was pleased with this subterfuge. But Domenikos was of two minds. "I hope you're right."

By comparison with the luxurious episcopal palace of the Roman patriarch, Bishop Gabriele Seviros' official dwelling was modest. It was a typical Venetian townhouse. Only when they had been ushered inside was any major difference evident, and what a difference it was. The atmosphere was votive, candlelit, somber, evoking in Domenikos a memory of Candia Metropolitan Church.

During this fortnight in Venice, there had been few sights to remind him of home. Now a wave of nostalgia assaulted him as he sat beside his silent uncle, waiting with other petitioners to be received by the bishop. Would he, if offered an excuse, return willingly to Crete? No. But he understood that his total certainty didn't preclude moments like this, when a recollection unexpectedly presented itself, shocking him with his loneliness, reminding him that on the best day he was a full month from his native island.

As they sat in the awkward stillness, Domenikos thought of Crete. Apart from the soft image of his mother and the more prickly one of Giorgio, he missed the countryside, the hot, rolling hills, the vineyards and groves and scrub. For there was nothing like it to be seen from teeming, sealocked Venice. These bittersweet reflections were interrupted by a touch on the shoulder. Manusos had risen at the bidding of a clerk, who indicated with a slight gesture that they should follow him. They were admitted to the large private cabinet of the bishop.

The old clergyman was seated on a black-lacquered throne. His beard was almost pure white, as was his bare head. So long was the beard that it reached a point just above the heavy jeweled cross that reposed magnificently on his ample breast. Manusos kneeled to kiss the episcopal ring, which must have severely impaired the circulation of the plump white finger it graced. Domenikos respectfully followed suit, trying to keep in mind his uncle's apothegm about the necessity for hypocrisy in the higher interest of self-preservation. As he was kneeling, he looked up into the eyes of the bishop; they were small and black, as brilliant, in the poor light, as the finish of his great chair.

They stood before him. Gabriele Seviros smiled with a studied, benevolent gravity, waiting for Manusos to speak.

"It's my nephew, Excellency. He's from Crete, my brother's son. And he would like to—"

The bishop silenced Manusos by lifting his right hand two inches from the arm of his throne. "But let him speak for himself." He faced Domenikos, barely moving his impressive head. "I take it you do speak."

Domenikos smiled. "I do, Excellency."

"You speak Italian?"

"I do, Excellency."

The old man was pleased. He smiled wearily. "Then by all means let us speak Italian. It is a much more civilized tongue than Greek. Of course, I would not want so dangerous an opinion to be generally known, but I am certain that I can count on my good friend Manusos for discretion."

Manusos solemnly placed a hand over his heart, and bowed deeply. "I'm known as discretion's very soul, Excellency."

"Exactly so." There was the slightest note of skepticism in the bishop's dry old voice. He inclined his white head once more toward Domenikos. "Forgive me. I interrupted you. You were going to say . . ."

"As my uncle said, Excellency, I'm from Crete, I'm a Candiot. I studied hagiography for ten years with Brother Constantine at the monastery of St. Catherine. I've come to Venice to learn painting." He paused, and took a deep breath. "I would like to study with Maestro Tiziano Vecellio, because his kind of painting is the sort I would like to be able to do."

The trace of a smile flitted across the bishop's antique features. "You show admirable taste."

Domenikos waited for the patriarch to continue, but he appeared to have nothing to add. "My uncle has very kindly given up most of his time during the past fortnight trying to arrange an introduction for me. . . ."

"Without success, I gather?" Seviros looked at Manusos.

The uncle sighed. "Alas, Excellency, I've failed."

"Exactly so. But I am surprised and disappointed that you did not think to come to me at once, Manusos."

"I hoped it wouldn't be necessary for us to disturb you, Excellency, knowing how occupied you are with more important affairs."

The old man shifted his position with difficulty and gazed reproachfully at his petitioner. "And what, in your opinion, could be of greater importance in my poor life than to help a promising young man to achieve a worthy ambition?" He turned to Domenikos. "I assume I may safely call you a promising young man?"

The youth flushed. "I'm proficient, Excellency, in what I've learned, but there's a great amount I've not yet been able to learn."

"It is good and proper to understand one's precise worth, without illusion. If a man leaves everything in this world to God's mercy, he will have difficulty accomplishing his just ends." Seviros shook his head sadly. "I fear that Venice has corrupted me. You probably know that I permitted some of my well-wishers to commission Maestro Tiziano to paint my portrait, and I must confess to you that at the time I never gave a thought to his not being of our faith." He paused, smiling. "He is a very rough and ready fellow, this Tiziano. But people who ought to know say he is without peer in his craft." He turned now to the clerk who had introduced them into his presence. "Brother Karyl, I wish to dictate a letter." His glance returned to Domenikos. "You are to listen carefully to what I say, and you must not hesitate to interrupt me if I make a mistake. Yes?"

"Yes, Excellency."

The clerk sat himself at a small writing table before Gabriele Seviros, holding a sharpened quill in his hand. The old man sank back on his throne, placed his head on the cushioned rest, and closed his eyes, addressing his words to the high, obscure ceiling.

" 'Maestro,' " he began, " 'the bearer of this letter is of a fine Cretan family with important connections in our city. He is said to be a painter of great ability in his native style of art, and he now wants to learn the craft as it is so wonderfully practiced by your noble self. You would do me honor. . . .' No, Brother Karyl. Stop, please. 'You would do me *further* honor by speaking to him and appraising his skill, and if you find him worthy, by taking him into your studio. I am informed that you have proposed no longer to teach. I would not, therefore, seek to impose on your time and energies were it not that I have reason to regard this young man so highly. It would seem to me a great pity if your virtues were not, once more at least, passed on to someone of such talents and eagerness. Please accept, maestro, this expression of my admiration and gratitude to you for your many considerations in the past, to which I would with much happiness add yet another debt, were you so disposed.' "

Gabriele Seviros moved his old head forward and opened his little black eyes. He spoke softly to Domenikos. "Would you find such a letter to your satisfaction?"

"It's far too generous, Excellency. It may be that I do not deserve such praise."

The old man smiled. "I respect your use of the subjunctive, my son. It suggests the possibility of doubt without granting its certainty." He lifted his ringed hand and moved it slowly across his chest, returning it finally to the arm of his throne. "No, I am sure that I do not exaggerate." He paused, his smile now benign. "You see, I have had a long letter from your Brother Constantine."

Six

Tiziano Vecellio was the kind of man who lied about his age. At different times during his life, he had allowed it to be believed that he had been born in 1472, in 1477, and even as recently as 1490. There may have been an explanation for this apparent coquettishness, but it was never offered. It could have had its source in vanity, or in convenience—social or material. The fact was, however, that this greatest of all Venetian painters was, in 1560, not a day less than seventy and perhaps as ancient as eighty-eight.

He was very rich, immensely admired, and eminently successful, regarded in Venice as a semipublic figure; indeed, he was a true "celebrity," covered with honors and titles, local and foreign. Yet for all his renown, Titian was not a bit better behaved than was demanded of him by a society already notorious for its looseness.

His bitterest foes conceded that he had come a long way since his birth in the Dolomites. He was a native of the provincial town of Pieve di Cadore where for centuries men of his family had served as soldiers, lawyers, and judges, distinctions that had been minor but that were distinctions nonetheless. Tiziano was not, as some alleged, merely a peasant whose career had flourished by accident of fortune. Beyond such personal force as he possessed, there lay a tradition of some magnetism and power, however minuscule this might appear against the background of an overwhelming Venice.

He had arrived in the Serenissima (just when, no one could now recall, so long ago was it) to study with Sebastiano Zuccato, an indifferent craftsman. Such was his genius, or so good were his connections, that within a short time he moved to the studio of Gentile Bellini, and still later worked with his celebrated artist's brother, Giovanni, the most highly regarded painter of his age.

Titian's circumstances during the period are mostly unknown. All that is established beyond doubt is that in the years 1507 and 1508 he collaborated with Giorgione da Castelfranco. They worked together on a series of frescoes for the façade of the Fondaco dei Tedeschi, a monument which ought to have raised Giorgione's already great reputation to the level of that of the Bellini. He died, however, barely two years later, leaving the legacy of this fame and success to Titian.

For Titian, there was no looking back. His rise was uninterrupted and rapid. By 1560, his name in Italy was rivaled only by Michelangelo's. In Venice and everywhere else on the Continent, however, he was the better known—Europe's master painter. To achieve this position, and then to retain it, he had on several occasions transformed himself as an artist. And to some degree he had modified himself as a person too, giving the appearance of moving readily and without remorse with the tastes and tempers of his long epoch. He was able at any moment to evince the sort of outlook and produce the sort of art demanded by those, of Church and the laity alike, who could afford his prices. A masterful opportunist, Titian gave evidence of having undergone drastic spiritual surgery when the Counter-Reformation tenor of the Councils of Trent became public knowledge.

After a lengthy period devoted mainly to portraiture, he reverted in midcentury to theological themes, subjects of purification and redemption that were consonant with the spirit of the Councils. If these themes were good enough for a Church attempting to save herself, they were obviously good enough for Titian. He may have felt it advisable to follow this trend, but it is doubtful that he felt his position threatened. He had important protectors. He had been a principal painter to the court of the emperor Charles V, and was now the favorite artist of Philip II of Spain. He seemed unassailable by the Church, even by the Pope himself.

Most of Titian's important later works were intended for export to Spain. The work he produced for Philip revealed a master at the very height of his power. And his force as a person had never been more impressive. He was unquestionably a giant.

Domenikos stood before the master's house in the Biri Grande. The white light of the midsummer sun blanched the pink brick, casting absurdly long, sharp, morning shadows on the protruding cornice and window ledges. Blinking frequently in this brilliance, he hesitated for only an instant. Armed with the bishop's letter, he felt that if he were hesitant now, whatever confidence he had mustered for the occasion would be dissipated. Want all, risk all.

He tried to control his trembling. He wondered if anticipation of things delicious would always affect him in this way. Would there not be a time when he could look forward to a moment of importance without finding that his palms were sweating? (He was recalling his tremors as he followed Serafina up the brothel stairs in Candia. The parallel was false, but the feeling was identical.)

Resolutely, he approached the great wooden door and knocked. He waited. The moments passed too slowly. At last, there were sounds of rattling chains and a bolt being thrown. A liveried servant, splendid in a particolored tunic and dark breeches, stared bleakly at him. The man's manner was one of decorous hostility, his lifted eyebrows alone denoting interest in the caller's business, none at all in his person.

"Yes?"

"I have this message for Maestro Tiziano." Domenikos offered his letter. The domestic accepted it gingerly, as if he thought it possibly contaminated. He contemplated the scarlet wax of the episcopal seal, turned the letter over and for a moment regarded the elaborate orthography of the address, gestures that amused the youth, who doubted that the man could read. He finally looked up.

"Is there to be an answer at once?"

Domenikos nodded. The servant stepped aside and with a brief, abrupt motion of his hand indicated that the visitor should follow him into the vaulted hallway. "Wait here, please."

The man disappeared beyond another door, leaving Domenikos in this cool limbo to study the arrangement of stone and mortar, the barreled arches, the fluted pilasters whose capitals were decorated with the traditional acanthus leaves of the Corinthian style. Only by great force of will did he compel himself to consider anything now except his future, which lay behind that door. His eyes could seem to focus on the architecture, but his thoughts strayed. Everything of importance was at issue, right now. His mind thrashed violently between daring to hope and the temptation to despair.

Wholly absorbed in his reflections, Domenikos failed at first to note the servant's return. The man's manner had perceptibly altered, was now distinctly deferential. "Would you be good enough to come with me, signore? The master will see you immediately."

An immense pair of doors gave access to the vast main studio. Suspended from all four of the extensive walls were paintings in various stages of completion. Just to the left of the center of this great room stood Titian, his back to Domenikos. He was short, heavily built. He wore a dark red velvet tunic, his arms encased in pale cream silk, the bald head partially covered by a black skull cap.

At the sound of the youth's approaching footsteps, the master turned to reveal a face at once fierce and curious, arrogant and humorous, sensitive and sensual. The pale domed forehead loomed over gray brows, over sharp, glittering, forbidding eyes, over a long, regular nose, a voluptuous mouth, a belligerent jaw whose beard grew outward almost horizontally, giving him an air of diabolical malevolence.

Titian glanced briefly, contemptuously, into his visitor's eyes; then his gaze flitted down to Gabriele Seviros' letter which he held, with evident distaste, in his powerful right hand.

"You had to have a letter from a bishop to give yourself the courage to present yourself at my door? You imagine that I'm likely to be moved by what some churchman thinks of you as a painter? You think I'm likely to be impressed by what the Doge himself tells me about pictures or painters?" He looked back to the letter. " '. . . a fine Cretan family.' There are no fine Cretan families. There are only fine Venetian families. The Cretans are our slaves."

Domenikos knew no more of Titian's temperament than the bishop's single admonition that he was rough and ready. He couldn't decide whether the man was serious or simply attempting to provoke him into making a sharp retort. He smiled weakly. "If you were a Roman, master, I think you'd feel that there were only fine Roman families. I'm a Cretan. I know what *I* think."

The hardness of Titian's expression threatened for an instant to dissolve into a smile, but he maintained his severity. " '. . . said to be a painter of great ability in his native style of art.' " The master looked up from the page. "Said by *whom* to be such a painter? By Michele Damaskinos, for example, that dreadful little sycophant?"

"No, master. The recommendation may be even more unreliable than that in your view, because it comes from my old teacher, Brother Constantine, in Candia."

Titian laughed coarsely. "Oh, God, now we have monks who want to be accepted as authorities on art. What next? And I suppose this 'native style' is icon painting?"

Domenikos nodded. "But I recognize its limitations."

"Do you now? Well, congratulations. I suppose you think that the last lecture is perception."

"It's a statement of fact."

"And why me, may I ask? What makes you come to me, of all the painters in all Europe?"

"Is there anyone else?"

Titian's laughter this time was almost amiable. "There is not."

"That's why I came to you, master."

"Another talent, for God's sake." Titian tapped his cap more firmly down on his bare head. "Oh, my sweet, gentle Jesus." He stared sadly at Domenikos. "And a Greek, by God, a primitive, a savage. Do they wear shoes where you come from in Greece, boy? Have you stopped playing with yourself yet?" He dropped the bishop's letter to the floor and turned his broad back to the youth, his words but an indistinct murmuring that blended with the clamorous sounds of the chattering craftsmen in the studio.

Titian whirled with astonishing rapidity, his old body still tense with energy and charged with a barely suppressed propensity to violence. "Well," he snarled, "tell me what you know. Can you stretch a canvas? Of course not, because they only use panels in the wilderness where you come from. Can you mix oils? No, because you've only been taught how to use tempera. Can you paint the blue of the sky or make the green of a leaf? No. Do you understand the delicacy of a flower or the beauty of a woman's nipple? Of course not. And why not? I'll tell you. It's because those mad coreligionists of yours have it in their heads that God won't permit art to advance beyond the point where it was fifteen hundred years ago when Christians were writing dirty words all over the walls of the Catacombs and calling it art, when they weren't eating each other, I mean." He took a quick, deep breath and continued. "Can you . . . ?" The voice trailed off, as if he had forgotten what further malice he had intended.

Emboldened by anger, Domenikos spoke. "What they wear on their feet in Greece, master, I can't say. I've never been there. But in Crete, most of the savages wear shoes, the ones, that is, who can grind the cost of them out of their Venetian masters. Not only that, but some of us manage to be educated. I'm able to read and speak and write three languages. I *have* stopped playing with myself, if that's really any concern of yours. As you say, I can't stretch a canvas, nor can I mix oils. I can't paint a sky or a leaf or a nipple or a face or a tear in the eye. That's why I'm here, because I want to learn them, because I must learn them. And I *can* learn, master."

As Domenikos spoke, Titian studied his expression, his own growing milder and more appreciative with each hot phrase. "Oh?"

"And I can learn *quickly,* too. I can be useful to you."

"Is that what they call Greek fire? Well, good for you." The master cast a half-despairing look in the direction of the men working at the canvases. Some were standing on the tiled floor; others were poised at various higher levels on scaffolding and ladders. "You see there?" he inquired. "Well, I have a dozen men working with me at the height of the season, and all of *them* are useful to me already. One of them happens to be my son. But there's not a single touch of genius in the lot of them put together. Not one. Plenty of hard work, though. And plenty of good will, too. Oceans of that." He paused, and looked once again at Domenikos. "I do wish God would preserve me from peasant boys who imagine that because they can draw a straight line and a curve they have a true vocation for painting." He lifted his gnarled, blunted, ringed right hand in a gesture of entreaty to the heavens. "No, whatever-you-call-yourself. Oh, no. I implore you. Go away. If, as you say, you truly admire me, just have mercy and leave me in peace. *You,* believe me, I have no need of."

Domenikos grinned. "Oh, I understand that, master. But I have need of you."

Titian pointed once more to his assistants. "But I've told you, I have a son there. Whatever energies I have left for teaching belong to him, not to a stranger, and least of all to a stranger who isn't even a Venetian. Who needs another Greek painter anyhow? I've already tried to teach one, and *he* was from Crete too, I think." He grunted huffily. " 'Maestro Domenikos,' he calls himself now. Can you imagine? *Maestro,* for the love of God. He learned nothing from me in the three years he spent here. But now he advertises himself as a former pupil of the great Tiziano. What do you think of that? And you should see his work. If I ever see him again, I'll wring his neck. But he's in Modena now, I'm told, creating monstrosities, I've no doubt, and still trying to hide himself behind my reputation."

Domenikos refused to yield or to be intimidated by this tirade. "But you've not seen my work, master."

"All right, then, where is it?"

"In my eyes."

The old man stared at him, at once annoyed, perplexed, beguiled, and moved. "Who told you to say that to me?"

Domenikos shrugged. "No one. It's the truth. If I'd brought you a painting, the kind of thing I'm able to make now, you would have laughed at me. And you'd have been justified. If I were content with what I can paint now, I'd not be here."

Titian grunted again, more thoughtfully this time. "Well, can you copy something then? For the moment, all I'm interested in is the level of your skill, what you can make your hands do. All savages can copy. That's all you've learned, isn't it?"

"I'm not a savage, master. I'm a Cretan."

"To me, boy, you're a savage."

"I'm a Cretan."

Titian stared long into the hot eyes of the slender young man, then turned aside, smiling. "All right, you're a Cretan. Have it your way. All Cretan painters can copy, can't they? Can you?"

"I'll try, master."

Imperiously, the great man snapped his fingers, and a man at once descended from a scaffold. He was in early middle age, wearing a smock and a demeanor that could only be called cowed. He was somewhat taller than Titian, whom he strongly resembled. He gazed at Domenikos as he approached, and there was no mistaking the suspicion and hostility in his eyes.

"Orazio, get me the model of St. Francis and Brother Leo, will you?"

Sullenly, Orazio nodded and moved toward a long, high rank of vertical stacks from which he selected, without evidence of hesitation, a small canvas. (It was the custom of Titian and other painters to maintain a file of miniature studies of all the important pictures they had painted, so that duplicates, when ordered, could be accomplished by assistants.) As Orazio returned, the master stooped over to pick up Gabriele Seviros' letter, which he had earlier thrown to the floor. Domenikos anticipated him, however. He handed it to the old man with a smile. Titian peered momentarily at the beautiful script, then looked at Orazio, who was standing beside him now.

"This is Domenikos Theoto . . . Oh, my God, Domenikos Something-or-other. It doesn't matter. This is my son." To Orazio he added curtly, "Go and get some eggs and dry pigments, and bring us a gessoed panel. I want to see what he can do."

"But I thought you said there were to be no more pupils."

"That's what I said. But there may be an exception now and then. This may be one of them. That's what I want to find out."

Orazio laughed sarcastically. "I swear to you, papa, you'll be trying to teach *my* grandchildren. There'll always be exceptions. I don't see why you bother making rules. All you do is break them."

"You think I should be governed by rules?"

The rough, oddly elegant old man chuckled delightedly at the preposterousness of such an idea.

"When you make them yourself," Orazio protested half-heartedly, "it might make a difference."

"I never set rules for myself. I set them for you."

By now, Orazio had set the model painting on an easel. Silent, he turned from his father and disappeared disconsolately in search of the required materials. Titian studied the little canvas. "You know, it's not bad at all. Not bad at all for something I painted so long ago."

Domenikos too had been examining this modest rendering of St. Francis receiving the Stigmata from the heavens while his old friend Brother Leo looked on. "Oh, I think it's much better than that, master. It's wonderful. 'Pondering what this vision might mean, he finally understood that by God's providence he would be made like the crucified Christ. . . .'"

Titian smiled appreciatively. "I know that. That's St. Bonaventura, isn't it?"

"It is."

"And how would a Cretan savage know about St. Francis of Assisi? He appeared after the Great Schism, didn't he?"

"Yes, master, but there are two Franciscan monasteries in Candia. I know quite a lot about him."

"Then you belong to the Roman Church?"

"I do."

"I hope you'll forgive me if I tell you I don't care. I selected this picture for you because it's simple."

"It's fine, all the same."

"You must never flatter me, boy. I won't tolerate it. Besides, what do you know about it, not the saint, but the picture?"

"Not enough. But I like it."

"Honestly?"

"Honestly, of course."

Titian nodded his approval. "That is the only valid test, you know. If *you* like it, then for you that's all that can count. To the devil with what anyone else thinks." He hesitated, and grinned. "Unless the someone else happens to be me."

Orazio returned with the eggs, some pigments, and a small panel that had been coated with plaster. An assistant followed him with a second easel.

"You understand," said Titian, "that I'm not asking you for a perfect replica, not the kind of thing they made you do in Crete. Make of it what pleases you, anything that comes into your head. Use it as the basis of another painting, your own painting. Be as original as you like."

Appalled, Domenikos protested. "But copying is all I know, master. I've told you."

The master shrugged as he moved away. "All right, then, copy it."

Domenikos stood for a time before Titian's model. St. Francis was kneeling, in a paroxysm of ecstasy, as he received the Stigmata on his hands, these splayed out, palms upward. The saint's narrow, haggard face, seen in profile, was inclined toward the sky. Brother Leo, half reclining on the barren, rock-strewn earth, shielded his face with a hand from the dazzling light of heaven. None of the representations he had seen in Candia of this vision approached in immediacy and intimacy the canvas before him. He memorized each detail as if it were the body of a beautiful woman whom he was unlikely to see again—the contorted tree to the right of the saint, the little valley with its green meadows and tree-lined stream, the angry sky shot through with God's light. It had on him, this picture, the effect intended; through it he relived St. Francis' precious miracle.

So intent was Domenikos in his examination that he failed to hear Orazio draw near him, and was startled when the master's son spoke to him. "You haven't started yet?"

Embarrassed, the youth shook his head. "I have to understand it first."

Orazio laughed, though not unkindly. "There's nothing in this studio that requires your understanding, except that you don't have to understand anything." He swept the great, lofty room with his hand. "We have two years' work to do, and in two years there'll probably be another three years' work to be done. There's no time for you to understand what this picture is about. The only thing that should concern you, *if* my father agrees to take you in, is how to do what you're told. Is that clear?"

Domenikos bowed his head. He would have to learn to live and work with this man. It was evident that Orazio could make life trying for him if he took a dislike to him. Deliberately now, he began to prepare his pigments, as Orazio looked on with tolerant disdain. While the youth blended the powders with the egg yolk, the man chatted. "How the devil did you persuade my father to let you get this far? I'd have sworn it was impossible."

"I had a letter from Bishop Seviros."

Orazio raised his eyebrows. "That's all?"

"Yes."

"It's astonishing." He was bewildered. "How is it that you call yourself again?"

"Domenikos Theotokopoulos, master."

Orazio laughed once again. "Oh, no. Papa will never be able to manage that. He'll call you something else, something easier—the Greek, perhaps, *il Greco*. I know him."

"But I'm not Greek, Maestro Orazio. I'm Cretan."

"It's all one, isn't it?"

It was Domenikos' turn to laugh. "Why, because we speak Greek?"

"Yes."

"But we're different in other respects. We may seem the same to you Venetians, but you'd make few friends for yourself in Candia if you said that there. The Cretans take those differences seriously."

"I'll bear it in mind. But how seriously do *you* take them, Greco?"

Domenikos grinned. "I'm not sure. When I was younger, they mattered to me very much, because they mattered to my father. I was brought up to believe in their importance. But after I became a Roman communicant, I began to see things otherwise. My confessor said to me, 'We're all children of God.' And that must apply equally to the differences between Greek and Cretan as it does between Eastern and Latin."

"How old are you?"

"Nineteen, master."

"And as an old man of nineteen, how do you see these things that everyone is talking about? *Do* you believe that we're all children of God, regardless of what faith we have or what land we come from?"

"I don't think it's meant to apply to *all* faiths. After all, though, there isn't much that separates the Latin and Eastern churches."

"You paid attention to what's happening at Trento?"

"Yes."

" 'Yes.' " Orazio parroted. "Well, in Venice, at any rate, you have to believe something of the sort. Otherwise, how can you account rationally for all the differences that God has made in people?" He paused and touched Domenikos lightly on the shoulder. "Work now, Greco. Your paints are mixed. Don't study this any more. Don't try to understand it. Don't even think about it. Just work."

It was a painstaking and agonizing task that consumed the daylight hours of four long June days. So absorbed did Domenikos become with the work that he remained throughout completely unaware of the snapping and bantering and the antics of Titian's assistants, which echoed resoundingly in the capacious studio. Even the master's own acerb comments and criticisms, which he ventured whenever he appeared from his own smaller, private studio, failed to penetrate the young man's consciousness, since they were not directed at him.

In fact, the old man made a point of staying away from Domenikos during this period of trial, this vigil, as it struck him, this test for a sort of knighthood. Domenikos was able even to ignore the summonses to meals, noon and evening, that drew all the others from their work. He wasn't hungry. He wasn't thirsty. This little rectangle of wood was his present universe, was all that mattered to him until it was completed.

With tempera, the work proceeded slowly. (Domenikos recalled Brother Constantine's observation: "Ah, it's slow, but when you're done with it, Domenikos, it will have a quality that only God and you can understand. So many layers invisible to others, known only to you and God, lie beneath the surface, beneath what others can see. Those are the layers of your soul, your life, your genius, your love of God and your passion for painting in the way He dictates.") To Domenikos, though he was no longer painting according to God's dictates, it seemed an accurate description of his labor.

He remained each evening in the studio long after the others had departed, stayed until it was too dark for him to continue, until he felt that his eyes were set out from their sockets on sticks. Weary, he would return each night to his uncle's house.

And then, incredibly, the little copy was completed. Domenikos stood back. Was it? It seemed so. Then area by area, almost stroke for stroke, he compared the original with the duplicate. Was it really done? It really was. He felt giddy, like one recovering consciousness, overcome with excitement and relief. Reflexively, he deposited a brush in a jar of clear water, then turned away from the panel. Slowly, ploddingly, as one walking through loose sand, he made his way across the studio to the scaffold on which Orazio was working.

"Master," he croaked.

Orazio looked down at him. He grinned. "So you're finally finished with it, are you, young Greco?"

Domenikos nodded, and found suddenly that it was difficult not to weep. Orazio slowly descended and carefully disposed of his palette and brushes. He patted the young man's shoulder, and with the same gesture pushed him aside, proceeding in the direction of Domenikos' working area. In silence he studied the panel for perhaps fifteen minutes, his eyes not bothering to travel from copy to model, for he knew the original by heart.

Domenikos rocked almost drunkenly, standing a few feet from Orazio, watching every movement of the man's face and body. All was soon to be decided, and he cared—oh, dear God, how he cared; but it seemed that there was little energy left in him to care with.

Orazio turned toward him at last. The face he offered Domenikos was a mask, the image of neutrality. "Go home, Greco," he muttered. "Rest yourself. My father will see it later, when he's returned from San Marco. There's no point in waiting for him. You're exhausted."

"May I not wait, master?"

Orazio smiled compassionately and pointed to a low couch against a wall. "Wait there, if you like. But I'm not sure when papa will be back."

"Thank you."

The young man moved slowly toward the couch. He lay down, and was sleeping almost as soon as his head came into comforting contact with the upholstery.

Seven

It was after seven when Titian returned from the Piazza di San Marco. It was his custom to proceed there in impressive splendor at least one afternoon each week during the warmer seasons, accompanied by no less than a pair of liveried servants, one of whom held a colorful parasol over the great man's head. Thus he displayed himself to the populace of Venice. "I do it to let people know I've not yet died. Tintoretto and Veronese have been spreading hopeful, nasty rumors about me," he would say. Here he would wave a mighty finger at no one in particular. "But they'll not have done with me so easily. Not yet."

The procession led eventually to Sansovino's magnificent Loggetta at the foot of the Campanile. Here, with a number of figures who were intimately associated with the affairs of the Serenissima, Titian indulged in what they chose to call discussion. Orazio characterized it less grandly as gossip. The master usually enjoyed these exchanges of information; and even when talk proved less spicy than he liked, he at least acquired bits of knowledge that might prove useful.

Today's excursion had been disillusioning, however. No murders, no rapes, not even an inspiring seduction; no burglaries or scandals in church or state had occurred to add an interesting blemish to the Most Serene scene; nothing more earthshaking than the suicide of a minor official of the Procuratie, whose peculations had been discovered.

"Really," he protested, as he swept with a petulant if regal dignity into the studio, "whom do these people take themselves for, Orazio? Whom do they think they're fooling by pretending to behave so well?

It's an outrage." He scowled, then began to rub his hands together briskly, enjoying a sudden access of hope. "But of course they won't be long in falling back into their accustomed squalor. It had better be so. We can't have them acting forever as if they thought themselves civilized, can we? My God, what mightn't they think of next? All the honest citizens might be murdered in their sleep."

Titian unbuckled his heavy leather belt, letting his glittering ceremonial sword in its scabbard tumble with a clatter to the floor. The noise aroused Domenikos from his fitful slumber. He failed to stir, however, and remained on his couch, locked between sleep and waking, prisoner of his exhaustion.

The master glanced about the studio with a practiced and suspicious eye. He noted at once what had been accomplished during his absence and measured it against his standard. Orazio knew he would find at least one point to object to. It was *de rigueur*.

"Who the devil is that?" Titian inquired sharply, pointing to the reclining figure of Domenikos.

"Your little Greek, papa. He's finished his copy."

"If he's finished, why didn't he go home? This is no inn, you know."

"I told him to go, but he refused. He wanted to know what you think of it."

"You're much too soft-hearted, Orazio, much too easy on people. You're too much like your dear mother, God rest her soul."

Orazio shrugged. It was an old story. He recognized himself to be a person of no importance. Yet he passed his time in peace, demanding of others only that they make life with Titian no more difficult than was bearable. "As you say, papa. But do look at what he's done."

The master grunted and walked to the corner where Domenikos had been working. There was a pause, broken for the youth only by the beating of his heart; he thought he would suffocate.

"Well?" said Orazio at last.

"It's incredible," Titian mumbled ambiguously. Then his meaning was plain. "Do you see what he's done?"

"I see that he's painted every one of your brushstrokes in perfect proportion to the original. Is that what you mean?"

"He's done that, yes. But there's something else, Orazio, something more important. He's understood my painting, understood it from inside. He's understood me. What do you think of it?"

The son's reply was muted. "He seems able enough."

"Then you think we'd be wise to keep him?"

"I know you want to keep him."

"You like him?"

"Well enough."

Titian's tone became exasperated. "Well enough for what?"

"I think he can be taught. I think he can be useful to us sooner or later."

"Yet you have an objection."

"No more pupils, you said. 'Whatever I may tell you, Orazio,' you said to me, 'I don't want you to let me accept any more pupils.' Those are your words, papa."

The old man chuckled. "And you want me to be consistent."

"I'm following your instructions."

"That may be, but the disturbing thing, the *intriguing* thing is that this boy interests me. He has ability. *You* see that. And he has courage. Did you know that? The very first time he laid eyes on me, he dared to put me down, in the face of the fact that he was risking everything he wanted. He understood me."

Orazio's tone grew plaintive. "Understanding, understanding. Just what is it you want *me* to understand?"

"For the moment," said the master softly, "all I want you to understand is that this boy is very important to us, to me."

"Because he understands you?"

"Partly. But I'm not completely vain, and I'm not a fool. That boy hasn't an idea of how much he already knows. Just think for a moment about what he was able to do with temperas. And what fire he has. I like that."

"We keep him, then?"

"We keep him unless you have a persuasive reason why we shouldn't."

"Do you suppose he has enough money to pay his expense with us?"

Titian laughed. "I am glad to see that you're my son where money is concerned. But have you ever met a Greek who lacked what he needed?" Before Orazio could reply, the master pressed on. "As a matter of fact, I've looked into the matter, and he's very well fixed. His father seems to have provided for him nobly."

"I'm relieved."

"But that's beside the point, Orazio. I'd have accepted him without a penny. He has genius, if I ever saw genius aborning."

"It's settled?"

"It is."

"Then I can tell you, papa, that I'm delighted. But I was afraid that if I said *I* wanted him to stay, *you'd* have found a reason for sending him away. You are a very perverse old man sometimes."

Titian grinned. "You might be right. If there's one thing I despise, it's to be agreed with. I don't much like being outwitted, even by my son, but I'll overlook it in a higher interest."

Orazio sighed, and looked over at Domenikos. "Should I wake him now?"

The master nodded, smiling. "You can go through the motions, but if I'd been in his position, I'd have been listening for every word."

Domenikos promptly sat up. He had the grace to blush.

There must be limits to elation—but what were they?

It was toward the end of Venice's dinner hour. The streets and canals were empty. In the darkness, Domenikos made his way across the island of San Marco to Rio dei Greci. The *campi* and *calli* started to fill once more. Yet the youth was only half aware of the bumping and brushing of shoulders as he walked. Nothing at this moment could have significantly intruded on his total self-absorption.

As he entered the dining room, Marica and Anastos were conversing. Manusos had already left to join his friends in the Piazza. Domenikos realized, as they looked up at him, that his expression gave his feelings away. Marica immediately rose from her chair and came over to embrace him, her strong arms threatening to crush him.

"Maestro Tiziano has accepted you." It was not a question.

He nodded, mute, and stood back from her, grinning broadly.

"But it's magnificent, Menegos." She shook her head. "You know, when your father first wrote that you wanted to study with Titian, I said to your uncle, 'But it's madness. It's complete madness. The boy has to be dreaming.'" She smiled, exposing her splendid Ragusan teeth, then threw back her head and laughed with all her heart, embracing him again. "But here we are. It wasn't madness at all, was it? It's happened. The dream has come true."

Domenikos remained silent. Marica turned to Anastos. "Isn't it magnificent? Could you have imagined it?"

"It's good," the boy said quietly.

"You should be more impressed, Anastos, because in a way, you're responsible. It was you who suggested that papa see Gabriele Seviros."

The cousin contrived a smile.

"But tell us everything, Menegos. What did Tiziano say to you?"

"That he liked my copy of his painting and that he accepts me as his pupil. And we settled the terms."

Marica drew him to a chair and forced him to sit. "Oh, there has to be more to it than that. Have some wine. Have something to eat. And tell us every single thing that happened."

Domenikos sighed, but he was delighted to recount the heady words that had been uttered in his presence that evening. When he had finished his narrative (after having to repeat, by request, several details, especially Titian's remark about his possessing genius), Marica turned again to her son.

"You must take Menegos to find your father. He has to hear all this right away."

"Must I, mama? Menegos knows the way to the taverna."

"You don't want to go with him?" She was astonished.

"I've heard the news already, haven't I? It's *his* success, not mine."

"But he's your own flesh and blood."

"I need my sleep, mama."

Marica was about to press the point when Domenikos intervened. "I know what he's feeling, aunt. I'll go alone. As he says, I know the way."

She shook her head, hurling both hands into the air in imitation of Manusos' gesture. "Well, all right. You may know what he's feeling, but *I* don't. Manusos has to be told right away. How happy he's going to be." She embraced her nephew once again. "How happy *I* am."

As he walked into the darkness, following the dimly lit streets toward the taverna his uncle frequented, Domenikos recalled young Anastos' reluctance to accompany him. Was he envious? It seemed unlikely. But he had said, "It's *his* success, not mine." Any success other than his own would have induced this jealousy. In the eyes of his brother Manusos there had been the same black look when Domenikos had told him that he had succeeded in persuading Giorgio to let him come to Venice—an expression of rue, of reproach for his having prevailed against the odds, against the gods. "You go," Manusos had said with some asperity, "and I'll never see you again." "But that's ridiculous," Domenikos had protested. "I'll be coming home sometime." The brother's face had relaxed into dry sorrow. "Back again, Menegos, but never home again. Me, yes. I could go to Venice a hundred times and come back here without being changed. But not you.

In fact, you're probably lost to us already, a stranger to us already."
Domenikos had sighed. "Then I've always been a stranger to you."

Their conversation had ended on this bleak note. And here were
its echoes. Domenikos shuddered. It was unfair that at so glorious a
moment he should find his joy stifled by dismay.

The lights, and then the sounds, of the taverna granted welcome
respite from this dark consideration. As it was still early in the evening, the gatherings of men here, mostly Greeks, Cretans, and Cyp-
riots, were merely garrulous; drunkenness had not yet set in. Domenikos scanned the room for the face of his uncle, at last discerning it
in the darkest reaches. Manusos was gesticulating with his usual vigor
when the young man approached his table. He looked up in mid-
phrase, his expression at first one of alarm. It cleared at once, then became jubilant as he divined the sense of his nephew's message. He
bounced to his feet, overturning his chair, and rushed to take Domenikos in his arms.

"It's true? The news is good?"

"It's marvelously true, uncle, thanks to you and the bishop."

His uncle grew suddenly casual. "Oh, you can forget about the
bishop. We didn't need him, did we?"

Domenikos straightened the chair and grinned. "Well, perhaps—"

The ebullient Manusos permitted him to proceed no further. "No,
no. We needed no one but ourselves. You with your talents, and me
with my connections." He grasped his nephew's arm and turned to
face the five other men seated about the round table. "This is the boy
I've told you about, the one who wanted to study with Maestro Tiziano." He paused to allow this intelligence to penetrate skulls already
partially numbed with retsina, and continued only when he thought
he had their full attention. "Well, what do you think? Titian has accepted him. What do you think of that?" He snorted. "And they dare
to say that Greeks can't get ahead in Venice."

At this point there was a wild outburst of mingled applause and
shouts of approval and the pounding of pewter mugs on the table,
most of them half filled with wine. Then followed great gusts of laughter and broken song. Domenikos was but dimly to remember the identity of the men to whom he was presented that evening, though he was
able to recall their faces, the scene more a tableau than part of
a drama.

He retained very few other details of his stay at the taverna. He
and Manusos remained until they were driven out by a weary proprietor and returned to the Rio dei Greci, arm in arm, singing the songs

of their native island, the renderings enthusiastic but imperfect, interrupted at irregular intervals by bursts of spontaneous hilarity. Not even the icy reception accorded by Marica could mar their joy.

Eight

A brilliant summer gave way to the mists and occasional frosts of autumn and at last to the bone-chilling winds and downpours, now of rain, now of wet snow, that marked the Adriatic winter. Domenikos made his passionate daily pilgrimage to Titian's studio. On Sundays and the numerous holidays afforded Venetian apprentices, Domenikos made repeated visits to the city's many churches, with Orazio frequently in his company. The master interceded for him, making it possible for him to explore the interior of the great basilica of San Marco and portions of the Ducal Palace not open to the public. He was chiefly concerned with contemporary painting—not only Titian's work, but pictures by the brothers Bellini, by Giorgione, by Raffaello, and by the only serious rivals his master enjoyed in Venice, Tintoretto and Veronese. He examined the sculpture in churches and public buildings, the architecture by the brothers Bon, Sansovino, and Palladio. He saturated himself in all the art to be seen in Venice, determined that he would be himself a master of all, sculpture and architecture as well as painting. Guided by Orazio, he pored over Titian's large collection of sketches and prints. Thus did he come to understand the origins of Italian art and the directions it was now taking.

His friendship with Orazio grew over the months, now almost a year, of their intimate association, despite the disparity of their ages. (Orazio had a son of thirty who was now in the diplomatic service of the Serenissima.) Domenikos was persuaded that the difference in their years may well have generated some of the warmth between them. Orazio enjoyed extending protection; he himself welcomed it.

Domenikos was grateful for Orazio's willingness to accept him both as person and painter and for his lavish praise for his progress. Never did he disclose a trace of bitterness or resentment, though under the circumstances this would have been comprehensible. And the young man was compelled to agree (in tactful silence, however) that of the two he was much the better painter despite his remaining technical shortcomings. Orazio himself frequently acknowledged the fact, ruefully but with a whole heart.

The gaps and defects in Domenikos' skill were being overcome so rapidly that even Titian was moved, if grudgingly, to congratulate him occasionally. "You were right, Greco. You *can* learn. But don't get puffed up about it. You still have a long journey to travel, and remember that you started it very late in life. When *I* was nineteen, I'd been at it ten years."

As soon as he was thought sufficiently proficient with oils to carry a share of the labors of the workshop, Domenikos was ruthlessly pressed into service alongside the assistants and apprentices, directed to put in his time of drudgery filling in the colors of sky, landscape, and drapery. He was at first appalled and indignant to discover how few of the larger canvases were actually from the master's own hand, although he signed them all. He was hardly mollified when he learned of the immense prices asked for them and so willingly paid. It seemed a case of gross forgery. He vowed that no matter how busy he might become when his career was launched, he would make as little use of assistants as possible. He would surely never permit his pupils to touch a picture to which he put the signature: "Domenikos Theotokopoulos made this."

However, during the first year of his work with the master, Domenikos' somewhat priggish views tended to modify themselves. He came to appreciate that if one proposed to market a large number of paintings, it would be impossible for a single man, however prodigious, to accomplish them alone. And whatever his reservations, he had to concede that the little effort, or so it seemed, which Titian contributed had a dazzling effect, transforming a routine canvas into a masterpiece. When Titian decided to make an addition of his own to a picture, the result, to Domenikos, was shattering. And he said so.

The old man was sly. "But of course, my boy. Isn't that what I'm supposed to do? I'm just the leader of a well-schooled army. I've trained my forces to fight, and then, as I ought to, I leave them to do the fighting. But once in a while I'm called in to do a bit of leading." He paused, his grin positively lurid. "And, naturally, it's I, as leader, who accept the rewards."

Domenikos toiled for the master in the afternoons, his recent work involving a vast interpretation of the celebrated Counter-Reformation scene of the Purification of the Temple. His mornings were reserved for practice and instruction. Shortly after this exchange, the young man began drawing, with charcoal on wide sheets of paper, his own conception of this theme. He was seated by a window overlooking the Isola di San Michele, Venice's island of the dead. (He had yet to determine whether it looked mournful for an intrinsic reason or merely because of its lugubrious associations.) The island lay on the lagoon, flat, silent, without animation, reminding him suddenly that he was mortal.

Orazio inclined to lateness, especially when he knew that his father was to be absent. By the time he entered the studio, Domenikos had sketched in outline the general form a picture of his own Purification would take. Orazio, greeting him amiably, peered at the paper and after a moment's examination began to laugh. "I see."

"What do you see?"

"That you think the time has come for you to improve on papa."

Domenikos felt the flow of hot blood flooding to his features. "No, no. Not that. It's just that I've been wondering if tnere isn't a different way of doing it."

Orazio seemed amused. "And you had no plans for improving it in the process?"

"You're trying to embarrass me."

"I'm just being logical. After all, if you don't intend to improve on papa's picture, what's the point of doing it differently?"

"I simply want to experiment with the idea on my own."

Orazio touched his shoulder. Domenikos turned and looked, briefly and shyly, into his friend's eyes. "You know, Greco, you're a bad liar. Now tell me. What is it about papa's version that you don't like?"

The young man smiled sadly. "I know it's presumptuous, but I think it out of keeping. It's too voluptuous." He stood up and led Orazio to the large canvas in progress that hung from a wall. He pointed to the figure of Christ driving the money-changers from the temple. "There's something almost depraved about Him. He's nothing but a well-nourished Venetian merchant." He made a broad gesture to comprehend the entire painting. "The scene is like an incident that might have interrupted a procession of the Doge across one of the squares here. It's not reverent. It's not a suitable representation of one of the most cherished stories in the New Testament."

"I never realized, Greco," said Orazio pleasantly, "that you were so ardent a religionist. How stupid of me. But here in Venice, you understand, we concern ourselves very little with these higher questions of doctrine. We believe what we believe because we've been taught to. We give it no thought. And I suppose papa's pictures show

it. They're in the Venetian style. They're colorful and dramatic, but
they don't strain for any special dogmatic accuracy. We make pictures
that people like."

"That's almost blasphemy."

Orazio chuckled. "No danger of that. We respect the Church well
enough, as an institution. We just leave these matters of theology and
doctrine to the Curia in Rome."

"They're a painter's concern."

"Your concern, you mean. You're God-struck, Greco. Papa and I
are not. Oh, I don't object to parish priests. I even can tolerate that ass
Father Antonio in San Canciano. Most of them are decent men doing
their best to save us, and now and then their best can be very good. I
don't even mind the bishops or the Patriarch."

"That's generous of you. What are you trying to tell me? That I
should live and let live?"

"Yes." Then, surprisingly, Orazio became angry. "Except for those
Franciscans and Dominicans. May God in His wisdom deliver us from
them. Those fellows are devils from hell—thieves, scoundrels, and
blackmailers, every one of them. I'll not willingly live with them or let
them live."

It was not the first time in Venice that Domenikos had heard so
ringing a denunciation. Orazio's view of the two mendicant orders was
shared by a solid majority of Venetians.

"I know, I know," he responded feebly. "But does that mean that
the Purification theme should be treated cynically, because you think
the Franciscans and Dominicans have become the money-changers of
today? A Purification seems to me meaningless unless it's painted as
pure."

"I agree. And you think this one isn't."

"Not for me."

"Then by all means continue this little project. I'd enjoy seeing a
Purification that *you* think pure." He laughed. "And I think papa
would too."

He decided to make this painting in tempera, for he wasn't yet sure
enough of his control of oils. Moreover, it was possible in a small
panel to obtain a refinement of detail in tempera not possible in the
freer-flowing medium, though the panel he selected was considerably
larger than the one he had been given for his initial copy of St. Francis
and Brother Leo.

With painful gradualness, the arrangement of the subject projected itself from imagination to panel. In all, the task occupied the better part of three weeks. As with his first trial, it was late in the day when Domenikos dropped the tip of the last brush into clear water, silently pronouncing the painting completed. There was no point in his studying the picture, though he did just that. "To be intelligently self-critical," Titian had told him, "is the first and most important obligation the artist has. Unhappily, it's almost always the skill he acquires last. And sometimes he never acquires it." This was certainly true of him now.

Beyond this incapacity to judge was the fact that he could no longer see the whole picture. Or perhaps he meant that he couldn't see the picture whole, so obsessed had he become with the fragments out of which it had been created. It was all details, all blurred. He must believe, as Titian had assured him, that the creative process was "like a baby learning to dress himself." It became easier with repetition. To think otherwise would be impossible. No one could forever endure the demands, physical and emotional, the anger, despair, and frustration; sooner or later, one must become used to the exigencies of creation.

Wiping tacky fingers on his gray smock and with the back of his slender hand brushing back the lank, darkening hair that had fallen across his weary eyes, Domenikos approached Orazio and Titian. They were painting the final touches to an immense rendering of the Rape of Europa, a favorite mythological scene that was much in demand. How prodigal of space and light and color this was by comparison with his own cramped little panel.

The master surveyed him coolly as Domenikos drew near him, the creased features assuming an expression of mockery. Titian turned to Orazio. "I think your young protégé has finished his latest effort."

"Ah?" Orazio looked at the young man. "Is that so, Greco?"

Domenikos nodded briefly. "That's so."

"Well, then, papa," said the son, plainly in a festive mood, "shall we see how he thinks you should be painting your pictures?"

Titian smiled gravely and followed Orazio to what had come to be called "Greco's Corner." The old man pointed an admonishing finger at Domenikos, who trailed after them, emptied of energy. "May I assume you'll not feign slumber this time?"

The young man smiled half-heartedly. "You may, master."

The three men stood before his picture. Orazio clasped his long, delicate hands behind his back, seeming to use them for support as he leaned backward, his face utterly impassive. The master folded his stubby fingers together over his modest paunch and rocked gently to and fro on the balls of his small, ancient feet, humming tunelessly to himself, the sound broken occasionally by a gasping pause for breath, for a grunt, for a sigh.

At last the great man ostentatiously cleared his throat, arrested his rocking motion, and extended a hand toward Domenikos, beckoning him slowly. His eyes were bright. "I see," he began, his tone dry, "that you've not spent *all* your time in my studio."

"Master?"

Titian pointed to the painting. "I mean, it's plain that you've been looking at the work of other Venetians, and even a Roman or two."

"Oh, yes." Then, wondering what was to come next, he added quickly, "Was that wrong?"

"Not at all. Didn't I make it possible for you to see the inside of San Marco and the Doge's apartments? No, I simply mean that your sight-seeing reveals itself here." He moved closer to the panel. "For example, I detect a touch of Sansovino's manner in your architecture, and perhaps even in these sculptures." He indicated the statues in the niches to either side of the entrance to the temple. "I take them to be Apollo and Athena."

"Not Athena, master, but Hera."

"Hera? I see. And that, then, suggests that this rather odd creature beside her is intended to be a peacock?"

Domenikos laughed self-consciously. "It is, master. I'm not very good at birds yet."

"That is more than amply evident. But let me pursue my thought a bit further. Looking is as instructive to the soul of a painter as practice is instructive to his hand. I'm delighted you've seen so much that you admired. I'll arrange for you to see some private collections, too." He pointed once again to the figures of Hera and Apollo. "Now while the style of these is Sansovino's, their arrangement suggests Raffaello Sanzio. Might you have had his School of Athens' in mind, Greco?"

The young man flushed and nodded. "I studied the woodcut you have of that picture."

Titian smiled. "I'm happy to know that you've been improving yourself with my prints too. After all, I never made the claim that I was the *only* painter in Italy, merely the best." He indicated the seated figure of a bearded old man, one of the infirm awaiting cure from the hands of Christ. He was dressed in flowing robes, placed in the right foreground. "Correct me if I'm mistaken, but don't I find something familiar in the face of that old gentleman?"

Domenikos looked blank, then gazed for a moment at the figure in question, and suddenly recognized the resemblance. "It's Michelangelo, master," he conceded, much embarrassed. "I honestly didn't intend it so. I've been looking at the sketches you made of him, and I must have held his face in my mind."

"The 'divine Michelangelo,' " said the master with a snarl. "I'd forgotten those drawings. I made them when I was in Rome sixteen or seventeen years ago." He chuckled, but there was iron in the sound. "He told me I didn't know how to draw. If I could draw, he said, I'd be unmatched on this earth, by which, of course, he meant unmatched except for him." He shrugged. "But I think I balanced the matter satisfactorily. I told *him* he didn't know how to paint, and that, God knows, is true enough."

"But he must be a good sculptor, master. I was looking at the sketches you did of 'The Day.' "

"But he's dreadful as a colorist, and if I had to choose a defect as an artist, I'd choose what he thinks mine rather than what I think his." The old man sighed. "I suppose that's natural. We learn to live with our own problems."

Domenikos agreed. "I learned to use line in Candia, not well, of course, but I much prefer what you can do with color to what I can do with line."

Titian looked at the painting before him. "If that's what you had in mind while you were making this, I hope you'll forgive me for saying that you are still a long way from achieving the effect you were looking for. There's no definition to your colors, Greco. You've used them very awkwardly, and chosen them with unfortunate taste."

"I still find them very difficult," he admitted quietly.

Titian grinned. "That's all right. There's still time for you. I must say I'm pleased that you liked my Ariadne. That's she there, isn't it?" He pointed to a half-clothed figure in a semireclining position to the left of Michelangelo, a woman quite as voluptuous as any the master had ever rendered. Here she appeared as a vendor of doves.

Domenikos laughed.

"Oh, wait, young Greco. Just wait. There's plenty of occasion for laughter to come. The Ariadne is mine, all right, but some of your other women look as if they'd been inspired by Veronese. And in the way you've posed these people, all of them"—he indicated the entire panel with a sweep of his ringed hand—"it appears that you were thinking much more of Tintoretto. Look at the odd angles you placed them in, Greco. Only he, and you, would imagine that human bodies could assume attitudes like that. The difference is that my erstwhile friend Robusto somehow makes this strangeness of his work now and then. *Your* people look as if they're suspended by invisible cords. If you want to paint like Tintoretto or Veronese, I'll send you to them. You're wasting your time here."

"Oh, God, master, what am I to do?"

"You don't like that suggestion?"

"You know I don't."

Titian shrugged. "I think Orazio has taught you all he can. On Monday, you'll begin to work with me in my studio."

Without a further word, he turned and stumped out, leaving Domenikos bewildered, breathless, and vaguely alarmed.

His mind reeling from the multiple shocks of dismay and humiliation and remorse and regret, Domenikos staggered toward the Rio dei Greci through the dusky Venetian streets, hardly knowing what to make of it all. He barely recalled eating supper and creeping up the stairs to his room and bed. When he woke the next morning, he discovered that he hadn't bothered to undress. Yet whatever clarity he could possess had returned.

In recollection, the colloquy with Titian the previous evening remained a hallucination. He was unable, throughout the long mass in San Giorgio dei Greci, to concentrate on the words of the liturgy. The same proved true when, later, he worshipped at San Canciano. Because of this wandering of his mind and because he had failed to make confession, he took no communion here, and this made a further contribution to his depression.

Constantly raking his consciousness were the contrapuntal themes that had characterized yesterday's exchange: He had failed miserably with his painting, and yet Titian thought well enough of him to bring him into his own studio; Titian was from now on to be his master. The impending desertion of Orazio was not, he guiltily reflected, nearly the source of pain he would have imagined. But it did concern him. As he knelt in San Canciano, he could hear his friend mocking him: "You should have been a priest, Greco. You're obsessed, you're even charmed, by sorrow." He hoped Orazio would not now become his enemy. No, that was improbable. The friend had surely been subjected to such treatment from his father before, but this time, Domenikos had been the occasion for this pain.

Emerging from the church, the young man remembered Titian's promise to introduce him to the private collections of art he had not yet visited. He paused in the summer sunlight. It would be superb to see at last the paintings in the Ca' d'Oro, in the Foscari, and the other palaces that were said to be treasure houses. He was sure as well that the master could gain him permission to make use of the books in the Libreria.

Just now, the idea of books was more attractive. Reading had become his principal delight when not at work. He enjoyed books on almost every subject. With the money he didn't spend on such diversions as drink and women, he managed the purchase of an occasional volume. In this, as in so many other things, he had been fortunate in having Orazio for a friend. Titian's son shared Domenikos' love of literature and learning, and it was he who had introduced him to a publisher and seller of books, commodities both dear and rare in the sixteenth century.

Recalling Orazio in this connection saddened him. Something ought to be said. Instead of directing his steps back to his uncle's house, Domenikos turned toward the Biri Grande. If Orazio were there, he might somehow soften his thoughts—if, indeed, they had been hardened against him.

Orazio and his family occupied extensive apartments in Titian's house, though they were less grand than those of the master. Domenikos found his friend seated in the shade of an arcaded gallery that flanked the *cortile*. He was alone, a large volume of Ariosto in his lap. He seemed to be dozing, but quickly roused himself on hearing the young man's approaching footsteps resounding against the masonry of the cloistered walk.

"Ah, it's you," he said, shaking his head. "The maestro is away for the day, you know, passing the times with the Doge, I believe. If it's something urgent, you'll find him at the Palazzo Ducale."

"It's you I came to see."

His friend smiled regretfully.

"As papa put it, Greco, there's nothing more I can do for you."

"That's what I came to see you about." Domenikos seated himself on the low wall beside Orazio's chair. "I'm sorry for what the master said."

"Why, in God's name? What have you to be sorry about? *You* didn't say it, Greco."

"I was responsible for its being said. I was the person at issue, so it was my fault."

"Your reasoning has flaws, but let's overlook that. You feel unhappy—"

"And," the younger man broke in, "I'm fearful that it might mean the end of our friendship."

Orazio laughed. "You despair too easily."

"You think losing a friend isn't a cause for despair?"

"I'm touched that my friendship means so much to you."

"You're the first person, the only person, I've ever been able to speak with about things that are really important to me. Even if you'd taught me nothing about painting, and you know how very much I did learn from you, I'd be grateful for everything you've helped me to understand."

"Very handsomely said, Greco. But now you have the very master himself to talk with, the true fountainhead of all wisdom, on all subjects, practical as well as spiritual. What further need do you imagine you have of me?"

"You're mocking me, Orazio. You know what I mean—philosophy, poetry. . . ."

"But you need friends who are nearer your own age. You've been associating with old men since you've been here."

Domenikos smiled sadly. "I agree, not that I think you old. But I've never learned how one goes about making friends. Where are they? How do I find them?"

"You must begin to live a different sort of life. You've withdrawn yourself too much, like a hermit. Have you never learned to open yourself up, Greco?"

"Never."

Orazio spread wide his fine hands and extended them outward and upward. "There's a whole world out there, outside yourself. Didn't you realize it?"

"Yes, but I don't know how to contact it."

"Have you tried?"

"Not adequately, I fear."

"There are thousands of people. Somewhere among them there's bound to be one person who'll interest you, whom you'll be interesting to. I think you've let yourself become too concerned with painting and books. The painting seems to consume you—"

"And the books repose me."

"Perhaps. But you've admitted that it's not enough. You need more than that to survive. Give yourself some room, some air, some light." He pointed at Domenikos. "I warn you, Greco, that if you don't, you'll always find that you're alone, and miserable."

"It's odd to hear that from you. Brother Constantine, in a different connection, I admit, said almost exactly the same thing to me." He paused, his expression doleful. "Does this mean that you'll cast me out?"

His friend sighed. "What a fellow. When you arrived just now, did I send you away?"

"No, but I have the feeling that that's what you're suggesting."

"Only in the sense, as I said, that I think you should meet other people."

Domenikos stood up, smiling, and offered Orazio a long, pale hand. "Thank you for that. I'm truly sorry for what happened yesterday."

The older man threw back his head and laughed—a bit forcedly, Domenikos thought. "Greco, your feelings of loyalty are moving. But there's really no need for you to be so concerned. That was just my esteemed father in one of his moments of candor." He became serious. "You have to know him, my friend, to appreciate that only rarely is he intentionally cruel. He was far more cruel, I think, in his treatment of you than of me. He was just saying what he thought. He can be a sycophant with patrons, when it's to his interest, but when he's dealing with people as people, he's never learned not to say what he thinks, to whomever he pleases. He doesn't know how to keep silent. He's never even learned how to whisper. But we live through it. He's the greatest man I know. And it's the regret of my life, and perhaps even more of his, that I'm not the son he wanted me to be. I try to make up in affection and understanding what I lack in genius. The gap is a big one, Greco, and in a way, you help to fill it." He smiled warmly. "Together, you and I can be his son, his talented, loving, compassionate son."

Domenikos shook his head. "But he scorned what I'd done."

"Nonsense. Do you think he'd take you into his own studio if that's what he felt?"

"But he said—"

"That's his way. He gives compliments with the back of his hand. If he didn't think you had genius, he'd leave you with me." Orazio hesitated, then added softly. "You *know* that, Greco. That's what made you come. And *I* thank *you* for that consideration."

Nine

During the week before Ascension Day, at the beginning of Domenikos' fourth year in Titian's studio, Venice was frantically preparing for the great celebration, the most important in the Serenissima's long calendar of festivals and holidays. Probably no one was more excited by the prospect of this event than the young Cretan, for Titian and Orazio had invited him, independently and evidently without either realizing that the other had thought of it, to join them on their barge for the public festivities and to attend a private gathering that evening in the Biri Grande.

Domenikos had already taken part in the colorful pageant. Hitherto, however, he had participated as a somewhat illicit member of the Scuola dei Greci, the confraternity of the Greek community to which his uncle belonged, sharing with his aunt and cousin a space in a specially decorated craft that followed, at a respectful distance, the Doge's own barge, *Bucintoro,* out into the waters of the lagoon. As Titian's guest, however, he would find himself much closer to that memorable golden galley.

He rushed back to the Rio dei Greci breathlessly to announce the good fortune of his invitation, confident that both aunt and uncle would rejoice in his delight. To his consternation, Marica received this information with neither approval nor joy. She was indignant, even hostile.

"But Ascension Day, the Feast of Bucintoro, is a family occasion, Menegos," she protested heatedly. "You had no right to accept that invitation. I don't care how important Maestro Tiziano is to you." She turned angrily to her husband for support. "Isn't that the way you feel?"

Manusos nodded rapidly, but Domenikos had known him to be more enthusiastic. "Well, my love, you're of course right in principle —" His voice was loaded with doubt.

Marica didn't permit him to continue. She clapped her strong hands together in exasperation, and began to rock from side to side as if she were about to keen, the classic Greek widow. "Oh, you," she snorted. "I should have known better than to think you'd agree with me. Get-

ting ahead. Getting ahead. That's all you ever talk about. I'm beginning to think it's the only thing that matters to you, to you *and*
Menegos."

Manusos sighed and stirred uncomfortably in his chair, wiping his
bearded face with the back of a hairy hand. "Well, you have to admit
that getting ahead has its importance. And after all, Menegos is almost
as much a member of his master's household as he is of ours."
He laughed uneasily. "He's with him much more than he's with us.
And just suppose he were to refuse the invitation. Suppose he *did*
come with us. And then suppose Titian were to take umbrage. How
would you feel about it then?"

She was adamant. "Suppose, suppose. My God. Suppose the plague
struck us again. What then?" She crossed herself hastily. "May God
forgive me. But all this supposing is sickening. *I* know how I
feel about it. Who knows what that old man might feel? And who
cares?"

"But that's just it," said Manusos. "Menegos cares. It's important
to him."

Marica looked at her nephew. "Do you care?"

"No, aunt, not about this. I don't think it makes any difference to
the master whether I go with him or not."

She confronted her husband, hands on her ample hips.
"You see?"

Deflated, Manusos shrugged. "I thought—"

She raised a hand, and for a moment Domenikos was certain that
she was going to strike his uncle. She merely held it by his cheek, however. "You thought. You thought. You think with your mouth, not
your head."

The young painter intervened. "I'd like to go with the master, aunt.
His galley will be very close to *Bucintoro*."

"It's against religion. Does your famous master belong to the Scuola
dei Greci? No. No good Greek should associate with a Roman
Catholic on Ascension Day."

"But I don't belong to the Scuola either," he said regretfully.

"That's only because you're not important enough to have been
asked yet."

"It's also because—" Domenikos cut himself off abruptly. This was
scarcely the moment to bring up his conversion. With Manusos' aid,
he had kept his secret well. Indeed, he had thought of it but little, except when Sundays necessitated his attending two masses instead
of one.

"Because what?"

"Because I'm not interested, I suppose," he responded weakly.

There was silence for a time, broken only by the sound of breathing. Manusos poured himself some wine; then, embarrassed to have been inconsiderate, he dutifully filled Marica's glass and then his nephew's. All drank without speaking, glancing furtively at one another and returning to a consultation of their glasses.

"I think," said Marica at last, "that this may be the time to tell you something that's been on my mind for months, Menegos. You should begin looking for a wife."

He had had no idea, as the words began to fall into the vacuum, what she planned to say, but it had certainly not been this. Domenikos burst out laughing, almost choking on the mouthful of wine he had been on the point of swallowing. "I'm sorry, aunt. You took me completely by surprise."

"Was it funny? Tell me the joke."

"It wasn't funny. I just didn't expect you to say anything like that."

"You disagree?"

"It's not practical, not for the moment."

"Nonsense."

"What made you say it just then?"

"I don't like the life you've been leading, and I don't think your parents would approve of it either."

"Is it wrong?"

"Very."

"Are you speaking of Ascension Day now, or of the way I live as a rule?"

"Oh, I admit that my disappointment about Ascension Day brought it to mind, but it's everything about you, Menegos. All you seem to do is read or walk about the city or work. It's unnatural. And you hardly ever talk to us, except at moments like this." She brushed a hand across her face.

Domenikos looked down, chagrined, at his long white hand that held the hollow stem of his glass. He responded without raising his eyes. "That's true, and you make me ashamed. But it's not for the reasons you might imagine, aunt. It's not that I can't think of anything to say to you in particular. I don't find much to say to anyone, except perhaps to the master and Orazio, but that's different."

"You see? I was right." Her tone was exultant. "I was right, Menegos. You need a wife to bring you out."

He shook his head. "I won't take a wife until I'm able to support her myself, not out of what papa gives me."

"And how long will that be? A couple of years?"

"No less than ten, uncle."

"You'll get no commissions for ten years?" Manusos was incredulous. "What kind of an affair is it to be a painter, then?"

"Oh, I'll probably get a few commissions before then, but not big ones, not the kind that will bring me enough to support a family. It takes a long time for an artist to establish himself."

"Ten years, to me," breathed his uncle heavily, "is forever. You'll be thirty-two in ten years."

Domenikos agreed. "So you see, there's really no need for me to hurry about making the choice of a wife."

"I still say it's unnatural," said Marica, sighing resignedly. She extended her hand across the table to her nephew. "But then, I suppose, there's nothing very natural about being a painter." She paused and, free of rancor, accepted her defeat with grace. "You'll want me to arrange some sort of costume for you, won't you, for the party after the festival?"

"I hadn't thought about it. Is it necessary?"

"Won't your master be giving a masked ball? That's what I've been told. A great affair," she scoffed, "for the finest ladies and most expensive whores. There's not much to choose between them, from all I've heard."

"The ladies," said Manusos pontifically, "are worse than the whores. I can tell you that."

During the two years that had followed his move to Titian's own studio, Domenikos was excited, depressed, and stunned as he watched his antique master at work. The old man's boldness assumed a character that gave the appearance of nonchalance, so casual was his vigor. Details over which the young painter had been instructed by Orazio to slave were of no consequence to Titian.

In the week before the great festival of Bucintoro, Domenikos had occasion to question him about a canvas that seemed to him particularly slipshod in its treatment of background; all was concentrated on the sense of movement and drama.

Titian was disdainful. "Who should expect me, at my age, to care for your precious landscapes and your marvelous architecture, Greco? When I was younger, I admit, they were important to me, but no longer. I'm seeking the very essence of my image now. I've no time to think of anything else." He grinned and wagged a finger at his pupil. "That doesn't mean *you* shouldn't learn to do these things, and do them well. It's only *after* you've learned them that you can afford to forget them. Because only then can you decide for yourself what's important. That's one of the ironies of art." He smeared a dark pigment onto his canvas with a palette knife and began with his blunt fingers to manipulate an edge of it on the picture. "Painting is the only thing. And in painting, no matter what Michelangelo thinks, color is the only thing of importance, to make it conform to your own plan for it, to shade it, to mold it, even to sculpture, as *impasto,* to give it a body of its own, a life of its own."

The old man paused and sighed, letting the palette fall momentarily to his side. "It's my only remaining battle, Greco. It's really the only battle I've had to fight all my life. And I'd be a liar if I suggested I was near to winning it. Because when I've achieved what I thought I was looking for, I no longer want it." Then, as if this confession had revealed a weakness he preferred to hide, he backed away from Domenikos, restoring his palette to its proper position. He continued bluffly. "You must never be afraid to paint with your fingers if neither the brush nor the knife will give you the effect you want."

"That doesn't worry me, master. It's the sketchiness of your backgrounds."

The master chuckled. "You think that a waste of canvas?"

"No, but it makes everything depend on the figure."

"That's what I want everything to depend on. It gives the figure the importance it deserves."

"You think this is what I should do?"

"I don't care what you do as long as you mean it and can make it work for you. No art is more pragmatic than painting."

"But I believe in details, in their symbolism. And how else can you make someone believe that the scenes you paint are real, are true, something that happened or that might happen?"

The old man nodded vigorously. "That's what you think now. But it will change when you get older. The great painter is an illusionist, a mountebank in the happiest sense." He paused and looked reflectively at Domenikos. "You read, Greco. Do you believe Dante?"

"I believe *in* him."

"Why?"

"Because he compels me to."

"And you accept his description of hell?"

Domenikos smiled. "I do and I don't. I do as I'm reading him, but when I've stopped, I rub my eyes and say, 'But *he* didn't know any more about it than I do.' "

"He just sweeps you along, doesn't he? He seduces you."

"Yes."

"And does the illusion he creates have anything to do with details?"

"I don't know, master. It never occurred to me to separate detail from whatever else you'd call it."

"Would you call it magic?"

"I might."

"Good. Now, tomorrow you observe the festival closely and then tell me whether it's the details that give it its special flavor or its magic, its atmosphere, the qualities that you and I and all the people bring to it."

In the week preceding Ascension Day there had been freakish storms blowing in from the Adriatic, and an alarming number of ship-wrecks had been reported. The atmosphere of high drama was en-hanced by the memory of a festival when several gondolas had cap-sized during a sudden squall, their occupants, in their heavy elaborate costumes, drowned to a soul.

Despite apprehensions, however, the sky seemed to bode well for this holiday. The morning dawned clear, mistless. The Sposolizio del Mare would take place under ideal conditions.

Soon after ten, the great flotilla of galleys, barges, and gondolas began to take coherent form along both banks of the whole length of the bending Canale Grande, each vessel assigned its position by a committee of the Consiglio. Pride of place, of course, was reserved for the Doge's own magnificent *Bucintoro*.

Domenikos met Titian and Orazio and the master's impressive en-tourage near the Orologio in the Piazza. (Orazio's family had been whisked away to a villa at Vincenza, presumably so that the evening's festivities might proceed without giving them offense.) They pro-ceeded with considerable pomp past San Marco and the Palazzo Ducale to the Molo, where *Bucintoro* was moored, glittering gold and red in the sunlight.

Titian's party arrived at the craft that had been prepared for him, a richly decorated barge, festooned with ribbons, newly painted a brilliant scarlet. The old man was lifted gently down to his seat in the stern. When Orazio and Domenikos had taken their places, the nu-merous attendants assumed theirs. The barge was propelled slowly out toward the middle of the canal, there to await the departure from the Molo of *Bucintoro*. Stationed in the center of the barge were three musicians, two with lyres, another with a lute, who began at once to play and sing some of the tunes, most of them extremely bawdy, that were in vogue that summer.

A servant timidly made his way aft to the master with wine and a basket of fruit, after which Domenikos and Orazio were served. It was a wholly delightful way to begin this gala promenade over the lagoon. The young painter looked back at the old man, who was propped up on a sort of throne, his aspect one of resolute, if somewhat baleful, majesty, his legs wrapped in blankets to protect him against the sea air and the possibility of spray.

"You seem to be enjoying yourself, Greco. You find this infantile spectacle to your liking?"

He grinned. "I'm following your advice, master. I'm trying to see in it what's important. Are you comfortable?"

Titian grunted. "As comfortable as possible under such appalling conditions. To me it's all a bore."

Orazio laughed. "He says that because he resents the fact that the Doge is taking part in it too. Papa hates to share glory."

At this moment, *Bucintoro* was released from her mooring and, her myriad oars flashing and reflecting the sunlight in perfect unison, moved to her prescribed position in the canal, taking the lead in the long procession that would terminate at the Lido. The voyage was accomplished without haste. There, the Doge preceded members of the Consiglio and others highly placed in the Republic, including a groaning Titian and his companions, into the Church of San Nicolò, where a solemn mass was offered by the Venetian Patriarch himself.

It was on the return journey that *Bucintoro* paused, according to a tradition established centuries before, so that the Doge might cast a gold and jeweled ring into the lagoon, murmuring as he performed this ritual the phrase, *"Desponsamus te Mare, in signum veri perpetuique dominii"* ("We marry you, sea, as a sign of true and perpetual rule"). Thus, the Serenissima reconsecrated her mystic marriage with the sea.

Just before this ceremony, Domenikos observed to Orazio, "This is a pagan celebration, you realize."

His friend grinned. "You *would* think of that."

"But it's true."

Orazio shrugged. "I've been told that even Easter has pagan origins."

Domenikos laughed. "I said that once, when I was a pupil in Candia. The monks nearly expelled me."

Suddenly conversation became superfluous. As the Doge made his elaborate gesture of casting the ring into the still water of the lagoon, all became pandemonium. His splendid galley moved off once more toward the Molo. The rite had been completed.

The remaining hours of daylight were given over to dancing in the streets and squares, to ogling the fantastic performances of the mountebanks who had set up their portable stages on either side of the Piazzetta, to examining the merchandise offered by eager vendors, to drinking and eating and doing one's best to protect one's purse against the legions of practiced thieves who patrolled the crowds.

Near dusk, Domenikos returned to the Rio dei Greci to dress himself for the masked ball that was to follow.

When Domenikos arrived at the Biri Grande, the noises of celebration could be heard in the street outside—singers and musicians, laughter and shouting, and the occasional tinkle of shattering glass. It was plain that the festivities had been under way for some hours. As he entered the house, he had the impression of walking into a solid wall of sound. Through all the echoing corridors and great rooms, the delighted giggles and outraged screams of the city's most esteemed ladies and most cultivated courtesans could be heard in the murky half-light of smoking oil lamps and teetering candles, these exclamations serving as chaotic punctuation for the music of the orchestra (lutes, lyres, violas da gamba, horns, and trumpets) which was playing in the large studio that had miraculously been cleaned, stripped of works in progress, and especially decorated for the occasion.

Here and there, orange in the penumbra, flashed gleaming naked thighs and bosoms, pawed by aggressive masculine hands, or the duller reflections of pewter ewers and jugs, oddly less metallic in their tone than glass goblets that glowed like polished silver in the lamplight.

In a corner of the studio the master sat in state, his eyes glazed with drink and fatigue, accepting the attentions of two pretty women. No longer able to partake actively of the fleshly pleasures afforded during his notorious revels, the old man nevertheless rejoiced in his role of *voyeur*. When Domenikos approached to pay his respects, Titian gazed up at him bleakly, his great black eyes wide with drunken anger. He brushed him off with a wavering but summary gesture of his hand.

"No time for you, no time for you," he muttered thickly. "Can't you see that, for God's sake? No time for men now, let alone puking boys. Go away. Get drunk. Find a woman and clap yourself on her back. Do you good. Get a little of God out of you." He laughed uproariously at this, and nearly fell from his chair. He was rescued by the women who flanked him.

Domenikos turned away from Titian, dismayed, disgusted, saddened. Like everyone present, he was masked, but only to those one didn't know was a mask an effective concealment of identity. "By the time the evening is over," Orazio had warned him that afternoon, "your face is probably the only part of your anatomy you won't have exposed."

He edged his way gingerly across the tiled floor of the studio, doing his best to avoid the dancers and the drinkers, not certain where he was going or what (or whom) he was seeking. Feeling exceptionally awkward and distinctly out of place in surroundings so familiar, he wondered why he had agreed to come.

As he neared the great double doors that led to the courtyard, a small, pale, ringless hand suddenly appeared on his arm, the touch so light and obviously feminine that even without at first looking toward its owner, Domenikos placed his hand over it. Then only did he turn to find a slender, diminutive figure with fair hair and dark eyes that peered at him brilliantly through the apertures of a mask which, like the gown, was whiter than her skin.

"You've just arrived," she said, her voice soft, as warm as her touch.

"How did you deduce that?"

Laughing, she drew him into the *cortile*. Here towering torches projected a flickering, golden light that disclosed an occasional couple, each much preoccupied. "Because you're so plainly, so painfully sober, and because you don't have a glass in your hand."

"I might have left it somewhere."

She shook her blonde head. "No. You haven't been drinking."

"I may not show it."

"You're not drunk. You're too timid to be drunk."

He pressed her hand more firmly. "You think drink would make me more violent?"

"It usually happens. Give a man too much wine and he's all over a woman like a sudden spring shower."

"I never realized that. You're very observant. What else do you know about me?"

They sat on the wall. "Many things. I know you're not from Venice."

"True."

"And probably not from Italy."

"Yes."

"You're Spanish."

"I'm from Crete."

"How exotic. But there, you see? I'm not so observant after all. I should have known."

"It was a reasonable guess. Most foreigners in Venice *are* from Spain. I happen to be the exception."

Her reply was soft. "In more ways than one, I've no doubt."

He flushed and looked away. "That's flattery."

"You don't like to be flattered?"

"I detest it."

"You seem unduly certain."

He laughed. "Well, I may enjoy it occasionally, but I never believe it."

"There's a nice distinction."

"Not a fair one?"

She didn't respond at once, but took his right hand and held it out with both of hers in the breeze-blown torchlight. Her delicate fingers made delicious little explorations of joints and palm. More firmly now, she held it palm upward and bent over to peer into it. "You use your hands in your work. They're not calloused, but they're very powerful."

"Yes."

She sighed impatiently. "I think you're the most uncommunicative man I've ever met."

"I'm curious about your deductions."

"You could be a little more helpful."

"But it's a masked ball, identities secret. People meet, incognito, in the night and depart the next day still unknown to each other. Tell me more of what you guess about me. It's amusing."

Her head inclined forward as she brought her nose and then her full lips into caressing contact with his hand. Domenikos touched the back of her neck, smoothing the soft skin that covered the stretched tendons, feeling the brush of vagrant strands of her fine hair. Then, laughing musically, she straightened. "You paint."

He joined in her laughter. "I should have washed my hands more carefully."

"Not at all. I've always thought the odor of paint very stimulating."
She paused. "Are you a famous painter?"

"I'm a person of no importance."

"Important to no one?"

"To hardly anyone."

She leaned over to look into his hand again. "Poor fellow. But I
see great things in your future. You'll be important to many people
someday."

"You read palms?"

"I do many things."

"Fascinating. What do you see in mine?"

She looked down again, tracing with tantalizing lightness the lines
of his hand. "You'll be very successful."

"In Venice?"

"I don't think so, not as a painter, in any case."

"What other kind of success might I have here? Painting is all I
care about."

"All?"

"All."

"What finality."

"You've not answered my question."

"I can't."

"Your vision is flawed?"

"Inadequate. I haven't the refinements of palmistry. And I don't
know enough about you."

"I thought the hand told all."

"Not to me." She fell silent, and when she continued her voice was
dark and low. "It may be that you'll be successful in love."

He laughed. "I've never thought of that."

"Never thought of love, or of being successful in it?"

"Does one ever think of love without imagining oneself successful
in it?"

Her eyes glowed strangely in the light of the torches. "I don't
know."

"Nor do I, really."

"How old are you?"

"Twenty-two. And you?"

She leaned back and swayed slowly from side to side, inclining her
head toward the star-marked sky. "Older than that, I'm sorry to tell
you."

"What made you ask *my* age?"

"Your answer was a young man's answer. I suppose, though, that it depends on what you mean by success. Everyone who falls in love wants the feeling reciprocated. Most men imagine they succeed, most of all when they fail—and most of them fail. I think they even realize in their hearts beforehand that they're going to fail."

"What a bleak prospect. That can be true only in Venice."

"I think it's true everywhere."

"In Crete, love isn't so frivolous as it seems to be here. I don't know about 'everywhere,' and neither do you."

"You think Venetian love frivolous?"

"You don't?"

"Not at all. What do you object to?"

"From all I've been told—"

"Oh," she interrupted, her tone dry. She gazed wearily at the sky. "You're speaking from hearsay, not from personal experience."

He blushed, a reaction happily lost in the light of the *cortile*. "Yes."

"Go on." Her voice was as weary as her expression. "I just wanted a clarification of the basis for your opinion."

"You think I've no right to one?"

"Of course you have. So does the Pope. Whom has he fallen in love with recently? And who's fallen in love with him? I'm sorry. That wasn't nice. Do go on."

"Well, from what I've been told, the men and women here fall in love for a matter of days, or even minutes. Oh, I know that they swear that each romance is going to last forever, but it's no sooner begun that it's ended."

She took his hand in both of hers and pressed it, suffusing his body with a provocative humidity. "You seem to have no faith in the eternity of each moment you're living in."

"I have trouble enough with the larger concept of eternity."

"You're confusing marriage with love, signore. They're not the same thing."

"But I thought they were, for women especially."

"That's a very provincial attitude. You'd never be understood in Venice. Here, women marry their husbands, but they love men."

"If I found out that my wife was unfaithful to me, I'd leave her. I'd have nothing more to do with her."

The young woman shrugged. "That's quite commendable. Your reaction is milder than some I've heard. There are husbands who arrange to have their wives *and* their wives' lovers assassinated. I think that something of an exaggeration myself. It's deplorable to take one's emotions so seriously."

Domenikos smiled. "I don't think I could go that far."

"Good. I despise bloodshed." She reached for his hand, and gazed into his black-masked face. "Yet you'd admit that if you *were* married, you'd consider taking a mistress. You think it's different for men than for women."

"I think it more pardonable, provided that the mistress isn't another man's wife." He hesitated. "This is all very hypothetical, because I wouldn't do such a thing myself, if that's what you were suggesting. When *I* find myself in love, it will be with a woman who, I hope, will become my wife, and there'll be no other woman in my life after that."

She threw back her head and laughed at the sky. "What a ravishing idea. And is it really that way in Crete?"

"It is. But I'll agree that this may be so, in part, because not many Cretan men can afford both a wife and a mistress."

Her response was mockingly grave. "Ah, yes, those economically depressed regions of the world make me sad. Money has its effect on the customs of love everywhere, I dare say. It can make things very confusing."

"Do you mind if I ask how often you've thought yourself in love?"

"I don't mind a bit, but it's a question I can't answer. Ask me instead how many times I've *known* I was in love."

"How many?"

"Hundreds. I'm almost always in love."

"With the same man?" As soon as he put the question, he laughed, although he had been very serious. "Forgive me. That must be a ridiculous notion to put before a Venetian lady."

"What an appalling idea."

He thought of the softness of her touch and trembled with pleasure as he reflected on her voluptuousness, the impure joy she evoked. "Are you married?" he inquired, almost in a whisper.

"No, of course not."

"Ah."

"And just what does that 'ah' signify?"

"Nothing. It's just that . . ."

"It's just that you've finally recognized me, haven't you? What I am, if not who?"

"Yes." He was humiliated, even shocked by her directness.

"And this makes you unhappy?"

"Surprised, rather."

"But why?"

"I don't know, really. You're so intelligent, so gay, so beautifully dressed, so. . . ."

She laughed again, her voice trilling and echoing in the *cortile*.

"You *are* provincial, aren't you? Isn't it permitted?"

"It's unexpected."

"*You* find it so."

He sighed. "It's just as you said. I'm provincial."

"And naïve."

"Oh, yes. That I certainly am."

"You won't, I hope, be offended if I find that charming, refreshing. I never thought, after so many years, I'd meet a man who's willing to admit that he's naïve. Most men, you know, would think that the most chilling of epithets."

Suddenly solemn, Domenikos edged slightly away from her and gazed into her eyes. "I think it would be very difficult for you to offend me."

"What a nice thing to say. But it's not altogether true, is it? I mean, now that your surmise about me has been confirmed, you feel differently, don't you?"

"No."

"Honestly?"

He nodded emphatically. "If anything, I'm even more drawn to you."

"Because I seem more accessible?"

"Less encumbered, in my provincial terms."

She squeezed his arms. "Will you dance with me?"

He stood up, drawing her to her feet. "With delight, though I warn you that I'm very inept. What I know are the dances of Crete, and they're very rustic by comparison with the Venetian forms."

"Never mind. Everyone else who's dancing is so drunk that you'll attract no attention at all."

They reentered the studio and joined the handful of couples who were dancing. Holding her in an arm's-length embrace, he felt an almost overwhelming desire to crush her to him, oblivious of all who were about them. He watched her bright eyes, followed the supple, graceful movements of her lithe body, and felt his mouth go dry with desire.

"It's enough," she murmured at last. "You see? I was right. No one noticed. And besides, you're not so awkward as you said. With a bit of practice, you could be an excellent dancer."

He laughed and took her arm, leading her once again into the *cortile*. "You must never tell me lies."

They sat down again. She stared at him evenly. "But that wasn't a lie."

He returned her gaze. "I believe you."

"Good. I think that you and I should get on very well. We both at least try to speak the truth."

"The truth?"

"As we find it."

"For your eternal moment?"

"Oh, yes, only for that, only for that. I could promise no more."

Domenikos sighed again. "So ends my adolescence."

She took his hand in both of hers and pressed it, almost maternally, it seemed to him. "You don't think it a little late for that to happen?"

He shrugged. "I was thinking about my illusions, not about making love."

She placed his hand against her well-displayed bosom. "Listen to me. That's one illusion you can easily spare, certainly about the women of Venice." She dropped his hand and took his firm, smooth jaw between her warm, moist fingers. "There are several kinds of women in this city. There are the virgins, whom you'd never find at a gathering of this sort. And there are the married prunes who are rich enough to have lovers but too ugly to find them. And there are the pretty married women who *do* have lovers whom they look after as well as they can. . . ."

Domenikos laughed darkly. "If only briefly."

"Briefly, perhaps, but sincerely. That's the point, the real point, isn't it?"

"So you say."

"Well, let me go on. And there are the courtesans, which is what I'm called." She turned his face to her. "They have lovers too, but on a somewhat different basis."

"A professional basis."

"That puts it crudely."

"But with accuracy."

"With some," she acknowledged. "But you keep overlooking the question of sincerity, however brief."

"And *you* overlook the question of fidelity. For you, fidelity is dead."

She nodded. "Except for the ugly wives, fidelity for Venice was never even born."

"But in Crete, it still lives."

"You're in Venice, my friend."

"You make me very uneasy, not for myself but for you. What will happen to you when this splendid prime of beauty you're in now has passed?"

"Am I beautiful?"

He caressed her white throat, inclining her face toward him. "That's a shameless question. You know the answer. I've never seen a woman who better understood how very beautiful she was, and just how far her beauty would be able to take her."

Her reply seemed genuinely humble. "Thank you for saying that."

"You've not answered me. What's to happen to you?"

"It depends. The logical end is for me to become a nun. I'll instruct old abbots and young priests in the ways of the world."

"I don't like it."

"I'm touched by your concern. I truly am. But you're in no position to like it or dislike it. You're not committed to me, after all."

He paused, almost breathless, before speaking. "Do I take it that you're instructing no one at the moment in the ways of the world?"

She smiled, almost demurely. "No one."

"Would you consider reserving yourself for a painter from Crete?"

"I find him very attractive."

"I'm afraid you'd have your work cut out for you. As you've said, he's very naïve."

"I have nothing but time."

"An eternal moment?"

"And you have a passion for something total, something permanent."

"No, not a passion, an inclination."

She smiled softly. "I accept that distinction."

"I have to tell you that I'm not rich. I have *some* money, but I'm not rich."

She laughed. "I know about you. You prefer to spend your gold on books."

"You know that?"

She was indignant. "Did you take me for a common whore of the streets? You don't imagine I'd choose just anyone, even a guest of Titian's, without learning something about him beforehand."

He grinned. "You're even cleverer than I thought. All those deductions and the palmistry were a hoax."

"An artful hoax, however."

"I agree."

"And do you think I'll prove an adequate substitute for a book as a way of passing an evening?"

"For a time, I think, you'll do nicely, but only for a time, until I've understood all there is to read in your body."

He held her face now with the tips of his fingers, gently, but with the certainty of possession. His expression became abstracted.

"What are you thinking?" she whispered.

"That you're the first woman I've ever had a real conversation with, except for my mother."

"Surely not."

"In Candia, in Crete, the unmarried are segregated."

"What a misfortune."

"Indeed, but I didn't realize that until now." He pressed her chin with his strong fingers. "May I kiss you?"

Her mouth was cool and sweet. With his free hand, Domenikos started to lift the mask from her eyes. She restrained him with a touch. "No, no, my love. There are few enough rules. We must obey them. Come with me."

Her apartment overlooked the Canale della Giudecca, at a considerable distance, by foot, from the Biri Grande. They walked it nevertheless. Her name was Veronica, and at approximately five o'clock in the morning, she became Domenikos' mistress.

Ten

News of his proposed liaison with Veronica was received somewhat enviously by his uncle, icily by Marica. "I suppose it's too much to hope that she's not a Roman Catholic," she commented initially. Domenikos reluctantly acknowledged this. His aunt then turned aside with the resigned observation, "Well, it's your affair, so long as you don't decide to marry her." The subject was dismissed, at least as a matter for discussion.

Though he continued officially to reside in the Rio dei Greci, Domenikos spent little time there now. At twenty-two, he had begun not merely a new life but a new sort of life, in an atmosphere that could scarcely have been more alien to any he had previously encountered. He rejoiced in the change, despite some of the shocks its earliest moments brought.

The fastidious Domenikos found to his horror, though ultimately to his amusement, that Veronica was utterly indifferent to the untidiness in which she lived. She reproached him, at first, when he attempted to create some order out of her chaos. "You're wasting time we could be spending in bed," she complained. "Leave that for the servants." "But you won't see that they do it," he protested. At this, she would throw herself on the large bed and cover her head with a cushion.

Yet this seemed her only source of petulance, and an adjustment was soon made; what she didn't carefully put away before his arrival, she hastily hid in cupboards. And when Domenikos discovered this new custom, he responded to it with a helpless grin. "I'm glad you're not my wife," he said, but gently. "So am I," she answered, laughing.

He learned much from her. It was only to be expected that she should educate him in the arts of physical love, in which her expertise was consummate. The refinements to which she introduced him were at the outset of their relationship far more shocking than her squalid housekeeping. In this respect, however, she was on firmer ground. To his expressions of revulsion, she pressed a hand over his mouth. "Be quiet, Menegos. We can only humiliate each other if humiliation is meant."

From Veronica, he gained as well an appreciation of food as a form of art. Since she regarded a proper meal as a necessary preface to a proper interlude of love, she was infinitely attentive about the preparation and presentation of each supper they shared. Hitherto, Domenikos had nourished himself thoughtlessly, indiscriminately. But Veronica's repast, served with such panache, made him understand that eating need not seem a penance, drinking simply a means of getting drunk, a condition he rarely enjoyed.

And she could learn from him. She listened with attention when he spoke or read to her, and responded with intelligent, perceptive questions about the subjects that interested him, especially his work with Titian. There were limits to her span of concentration. After an hour of seriousness, she would frown and break the mood. "If I'm not careful, you'll ruin me for any other man. No man wants a woman who's better informed than he is."

They loved each other. Whatever reservations she had expressed when they first met at the Biri Grande, Veronica appeared unstinting in her devotion to Domenikos, unguarded in her praise of him as a man, as a lover. She gave him a kind of self-confidence he had previously lacked, security as a male, as one attractive and satisfying to women, to a woman. She never gave him cause to doubt that she was absolutely his. Her only genuine complaint was that he spent too much time with Titian.

His love for her, if ostensibly as unquestionable, had its unmentioned restriction: he couldn't marry her, and for that reason he wouldn't permit himself to love her completely. In the absence, however, of one to whom his devotion could be total, he gave only occasional thought to this shortcoming.

The advent of Veronica had brought a roundness, a fullness to his life. He was less tense, less introspective. Orazio noted this frequently. But it was for Titian to make the conclusive comment: "Greco, you've at last begun to grow up."

Michelangelo died in February of 1564. Venice may have trembled less than did Florence or Rome on receipt of this news, but her master artists responded to it with prudence. Even Titian, conscious of his role as dean of the unofficial Venetian academy of painters, sculptors, and architects, was impelled to send a moving letter of condolence to Michelangelo's erstwhile patron and longtime protector, Duke Cosimo de' Medici, of Florence.

In private, the master admitted that his words to the duke were far loftier than his thoughts. "I never liked Michelangelo. But I never pretended to. And I'll not miss him," he observed grimly to his son and Domenikos. Then his mood changed abruptly, and he rubbed his hands together energetically. "I'm at least as old as he was, and there's still plenty of life and work left in *me*."

The death of the great Florentine occasioned unhappy echoes the following June, when the edicts on art of the Councils of Trent were officially published. Almost simultaneously the Pope had ordained that the nudes depicted in Michelangelo's "Last Judgment," the chief ornament of the Vatican's Sistine Chapel, be expurgated by the artist's old friend and assistant, Daniele da Volterra. "Even if I didn't like him," said Titian sorrowfully, "I respected him. It's tragic that his life should end on such a note of defeat."

The Council's decree on religious art provoked a number of stormy meetings of the Venetian academy. Although he couldn't yet claim membership, Domenikos heard from the lips of Orazio and the master the gist of the long debates. Naturally, it was Titian who held the more forceful opinions.

"If we follow these rules strictly from now on, our paintings will be as interesting and lifelike as those stiff little icons you were running away from when you first came to Venice, Greco. How does that strike you?"

"That would be catastrophic, master, but I can't believe it will be nearly so serious as that. It doesn't make any sense, not when the years of our religion are piled so high."

"Oh," said Titian with a tremor of indignation, "I'm delighted that your faith hasn't been shaken. Blessed are the converts, for theirs is the kingdom of credulity. The Church, my boy, is in the process of denying artists a freedom they've enjoyed ever since Giotto and Dante opened the world to us."

Domenikos shook his head. "I won't believe that."

"Of course you won't. But it's true just the same. As far as painting is concerned, the Church of Rome is becoming as doctrinaire as your former Church of Constantinople. Oh, how the heretic Martin Luther must be chortling in his grave about this. The bishops at Trento were doing their best to woo the Protestants back into the fold."

"Can that be wrong, master?"

"Not in itself. But the way they chose will have the effect of destroying, at a single blow, all our old concepts of beauty." Titian laughed angrily and began to pace the floor of the larger studio, his hands folded tightly behind his capacious rump. "Savonarola could have written that decree, all by himself. If he were alive today, the cardinals would probably make him Pope instead of burning him at the stake. The next thing you know, they'll be behaving as he did, burning books and pictures." He marched to a table and picked up a printed abstract of the Trent decree. "Just listen to this. 'If any abuses shall have found their way into these holy and salutary observances, the holy council desires earnestly that they be completely removed, so that no representation of false doctrine and such as might be the occasion of grave error to the uneducated be exhibited. And if at times it happens, when this is beneficial to the illiterate, that the stories and narratives of the Holy Scriptures are portrayed and exhibited, the people should be instructed that not for that reason is the divinity represented in pictures as if it can be seen with bodily eyes or expressed in colors or figures. Furthermore, in the invocation of the saints, the veneration of relics, and the sacred use of images, all superstition shall be removed, all filthy quest for gain eliminated, and all lasciviousness avoided, so that images shall not be painted and adorned with a seductive charm, or the celebration of saints and the visitation of relics be perverted by the people into boisterous festivities and drunkenness, as if the festivities in honor of the saints are to be celebrated with revelry and with no sense of decency.' "

The old man puffed mightily after reading so extensive a citation. ". . . 'completely removed,' " he said. "The emphasis, of course, is mine. Removed to where? To the flames. Mark my words." He peered intently at the document once again and then waved it dramatically beneath the noses of his listeners. "No superstition. There goes mythology. No false doctrine. There goes the Apocrypha. No grave error. Here comes the Holy Inquisition. 'All filthy quest for gain eliminated.' " He stared hotly at Domenikos. "What's that mean?"

The young painter laughed. "From now on, we're to paint for the love of God, not money."

"Precisely, precisely." Titian hunched his shoulders. "And you think that amusing?"

"It has its humorous side, master."

"The Church is content to take her tithe from us, but from now on, we artists must settle for the thanks of some decadent bishop and hope that we'll receive the remainder of our reward in heaven, if we're fortunate enough to reach heaven."

"I was joking, master," Domenikos protested. "Surely, that passage means that we're supposed to introduce nothing into our paintings that's intended to make them more desirable or more interesting than would be indicated by the scene itself. We're not to try to attract people to faith for the wrong reasons. The phrase you read is admittedly open to another construction, but I can't believe yours is the right one."

"I hope you're right, Greco, and more for your sake than my own. I hardly sell pictures to churches any more. They can't afford my prices, or so they tell me." Suddenly he grinned. "If you're right, I wonder how His Most Catholic Majesty of Spain will feel. He likes the little touches of lasciviousness I put in my paintings for him, the ones for his palace, I mean, not the ones for the Escorial. That is one of the reasons he likes my work so much. I pander to his taste." He shrugged. "But why not? Now, if you're correct, he'll have to find some new diversion when the Inquisition has no auto-da-fé for his entertainment."

Domenikos took the sheets of paper from the master's hand and studied them for a moment, then shook his head. "In any case, this seems only to apply to paintings for purely religious purposes. Still, it may not be completely mistaken that kings be protected from their baser instincts. I assume they're no different from anyone else in the eyes of God."

Titian chuckled. "King Philip would hardly agree with you, if I know him. But do I understand you to be saying that we must all seek church protection from our 'baser instincts,' as you put it? Does that, for example, include your own?"

"I didn't quite mean that."

"You mean there are baser instincts and baser instincts."

"There are base instincts and basic instincts."

"Yours, I suppose, are basic."

"They're more common."

The old man's eyes filled with facetious astonishment. "And how would you know that? You mean that we hear more pleasantries about a man and his mistress than about a king whose pleasures are what you'd probably call perversions?" He sighed. "The pleasures, the nasty, odd little habits that Philip and I share may be all that are left to old men. You mustn't gloat, Greco, simply because you have the youth and the funds to maintain a woman. Be a bit more compassionate about others, for your time will come."

Domenikos flushed and gazed at the floor in mock contrition. "We've lost the point, master," he said at last. "If the Church is serious in her intention to purify her temple, I don't see how you can expect that art should be excluded. We're constantly told that art is the 'Bible of the illiterate.' Of course, everything depends on how the bishops, individually, interpret the decree. But the idea isn't wrong as such, and it may sometimes be absolutely necessary. If it's reasonably done, I don't see that we have much to worry about."

Titian threw his hands in the air and moved toward the door to his own studio. "You don't have to take my word for it. If you think I exaggerate the danger, talk to some of the others. Talk to Tintoretto. You say you admire him, though God alone knows why. Ask him what *he* thinks. Then perhaps you'll not be such an optimist."

He left the great room, slamming the door behind him.

Domenikos had encountered Jacopo Robusti (called Tintoretto because his father had been a dyer) on many occasions; all their meetings heretofore, however, had been casual exchanges in a taverna near the Piazza. Each time they met, the young painter had been impressed by the almost black vigor evinced by this native of Venice. Tintoretto had begun his studies with Titian at twenty-five. His association with the old master was brief. Their personalities and their artistic inclinations conflicted too sharply for them long to remain in anything resembling double harness. Their failure to harmonize had little effect on Tintoretto's career, for he rapidly established himself as second only to Titian among the major painters of the Serenissima, Veronese being his other significant rival.

That Domenikos had so long delayed in paying a visit to Tintoretto's studio was not a mystery. It stemmed from Titian's unaccountable jealousy of the younger man's success, an emotion he customarily disguised as a violent distaste for his style of painting. He had repeatedly made it clear to Domenikos that were he to make any sort of overtures of friendship toward the flamboyant artist, he would consider it nothing less than treachery. The master's offer to arrange for his pupil to study with Tintoretto or Veronese, made after he had completed his version of the Purification of the Temple, left Domenikos in no doubt about Titian's viewpoint.

Thus, although he really cared little to have Tintoretto's opinions about the decree of the Trent Council, he seized on the old man's suggestion that he consult with him. It was the first viable opportunity offered him.

Domenikos found Tintoretto at his usual table in the taverna and gratefully accepted an invitation to accompany him to his studio. The older man was in a particularly cheerful frame of mind, laughing to himself as they walked, clapping his hands together with delight. Domenikos restrained his curiosity, supposing that if his host wished to share his joy he would explain. It was only when they entered his studio (somewhat smaller and much more cluttered than Titian's) that the secret of his pleasure was disclosed.

They were standing in the center of the room, amid torn sheets of drawing paper, fragments of stretchers, and broken paint pots. Tintoretto pointed to an immense oval canvas nearing completion. It depicted a religious scene unfamiliar to the young painter. Robusti burst out laughing again. "You don't know the story of this, I suppose."

"Should I?"

"I just wondered how long the secret could be kept." He indicated the men who were applying final glazes to the painting. "In Venice, you never know."

Domenikos laughed. "Do you plan to explain?"

Tintoretto shrugged, then drew his guest from this studio into an adjacent sitting room, nearly as untidy as the workshop, and indicated that he should sit. After pouring glasses of strong red wine, the artist took a chair and chuckled once again. "Do you know the Scuola de San Rocco, on the other side of the Canale Grande?"

"I've visited it, a great loft of a place."

"That's it. Or that *was* it. But not for much longer." He aimed a long, thick index finger in the direction of the studio. "That's for the ceiling of the great hall."

"Congratulations, master."

"I accept them, Greco. They're completely deserved, but you don't yet know why."

"Because you obtained the commission, I assume."

"Ah, but you see, I've not obtained the commission. That's why I deserve the congratulations."

"Is it a riddle?"

"Have some more wine." Tintoretto stood up and in the process knocked a shin against the small table that separated them, overturning their glasses. Domenikos helped him to right the situation, and nodded his thanks as his supply was replenished. The artist sat down. "Not quite a riddle, but very much a joke." He sipped from his glass before continuing. "You may have heard from your master that the directors of the scuola are holding a competition to determine which painter will do the pictures and gilding of the Albergo, the great hall."

"No."

"I'm surprised, because of course he was invited to submit a design."

Domenikos smiled. "He no longer competes for anything. 'If they want Titian,' he says, 'they want only Titian.' "

Tintoretto nodded. "An enviable position I hope someday to occupy myself. Well, no matter. He *was* asked, whether he mentioned it to you or not. So was I. So were Veronese and Salviati and Zuccaro and Schiavone. A very representative group, I think you'll agree. All are to submit sketches, and a committee will decide."

Domenikos inclined his head toward the studio. "But that's not a sketch."

Obviously delighted with the young painter's reaction, Robusti nodded vigorously and laughed again. "Exactly, exactly. That's the heart of the joke. Let me tell you, because it's too rich to keep silent about any longer, only you must promise to tell no one, not even Titian, until the arrangements are settled. Since he's in no way involved, your silence won't affect him."

"I promise."

"Right, then. I considered the matter carefully. It's a very rich commission in itself. But there's more to it than that. Because whoever gets the original contract will almost certainly be offered the opportunity of finishing the whole building, all the rooms. So I said to myself, 'Robusti, this is an occasion for ingenuity.' I went to the scuola on a Sunday afternoon and had an interview with the portiere." Here Tintoretto rubbed the thumb and index finger of his right hand together, his expression owlish. "It was interesting. I was able to persuade the good old man to measure the exact dimensions of the oval in the center of the ceiling of the Albergo. Then I returned home and on the canvas you saw there I made this painting of a scene from San Rocco's life. That's the theme of all the pictures for the room."

He stopped speaking and stared expectantly at Domenikos, who returned a bewildered gaze.

"You don't understand?"

"Not yet."

"It's so simple, Greco. All the other competitors are going to submit sketches. I'm not only going to submit a finished painting, but I'm going to have it installed in the ceiling."

"Isn't that risky, master? The committee doesn't have to accept your design, installed or not."

At this, Tintoretto's laughter all but overwhelmed him. It was almost a minute before he recovered his composure sufficiently to proceed. "But they *do*. It's in their bylaws. They may reject no gifts."

"But they can still accept someone else's design. They can shift your picture."

Offended, his host stood up and beckoned Domenikos to follow him back into the studio. "You didn't look at it carefully enough, Greco. They'll take my plan. I'm not concerned about that."

The picture was of San Rocco in Glory, a blaze of yellow, violet, and ultramarine; the saint was transfixed as he observed the descent of God from heaven, while attending angels bore the holy man's symbol of pilgrimage. Domenikos studied it in silence, full of uncertainty, for its distortions of the figures were disturbing, a quality of Tintoretto's art that nevertheless intrigued him, attracted him, appealed inexplicably to his emotions. But of this painter's use of light, he felt pure admiration.

At last, he turned to the older man who stood silent, confident, beside him. "I don't know," he said quietly. "It's very daring. For your sake, I hope they approve, but I'm not sure."

"I know why you feel this way, Greco. You're seeing it from the wrong position. You have to imagine it directly above you, nearly fifty feet above you at that."

Domenikos looked at the picture again, then nodded. "So the distortions will cease to be distortions?"

"Yes. The eye plays tricks. Haven't you noticed it?"

"But it never occurred to me that a trick of proportion could overcome them." He paused and grinned. "I'd like a hand in this adventure. Let me help with the installation."

Tintoretto slapped him on the shoulder. "But of course."

A few days later, just as darkness settled over the city, an odd procession set out from Tintoretto's studio. The artist and Domenikos took the lead, followed by a hand-drawn cart which bore the carefully wrapped painting of San Rocco in Glory. Several assistants, all in as bibulous a condition as their master, brought up the rear. They noisily traversed the Piazza and made their way chaotically through the labyrinth of contradictory streets and alleys to the Rialto Bridge, the cartmen and assistants uttering violent oaths as they pushed the rattling vehicle across the canal. By the time they reached the Scuola de San Rocco, a modicum of silence, induced by fatigue and excitement, had imposed itself on the drunken group.

Domenikos laughed nervously as he waited with Tintoretto for the *portiere* to open the door. "I feel like a thief."

Robusti demurred. "Not at all. You're a Greek bearing gifts."

The sound of the great bolt being thrown silenced them. The door opened a crack, and in the light of a single torch (borne by one of the helpers) the reflection of an alarmed eye appeared. Then, perceiving the identity of the intruders, the servant threw wide the door, eagerly taking Tintoretto's gold-filled hand.

The installation of the painting required hours. Domenikos was disappointed when the artist insisted that it be covered with muslin sheeting until it was revealed to members of the scuola. "I was going to wait for daylight so I could see what you meant about the distortion being corrected."

"No. There has to be an official unveiling. I'm taking no chances at this point."

Reluctantly, with a final look over his shoulder, the young painter wearily descended the broad staircase and emerged with Tintoretto into the small square. It was almost full morning as he returned to the impatient arms of Veronica.

The officials of the scuola behaved precisely as Tintoretto had predicted. Some were outraged by his high-handedness, but even they conceded a grudging admiration for the artist's audacity. The competitors were, understandably, less generous, accusing Robusti of the foulest sort of play. But their protests were unavailing. He was awarded the commission, and to Domenikos' astonishment he agreed to complete it within a year.

"It's not possible," he protested.

Tintoretto shrugged. "It's possible. I work quickly. I did the first one in less than three weeks. But if you don't think your master would disown you, I'll confess I could use some assistance. Would you work with me this summer, while he and Orazio are in Vincenza?"

The young painter considered this. "I'm honored, of course. But I'll have to ask him very carefully."

Titian's reaction to Domenikos' request was half of amusement, half of arrogance: "So you want to play nearer the fire."

The pupil grinned. "You think him dangerous?"

"I doubt that he can do you much harm in two months. But I warn you, Greco, if you come back to me painting in his manner, I'll have nothing more to do with you."

"There's no need to fear that, master."

"You're not thinking of leaving me, are you?" The old man's apprehension was touching.

"You should know that to be the farthest thought from my mind."

Titian grunted characteristically. "I only hope you feel the same way when September comes."

"I shall," the young man responded earnestly.

So it was arranged.

The methods employed by Venice's two greatest painters differed markedly. It was, for one thing, Tintoretto's custom to paint by himself most of the pictures intended for local installation, leaving those to be sent abroad largely to his assistants after he had blocked out the basic elements. "I see no point in soiling my own nest," he said.

He had developed an ingenious device for demonstrating the spatial essentials of a painting. It was a shadow box whose interior was fitted with vertical and horizontal cords, tightly drawn, in a three-dimensional grid pattern. On these cords he suspended models of the figures to be included, which could in this way be viewed in their relative positions and perspectives. When Domenikos expressed admiration for this invention, Tintoretto assented. "I don't believe in letting my assistants think for themselves if there's any way of avoiding it."

"In that respect, at least, you and Titian are agreed."

Robusti, ebullient, swarthy, middle-aged, was standing, arms crossed before his belly, surveying the beginning stages of another picture for the confraternity of San Rocco.

"You know, Greco, I'm trying to think what made me suggest that you help me this summer. I'm sure you're a spy for that old man."

"He'd never send *me* on so important a mission. Besides, why would he want to spy on you? He already has more commissions than he can manage."

"My secrets."

"He's much too old to learn new ways."

Tintoretto appeared at least partially to accept this. "All the same, I don't owe him any favors. Do you know how long I was with him before he drove me out of his studio? Ten days. He gave me only ten days. Can you imagine it? He said I was 'too formed' for him. He couldn't teach me anything." He laughed harshly. "What he meant was that he didn't like my drawing. It was too much like Michelangelo's."

"No, he wouldn't like that very much."

"He may have been right, though, in sending me away. He thought me a threat to everything he so deeply believes about drawing. And in that sense he was right. I *was* formed before I came to him. I was a man." He hesitated. "You understand, Greco, that I'm not inviting you to be disloyal to him in any way. But you should know *my* position. You already know his, I've no doubt."

Domenikos shook his head. "You've no need for concern, master. I have no illusions about him. He's been very good to me, and good *for* me, I think. But I know who he is and what he's like."

"So do I. And he's a great painter, the best of our time." Tintoretto sighed and rubbed his black-browed forehead with a heavy hand. "It's ironic. From the moment when I began to have informed thoughts about such things, I've meant to paint like Titian and draw like Michelangelo."

"I know the controversy only too well."

"You know Titian's side of it."

"But until I see Michelangelo's work, I'll keep an open mind."

Tintoretto turned and pointed to a work in progress that hung on the wall opposite the one he had been considering. "Michelangelo is there, Greco. He's in everything I paint. Precision is the thing. But of course, you'll not be able to decide until you see his work in Rome. It's dazzling. When I first visited the Sistine Chapel, it was like finding myself endowed with a new kind of faculty, a new way of seeing. Oh, Titian can say that Michelangelo didn't know how to paint, didn't know about color, and in *his* terms I suppose he's justified. But my God, Greco, how he could *see,* how he could visualize, how he could *conceive* on a really grand scale. Overwhelming."

"But he was a bit strange, I gather."

Tintoretto pursed his lips and frowned. "Even a madman, according to some. But what's that matter? He loved boys. What has that to do with his art? There are monks in Venice who probably debauch more children in a week than he did in his lifetime."

"Titian complains about his women. He says they're not feminine."

The older man laughed. "He means they're not like his own women, not voluptuous. They have something else, though. They're superhuman, transcendant. Titian so despised him, so feared him as a competitor, that he'd see him buried without a trace."

"He doesn't feel so strongly as he did."

"Now that he's dead, you mean, there's no longer a need for *wishing* him dead. You don't know, Greco, how badly Titian wanted to be in Michelangelo's position. How he cultivated the Farneses, and how bitter he was when the Medicis proved more powerful, because they were behind Michelangelo. He wanted to be in Rome, not Venice. He wanted to make the earth tremble, as Michelangelo did, and he couldn't. And now he's too old to make anything tremble."

Domenikos disapproved of the turn in conversation. "Your ideas and Titian's are so different, it's not possible for you to agree about anything important."

Tintoretto laid a hand on the young man's slender wrist. "Listen, Greco. I'm not trying to turn you against him. He's a great painter. I've said it before. But he hasn't any convictions."

"How wrong you are. I think he's got a much more profound conception of his art than you do. I'm sorry to say that. But you've invited it. He's after a simplicity. You pursue the pageant. You're concerned with life. He's concerned with an aesthetic."

The artist was silent as he stared at Domenikos, his expression revealing no offense, but rather an intense interest, even a kind of rueful pleasure. "That's right," he finally muttered. "That's exactly right. I try to tell a story. That's one of the really tempting things about this San Rocco project. I can paint San Rocco's whole career. If Titian were given the commission, it would be a series of studies, tableaux. Mine will be, as you put it, a pageant."

"It wouldn't do if you and Titian painted alike." He smiled. "If you painted alike, I'd not be here to learn from you."

This truism seemed to break Tintoretto's speculative mood. He clapped his hands together, his voice strong and full of enthusiasm. "You know, Greco, this commission poses some interesting problems of light. The Albergo is so dark, even on the sunniest day. But by knowing in advance exactly what position each picture is to occupy, I can make allowance for the amount of light each receives." He slapped the young painter's shoulder. "Let me show you what I mean."

By the time Titian returned to Venice from his customary respite at his villa in Vincenza, Domenikos had mastered the principles of illuminating his canvases as they were propounded by Tintoretto.

When Domenikos left Robusti's studio following his final day of work with him, he expressed his gratitude warmly. The master reciprocated. "You really helped me, Greco. It was a true gesture of friendship."

"I meant it so, Jacopo."

"See that Titian doesn't keep you all to himself now."

The young man shook his head. "He'll not keep me from a friend."

Eleven

It was a perfect day in early June. The noontime sun of Crete cast short, precise shadows on the parched ground. The clusters of black-clothed mourners, gathered by the modest grave markers in the shabby little hilltop cemetery, were timeless in their movement and bearing. They might as easily have been standing beside the grave of some fallen hero of an antique civilization as by that of Giorgio Theotokopoulos in the year 1566.

The bruising intelligence that his father was desperately ill had come as a shock to Domenikos, for there had been no preparation for it, no news of a decline in health. Yet it seemed, in the context of that winter and spring in Venice, wholly in keeping with the tone of somberness and sorrow with which those seasons were marked. As he reflected now on the sequence of disasters, minor and major, that had beset him in recent months, he was moved to believe that in some fashion God was seeking to redress an imbalance of good fortune and joy which He had accorded the young Cretan during the first years of his stay in the Serenissima, an imbalance of happiness that had extended over his whole lifetime.

If he accepted these unhappy events with a resignation that appeared stoic, it was because he had come to regard himself as an object of celestial disapproval. He could even feel guilty about the guilt he now felt, because he considered it appropriate, a source of painful joy, a hairshirt he willingly wore.

The sharp change in his fortunes had its inception just after Epiphany, when he was visiting Tintoretto. The two painters had worked together a second summer; their friendship had grown in intimacy. Domenikos no longer remembered with absolute precision the remarks that had produced the explosion, so shocked was he when it took place. But the words, as they fell into position, provided an arrangement of mounting and mutual hostility. The subject, inevitably, had been Titian. Robusti, slightly drunk after a prolonged Sunday meal, had disparaged the master once too often. The dam burst.

"Why do you keep saying this kind of thing about him to me, Jacopo? Can't you keep quiet? Think of the position you place me in. If I agreed with you, it would be tantamount to admitting that I'd wasted five years of my life."

The impatient Tintoretto dismissed his friend's protest with a brusque gesture. "You're much too sensitive, Greco. Your loyalty to the old man is very moving. You sometimes make me want to cry. But you're much too good a painter to be impressed by those overblown Virgins of his. He used to have vigor. He really was somebody. But now he's sterile, no matter how philosophical he's become. He's nobody."

"You didn't used to think that. You said he was the greatest painter alive."

The older artist laughed scornfully. "That's when I was sober. When I'm drunk, I tell the whole truth."

"That's despicable. *You're* despicable."

Superficially, the wound thus made had been healed. But friendship had dwindled to a perfunctory acquaintance.

Barely a week later, his aunt Marica had learned, through an accident virtually identical to the one that had revealed the truth to his uncle, that Domenikos was a communicant of the Roman Church. Her rage was astonishing, beyond her control. She ordered him to leave her house forthwith. "It's bad enough that you take a Catholic mistress, but that you should have betrayed me in *this* way, and for so long, is the last straw."

As far as Marica was concerned, Domenikos' soul was lost, forever damned. She would no longer tolerate his remaining under her roof. (This had its comical side since in fact he spent virtually no time beneath her roof in any case. "It's the principle," she said.) So, early in February, he removed his possessions to lodgings provided by the amiable wife of Francesco da Ravenna, an assistant of Titian, convenient to the Biri Grande and San Canciano.

Certain that his aunt would now communicate the news of his conversion to Candia, Domenikos himself composed a letter home conveying this information as diplomatically as he could. He attributed the decision to his impressionable youth—which was true—but assured his parents that as time passed, he was increasingly persuaded that the Latin faith was "better suited to my religious needs and to my view of life." Reaction was more disappointing than, at his most pessimistic, he had feared. A letter from Cleo informed him that she had kept his missive from Giorgio. "But you have broken my heart, Menegos, not only by what you have done, but because you only told us when you saw no alternative. As it happens, Marica has written nothing yet, save that you are no longer living in her house. Out of consideration for your father, I beg you to say nothing of this in any future letter you may send."

On Ash Wednesday came the next calamity. Veronica announced to Domenikos that at a gathering they had both attended the previous evening she had met a Venetian gentleman of considerable wealth and influence to whom, as of this very day, she intended exclusively to devote her favors.

In view of the apparent tranquillity of their relationship, its pleasant

routine, her dismissal of him seemed cruelly airy. "You were beginning to bore me. It's not that I don't enjoy talking about serious things,
art and what-not. I find them elevating. But my God, Menegos, if
you ever want to please another woman for more than a few months,
even if she's married to you and can't escape at all, you'll have to
train yourself to have more low thoughts. Nobody, no woman certainly, enjoys being elevated all the time."

It seemed plain that nothing more could happen. It was difficult for
Domenikos to decide whether his heart or his pride had suffered the
greater injury as a result of Veronica's abrupt defection. And in the
end, he concluded that the question was irrelevant. He was suffering.
The fabric of his life in Venice, woven with such care, had been ir-
reparably shredded. All that remained was his tie with the Biri
Grande. Save for Titian and Orazio, he was alone, even more alone,
because he had tasted intimacy with others, than on his arrival here
nearly six years before.

Late in April, he understood his error. Worse *could* occur. Word
then reached him of his father's terminal illness. Somber in mind,
blacker in spirit, the inner Domenikos reflecting his outward appearance, he had boarded the first vessel for Candia, praying only
that God would spare Giorgio at least until the prodigal's return from
Venice. In this, too, he was disappointed. His father died the evening
before Domenikos' ship cleared the breakwater of Candia's little harbor.

For the Roman Catholic world also, lay and cleric, the year 1566
was agonizing. The Ottoman Empire continued to apply pressure
against the Serenissima's bases in the eastern Mediterranean. The
Consiglio was giving consideration to the Pope's suggestion for the
creation of a Holy League, an ill-assorted alliance of the Papal States,
Venice, and the Holy Roman Empire: Spain, Naples, Austria, and the
Low Countries. Formation of the Holy League, however, would be
delayed another four years; only when Cyprus fell to the Turks would
Venice throw in her lot with the detested King Philip of Spain.

The Church found herself in greater trouble after the decrees of
Trent had been published than before. Debate on their merits was
prolonged and acrimonious, and it was increasingly evident that the
bishops participating in the Councils had been less than unanimous
in their support of proposals, most of which had been made at the
demand of Pope Pius IV.

That there was disagreement among her own was disturbing to the

Church. Her new policy with respect to Protestantism included a revival of the Church Militant, a Europe-wide crusade to stamp out the most virulent heresies. The Jesuits were given a broader mandate, the Holy Office strengthened.

Much of Europe was in torment. Wars of religion raged almost everywhere. Held to be illegitimate and a usurper by her own bishops, Elizabeth of Britain reestablished the Protestant Church of England, which had but recently been declared anathema. With her aid, the Huguenots in France were threatening not only the Church of Rome but the enfeebled monarchy as well. Long dominated by the Empire, the Low Countries found it possible to mock their masters and their masters' Church. Similar implosions occurred in Switzerland, in Scandinavia, and in northern Germany. Of the western countries beyond the Italian peninsula, only Spain appeared largely unaffected by Reformation movements, and there another holy war was soon to be mounted against the Moors and the Jews.

Domenikos' interest in these events was imperfect and intermittent. He said more than once to Orazio, "It's difficult for me to become too deeply concerned about matters that don't affect me directly. That doesn't mean I don't care, but just that I can't afford to squander emotion on anything but painting. Perhaps I'm too detached."

The handful of Cretan earth he now cast into his father's grave seemed a trifling, pathetic gesture to the memory of a man so beloved, so generous, so forceful. Domenikos wept, and in silence turned away.

As he and his brother led the shrouded Cleo back along the dusty road toward the house of the family's vineyard in Fodele, Domenikos gazed at the familiar landscape of dry plains, undulating groves, and ordered rows of vines. He looked at Mount Ida, bare and snow-capped, its summit gleaming in the light of the towering sun. There was in these harsh vistas a tug of affection, but the nostalgia was for a childhood now utterly lost.

There were few physical alterations in Candia or Fodele. Yet his six years' absence had produced other changes that stunned Domenikos. Death had taken not only his father, but Brother Constantine two years before and Father Vincenzo the previous autumn. He couldn't believe, as he looked down at her, that his mother, weary and seemingly frail, could live much longer. Only his brother would remain of his boyhood here, and their ties were tenuous indeed.

As if she guessed his thoughts, a tearless Cleo peered up at him through her black veil. "When do you return to Venice, Menegos?" Her left hand gripped his forearm firmly.

He studied his dust-covered boots as they paced over the powdery white surface of the country road. "I don't know, mama. I've made no plans."

"Why don't you stay on here?" Manusos asked eagerly, but as he looked at his younger brother, his eyes were hopeless.

"No," said Cleo decisively. "It wouldn't be wise for him. I don't think it would be wise for *you,* either."

"But why not, mama, if he wants to? You wouldn't order him to leave, would you?"

"Of course not. But he doesn't want to stay." She looked up once again at Domenikos, her face gray beneath the veil, the sunlight casting a black shadow of her nose on her pale cheek, her eyes dark and recessed, almost invisible. "There's nothing left for you here, is there?"

It was true, but it appeared something he should deny at this moment. "You and Manusos are here." Then, more softly, he added, "I'll do what you want."

"I know you will," she replied tranquilly. "You must go. We're not the kind of people a painter, your kind of painter, can survive with for long. We're just country people, Menegos, and it's no good pretending we're not. Besides, it's important for you to finish the thing you've started so well. And the sooner you leave, the easier the break will be."

"But if you need me . . ."

"We *don't* need you," she said dully.

"Of course we need him." Manusos' shrill tone surprised his brother.

Cleo shook her head sharply, causing her veil to fly out from her narrow shoulders. "No, Manusos, we mustn't press him. It's not fair. I'll be able to help you."

"But you don't know the first thing about papa's business," he protested, a note almost of panic in his voice. Then, apologetic, he continued. "I appreciate your offer, mama, but it's complicated. It's man's work."

Cleo's laughter, emanating from beneath her veil, was incongruous. "I may not understand everything, but I knew most of what Giorgio knew. I checked all his calculations."

Manusos suddenly became sullen. "I suppose that means *you're* planning to run things now."

"It means what I said. I'll help you. The authority is yours."

The older son made no response. They accomplished the remaining distance to the house in silence.

Domenikos could not easily dismiss the feeling that he ought to remain in Crete. For the generosity he had received, it seemed that he offered nothing in return. Testing himself, he spent the days before the next ship sailed by walking up from Candia into the low hills, to the Roman ruins he had sketched as a boy. He made some drawings, but his interest was only desultory; landscapes, except as backgrounds, were of little appeal to him. But the land itself retained its hold on him, as distinct from the culture he could now discern with some degree of objectivity. Candiot society, even that of the Venetians there, was almost implausibly provincial. He wondered that he had ever imagined a future for himself here. Venice had corrupted him.

Giorgio had done handsomely by his younger son. The sum he left him in golden ducats, if not princely, would nevertheless assure his independence for years to come, even were he to secure no commissions at all. He had become a young man of property.

The remainder of Giorgio's estate passed to Manusos, the houses, the lands, the warehouses. And it seemed a certainty that the older son would also inherit his father's post of tax collector. Although Cleo's dowry had been restored to her as a consequence of her husband's death, it was understood that the unmarried Manusos would care for her as long as she lived.

When the testamentary documents had been witnessed and filed in Candia, Manusos once again grew expansive and relaxed, the man Domenikos recalled. They sat together in the dining room of what was now Manusos' house, drinking retsina.

"Well, Menegos. Aren't you pleased? We both have what we want."

Domenikos marveled at the resemblance of brother to father. "Oh, yes. Papa was good to me. I had no right to expect such generosity in his will. I do feel guilty, though. Will you be able to manage?"

Manusos wiped the wine from his broad moustache with the back of his hand. "Oh, for God's sake, now you're beginning to sound like papa. Do you think I know nothing?"

"I didn't mean it that way. I just wondered if you have people you can rely on. I remember papa cursing the knavery of his clerks and the thievery of his overseers."

"That was his way. He didn't mean to be taken seriously. He liked to complain. This is Candia, not Venice. We all know each other. I'll be all right."

"I'm sure you will, and I'm sure you'll carry on where papa left off." Domenikos was sure of no such thing, but there seemed no purpose in annoying Manusos over a matter beyond his control.

"Oh, I'm going to do better than that, Menegos." The older brother poured himself more retsina and drank deeply before continuing. "Papa was wise and clever, but he was timid. . . . No, he was cautious. He never took chances."

Domenikos did his best to conceal his apprehension. "You're going to take chances?" he inquired blandly.

Manusos pushed the ewer of wine across the table. Domenikos filled his goblet. "Well, not exactly chances. Risks might be the better word, if you understand me."

"What's the difference between a chance and a risk?"

"When you gamble, you're taking a chance. When you invest in something, you're taking a risk, because you have more than just a hunch to go on. You have information."

Domenikos nodded. "And what's the nature of this risk you plan to take?"

"Piracy," was the cool response.

The younger man stared at him. "Piracy? You're not joking?"

Unconsciously emulating his father, Manusos slapped his thigh with delight over this startled reaction. "I thought that might surprise you."

"Surprise me? I'm staggered."

"You shouldn't be, Menegos. Quite a few Candiots are doing it already, and making handsome profits too. It's legal, you know."

"From whose point of view?"

"The Republic's. All you need is a license from the Consiglio, and a ship, of course. As a matter of fact, the Serenissima will provide the ship in exchange for a share of the takings." He grinned. "It's understood, of course, that we raid only Turkish shipping, and the odd Genoan now and then."

"It sounds very dangerous. Have you told mama?"

"Not yet. Oh, I suppose there's a certain amount of danger, but the gains can be enormous. You have no idea, Menegos, especially if we capture a merchant ship."

"And when do you think you'll start out on this remarkable venture?"

"Well, it's all indefinite at the moment. I mean, it's not exactly the sort of thing you'd organize with just any fellow you happen to find in a taverna, is it? You have to know your men. And there are complications." His tone became confidential. "That's one of the reasons I'm telling you about it. When the time comes, you could be very useful to us in Venice, you and Uncle Manusos—if you're willing, that is."

"If you're actually serious about this, I'll think about it, but only when you have a specific proposal." Domenikos shrugged. "How could *I* help?"

"You could petition the Consiglio for us."

"Us? You haven't even chosen your people yet."

"When the time comes, I mean."

"It seems very impulsive to me, Manusos. I don't like it."

"I admit that I've only begun considering it carefully since papa died. But I've had it at the back of my mind for a long time."

"Did you ever discuss it with papa?"

Manusos roared with laughter and slapped the heavy table with the flat of his hand. "Dear God, Menegos, can't you just hear what he'd have said? He'd have been carried off in the next moment, from shock or outrage or both."

Domenikos sighed. "I hate to seem skeptical, but I don't think this is the time for you to be planning anything so ambitious. You have all these other business matters to worry about."

"Worry? Who worries?" Manusos exuded confidence. "Besides, it's not going to happen tomorrow. These things take time to arrange."

Domenikos changed the subject. "Since you're planning to become a pirate . . ." He began to laugh. "I'm sorry, but that's how it strikes me. If you *do* become a pirate, I assume you've given up any thought of getting married."

The older brother grimaced. "Marriage has never interested me much. You know that. It upsets mama, and papa was always urging me to marry. But I have no great desire to have a woman constantly around the house. I enjoy living alone. A whore now and then is all I need. No obligations, no bickering, no children underfoot. And now I have mama to look after. She's all the woman I require."

"What about the family name?"

"What about it? It's of no concern to me. And you'll carry it on, won't you?"

"You think I'm going to marry?"

"Decidedly."

"What makes you think so?"

Manusos chuckled. "I understood it the night I took you down to that brothel on the quay. Do you remember?"

"Vividly."

"My God, how shy you were. That was when I knew you'd marry."

"But why?"

"You were so damned solemn about it, so serious. You didn't think of it as a game, as a way of passing a few minutes. It was something important and mysterious. Or that's how it appeared to me."

Domenikos briefly regretted thinking of his brother in Giorgio's terms; he *was* perceptive. "But you know that I went back there again. I went back fairly often, as a matter of fact."

"I know you did. But you did it in spite of yourself, didn't you, against your better judgment? You had to go."

"Precisely. But I don't see what that has to do with marriage."

"You want something permanent."

Domenikus nodded. "That's true."

"So you'll marry. What's more permanent than that?"

"I have nothing against it."

"Then don't wait too long, Menegos, or you'll be too old to enjoy it."

The younger brother laughed. "Don't worry."

"When you get married, I'll come and visit you in Venice."

"That would be fine, but I'm not sure I'll be living in Venice for the rest of my life."

"I thought you were happy there."

"I'm happy enough. It's not that. And I haven't any desire to leave. It all depends on whether I can get the commissions I need. I'm not going to work for Titian forever."

"I don't know why you stay with him any longer. You have money enough to be on your own now."

"It's not a question of money, brother. I have more to learn from him."

Manusos was bewildered. "How can anything take as much time as that? What is it, six years? And there's more to learn? How much longer?"

"I've wondered the same thing." He grinned. "Maybe I'm waiting for him to push me out the door."

"Not likely, if you're as useful to him as you say."

"Well, I may push myself out the door, but I'm not ready for that yet."

"How will you know when you're ready?"

"When I want to paint everything differently from Titian's way."

The time had passed. It grieved Domenikos to reflect that it had seemed to pass so slowly, made him feel a traitor that he should be so anxious to take leave of the two in Candia who loved him. But here his separateness and his insularity were even more marked than in Venice.

"I'll say goodbye to you here, Menegos." Cleo was standing beside him in the courtyard. Below, in the harbor, the ship was being prepared for departure. "Manusos will go down to the quay with you." She smiled sadly and took his hand. "Go with God."

"I hope so, mama. And you too. Take care of yourself until I see you again."

She clasped her arms tightly beneath her narrow chest and shook her gray head. "No, I don't think we'll see each other again in this world."

"Of course we will."

"You'll never come back to Candia."

"You make it very painful."

"Life wasn't meant to be amusing."

"I *would* return, if you sent for me."

She looked down at the stones of the terrace. "But I'd never send for you. I have Manusos. He's a very gentle fellow. A bit reckless, as your father used to say, but good and kind and considerate."

"Unlike me, you mean."

"Unlike you." She sighed. "But distance is such a harsh thing. It makes us forget."

"I should have written more often."

"You should have."

In the ensuing silence, only the soft brushing of the August breeze against the leaves on an olive tree could be heard. "I'll try to be more diligent," he said at last. "I'll write a letter for every ship that leaves Venice for Candia."

She stayed him with a hand. "Don't say that. Don't try to make me believe it. It would be cruel to let me hope."

He turned from her and looked down on the ships in the harbor, at the breakwater lapped by the easy swell of the sea. "You seem determined to make me feel even guiltier than I do already."

COLOR FROM A LIGHT WITHIN   154

"I was only speaking the truth."

"I know."

"It's better to be truthful."

"Yes."

"There are such changes in you," she said. "It's not just your body. That was to be expected. You were young when you left. There are changes about your eyes. It's rather unnerving. When you left, you were only beginning to be the man you've become. I hope it matters that you've become the kind of man I'd like, a man I'd admire if I had a chance to know you."

"I'm not sure about that, mama. I'm not sure I like knowing myself."

"We rarely like ourselves much. It's all very strange and perverse."

"I find it so."

Cleo looked into her son's eyes and wept. Then she forced a smile. "In his own fashion, your father would have been pleased with you too."

"I only wish I'd been able to make him understand why painting meant so much to me."

She nodded. "You're right only in a sense. He didn't understand why you were as you were. But he was delighted that you were succeeding. He was proud of you."

Domenikos gazed at his feet and took a deep breath, exhaling it forcefully. "You're going to say nothing about my conversion?"

Cleo shook her head. "What's to be said?"

"I thought you'd have something to ask me."

"What would you like me to ask?"

"Why I did it, I suppose."

"You explained that in your letter."

"Did you tell papa?"

"Never."

He pawed the terrace with his boot. "Don't you want to chastise me?"

She laughed softly, sardonically. "*That's* what you want, isn't it?"

"It's what I deserve."

"Oh, no, Menegos. I've given you what you deserve, total silence. Isn't that what you gave us?"

"Yes."

"All right. That's that. But perhaps you'll realize that it's wrong to pretend or to lie with people who know you and love you. It was childish. I think that's about the kindest comment I can make about it. Giorgio would have understood if you'd told us right after you got to Venice. He wouldn't have liked it, but he would have understood at least that your motives were pure. By waiting so long, you'd have hurt him mortally. That's why I didn't let him know."

"I realize that it doesn't alter things, mama, but it was Uncle Manusos who persuaded me to say nothing at first."

"I believe you, and as you say, it alters nothing. *You* should have known better, even if he didn't."

"He was afraid of what Aunt Marica would do when she found out. And he was right."

"With your father's death, I'm sure she'll not hold it against you any more. She's a decent woman."

Domenikos rubbed his cheek and smiled. "If she lets me enter her house again, she'll probably try to marry me off to a girl of her church. She used to talk of nothing else."

"And you have other ideas?"

"Not yet, mama."

"Well, it doesn't matter to me." She paused, then began again. "It *does* matter to me. I'd be more comfortable if you married a woman of my faith. But that's not the same thing, is it? I do hope, though, that whomever you marry, Menegos, you'll marry well. Marry somebody, not just anybody. I'm not thinking in terms of a dowry. Marry a person."

Manusos appeared in the doorway. Behind him, two Candiot laborers were struggling with Domenikos' belongings.

"Is it time?" Cleo asked plaintively.

The older son nodded.

"Well," said Domenikos, embracing her closely.

She detached herself and pressed a finger to his lips, her eyes filled with tears. "God be with us all," she whispered. "Your God and ours."

Twelve

"Do not mourn, Greco," said Titian, bowing his ancient bald head. He laid a heavy hand on the young man's black sleeve and looked up, seemingly embarrassed. "I'm never sure how to show sympathy."

Domenikos nodded. "I have the same difficulty."

"I'm saddened, of course. You've lost something, someone precious, and that makes *me* sad." He sighed profoundly, as if feeling inordinately the burden of his years. "But God is wise, or that's what we have to believe when something takes place that we don't understand." The old man laughed sorrowfully. "I know it's easier for me to think that, or say it, than for you. The loss is yours. But I *do* remember, Greco. I *can* remember, believe me, the day I lost my beautiful Cecilia." Suddenly the black, fierce old eyes filled. "When that happened, I was certain that God had gone mad. So there you are."

It was Domenikos' turn to be embarrassed. He looked away, his eyes tearful now, more because he was moved by Titian than by the sense of his own loss. "Are we ever ready for death, master?"

"Oh, for our own deaths, I think so. I've been ready for mine for years."

"Ready, or prepared?"

"Ready. To be prepared, one need only be in a state of grace."

"You're alone in your readiness, then, master. What a shock your death would be for the rest of the world."

"You forget how many enemies I have."

Domenikos laughed. "Not any more. You must have outlived most of them."

"There are still quite a few. And they'll cheer." He hesitated. "No, that's not so. In their hearts, they'll cheer, but in public their voices will sing my praises." He grinned. "Do you know what I've just finished doing? I tell you this simply to show what I mean. I've written a letter to Duke Cosimo de' Medici requesting that members of the Venetian Academy be permitted to contribute their skill to the making of the catafalque for Michelangelo in the *duomo* in Florence." He sighed. "But God isn't deceived."

"Then why did you write?"

"Because I was asked to. Because my colleagues thought it politically unwise, whatever that suggests to you, for them to be left out. They feel their names should be associated with the great man's tomb."

"What benefit can they expect from Florence?"

"My very question. It's more that they fear they might be held in disrepute if they weren't directly involved."

Domenikos smiled. "That's the way my uncle thinks: the right action for the wrong reason."

The old man shrugged. "Nothing is more comfortable than hypocrisy, if you learn to live with it."

"Not for me."

"And have you come to an understanding with your uncle and his good woman, Greco?"

"Yes, master, right after I returned from Candia, while you were still in Vincenza. My aunt even invited me to come back and live with them. I thought that a mistake, but I see them quite often." He sighed.

"The reconciliation doesn't seem to fill you with the joy Our Lord tells us will accrue to the peacemakers."

"No. It's difficult. My aunt can speak of nothing but finding me a wife."

"Well, far be it from me to try to make decisions for you, but she's right, you know. It's time you thought of marriage."

"You too?"

"It's unwise for a young man to pass all his time locked up within himself."

"I don't, master. There *was* Veronica. I'm not a hermit."

"Ah, but mistresses are different. You have no commitment to them."

Domenikos rose instantly to the bait. "My only commitment is to painting, and it will never be to anything or anyone else. . . ."

"If that's true, Greco, and I can't believe it—"

"You have to believe it."

"Then you've elected to go through life half starved." Titian spread his arms. "Life is so rich. There are so many things to be enjoyed. How can you think of so depriving yourself?"

"You misunderstand me, master. You were talking of commitment, not enjoyment. I'm not opposed to marriage. In fact, and I hope you'll not think me impudent for saying it, I think I'd be a better husband than you were. But painting is the place where I'll always live."

"I'm perplexed. If you have no objection to marriage, why does your aunt's suggestion upset you?"

"Because I think I'd be unhappy with the woman she chose." He laughed. "And the subject, as she presents it, bores me."

"Your aunt's standards, I gather, aren't yours."

"It's a question of faith, principally. My aunt is obsessed. She's convinced that if she finds me a wife of the Eastern faith, I'll be lured back."

"And you don't want that to happen."

Domenikos pulled at his right ear and shook his head. "If I were persuaded, I'd return, and neither my aunt nor my uncle would have anything to do with it. It's not a question of pride."

"What *has* religion to do with it, then?"

"I just think it's silly to create a problem where none needs to exist. Why should I marry outside my faith?"

Titian stroked his scraggly beard. "And I suppose you're afraid too that your aunt mightn't choose you a woman you'd enjoy talking with."

The young man nodded. "Perhaps. She's a fine person, my aunt, but the things of the mind are lost on her."

"What would you think of *my* finding you a wife?"

Domenikos contemplated this question. Was he just being stubborn? He covered his lean features with both hands, pressing his eyes with his fingers until little darts of light shot through his vision. It was absurd, wasn't it? He dropped his hands to his sides. "I think I'd entertain the notion favorably."

The master chuckled and nodded. "That's very lofty and condescending of you. I'll see what I can do." He rubbed his hands together enthusiastically. "This ought to be very amusing. I've not tried anything like this since I arranged things for Orazio. That's been some time."

"You did very well for him."

Titian ignored this. "What coloring do you prefer?"

"It's a matter of indifference, master."

"Must she be rich?"

"No, but if she's extravagant, she should have a dowry large enough to support at least a good part of her taste."

"Very reasonable. And what attributes do you look for most? Loyalty? Virtuousness? Intelligence? Education? Appearance? Breeding? Piety? Good temper?" He paused for breath.

Domenikos stared at the floor. In the silence, they heard the high, strangely doleful cries of the gondoliers as they signaled their approach to a corner.

"I suppose," he muttered finally, "that I admire all those qualities."

Titian snorted. "So do we all. But it's a question, isn't it, of emphasis? It's a question of what order we'd like them to be arranged in, and in what proportion?"

"Just so."

The old man pinched his nose and sniffed. "You'll give me no more assistance than that?"

"I'll help you all I can, but it would seem wiser to wait and see what sort of woman might be interested in me."

The master smiled knowingly. "There'll be a wide range of choice, Greco. With your fortune and your prospects, you're admirable material." Abruptly, he dismissed the subject with a wave of the hand. "Well, well, I'll see what I can arrange. It's quite exciting, something to brighten the days of my declining years."

"There's no need for haste, master."

"You might change your mind."

Domenikos shook his head. "I might reject your selection, but I'll not change my mind."

"You mustn't be too particular, Greco." Titian chuckled. "It's not as if you were choosing a mistress. She's only going to be a wife."

The young man realized that he was supposed to respond with laughter. Instead he recalled his conversation with Veronica on the occasion of their meeting, and he became solemn, his dark eyes hard. "It's very important to me, master. And I'll take no mistresses after I'm married."

The old man stared at him, amazed, then burst out laughing. "I wonder how many pious young men have promised that over the centuries."

"I'm serious."

"Of course you are. So were all the others."

"I'm going to keep *my* promise. There's no doubt of it."

"None at all."

"No matter what the temptations may be."

"Oh, I believe you, Greco. You don't have to say more."

"You don't believe me at all."

The master grew reflective as he studied the intense, pale face. He smiled at last. "Oddly enough, I think I *do* believe you."

They fell silent. At length, Titian brightened and slapped Domenikos gently on the cheek. "Well, now, that's settled. Let's see if your travels among the savages and six months away from my cultivating influence have done anything to harm your craft. I want you to paint me a picture, any subject you like."

The theme of Christ healing the Blind had long appealed to Domenikos, not only because of its relevance to the Counter-Reformation, but for its personal application: "According to your faith be it unto you," was the way Jesus had put it, according to St. Matthew. It seemed a concept peculiarly germane to him.

He worked very swiftly, reverting to tempera, which he now used only for studies. He felt himself restored, at peace with all about him, because after so long a lapse he was painting again. The idea of the picture came to him as a single vision, a revelation, like the act of faith it depicted.

The setting was a paved square with a Venetian gondola stage in the right and center foreground, the arcaded façade of a palazzo extending from the left foreground and terminating in the middle distance with a small *tempietto*. The upper portion of the right side of the panel was filled with a wild, windy, Adriatic sky, clotted with variegated clouds, punctured by patches of intense blue.

The Savior stood just to the left of the center foreground, His body slightly inclined, His left hand holding that of a blind victim, the right touching the eyes of the kneeling man. A young man with dark, curly hair bent over the blind man, giving him support. Behind this group was a quartet, three men and a youth, engaged in conversation. To balance this arrangement, Domenikos portrayed a larger assembly of men to the right of the painting and, at a greater distance in the center, a pair of figures seated on a step. On the landing platform was a crouching dog that protected a sack and a gourd, the property of the man seeking Christ's mercy.

"It's cleaner," said Titian with obvious pleasure. "Much less complicated, much less cluttered."

Domenikos beamed. "I tried to remember all you said about leaving things out."

The master raised a protesting hand. "I don't want you to imagine yourself cured of all *your* ailments. You still have problems to solve, Greco. There are some awkward things here." He pointed to a hand appearing across the breast of a man in the group behind the Savior. "Whom does that belong to? It looks as if it were coming out of that boy's chest." He became silent, studying the picture more closely, standing back from it, then approaching it once again. "No, it's really quite a good thing, you know. I can think of no reason for not saying so. The dog is superb, the best single creature you've ever painted. Now *he's* really alive. I can almost hear him bark." He turned to Domenikos and smiled. "You still have trouble capturing the human being in motion, but you've done it much better here. Your people are still frozen, though. I think it has to do with the way you paint their clothing. Work on that. But don't fret, Greco. It will come." He laughed and slapped Domenikos on the back affectionately. "I like it. I like it very much. It was good for you to get away for a while. It gave you time to think."

The young man nodded. "I felt the same way while I was painting, master. I was refreshed. My eyes were renewed. And I never hesitated. I knew just what I was trying to do."

Titian turned and pointed to a large painting of the Martyrdom of St. Lawrence that hung on the opposite wall of his small studio. "Since you appear to be so full of yourself, perhaps you'll give *me* some help. Our brave King Philip has been snapping at my heels for it for several months now." He grunted angrily. "My informants in Rome tell me that the Spanish ambassador there has been saying I'm past my prime. And you know, Greco, when I think of the trouble I've been having with this, I wonder if he isn't right."

Domenikos made a show of putting his hand to his mouth to suppress his laughter. "That's the most shameless begging for a compliment I've ever heard from you, master, and it deserves no comment."

Titian shook his head wearily. "Then why am I having so much trouble?"

"Perhaps you should have stayed at Vincenza until you'd finished it. There are too many distractions in your life here, too many visitors, too many gatherings. . . ."

"You think I should make sacrifices to art at my age, just because a king is goading me? I know you mean well, Greco, but I enjoy life. It's what I was trying to say to you the other day. Life is for enjoyment, and the more so when you reach my age."

"We have different temperaments, master. I require tranquillity."

"In modest doses, tranquillity isn't a bad thing. I don't object to it when it's thrust on me. But nothing pleases me more than to see my friends, to talk, to gossip, as you and Orazio call it." He paused, smiling. "My old friend Giorgio Vasari of the wicked tongue and pen was in Venice while you were away. You'd have enjoyed his visit, I think."

"I'm sorry to have missed him. But the fact remains, master, that his visit kept you from working. Nothing should be permitted to do that."

"Don't try to dictate the way I live. I'm too old to be reformed. Besides, Vasari is going to write about my life in his book on Italian painters."

"How could he do otherwise?"

"But he'll tell the truth. He'll not be like Aretino, who used to boast in public that I'd never have sold a painting if he hadn't publicized my talents. He himself had no ability, except for exploiting others. But what an art he raised that to. Even the people he blackmailed were made somehow to feel vaguely pleased because of the attention he paid them. But what a dangerous enemy he could be. That was part of his attraction, I dare say. If he turned on you, you knew you'd be in terrible trouble." He suddenly grew serious. "Painters can't afford important enemies, especially early in their careers." Then he laughed. "But I forget that you've no interest in money."

Domenikos grasped the back of his neck and looked at the ceiling, exasperated. "You keep teasing me about that, master, and you keep missing the point. I'm concerned with money, with selling pictures. I want commissions, but—"

"But you think it undignified to display your wares in a place like the Banche de le Pintori. That's rather it, isn't it?"

"No."

"No?"

"Well, naturally, I'd prefer not to have to do that, but I've never ruled out the possibility."

"You're a liar, Greco. What pride you have. It was good enough for your friend Tintoretto. That's how he got his first commission here. Did you know that? He showed his pictures under the arcade of the Piazzetta. I bought two of them myself, through an agent. I'd not have wanted him to know it. How long do you think you can afford such pride?"

"It's not pride. When I'm ready, I'll get my commissions. I'm in no hurry."

"Arrogant, too. I never realized that. You're mistaken, you know. You're going to fail if you persist in that attitude. If you intend to play the role of a fish, my young friend, you'll have to learn to breathe water, like all other fish. There's no alternative."

"When I find that I must become a fish, master, I'll learn to live in water, but not one moment before it's necessary. I have time, fortunately, and patience."

Titian's laughter was edged with anger. "What a big man, what an important fellow. Don't imagine yourself an established artist because I praise a single picture. Don't imagine that people will beg you to accept commissions because you once worked with me. You'll have to struggle to find work. You'll have to lie, to cheat, to praise when you'd love to condemn. You have to bow and scrape, to kiss ugly, stinking hands, to flatter. It's a dirty business, Greco, dirty and degrading, this business of getting a major reputation."

"I've never seen you do anything of the sort."

"I don't have to any longer, thank God. But when I was young, in the days when I knew Aretino, when I had a family to care for, it was different. Yes, people come to *me* now. They implore *me* now. I can command my own prices now, choose among offers as I please. But it wasn't always so. And believe me, young Greco, you'll find things even harder than I did. There are more painters than there were seventy years ago, and as a group they're more skilled. The competition is very unattractive."

Domenikos listened with polite interest and abundant skepticism. "I understand, master. But when I'm ready, I know what I'll have to do."

Titian sighed profoundly and shook his head. "I hope so, my boy. I hope so. But your pride makes me tremble. There are so many rocks in the water you must learn to breathe. Don't swim with your eyes closed, I beg you."

Her matchless person every charm combined.

Ariosto's line came at once to Domenikos' mind when he was presented by Titian to Maria, only daughter of a widowed Venetian merchant, Mario da Verona. She stood by the high double doors of her father's drawing room, her pale, slightly angular face held high, her deep-set brown eyes clear and bright, her mouth thin and even in its well-controlled smile which conveyed at once politeness and arrogant self-assurance. A gown of deep green silk, superbly cut, delineated a form that was lithe, youthful more than womanly. She was eighteen.

Titian's introduction was characteristic. "This is Domenikos Theotoko . . . Dear God, I've never learned the terrible rest of it. And it doesn't matter anyhow. In Venice, everybody calls him Il Greco."

Maria inclined her dark head downward, briefly closed her eyes, then looked up again, extending a small, soft, unused hand. Domenikos took it with both of his and soberly kissed it, inhaling with an animal thrill the musky perfume with which she had thoughtfully scented herself.

"And how do you call *yourself*, signore?" she inquired mockingly. The tone was unimportant, so richly and purely modulated was her voice.

"My full name, signorina, is Domenikos Theotokopoulos."

She laughed, and then she coughed, embarrassed by her impoliteness. "Surely you can't expect me to call you by so long a name as that, beautiful though it sounds to my uninstructed ears."

Domenikos smiled appreciatively. The girl wasn't stupid. "In Candia, in Crete, where I was born, I'm called Menegos. In Venice, as the master said, I'm called Greco. But you, of course, may call me what you like."

She nodded and took a step back from the doorway. With a minute, delicate gesture of her head and hand, she indicated that Domenikos should follow her to a broad, upholstered couch in the center of the elegantly furnished room. With surprisingly exemplary discretion (marred only by a grin and a wink), Titian withdrew, closing the doors behind him, in the process making a conspicuous clatter.

The young man's eyes were drawn at once to a large tapestry that covered an entire wall of the bright salon. He stared at it, wholly oblivious to the beautiful young woman. She turned, surprised, and noting his concentration candidly studied this strange, intense, darkly handsome artist whom her father and Tiziano Vecellio were so anxious for her to take as husband.

His style of dress could not be thought even remotely fashionable by Venetians who knew about such things. If they married, the black of his tunic and breeches would have to give way to bolder and more cheerful colors. He couldn't forever mourn a father, however beloved, could he? But this minor defect aside, physically at any rate, he appeared quite acceptable, especially so when she took into account that he was, of all things, a painter.

He was tall enough, carried himself very well, was very clean. He seemed endowed with poise and manliness and manners that she thought adequately respectable in one not to Venice born. He spoke well, too, his voice warm and dark, almost melodic, the slightest trace of an accent alone betraying his alien birth, and she found this not at all an unattractive trait. She was sure that if he sang, he would sing pleasantly.

It was, however, his face that drew her greatest attention. (He remained engrossed by the tapestry, which, because perhaps she had lived with it all her life, she found unspeakably dull.) His large, candid eyes stared at it without blinking; hot, they were, capable of great anger. She was sure of that. The long, rounded chin was firm and strong, cleanshaven, thank God; her father's beard scratched her skin. The nose was slender, delicately made, slightly pointed. The mouth was full-lipped and sensual. Between his nose and mouth there was a small, attractive cleft. The hair, cut short for Venetian taste, disclosed a high forehead. She wasn't sure that this was invariably a sign of intelligence, but it must be in his case. Tiziano had described him as brilliant, well educated, a man of many languages. She repressed a smile. The master also described him as rich.

Not that her appreciation of him made much difference. Her father had made it clear that if this young man approved of her, she had no choice in the matter. Poor papa, deeply in Titian's debt, would be released from all his obligations. For so great an amount of gold, the master must indeed think highly of Domenikos, and hold him in deep affection. Titian had even offered to contribute heavily to her dowry.

Although she well understood the meaning of making a virtue of necessity, it suddenly dawned on Maria that Domenikos was more than attractive to her; he was desirable. Here indeed was irony. Now it was she who must hope, and for a reason more persuasive to her than the temporary resolution of her father's financial difficulties, that he wanted her. Yet it was not in Maria's youthful nature to be straightforward.

"You admire the tapestry?"

"It's magnificent, one of the finest I've seen."

"Papa had it made a long time ago, in Flanders."

"Really? But the design must have been made by Raffaello."

"I've heard papa say something like that, yes." She bowed her head and laughed lightly. "There's much about art that I've never learned."

He smiled. "Well, then, you've improved yourself today. For I can assure you that Raffaello Sanzio painted the cartoon for that tapestry."

"You can't know, signore, how grateful I am," she replied with elaborate gravity, "to have been improved by so great an authority on art."

He acknowledged with flush how richly he deserved her mockery for that bit of sententiousness. He clasped his hands. "May I sit down?"

"Oh, yes. Forgive me. I should have asked you."

"Yes, I believe the rule is that I should have waited for you to ask me. But even after six years in Venice, there are many things about society that I haven't learned."

"Surely not, signore."

Was she mocking him again? Domenikos looked about him as he placed himself beside her on the coarse-woven tapestry of the couch. "Is it your father who chooses the decorations?"

Maria inclined her head toward her shoulder, considering sagely. "Papa selects, but I must express my approval."

"That's very interesting."

"I think papa has very good taste, don't you?"

"Excellent. But what happens if you and your father disagree?"

She laughed. "You give me the feeling that I'm being tested."

Domenikos nodded briefly. "Perhaps. This is an odd and rather painful situation for us to find ourselves in, isn't it?"

She shrugged delicately. "Is it? I'm rather enjoying it."

He became severe, annoyed by what appeared her frivolous view of a matter that was of almost limitless significance to him. "It's not a bit amusing, signorina, this thing you and I are considering. It's no game we're playing. I see nothing enjoyable in the fact that we're confronting each other this way, surveying each other, with the idea that if we don't find each other too objectionable, we shall marry and spend the rest of our lives together, and I must warn you at once that I come from a stock which, as a rule, lives a long time."

She opened her mouth, but Domenikos silenced her imperiously. "I enjoy your company. I mean, under normal circumstances, I think I'd enjoy it. You're beautiful. You're young. You're fresh. You seem intelligent. You have humor and grace. All the suitable elements seem present. But this is difficult for me, and it's fateful for you."

"Thank you," she said softly, ironically, "for conceding me that."

He blushed again. "I suppose that the only thing that commends me to you is that Titian is your father's creditor."

"It *is* a factor," she murmured, restraining a smile. "But since it appears that you mean to test me on several levels, there must be more than that you need to know. Let me see. I eat a great deal, but I'm not heavy for my age. I drink when I'm asked to. I sleep on my right side. My kidneys are in perfect condition. As far as I know, I'm capable of bearing children. I play the lute well, but I sing badly. I despise almost every line of Latin I've ever been made to construe. I can sew, but I don't like to. I enjoy a fine meal, but I cook indifferently. I shall expect servants to do everything in my house."

Domenikos smiled ironically. "Forgive me for thinking you might be a serious person. It should have been obvious—"

"That the daughter of a man so deeply in debt couldn't be serious?"

"That anyone so young and beautiful—"

"Oh, signore, those words sound very cheap."

"Completely honest, nevertheless."

She considered him for a moment, her fine eyes holding his almost fiercely. "You mean it, truly?"

"Truly."

Maria extended a graceful, green-sleeved arm, and then bent it across her ripening bosom. She offered him a smile, her eyes half grave, half mocking. "Shall we call a truce? This doesn't seem a very promising way of beginning a courtship, if that's what we're doing."

"I agree. A truce, then." He responded, smiling in relief.

"I'm really not so frivolous as I must have seemed to you just then. I don't know why I behaved that way. I can be serious now and then." She smiled disarmingly. "But not for too long, please."

Domenikos nodded. "Perhaps the idea of being tested, as you put it, didn't appeal to you."

"It was to be expected, wasn't it? Isn't that why you're here?"

"But it's so crude."

"It's the way."

He sighed. "And we must accept it."

"Is there an alternative?"

"My candor annoyed you."

She laughed. "In mentioning papa's debts? No, signore. Everyone in Venice knows. Your master sees to that," she added grimly. "He never lets papa forget."

The young man frowned. "My master isn't always very discreet."

Maria shrugged again, then glanced toward the doors. "You do understand that when we leave this room a definite answer is expected of you."

He looked away, delighted and distressed, uncertain to which of these emotions he would prefer to surrender in this moment. He was immensely drawn to this girl. But would he be able to abide the woman who was in her, the person she would become? Was Maria the wife for whom he would renounce any future mistress?

"Is an answer expected only of me, signorina? What is yours?"

"My hands are tied. You know that."

"But if you were in a position to choose . . ."

"If I were in a positon to choose, I'd be inclined to say that the idea of marrying you is absurd."

"My very thoughts."

"How can they expect us—"

"To come to an agreement of such importance when we know so little of each other?"

"Yes."

He reached out a hand, touched hers, and withdrew it at once, scalded by this contact. "We're not obligated, signorina. We don't have to accept each other."

"My case is clear. I can't question it."

"Why ever not, in God's name? How can you be so resigned to your fate, at eighteen?"

"It's the way."

"But we have to live with the results of this decision, whatever happens. I couldn't live with you if I had reason, the slightest reason, to think you'd married me against your will."

Maria suddenly became alarmed. "You'll not accept me, then?"

"I *do* accept you."

"But you have reservations."

"Many. But I'll confess that I'm prepared to think that in this case an arranged marriage has advantages I'd not thought of."

She shook her head. "That's flattery."

"Not from me, signorina. You'll never hear flattery from me."

"Thank God. You'll not hear it from me either. I detest it."

"Good. You see? We agree about something important already."

She seemed shy as she turned to him. "There's an important question I'd like to ask you, signore."

"Please."

She shifted her position on the couch so that she faced him squarely, their knees nearly touching, her expression unexpectedly severe. "*Must* you paint?"

He stared at her evenly for a moment. "Does it matter?"

She lay back against the upholstery and gazed at the splendidly carved beams of the ceiling. "I should have thought that nothing could matter more," she muttered.

"I suppose not."

Abruptly she sat up, confronting him earnestly once again. "So?"

"So. Well, yes, I must paint. It's the single true imperative of my life."

"But why?" she persisted, her voice suddenly very small.

Domenikos stood up and paced the floor in front of the couch, aware of a strange sense of self-consciousness, aware that he was emulating the master when *he* was posed a difficult question. As he spoke, he looked at Maria, whose complete attention he at last commanded.

"In the first instance, I don't know. That's the short answer, but I presume you'll require the longer one. It's a compulsion. Oh, I sup-

pose I could give it greater dignity by telling you that I'm a painter because I have a desire to create beauty with my hands, or because,
through my painting, I have a desire to glorify God. And that would
be true enough, I promise you. But that answer only describes the result, not the cause. Why is it the strongest drive, perhaps the only
drive, in my nature? I can't explain. It *has* been ever since I can remember. It's something primordial, like the urge to suckle, or to make
love."

Maria laughed. "Your reference to love-making is lost on *me,* signore."

"Don't be coy. You may be inexperienced, but you know what I
meant."

"I *may* be inexperienced? Are you in any doubt?"

He sighed. "Can you *not* be serious?"

Maria nodded, her mouth expressing remorse, her eyes amusement.
"Forgive me. You say you feel this need to paint in your bones."

"In my soul," he retorted angrily.

"Oh, my."

"You think it derisory?"

"Not for a moment, signore."

"Then what is it that compels you to treat everything as if you did?"

"Because, as you've observed yourself, I'm just not a very profound
sort of person. I have serious responses. There are sights and sounds
and odors and textures that I react to vividly. There are even a few
people who can stir me. But you see, I'm possessed by nothing, obsessed by nothing. Do *you* understand *me?*"

Domenikos sat down beside her again and looked intently into her
brilliant eyes. He smiled. "It might not be so bad a thing, the differences between us. We might balance each other nicely—you so cool,
me so hot."

"Is that a definite proposal of marriage, signore?"

He laughed. "How disingenuous you can be. You never doubted
the outcome, did you?"

"I did indeed. My own acceptance was understood. Yours is volun-
tary."

"My best hope would be that your enthusiasm is half as great as
mine. Have you any at all?"

"It doesn't matter."

"It does to me, as I said. Nothing could matter to me more."

She smiled, and then, as an afterthought, she reached for his hands.
"Let me say, then, since you find it so important, that if my enthusi-

asm isn't so great as yours, it's only because my temperament is cooler, as you so handsomely phrased it. If I *had* a choice, signore, I would accept your proposal with eagerness."

He laughed nervously and pressed her hands. "Good. Because I have to confess to you that, privately, I've been devouring you already."

Maria giggled. "How exciting, and how convenient."

"Convenient?"

"Yes."

"You're certain that your feelings about it are arranged in that order?"

"You have my word for it."

Thirteen

Maria and Domenikos were married immediately after Easter, in 1567. Mass was offered in the Church of San Canciano. The wedding breakfast was counted one of the most elaborate in many seasons. Maria explained this splendor to her new husband: "Papa wants to let everyone know that he's out of debt, and ready to plunge in again." The affair was well attended "by all the people of Venice who are in some way obligated to Titian," a drunken Tintoretto complained to his erstwhile friend Domenikos.

The young man's aunt, uncle, and cousin were present. Marica, though she still smarted from his having declined *her* offer in favor of Titian's, comported herself with a rather grudging propriety. She even noted with some approval the comparative brevity of the Latin nuptials, and partook eagerly of the refreshments. Manusos appeared enraptured. He darted from guest to guest, presenting himself ingratiatingly to those he knew and those he didn't know, announcing to all his close relationship with the bridegroom. To Domenikos he repeated as often as he could, "Congratulations, my boy. Congratulations. You've done splendidly, splendidly. You're really getting ahead now."

Every possible amenity was provided in the way of entertainment, music, and a copious collation. Some called it a matutinal revel on a scale matched only by Titian's nocturnal ones. A few critics considered the reception in doubtful taste, reflecting in an unseemly way an affluence to which the couple being celebrated could hardly soon aspire. The master retorted hotly that it wasn't a bit more ostentatious a display than was deserved by the young painter who would keep his name alive and bright after his own demise—"which is coming," he added gloomily, "which is coming."

Mercifully, Maria and Domenikos were spared the more orgiastic excesses that were a feature of the reception's later hours. They were permitted to escape by the gaudiest of gondolas to the mainland, whence they were borne by a springless carriage over the bumpy road (built by the Romans nearly two millennia before) to Titian's gracious villa near Vincenza.

There, in the warm mornings and afternoons, they slowly came to discover and understand each other's characters and idiosyncrasies. In the cool nights, they explored each other's bodies, the groom a willing instructor to a bride anxious to learn. As her knowledge of the rites of love grew deeper, Maria proved a far more exigent partner to Domenikos than his languid Veronica had been. He responded happily to her demands, himself caught up in a passion reborn after each moment of satiety.

He perceived that Maria, though quite as spoiled as she had described herself, was never petulant, always prepared to change a position if convinced of its necessity. Her convent upbringing had taught her obedience; her husband's gentleness made obedience not only bearable but a source of pleasure.

The sound of his voice as he read to her—from Dante, from Aristotle, from Ariosto—more than compensated for the discomfort of having to sit still, of trying to follow, to comprehend. "I like it best when you read in Greek," she said. "Then I don't have to understand what you're saying. I can just listen to the music of your voice."

Domenikos laughed. "But I'm going to teach you Greek, *cara*. Then you can be bored in three languages."

He made her pose for him, clothed at first, then in the nude. When he asked her to undress, she balked, giggling pruriently. He rebuked her gently. "Surely you can't object to my drawing what I've so often seen and touched."

She blushed. "It feels odd, Menegos. When you have a piece of charcoal in your hand, you seem different to me, someone I hardly know. Would I undress for someone I hardly know?"

Yet she complied. She sat for him patiently, tirelessly, moving only when muscles grew stiff, or to shiver in a sudden current of air or laugh at something he said. For all the discomfort of posing, she enjoyed being the object of his total attention. And she loved the finished sketches of herself, always taking them from Domenikos and placing them in a large, soft-leather folio he had given her.

The tranquillity of these earliest days of marriage was different from that of his liaison with Veronica, for he was committed to his wife. Her dedication to him seemed equally profound. She was quick to note and accommodate his preferences in food and drink, his appreciation of flowers, and to change her method of arranging them to suit his pleasure—eager in every way to please him.

Far from influencing him in *his* style of dress, Maria willingly and even delightedly permitted her husband's taste to guide her choices for herself in this matter. She wore her hair in a more severe fashion because Domenikos insisted that it better suited the prominence and beauty of her forehead, the sharpness of her features.

Their month's idyll at Vincenza brought them not, perhaps, to a state of perfect intimacy and complete harmony, but at least an appreciable distance along the road. They returned to Venice and installed themselves in apartments generously offered by Maria's father in a wing of his imposing house, which, like Titian's, overlooked the lagoon and the bleak Isola di San Michele.

Although she had brought as part of her dowry a number of pieces of furniture, including a magnificent chestnut bed with a red silk damask canopy, and though Domenikos had quantities of pictures and objects of virtue, much remained to be acquired for them to complete the setting which he, and therefore she, considered ideal. With Domenikos, Maria rejoiced almost childishly in exploring the more obscure corners of the city, where occasional purchases were made.

If not quite so appalled as Domenikos had been at a first view of the scenes of poverty they encountered now and then during these strolls, Maria was nevertheless distressed and uncomprehending. "With so much wealth as there is in Venice," she protested, "how is it possible for so many to be so wretched?"

His attempts to explain were inadequate, for in fact the reasons were not clear to him. She was repelled by the grimy, ragged, toothless cripples and the barefoot children who reached out to her for alms.

"Oh, please don't take me back there, Menegos."

He chided her gently. "Our not going back isn't going to alter things, you know. Those poor people aren't going to go away."

She insisted. "But what I don't see, I don't have to think about."

He pressed her. "Once you've learned something, *carissima,* you can't unlearn it just because you want to."

She complained mildly. "You always pin me down so firmly. You leave me no room."

His response was sorrowful. "It's not I who do that, it's life."

"I don't care what it is. When I don't want to see something, I don't want to *have* to see it. I just want to crawl into my burrow and hide."

"You can't hide."

"I must."

In June, it was definite that Maria was pregnant. Domenikos was overjoyed. He would have a son. His pleasure was gratifying to her, although she confessed herself apprehensive about this adventure her body was about to take her on. The young painter readily accepted Titian's invitation to share his villa at Vincenza for the summer months. For Maria, it was a return to the scene of those moments of delight when she had first come to know her husband. For him, it meant that she could be more comfortable than in the stifling city and that he could continue his work with the master and Orazio on the great Martydom of St. Lawrence, which they had transported to Vincenza. When they returned to Venice, early in September, the painting was considerably advanced, though still unfinished.

Pregnancy added to Maria's natural ease and good temper a radiance that made Domenikos want to paint her portrait in the guise of the Virgin with Child. The project, suggested shortly after their arrival in Venice, seemed to disturb her. "You don't think it might be better to wait until after the baby is born? It might be tempting fate."

He responded with mild wonder. "You're superstitious. I never realized that."

"Not normally. But when it concerns a baby, a first one . . ."

But when he insisted, Maria offered no further objection. She sat for him willingly. Her expression was contemplative, endowed with a tranquillity that he interpreted as evincing the patience induced in women by this condition. She wore a pale blue cloak with a cowl, a garment frequently painted by Titian. The shadows that it cast across her angular features gave this small picture an air of somberness and mystery.

Maria was enchanted. As she stood before the finished painting with Orazio and Titian, she clapped her hands together and embraced her husband. "I've never seen myself that way. Do I really look like that?"

"Of course not," answered the master tartly. "You haven't had the baby yet."

Maria laughed, releasing Domenikos from her arms and turning to
Titian. "You didn't understand what I was asking. I was speaking of
my expression. I look quite holy, don't I? We must show this to Father
Jacopo. He's always complaining that I'm not pious enough."

The master nodded. "But *I* was speaking of your expression too,
my dear. Don't you see what your fine young man has done for you?"

Bemused, she returned her gaze to the picture, shaking her head.
Then, having studied it, her young face cleared. "This is the way I'll
look *after* I've had my baby?"

"I'm sure of it," said the old man huskily.

"But how could Menegos know that?"

Titian nodded in Domenikos' direction. "Ask him."

She looked at her husband, her dark brows raised. He smiled and
touched her small white hand, then impulsively drew it to his lips.
"I've understood you because I love you. That's what the master
means." He chuckled. "Of course, I may not have understood you at
all."

She spoke quietly, her eyes bright. "That's very nice. I like that explanation. But there's one thing I insist on. You must paint a portrait
of yourself, for me."

Titian cleared his throat to break into this moment of intimacy.
"This is a workshop, Greco, not a bedchamber."

"How do *you* find the picture, master?" asked Domenikos.

"You're learning more about colors," he replied gruffly. "And the
subject appears to suit you."

"Yes," the young painter said happily. "My model is superb."

"Since she pleases you so, why not use her in something more ambitious, Greco, like the Annunciation or the Nativity, or perhaps one
of the Adorations?"

Domenikos agreed to this proposal and selected as his theme the
Adoration of the Shepherds. Though it was a scene Titian had often
painted, the pupil's conception of it would be somewhat different, giving him an opportunity to experiment with exaggerations of light and
shadow, chiaroscuro, a technique of Tintoretto's and Bassano's that
much interested him.

Throughout the autumn and early winter of 1567, he painted steadily on this the first of his studies to be executed in oils. The theme,
he believed, demanded a dramatic use of contrasting brilliances and
obscurities to evoke the tenderness, the pathos, and the awe that the
scene must convey. His setting was a shed, deprived of a portion of its
stone walls and all but the heavy beams of its roof. In the foreground,

just left of center, lay the infant Jesus, His plump, white body fully disclosed, a dazzling light concentrated on His figure establishing Him as the focus of all attention, a well-articulated right arm reaching out imploringly to His mother. The drapery of the manger was of the same tone of ultramarine as that of the disturbed sky, a color predominating as well in the garment of a shepherd who clutched a lamb.

The Virgin herself, of course, was Maria, depicted here in a flowing gown of rose and blue which contrasted vividly with the yellow-ochre robes of St. Joseph, who stood behind her, his head and torso silhouetted in a window. Through the window could be seen a lone horse and rider bathed in the light of the guiding star. To the right of the child was a youth dressed in a robe of pale blue. The yellow of St. Joseph's attire was picked up on the opposite side of the canvas in the rough tunic of another shepherd who wore bright green breeches and carried, in his high-held hand, a cap of rose.

The background was subdued, gray-toned, somber, a barren Cretan landscape, broken by gray-clothed shepherds huddled together with their horses and flocks. Above them, on this wonderful night, was a tormented sky, portentous.

Titian stood before the completed painting for fully twenty minutes, expressionless, soundless, his bearded jaw working deliberately, the hooded eyes blinking rapidly, the clever old fingers opening and closing as they rested on his paunch.

"Well," he said at last, "you've finally come to the conclusion that you're somebody else."

"Not somebody else, master, just somebody."

"No longer Titian's man at any rate. That's plain."

"I'm your pupil, master, but I never thought myself your creature."

The old man grunted, and spoke without removing his eyes from the picture. "You realize how derivative this is."

Demenikos shrugged. "How could it be otherwise? I'm still experimenting, still learning."

"I see other painters here, but I have to admit that it's mostly Titian, especially in the way you've used your colors. You've managed that pretty well, Greco. The plan seems mostly your own, but that's something you've been able to do before. It's not an arrangement I'd choose myself, but it does have a quality I find interesting. It's original."

"Thanks for that word."

"No need to thank me. You painted the picture. And I say it's original."

Titian abruptly retreated to a disordered writing table. He returned at once, the old feet shuffling slowly. He held two large sheets of writing paper.

"Just listen to this." He glanced at the pages covered with his cramped script, then looked at Domenikos, smiling affectionately. "I've been watching you since you got back from Crete. Now listen to what I'm writing to His Most Catholic Majesty, my esteemed Spanish patron." The master's voice droned as he mumbled the opening passages of his letter, which were an explanation of the delay in completing the Martyrdom of St. Lawrence. Then his tone sharpened, increased in volume: " 'In the completion of this great picture I have been aided by my son Orazio and by a pupil, a most gifted young man. . . .' "

He handed the letter to Domenikos. "That's what I think of you. And if *I* were a young man, that's where I'd go today."

"To Spain? Why?"

"It's the seat of Europe's power. And where there's power, there's money. And if there's money, there are people willing to pay respectable fees for paintings. I've been told it will take twenty years for Philip to finish this fantastic Escorial he's building. Just think of the commissions you could have."

Domenikos shrugged. "Perhaps. But there are so many places in Italy I've not seen yet. And now that I'm married . . ."

The old man chuckled. "You're way ahead of me, Greco. I wasn't suggesting you leave tomorrow, or even the day after. But eventually, you understand, you'll have to give thought to where you're going, not necessarily even from Venice, but certainly from me. I was simply suggesting that if everything else fails, you go to Spain."

"Might everything else fail? Is that what you believe?"

Titian looked toward the ceiling, shaking his ancient head slowly, and sighed. "Ah, we can't know, can we? That's one of the charms of being alive. There are so many surprises."

"But Spain?"

"What could be wrong with it?"

"It's so far away. I don't speak the language. I don't know how Maria would like it."

"You're gifted with languages. I have that on your own authority. You're not a xenophobe, are you?"

"I have no friends in Spain."

"I thought you were intelligent, Greco. I'm assuming that you'll make Spanish friends before you go. We need friends wherever we are."

Domenikos remained doubtful. "I think I prefer to stay in Italy, and especially in Venice. I want to travel, of course. But if only for her sake and yours, I hope I can manage to stay here."

"Don't worry about your wife. She'll go where you go. And whether you like it or not, Greco, you'll have to strike out, in some way, for yourself."

"Yes, but . . ."

"You prefer to wait until I die?"

"It's an important factor, I know, but I don't like to dwell on it."

Titian responded disdainfully. "Don't be soft, Greco. It's a subject I dwell on all the time. I have to. I'm ninety years old. And after I'm gone, I don't think Venice will be the place for you." He paused and looked sorrowfully at his beloved pupil. "Tell me something. What do you want your work to bring you?"

"In what sense, master?"

"In any sense you think important."

"What it's brought you."

"Money?"

"I don't know about that. Money, yes, if I find myself in need of money, but not money just for the sake of possessing it."

"You think me a miser?"

"A collector of gold."

The old man laughed sharply. "But you like what gold can buy. How else could you afford your books, your fine wife . . . ?"

"Agreed. I like much of what it's brought you, too." Domenikos grinned. "Especially the music, I think. If I could manage it, I'd have an orchestra playing every evening."

"Nothing else?"

"Satisfaction." He shook his head brusquely. "No, I mean joy. And I'd naturally like the good opinion of others who are entitled to an opinion. But I don't think I'd go out of my way for that."

"Good." Titian's tone became mocking. "And what about the 'glory of God' you speak of?"

"That, yes." Domenikos' voice was almost menacing in its flatness. "I'm not ashamed of seeking the glory of God, master. You think I take my faith too seriously, but *I* think I don't take it seriously enough. I suppose no one ever does. No one ever can. But you'll have to concede that I've never tried to impose my faith on you."

The old man chuckled. "In other words, if you've been able to hold *your* tongue, why shouldn't I hold mine?"

The young painter's face relaxed into a smile of embarrassment. "The thought did cross my mind."

"You'll have to leave Venice, Greco, one of these days. If you don't go as far as Spain, then think about Rome. This is no place for a man with such strong religious convictions, especially a painter."

"But is Rome different, master? I've heard that everyone there is still obsessed by Michelangelo's style. That's certainly not mine."

"He's dead. You might be able to change Roman taste."

Domenikos nodded. "That *would* be a challenge. But it's academic. I'm going nowhere just now. I have to wait for the birth of my son . . ."

"And the death of your master?"

The young man grinned. "I'll leave that for *you* to dwell on."

Domenikos' son was born in February of 1568. There could have been no more radiant parents for a newly baptized child—named, naturally, Tiziano. The young painter continued working during the earliest months of the infant's life, but it was evident to a touched and flattered godfather that his pupil's efforts were, at best, only routine in quality. It seemed that all his creative energies were expended in his delight, in reflecting sadly how Giorgio would have liked to see his first grandchild, in projecting a successful, perhaps a noble, future for this little black-haired boy.

On one occasion during the later days of spring, the master chided him. "Perhaps you ought to show a little more concern for Maria, or even for your art, though I hope you'll forgive me for reminding you of your inspiring talk about 'commitment' to it."

Domenikos flushed. "You're not suggesting that I neglect my wife."

Titian laughed. "I'm suggesting that you're obsessed just now with neither art nor matrimony but with the continuation of your line to the exclusion of everything else. If you act this way every time a child is born, you'll never do another stroke of useful work."

"As serious as that?"

"Quite."

"I'll try to bear it in mind."

Yet he created no new subjects in the following months, and such repetitions as he painted were simply copies, meticulous reiterations that were mechanical and demonstrated little progress.

As spring yielded to summer the tiny Tiziano's health started to falter. Slowly, inexorably, the baby's strength waned. The end came in the first days of September just after their return from Vincenza. Maria and Domenikos, numbed, could merely stare at one another, able to communicate their misery and bewilderment only through their eyes and by the meeting of their hands.

The idyllic period of just a bit more than a year was abruptly and cruelly ended. "Oh, Father, why hast Thou deserted me?" These words of Christ echoed and reechoed in the painter's mind. Only God could have done this thing to them, and only God could have determined at first which of them was the more stricken, the more afflicted, the more affected. Soon, however, it became plain to everyone.

At the outset, the deterioration in Maria's health had seemed a temporary reaction, a depression that would pass. Domenikos told himself that infant mortality, so common a thing, was a condition with which every parent had to cope. To console her, he recounted to Maria his aunt Marica's experience of losing not one son, but two.

"We'll try again, at once," he said.

She shook her fine young head. "You don't understand, Menegos."

"What don't I understand, *cara?*"

"It's in my blood. The same thing happened to my mother. She died after my brother died. Papa told me. I was too young to know it."

"But *her* dying has nothing to do with you, my love."

"She'd failed. I've failed. It's the same thing."

"Not at all. We'll try again, and hope that God lets the next child survive."

She revolved her head, more slowly this time, more determinedly. "No, Menegos. The spirit isn't in me."

She was lying in bed. Now she rolled her body away from him, the first sign of rejection she had ever shown. Domenikos sighed and left their bedchamber.

He consulted his father-in-law. "She speaks of her mother."

The dapper little Mario da Verona raised an eyebrow and pressed a well-kept finger to his lips, drawing the painter into the salon, the room where he had first met Maria. "What does she say of her mother?"

"That she died after she'd lost a son. Maria expects the same fate."

The father pursed his lips, nodding. "I have to tell you. She doesn't know, my little Maria."

"Doesn't know what?"

"Her mother is alive." He pointed a finger at his temple and revolved it rapidly. "When the baby died, she became depressed, and then she went mad."

"My God."

"But it won't happen to Maria. She has *my* blood in her. She'll be all right, Greco. You'll see. She'll be fine."

"But her mother, your wife, where is she now?"

"In a convent for the mad." He shrugged easily. "It's not a bad place, you know. The nuns are very gentle with her. But poor Alicia, she knows nothing, recognizes no one."

"And is she, was she, as gay and bright and calm as Maria?"

"Much the same."

"My God."

"Don't fret yourself, Greco. As I say, Maria has my blood in her veins. She'll be all right soon. There's no need for despair."

But as his father-in-law spoke, Domenikos recalled Maria's remark about retreating into her burrow when seeking respite from something she couldn't bear.

Never an early riser, Maria now remained in bed most of every day, dragging herself to her feet and dressing only in anticipation of her husband's immediate return from Titian's studio. Within three months of the baby's death, as the cold air from the Dolomites swept angrily across the Venetian plain, even this pretense of participation in their collective life was abandoned.

Maria could no longer abide the daylight. Through each short winter's day, as 1568 became 1569, the curtains of the bedchamber remained drawn. Through each long winter's night, she would barely stir in response to a despairing husband's words and gestures of tenderest solicitude. The fine dark eyes stared vacantly in the orange flicker of the candlelight. The sleek black hair went lank. The frail, delicious flesh became pulpy. She appeared to be disintegrating before his horrified eyes.

There seemed no help. Domenikos turned for aid to Maestro Pietro Fiorentino, one of the wisest physicians in Venice. This fussy, pompous old fob merely pontificated at appalling length on the subject of melancholia, the malady he ascribed to Maria, and prescribed unguents, inhalations, and infusions which, though conscientiously administered, proved unavailing. Her condition worsened.

At last exasperated, Domenikos sarcastically inquired of the physician, whom he now took for a charlatan, if he knew of no incantations that members of the desolate household might mutter over the victim.

Fiorentino's response was earnest. "Why yes, I know of several. But the Curia has forbidden us to advise them any longer. They're said to smack of witchcraft."

Maria's mental state continued to deteriorate. Though she grew pale and her flesh assumed an unhealthy tone, she ate well and appeared, if anything, physically stronger than she had ever been. It was as if the body were thriving on the mind's decay.

In his despair, Domenikos was driven out of himself. He sought companionship, the knowledge of another human presence. Not for some months had he visited his aunt and uncle in the Rio dei Greci. Now he called frequently, and was touched by their concern, their hope for Maria's complete recovery, for the restoration of his joy.

As he hadn't done since his return from Candia, he visited the taverna frequented by Tintoretto and other artists. In search of oblivion, he drank more wine than he could sustain, lurching homeward in the darkness, his brain filled with hallucinated anger and outrage. Yet there was relief in these visits. With casual acquaintances he could speak objectively and assert in their presence what he recognized to be the fact: Maria's condition was hopeless. Whether she lived or died, she was lost to him forever. In his heart, however, he persistently rejected this knowledge. He wasn't ready for it yet. He felt now that he would never be ready for it.

From Father Jacopo, the intelligent new parish priest of San Canciano, Domenikos drew a small measure of solace. The curate laid a hand on the painter's shoulder. "When medicine has done all it can, Greco, we must leave it in the hands of God. We must pray for a miraculous healing."

"As when Christ healed the blind man?"

"Precisely."

"But I have to confess, father, that since it's becoming very difficult for me to believe in God, even prayer seems hopeless."

"*That* you mustn't permit yourself to feel. To God, nothing is hopeless. Don't lose your faith."

"But I'm not God. I want action. I want to know what I can do to help my poor Maria, to bring her back to herself, bring her back to me."

"Do you think she's in physical pain?"

"No, not in her body in any case, but her soul must be in agony. I remember now, when we first knew that the little Tiziano was dead, there was death in her eyes. And, fool that I was, there seemed nothing I could do for her. I couldn't find the words that would comfort her. Even the idea of having another child was of no use. 'Mother of God, Menegos,' she said. 'Do you really think we could go through this again?' I'm sorry to say this to you, father. I was too distressed myself then to realize what was happening to Maria. But I'll never understand it."

"God understands, Greco."

"That's not good enough for me now."

"Don't you see that you're fighting Him? You say you want to understand, as if understanding were a solution. Perhaps you're not meant to understand. And what we're not meant to understand, Greco, we must simply accept as the will of God. You have to find peace of soul for *yourself*. If you don't, you'll soon be following Maria. And whom would that help? Only the devil."

"I can't be made to believe that Maria's illness is God's will. There's no sense in it. She's good, she's only a child. And the little Tiziano, was his death God's will too?"

The priest replied softly, his tone gently sardonic. "Has it occurred to you that God might not be striking at Maria at all, or at the child, but at you?"

Domenikos stared at him for a long moment, then averted his eyes. "Would God strike at one person for the sins of another?"

"God's ways are mysterious. It doesn't help us to question them."

The painter suddenly recalled Brother Constantine's reproach: "You ask the wrong questions."

He looked at the priest despairingly. "Do you suppose that God means for me to be alone?"

"Who can say, Greco? You feel that He meant for you to be an artist, don't you?"

"Yes. And this is a punishment for my sins?"

"Perhaps."

Domenikos bowed his head. "I can accept that idea, though I wonder if I've sinned in proportion to such a terrible punishment."

"It must be for the best. We can't think anything else."

"But poor Maria, father. I only hope that God hasn't gone mad." Titian's phrase about the death of his wife was blasphemous, yet how accurately it conveyed Domenikos' feelings now.

"For your sake, Greco, I hope that *you've* not gone mad."

The young man smiled wryly. "Oh, father, if you could only

imagine how I'd welcome a taste of that sweet oblivion now. I feel myself the accursed of God."

The transition was gradual. Not with a single, drastic gesture could Domenikos compel himself to desert her, to recognize once and for all time that his beloved Maria was conclusively beyond his reach, beyond his assistance.

He moved from their bedchamber to another just across a corridor. For a further period, however, he continued his nightly vigils at Maria's bedside, hoping against all logic, searching her now-ravaged features for some sign of comprehension or recognition. There was none.

When he was certain that she slept, he turned away. At first he wept. Later, resigned, he found that his tears were dwindling, and at last they fell no more. He felt that he had expended his full supply, that he would never weep again.

The vigils shortened, became sporadic and perfunctory, then ceased altogether, to be replaced by numbness. Unable to forget who Maria was, he could no longer remember with such poignant vividness who she had been. The shape discerned in the semidarkness, huddled beneath the covering of sheets and blankets, was no longer a person, merely the clay from which a person had once been formed.

Not since the days beneath his uncle's roof had Domenikos read so much as he was doing now, voraciously, almost indiscriminately, grasping at every available printed word, purchased or borrowed or discovered in the magnificent collection bequeathed to the Libreria by the patriarch Bessarion. It was as if he sought a single word or phrase, an idea or proposition that would release him from what remained of his bondage to memory and remorse.

He painted as furiously as he read. He drove his hand quite literally beyond the limits of its endurance. The brush fell from his exhausted fingers. Yet his mind, his spirit, remained strangely fresh. He found in this recklessness a sense of freedom, of adventure. In his audacity, he discovered new elements in his skill. Repeating themes he had painted earlier, he made modifications that Titian was moved to note with gratified astonishment. The agony of his life was honing the edge of his genius.

He painted the self-portrait that Maria had so often requested and presented it to his delighted master. He added a new subject to his repertory, the Flight into Egypt, a tempera study.

"Why did you paint this?" asked Titian. "I'd have thought you'd try something more grandiose in your present frame of mind."

"I'm not sure. It occurred to me one night, while I was reading, that I'd like to paint it."

The old man nodded. "I think I know why."

"Then tell me."

"It's not plain? There is Maria, and this is the little Tiziano. They're being pursued. And yet the donkey—he's very well done, by the way—the donkey, which I take to be life, seems reluctant to go on. So *you*, St. Joseph that is, are dragging him along with a cord."

Domenikos was amused and intrigued by the analysis. "Do I really resemble this St. Joseph? You must think I've gone mad."

Titian smiled. "Call it a portrait of yourself not as you are but as you feel just now. Isn't it possible?"

"It's ingenious." Domenikos looked at the little panel. "Yes, it's possible."

"If you make a larger oil of it, I'd like to have it, Greco."

The months passed slowly. No longer even remotely aware of the world or of any part of their former life, Maria existed like a vegetable. Attendants were required for her every moment, for her every pathetic need. Mario da Verona at last approached his son-in-law.

"We must put her in a hospital, Greco."

He had long expected this message. Now that it had come, he felt a tremendous burden had been lifted, only to find that another, and similar, burden had replaced it. "Must we?" he asked plaintively. But he knew the answer.

Mario wept. "The doctor says it's just like my poor Alicia. She might live for years like this, her body surviving, her mind starving. It's too much for any of us, for the servants, for me, for you above all."

"But I don't think I could live with the thought of Maria in a madhouse. I'll find some place to move her to."

The little man laid a gentle hand on his son-in-law's cheek. "Listen to me, Greco. I've been through this. I understand what you're feeling. But don't be a fool. Father Jacopo knows you love her. Maestro Tiziano knows it. Everyone knows it. You know it yourself. But there's a difference between love and self-crucifixion, self-destruction. That's what you're suggesting. Everything that could possibly be done for her has been done. She's gone. She's dead, if you like, but still alive. She has to be confined, and it makes no difference if you take her to another house. What has to be done simply has to be done."

"I couldn't go on living here knowing that she was locked up just a little distance away. I'd be haunted. Have you seen those places on the Isola del Desole?" He was at once apologetic. "Yes, of course you have. The thought of her there would horrify me. How could you have done that to your wife?"

Mario shrugged. "Alicia doesn't understand, and neither will Maria."

"How can you be certain?"

"Look at her, Greco. You can see that she has no idea where she is now."

Domenikos reluctantly acknowledged this. "Perhaps it's only myself I feel sorry for."

"That's understandable. But be sensible, Greco. Let me take care of this. She won't suffer. I'll not send her to the Isola del Desole."

"You promise?"

The man wept once more. "Do you think I could bear for her to suffer more easily than you could? You think me heartless? She's my daughter."

The young painter embraced his father-in-law. "Forgive me."

Mario drew back, wiping his eyes. "I have your consent, then?"

"Reluctantly."

"It's the only thing to do."

"I see that. But I won't be able to stay here. I'll have to leave. I couldn't abide it."

"Yes, I'm sure you'll have to go, but it saddens me."

"I agree," said Titian. "But where will you go?"

"To Rome, master, as you suggested."

"But I suggested Spain."

"Rome is nearer. If I fail, then I can think about Spain."

The master shrugged. "Well, of course, it's up to you. But will you listen to some advice?"

"Gladly."

The old man laughed skeptically. "You say so. But I don't expect you to follow it." He paused for a deep breath. "I think you're destroying yourself, Greco."

"Over Maria?"

"No, your books, your constant thinking and brooding, your religion. I know what they mean to you, but you're wrong. Books aren't for painters. Thinking isn't for painters. If you mean to become a great master, you'll have to stop thinking. It's bad for you. Painters must feel things, enjoy themselves, laugh and cry at the very same moment, shout, rage, bellow, scream. They have to unwind themselves. You've never learned to do that. You can't learn that in a book."

Domenikos was about to speak, but Titian silenced him. "Hear me out, will you? Tell me something. How long has it been since you came to one of my evenings?"

"A long time, master. Since before my father died, I think."

"Why? They no longer amused you?"

"I no longer felt the need of them."

"You found them disgusting, didn't you? Tell the truth."

"I didn't feel so strongly as that. But it's true that they didn't attract me."

"You think it sinful that people should take leave of their senses now and then, their daylight senses, I mean?"

"It doesn't appeal to *me*."

"You think our senses should be inspired by the head, not the heart?"

"The head isn't always the worst guide, master."

"For a painter, the head is always the wrong guide. For us, the needs of the flesh have to be the guide."

"You speak for yourself, not for me. For me, it's the head, not the body. It's the soul that shows me the way. And I have no choice but to follow."

Titian was at his most contemptuous. "What nonsense. You speak of the soul as if it were pure and sweet, all gold and rose, like Simone di Martini's pictures. But let me tell you, Greco. If you scratch the surface of most souls, men's or women's, it doesn't matter, you'll find the blackest gloom. You'll say some are white. Who cares? Black or white, if people just let themselves be ruled by their senses, there'd be less trouble in the world. And if *you* did it, which is what I'm saying to you, you'd be a better painter. You've got to learn to let yourself feel."

"You think the way my uncle does, master. You amaze me."

"If that's so, he's not the fool I thought him."

"If people behaved as you suggest, we'd be no better than animals."

"And just how much better than an animal do you think you are now, in your present state of grace?"

"Not much, as I am. I agree."

Mildly frustrated, Titian grunted. "Well, what's so wrong with being an animal? Most people are, you know."

Domenikos laughed. "You're arguing on my side now, on the Church's side."

"Don't tell me about the Church. I'm ninety-three and I'm in a better position than most men to know what people are like. We may have souls, as you and the Church keep saying, but it's our instincts that tell us best how we ought to behave. You're fighting nature."

"All the way, master." He was beginning to enjoy the old man's harangue.

"Why do we reproach animals? Do they kill their own kind without cause? Do they confuse clear emotions with garbled thoughts? Not for a moment. That's what I'm talking about. You have to forget your reading and your philosophy. You can be a good painter, perhaps even a great one, but you can't be a theologian or a philosopher at the same time. Painting is what you see and feel, not what you think. It has nothing to do with reason. The moment the intellect begins to instruct a painter's hand, he's finished as a painter."

"We're talking at cross purposes, master. The more I improve my intellect, the more I improve my soul. The more I improve my soul, the better I am as a painter. I can see more plainly with my soul, in some ways, than with my eyes. And forgive me for saying so, but it's the same for you."

"If you believe that, Greco, you're more obtuse than I ever thought possible. Besides, that's the remark of a prig." The old man folded his hands and gazed at the floor. "The subject is closed. As you say, we've been talking at cross purposes." He looked up. "Rome may be just the place for you at that. It's filled with people like you. Most of them are Spaniards. What annoys me is that all you God-struck meddlers worry about *my* soul as well as your own." He heaved a great, exhausted sigh. "I'm going to give you a letter to my old friend Giulio Clovio. Have you heard of him?"

Domenikos nodded. "There are two or three books that he illuminated in the Libreria."

"You and he ought to get on well. He's from one of your savage countries. Over there somewhere." With a broad gesture, Titian indicated the general direction of the Adriatic. "He's a good man, though, and he'll help you if he can. He's on good terms with Cardinal Farnese. I did a portrait of *him* a number of years ago. He liked it, so your connection with me won't do you any harm."

"I'm grateful."

Tears suddenly filled the old man's eyes. He wiped his nose roughly with the back of his hand and sniffed mightily. "You're right to leave. But I'll not pretend it doesn't pain me. I suppose that's why I spoke so sharply just now. But I meant every word, Greco. On the other hand, I know that each of us has to fatten himself in his own way for his own slaughter."

"I guess that's true."

Titian recovered his composure and became businesslike. "I want you to take studies of your good pictures. And take that self-portrait. It's the only thing of the kind you've done."

"No, that's for you, master."

"You can leave it to me when you die."

"If I offended you, forgive me."

The old man snorted. "You mean just now, when we were arguing?"

Domenikos nodded. "I spoke harshly. I'm sorry."

"Nonsense. That was just talk between men." He smiled sadly. "When you go, I doubt that I'll ever see you again." He moved to embrace his pupil, sniffing loudly. "Come to see me before you go. I'll give you that letter to Clovio." He turned his back to Domenikos. "Now I want you to leave me. I have work to do."

PART III:

Rome (1570–1575)

Fourteen

ONCE Domenikos was certain that he must leave behind him, insofar as he could, the anguishes and despairs of Venice, his preparations for departure were feverish. He must go quickly. To prolong his stay was only to prolong his feelings of guilt and remorse, a pain that at times was physical, a gripping in his chest, an anxious shortness of breath, recurrent headaches. After each day of packing, or arranging the objects he planned to leave in his father-in-law's care, he found a fitful, tormented sleep, intruded upon by frequent dreams which evoked his qualms about the future, about deserting his poor Maria and his beloved Titian, and about his own loneliness that in his waking hours he managed to suppress.

Saying farewell to those he loved in Candia now appeared carefree by comparison to his valedictory to Venice. Indeed, he was unable to give a parting embrace to the one he most regretted leaving; Maria was now confined to a convent. Mario da Verona did his best to console the young painter, promising weekly visits to ascertain his daughter's state and periodic letters to Rome. Domenikos was unable, however, to dismiss the feeling that his departure from her was somehow treasonous.

Hardly easier was it to say goodbye to Titian. With Orazio beside him in the arched entrance of the house in the Biri Grande, the old man made at first a considerable fuss about Domenikos' letters of introduction to important persons along the route of his progress to Rome. As he had done repeatedly during the young man's week of preparations, he reiterated the sights he must on no account overlook along the way: Padua, Mantua, Parma, Reggio, Modena (to see the triptych by his namesake, Maestro Domenikos, of whom the master still spoke in anger), Bologna, Ferrara, Ravenna, and finally Florence.

But in the end, there were tears.

"We'll not meet again," said Titian softly. "And it may be just as well, Greco. We'd not like each other. You'll change, and I wouldn't be happy about it. I won't change, and you'd despise me for that." He sighed. "Now, for God's sake, go."

Travel between the great towns of Renaissance Italy was arduous at its most salubrious, the more so when it involved the transport of one's possessions. Although he took only those articles that he thought indispensable to his life in Rome, no less than eight donkeys were required for each of the stages of his long trip. To these beasts were added their drivers, and a pair of mounted guards to protect this caravan from attack by brigands who haunted the narrow, tortuous roads. Domenikos rode a horse since it was safer than a carriage (one might, with luck, find refuge in the brush were an ambush to occur), and it could hardly have been less comfortable, given the appalling state of Italy's mountainous highways. There were, fortunately, no untoward events to mar the journey.

He reached Rome early in November, 1570. With no more ceremony than the consumption of an extra flagon of wine, he had recently celebrated his twenty-ninth birthday in Florence. The nine months that separated his departure from Venice and his arrival in the Eternal City were almost too exciting, too edifying. His eyes were weary, his senses dulled by so much to see, to take in, to make a relevant part of his experience. As with his first view of the Basilica of San Marco a decade before, Domenikos found himself recalling details of his journey—Giotto in Padua, Mantegna in Mantua, Correggio in Parma, Piero della Francesca in Ferrara, the mosaics of Ravenna. Only Florence, where he remained for two months, stood out distinctly in memory—vivid, brilliant, elegant. There he at last appreciated the near-idolatry that Michelangelo enjoyed. It was tempting to remain longer in the city by the Arno. Yet he was eager to proceed to Rome, where his future lay.

Because she had for so many centuries dominated the history and culture of the western world, Rome lay in Domenikos' imagination like a unique and flawless diamond on a black velvet field, different from all other cities. It was the stronghold of Christianity, the symbol of his chosen faith, the place where the promise of his talent was to be tested, his genius at last made manifest: Domenikos Theotokopoulos, Il Greco, the most godly of all artists, depictor of the Faith.

The Rome of his image was not the Rome he would find. At the time of his arrival, the city lay in spiritual ruins. Still shocked by the terrible sack of 1527, the capital of Christendom was as yet far from having recovered its customary bouyancy, equilibrium, and sophistication. The decrees of Trent and the installation of a new Pope (Pius V, who rejoiced in the sobriquet "Father of Poverty") had combined to create a dispiriting effect on a Rome hitherto gaudy in its style, bawdy and roisterous in its way of living. The city was seeking a new direction and sense of purpose. The goals proposed by a reforming clergy, however estimable, were ones to which the rowdy and sensual Roman past offered few clues. It was a city bewildered, floundering.

Physically, too, Rome was but slowly recovering from the appalling destruction of 1527. Much had been done by Michelangelo and others toward the completion of the new Basilica of San Pietro, but more remained to be done. Vignola was supervising the construction of the mother church for the Society of Jesus, the famous Gesù that was to revolutionize architectural taste on the Continent and in the New World as well.

Energy was returning, but there was little of the old fire in the Roman eye, little of the previous passion for dispute in the Roman throat, and little if any inspiration in the hands of Roman craftsmen. Still reeling from the shock of Michelangelo's death six years before, the arbiters of taste, lay and cleric, were in desperate search of a new artistic bellwether. A number of established but minor masters had sought recognition as informal dean without making much of an impression. Each was compared to the great Florentine and found woefully wanting. The hand of Michelangelo governed Roman artistic judgment, as it did that of Florence; a dead hand, Domenikos thought, must point only to a dead end. It may have been, as Venetians insisted gleefully, a city cursed. To the young painter, who felt himself a man cursed, it seemed to offer the challenge he required.

He made his entry into Rome through the Porta del Popolo, beyond which he found the Piazza del Popolo. To his dismay, accustomed as he was to the urban refinements of Venice and Florence, he discovered the large square unpaved, its muddy surface indented with hoof- and footprints, rutted by wheels of cart and carriage. The slender obelisk standing in the center was a curiosity of the first magnitude, evoking reveries of the Near Eastern past. Flanking this unimpressive square were low, shambling houses whose

ground floors contained shops and kitchens, a few inns catering to
travelers arriving from the north, and the Church of Santa Maria del
Popolo. (Here, though Domenikos only learned it later, the young
Martin Luther had paused in 1510 to give thanks for his safe journey
from Germany. His mission to Rome on that occasion could scarcely
have been more fateful.)

The painter's long train of donkeys moved slowly from the piazza
into the recently widened Via del Babuino that skirted the Pincio.
Eventually, the mounted guide indicated a halt in the Piazza di
Spagna. There, in the shadow of the glowing fifteenth-century
Church of Trinità dei Monti, Domenikos found lodgings for himself
at a noisy inn.

The rustic atmosphere of this quarter, which made it popular with
Greek visitors, impressed him as odd when contrasted with the central portions of Venice. To the physical differences of the two cities
were added the differences in populace which reflected Rome's comparative lack of development. Domenikos was less than heartened
by his initial view of the city where he hoped to make his reputation.
He realized it was too soon to pass firm judgments, but he would have
been happier had he found himself in more elegant surroundings. He
took modest hope from the notion that Rome was a city under construction; it would offer him scope.

Within a week of his arrival in Rome, Domenikos had sought out
Don Giulio Clovio, whom Titian had recommended to him. Clovio
received him in the library of the magnificent Palazzo Farnese,
which Michelangelo had helped to design. The room pleased
Domenikos with its elegance, the first Roman interior he had seen
that gave him an impression of true light and prodigality. His explorations of the city had done little to counteract the first feelings of disappointment. But he had managed to continue his suspension of ultimate judgment. "Rome is not Venice," he had written Titian, "but
that is hardly surprising. I shall not, however, join my uncle in saying
that *nothing* is Venice's equal."

Before their interview was concluded, Don Giulio had agreed to
write his patron, Cardinal Alessandro Farnese, recommending that
Domenikos be given quarters in the upper portion of the Palazzo.
Old Clovio revolved the sheet of foolscap so that the painter, seated
opposite him, could read the letter. "There," he said, his throaty accent foreign to Italy, "does that seem suitable?"

Domenikos made a brief perusal of the paper and pushed it back to his questioner. "It seems admirable to me. But you have the advantage of knowing His Excellency."

Clovio assented. "I think it will suit our purpose. He's a good sort of person, the Cardinal. I'm sure he'll let you stay here until you find something more suitable than that stinking inn you chose for yourself."

"It's not so bad, Don Giulio. I rather enjoy the noise and confusion and the cooking smells. I got used to it while I was traveling. And besides, there are quite a few Greeks staying there. I've been able to catch up a little on what's been happening in our part of the world since I left Venice."

Don Giulio was loftily severe. "That may be. But in Rome it won't do. If your potential patrons knew you were living in a place like that, they'd not be a bit impressed. And here you have to impress people. You have to seem important. You must have important connections, important protectors—"

"Like the Cardinal?"

"Like the Cardinal."

The newcomer grinned. "I appreciate that, Don Giulio. I've no intention of staying at the inn any longer than I have to. And I'm grateful to you for writing His Excellency."

Clovio leaned back in his cross-legged chair and folded his arms complacently. "You needn't imagine, Greco, that I'm going to let you off with a word of thanks. I want you to paint my portrait."

Shortly after their first meeting, Clovio suggested to Domenikos that the self-portrait which he had brought to Rome, along with the other paintings, be hung in a small gallery just off the library. The artists, scholars, and clerics who passed through the palace each day responded with gratifying warmth.

It was at this point that Clovio referred again to the portrait of himself that he wanted Domenikos to paint.

"I'd be honored, Don Giulio."

The old man produced a sheet of paper and began to make a sketch. "I'll show you precisely how I'd like you to paint me."

Domenikos frowned. "I'm afraid that's out of the question. The pose and manner are the painter's concern. I'll paint you as I see you."

Clovio studied his guest, his face registering no emotion. Yet there could be no doubt that he had been offended. "So? *You* presume to tell me?"

"No, Don Giulio. I presume merely to know my craft."

"I see."

"A painter can do his best work only when he's free to select his own terms."

"That viewpoint, young man, isn't going to help you in Rome. Not even Michelangelo succeeded in asserting his rights over the patron's. The artist is expected to do what he's told."

Domenikos laughed. "I intend no scandals, you understand, no outrages. I simply mean that if I'm to paint you as best I can, the pose and manner I choose are important."

Clovio eyed him suspiciously. "You meant no more than that?"

"Well, yes, perhaps I did. I meant, too, that I hadn't come all the way from Venice, where I did what I was told for ten years, to find the same situation in Rome."

"But it's the same everywhere, Greco. What can you be thinking of? Do you really expect to receive a commission to do a great altarpiece, for instance, without receiving specific instructions?"

"It depends on how specific the instructions are."

"Ah, language is a wonderful thing." Clovio sighed and rose from his chair, walking to one of the large windows that overlooked the superb cortile with its collection of statuary. He turned back to Domenikos after a moment. "I beg you not to close your mind completely to what I've said. You must bend, Greco."

"I think it would be wiser, Don Giulio, to face each problem as I come to it. For the moment, we can leave it that, as I said, I'd be honored to paint your portrait."

"But as you see me."

The painter's expression was almost grim in its stubbornness. He merely nodded.

There the matter rested. It was agreed that Clovio's sittings would begin only after Domenikos had moved to the palace. In the meantime, the artist, conscious of the importance of this commission, took every opportunity of studying his subject's face, as the old man recounted his life story with a relish he appeared to display for no other subject.

Now in his seventies, Giulio Clovio was no longer at the height of his modest powers as an artist, though he was enjoying his period of greatest success. A Croatian, he had witnessed the terrible depredations of the Turks upon his native land. And later, when in the service of the Hungarian Louis II, he had once more suffered at Ottoman hands.

He had sought refuge in Rome, finding employment as an assistant to Giulio Romano, Raffaello's pupil and eventual successor. To this task, he had brought a technique identical to that which Domenikos had mastered in Candia. Clovio had soon found that he was unable to emulate the romantic Romano, who worked on a grand scale.

He much admired and often copied in miniature the paintings of Titian and Raffaello, but it was Michelangelo whom he came to revere; his replicas were little masterpieces of delicacy and accuracy. He achieved his present state, however, only after the third disaster of his life. Within a year of his arrival in Rome, the sack of 1527 took place.

There is no accurate estimate of the number of dead, the tortured, the maimed, and the raped whose fate marked this occasion as one of history's least comprehensible and most atrocious massacres, one made the more terrible for the participation of Italians themselves in the ravaging of their greatest city. Clovio was beaten and, without apparent cause, tortured, then left with both legs broken to starve in prison. The pillagers, sated, left Rome; and the plague arrived.

Clovio vowed to join a monastic order if God saw fit to spare his life. He at last escaped prison and became a lay brother in an order of penitents whose mode of worship included mutual flagellation, a practice that must, when compared to what he had already endured, have seemed mild suffering indeed.

He was discovered by Cardinal Grimani, who thought Clovio's talents as an artist of greater use to God outside monastery walls. He was soon afterward invited to join the service of the rich and influential Alessandro Farnese, under whose protection he gratefully prospered thereafter.

Within a week of his receiving Don Giulio's letter, the Cardinal instructed his majordomo to provide the young painter with quarters —two rooms on the top floor of the palace, one of which overlooked the cortile, the other the broad, muddy, winding Tiber, with a glimpse of the crenelated Castel Sant'Angelo, the Pope's personal fortress. Domenikos requested that one of the rooms be stripped of its furnishings; it was here that he set about painting the portrait of Don Giulio.

The completed portrait was unmistakably Venetian. It possessed none of the decorative frivolousness that characterized much of the art Domenikos had so far seen in Rome. The atmosphere was one of stillness, of a calm, gentle resignation to the realities of age. Domenikos was both pleased and discontented with this picture. It was undoubtedly his most carefully executed. There was about it an elegance that he hoped always to preserve in his painting. He had endowed old Clovio with an aura of dignity that was suitable. But there his pleasure in it ended.

What was wrong? Despite Titian's scorching admonition that he avoid thought, the painter felt that only by thinking could he put his finger on the problem. He contemplated the portrait as he applied the final glaze. What did it lack? Then he understood. The painting lacked conviction, penetration, affection—love. It was superficial. He liked Don Giulio, respected him, but he didn't love him, didn't "understand" him in the sense that he and Titian had come to use that word.

Clovio, however, had no reservations. He stood before the portrait, hanging now in the gallery downstairs, his posture almost soldierly, the old eyes blinking rapidly to hold the work in focus. Only when tears blurred his vision did he turn aside, sniffing noisily. "It's superb, Greco, superb. Titian himself couldn't have done a better thing. It's much finer than I dared to dream possible. I congratulate you, and I thank you."

Domenikos bowed his head, touched by Clovio's delight. He was dismayed too, even slightly angered, that one purporting to be an expert should be so unequivocal in his praise, so plain did the picture's flaw seem to him. Yet he kept his peace, recalling Titian's adage about fish having to breathe water.

"I'm happy you find it to your taste, Don Giulio."

Fifteen

Until Alessandro Farnese was shown the portrait of Clovio, his relations with Domenikos remained distant. It wasn't that the Cardinal made a point of avoiding the painter. There was simply no occasion for a lengthy interview. Hitherto, he had acknowledged, in the annoyingly offhand way so often affected by the benevolent rich, the young man's expression of thanks for his hospitality, which was a matter of routine for His Excellency. The Palazzo Farnese was crawling with the artists and scholars to whom it gave shelter, often furnishing board as well as lodging.

Domenikos was working in his room at the top of the palace when summoned by a page. "His Excellency requires your presence at once."

The painter hastily changed into a fresh blouse, despairing of the odor of turpentine that would, he knew, imbue him until he washed, something for which there was no time. He descended the broad stone staircase and was told by the boy who had called him to go into the gallery.

The Cardinal stood before the portrait, conversing with Clovio and his librarian, Don Fulvio Orsini. As Domenikos entered, bowing hastily, Farnese pointed to the picture with an eloquent right hand.

"I want you to paint my portrait."

The painter's bow was more formal. "Of course, Excellency."

"I shall be interested to see whether *you* can do for me today what your master did twenty-five years ago. You've seen that portrait?"

"I have, Excellency. You may ask more of me than is quite fair."

"Nonsense, not if you can paint Don Giulio as you have. It's a wonderful likeness, and Orsini here tells me it's a fine picture too."

Domenikos turned quickly to smile at the stocky librarian, then shifted his eyes once again to the Cardinal. "I shall do my best, Excellency. When would it be convenient for you to begin?"

"At once." The Cardinal moved through the library toward the stairway, pausing to look over his shoulder and chuckle ominously. "The humor is on me, Greco. And when a Cardinal wishes to do something, there's only the Pope to say him nay, and that not invariably." He started to mount the stairs, followed now only by the astonished painter.

In the Rome of early 1571, Alessandro Farnese was something of an anachronism. In his demeanor and his way of thought and life, he reflected an age, a spirit, a taste and exuberance, a temperament and intellect that placed appreciably less emphasis on inward than on outward manifestations of style, grace, and religious conviction. He was a high-Renaissance man, a breed that was losing fashion throughout the Catholic world of the Counter-Reformation.

His background explained a lot. For even if one accepted as standard the patterns of immorality and corruption typical of so many earlier masters of the Church, Farnese could point out as remarkable the fact that his grandfather had been Pope and his great-aunt Julia *maîtresse en titre* to another pontiff. The Cardinal's father, bastard son of Pius III, had proved himself a distinguished villain in a spectacularly fast field and had been foully but deservedly murdered.

Fifty now, Alessandro Farnese had been a cardinal since the age of fourteen. (This was nothing like a record; boys of five had been designated to wear the purple.) It was an office to which he brought considerable charm and wit and a genuine passion for art and scholarship; his palace was a center of culture for the whole of Italy. In his view, the arts and philosophy were quite as consonant with the works of God as were the gestures of purification and penitence demanded by the present rulers of the Church—and they were a good deal more pleasant. It wasn't surprising, therefore, that he felt less than a wholehearted sympathy for the edicts of Trent.

He most actively deplored—and completely ignored—the Councils' ruling on books and the index of forbidden literature promulgated by the Holy Office. The disappearance from legitimate circulation of such writers as Boccaccio, Machiavelli, and Ariosto was repugnant to him, a fact which endeared him to Domenikos, who, though recognizing his rashness, had found it impossible to be separated from his growing library, which included a number of proscribed volumes.

The portrait of Farnese seemed to the painter to suffer from the same defect as Clovio's. Its elegance was cold, distant, austere. But it proved, if possible, even more gratifying to its subject, who ordered its permanent display in the library rather than in the adjoining gallery. The Cardinal's pleasure seemed a most auspicious augury for Domenikos' career in Rome. His success seemed assured; he could now proceed only from strength to strength.

The suave Alessandro Farnese was, of course, the most valuable of Domenikos' early connections in Rome. His promise of further patronage and influence in the securing of commissions elsewhere was of crucial importance to the painter's future. Yet the role of first friend, a need almost as vital, fell to Fulvio Orsini, the Cardinal's librarian.

The illegitimate offspring of one of Rome's most illustrious families, Orsini had joined the Farnese entourage while still a youth. After taking lay orders, he became his master's principal adviser on all things cultural and scholarly, curator of his important collections of paintings and sculpture, and custodian of his magnificent library.

In the process of accumulating art and literature for the Cardinal, Fulvio had amassed for himself an impressive number of books and paintings and a major collection of ancient sculpture. He was considered Rome's greatest expert on the literature of Greece and early Rome and was consulted whenever an old manuscript was rediscovered.

Orsini first came to Domenikos' attention by his endorsement of the Clovio portrait as art. He proved no less enthusiastic of the artist's rendering of Farnese and at once commissioned a painting of himself. It was during his sittings that he first discerned in the artist not merely a craftsman of distinction but an intelligent, well-read intellectual who expressed his ideas with pungency and vividness.

"You're the first man I've met who can do things well with his hands," he observed tactlessly, "who can do them as well with his brain." And to Alessandro Farnese he said as unequivocally, "Greco is the best the Greeks have to offer us. We should cultivate him."

In Orsini, Domenikos perceived a man with whom he could enjoy a conversation, serious but clever, wise but never pontifical. It was Orsini, moreover, who offered to introduce him to what he called "internal Rome, what you can't see from the gutters."

It would have been difficult for Domenikos to find a better-informed, more broadly interested, or more enthusiastic guide than Fulvio Orsini. A Roman of the Romans, he understood his native city, thought it unreservedly the finest place in the world, and was able to convey his affection with an energy that seemed limitless.

Orsini's passions and zeals were so many that Domenikos at first found it difficult not to think him frivolous. Indeed, at times, he was, but infectious too. A small, cheerful, bouncy man who inclined to a puffiness his diet did nothing to discourage, he succeeded in communicating his worldly gaiety to a Domenikos who had always found this quality elusive and never more so than since the death of the little Tiziano and his dear Maria's illness.

Unlike Venice, Rome was a city in which it was possible to walk from one place to another in more or less a straight line. With the Palazzo Farnese as their starting point, Domenikos and Orsini scudded from palazzo to ruin to church in the lengthening days of 1571. As they walked, they conversed, seriously or lightly, about the things that mattered most to both—philosophy, theology, history, art, the gossip on everyone's lips. When the weather was inclement, they passed their afternoons in the library, confronting each other across a broad table in the failing light.

They explored each other's minds in much the same way that they roamed the city, probing deeply here, just nodding in there, and came to understand the differences of their temperaments. For Domenikos, this wasn't an altogether easy matter, so inherently suspicious was he of anything that smacked of the purely whimsical or the willfully foolish. For Orsini, too, the process of becoming this brilliant young man's intimate was not without difficulty. A skeptic, he normally held little sympathy for intensity, as distinguished from profundity. A logician, he suspected the emotions. A scholar, he despised arid erudition.

While immediate recognition by each of the other's genius drew them together, it was a tolerance of the other's peculiarities that held them close. Domenikos found in Orsini the first person to whom he could confide the whole of his experience, his frailties, his faith, his love, his reading, his observation, his pain and despair, and the sources of his joy without feeling an accompanying need for elaborate explanation or defense.

For Orsini, the young painter was intriguing in his contradictions —the intellectual at war with the passionate, the religious mystic in conflict with the disciple of Aristotle. He frequently complained that Domenikos would enjoy martyrdom.

If their friendship required sealing, this occurred when the artist permitted Orsini to watch as he painted a study of the Michelangelo Pietà that the librarian took him to see in the garden of a Roman merchant. For the better part of a day, the older man sat speechless in the shadows of Domenikos' improvised studio in the palace as Domenikos transformed the original image into a conception wholly his own. For the first time, Orsini thought he could comprehend not only the concentration and the discipline demanded, but the creative process itself. Yet of this day he never said anything.

"A little more than a year has passed since I came to Rome. It seems both impossible and too true as I consider it." Thus Domenikos wrote Titian.

There had been periods of loneliness and self-doubt when time had seemed to creep pointlessly by, but they had been relatively few and of short duration. He had met important Romans, notably clerics, who could prove useful to his career. Yet little of importance had materialized by way of commissions, nothing but a steady commerce in portraits of the nearly illustrious.

"I'm not yet anxious," his letter went on, "nor even greatly frustrated. But it would be pleasant to report that at least one of the studies I have made for altarpieces to be installed in one of several churches under construction had been accepted. There have been as yet no major patrons. But I have learned to appear patient. That should amuse you."

He had, in any event, finally succeeded in organizing his domestic arrangements. He had rented a house that was close to the Palazzo Farnese, retaining the Cardinal's residence as a base from which he hoped to launch himself impressively upon the Roman scene. Even in burgeoning Rome, it had been difficult to find a suitable dwelling, one with a room facing north that was large enough for him to use as a studio. The furnishings provided by a landlord skeptical of an artist as a tenant were simplicity itself. Nor was Domenikos much tempted to augment them, for it remained uncertain that his establishment here was a permanent thing. Beds, a few chests, chairs, and crudely made tables, all of them in less than pristine condition, were the extent of the objects adorning his quarters at the beginning of his occupancy. To these he had reluctantly added a meager supply of cooking utensils, glass, and crockery whose quality reflected the indifference of their owner to solitary nourishment or comradely conviviality.

He had, moreover, so far resisted Orsini's plea that he employ a domestic, maintaining that he couldn't indulge himself with such a luxury while his poor Maria was locked away. Even more maddening to his friend was his steadfast refusal to cultivate conscientiously those members of Roman society who might become his patrons.

As both realized later, one of their most relevant discussions about Domenikos' future took place on the day on which all Rome buzzed with the important naval victory of Lepanto on October 7, little more than a week previously.

An immense fleet under the leadership of the bastard Don John of Austria, comprising ships of Spain, Genoa, and Venice and sailing with the highly valued blessings of the Pope, had met a substantial force of Ottoman vessels bound for another Mediterranean island invasion. In the Gulf of Corinth, the fleet of the Holy League inflicted a sharp defeat on the Turks. It was being said, in the flush of triumph, that the Infidel hordes had at last been conclusively suppressed and that the Holy League, galvanized by success, would now begin to drive the enemy from the mainland and its island holdings.

This optimism didn't reflect the views of the politically astute Fulvio Orsini. Domenikos was impressed by his friend's objectivity. Orsini was to be listened to, if not always believed, because his mind was analytical, because he had a sense of history, and because, in those days of venality at all levels of society, he had no personal stake in the outcome of events that took place outside the Palazzo Farnese.

"If the Holy League stayed together," he said that afternoon in

October, "what the wishful thinkers have been saying might be true. For that matter, as long as the league does stay together, it *will* be true. But it will come apart in the long run."

"I wish I had your clarity, Fulvio, but I don't."

The librarian heartily agreed. "No, you don't. You wish the world would go away and leave you alone. You're not in the least interested, are you?"

Domenikos walked for a time in silence. "Well," he said at last, "that puts it too strongly. I'm interested in what affects you and me and my friends and my family. But when it comes to wars and rebellions and acts of God, I can't say that I feel very intimately involved. Besides, what could I do to change things?"

"Nothing. But you might be a little more interested."

The painter laughed. "I'm aware, but not interested. I can't afford to waste my passion."

"What is it you seek, Greco," asked Orsini, pointing to the church, "apart from glorifying God in paint?"

"Peace."

They walked on. "That's for the grave."

"Is there any place in the world that's safe and peaceful? Not Rome, not Venice, and certainly not Crete."

"Things aren't so bad as that, Greco. If it's remoteness from the real world you're looking for, I suppose Spain would be the place for you. But I doubt that it *is* what you want. You're not a tranquil fellow. Oh, on the surface you are, but to one who mistrusts surfaces and looks beneath, you present quite another impression."

"That's just it. I have enough anxieties. I don't want them imposed on me from the outside. You seem to enjoy the world's violence, Fulvio. I don't. I like peace. There was a kind of peace in Crete. When I was a boy, I could spend hours in the ruins near Candia and never hear a sound except the rush of the wind."

"But you say you can't go back there."

The painter smiled sadly. "That would be paying too high a price."

"You're very fussy, Greco."

"Very. But what's different about Spain?"

"Spain is secure. The Turks won't invade her. She's strong. She could resist attack." He laughed ironically. "Venice has to fight her land wars with mercenaries. All she has are ships and gold. Spain has those and she has men too." He paused for emphasis. "*And* she has mountains. The Pyrenees, I'm told, are almost as high as the Alps.

They protect Spain from France." His tone became dry. "You'll have noted that Philip has fought all his battles with France north of the Pyrenees. It's not stupid to have a mountainous boundary. Of course," he went on musingly, "a boundary like that can have its drawbacks. It cuts one off from other civilizations." He became oddly eager. "They're a curious lot, the Spaniards. You'd admire them. You have something in common, a love of suffering and death."

Domenikos protested mildly. "I never said I loved suffering, Fulvio. And I accept death as a fact. I certainly don't love it, don't seek it."

"But you do think of death as the last victory, don't you, not the last enemy?"

The artist considered this. "Perhaps," he finally agreed.

"But there you are, Greco. What we don't love we hate. We must fight it. And of all things inimical to life, what could be more so, by definition, than death?"

Domenikos laughed. "How you love to play with the language. You really are a casuist."

"You malign me, Greco. Let's leave death aside for the moment and talk about suffering. The Spanish seem to adore actual physical pain. It's one of the reasons why they make such good soldiers, why they create so many saints, too, because martyrdom is a sort of racial passion for them, an ideal. I suppose the counterpart is that it explains why there are so few Spanish artists and poets. They're the most joyless people I've ever encountered." He grinned maliciously. "Unless, of course, as *you* seem to, one regards suffering as joy."

The painter shook his head. "You're wrong. I have my joys, ones that aren't painful, I mean."

"You take me too literally. I recognize your occasional gaiety. You manage to laugh with your whole heart now and then. You can even joke a little. But in your heart, my dear friend, you're dark, gloomy, and introspective, full of the need to suffer and be penitent for all the sins you imagine you've committed. What a depressing thing it must be to have so low an opinion of sin and to despise yourself for having yielded to its delights—if, in fact, you ever have yielded to its delights. You nod your head. That means you agree, or that you've yielded?"

"I've yielded."

Orsini permitten his skepticism to describe itself broadly on his full face. "Really, Greco? Let's see. Let's talk of something small. For instance, tell me when you were last drunk."

Domenikos scowled, recalling the occasions in Venice when he reeled homeward to Maria's bedside, momentarily released from the anguish of her illness. "A couple of years ago," he mumbled.

"And when were you last with a woman? I'm not speaking of your wife, of course."

The painter flushed angrily. "I don't think—"

"I know. You think it an improper question. It causes you pain. But I'm trying to make a point I think important. When?"

The young man grimaced uncomfortably. It was absurd to feel so uneasy. He had nothing to be ashamed of. Yet he knew that his reply would invite Orsini's scorn; he knew Orsini's outlook. It was similar to Titian's. So his response was reluctant, embarrassed.

"Not since I was last with Maria."

His friend reacted as Domenikos had known he would. He was incredulous. "Two years ago?"

"It's more like three, even longer perhaps. She was ill for a long time before I left Venice." He hesitated, reddening. "To have tried to touch her then would have seemed like a sort of violation."

Orsini was embarrassed, but he was not to be distracted. "That long? My poor Greco. You can't be serious."

"But I am, Fulvio." He smiled dolefully. "It's not that there've been no temptations . . ."

"Thank God for that. At least you're human. But that you should have resisted . . ." He shook his head wonderingly. "No, it's not possible, not in this century."

Domenikos responded softly. "I made a promise."

"To whom, for God's sake?"

"To myself."

"Preposterous."

"But true. Before I married Maria, I vowed never to be unfaithful to her."

"But surely now, Greco, with your wife mad—forgive me for putting it so boldly—but surely the situation is completely different from anything you could have anticipated."

"But that doesn't alter the fact of my vow."

"You astonish me, and not for the first time. Can you be that hard on yourself? Can you keep to the promise for the rest of your life?"

Domenikos was shaken. Having simply proceeded from day to day, he had not, he confessed to himself, considered the implications just evoked by Orsini. He nodded weakly. "I have to try."

"You're mad, I tell you. God in heaven, we'll have to do something about this right away."

"No," said the painter, his expression grimly stubborn. "No, Fulvio."

The librarian ignored this. His rich voice assumed its most persuasive tone. "There can be nothing tawdry about it, nothing dirty or mean. I see that. Just a nice, clean, strapping girl from the country, one who's hot on for the game. But no complications, no love affair, no emotions to trouble your sleep." He paused, smiling warmly. "How does that strike you?"

For a time, Domenikos couldn't look into Orsini's eyes. It was devastating, like watching as one's home burned to the ground, all possessions lost, leaving only a few charred remains and memories of the irretrievable. The irony was that as soon as his friend had made his suggestion, the painter had felt the sudden, stinging stirrings of desire, so long dormant. Defeated, he raised his eyes, smiling ruefully.

"You're a wicked man, Orsini, a disgrace to your Cardinal. 'Lead us not into temptation.' "

The plump librarian was jubilant. He laughed. "So perhaps, very slowly, we shall make a normal man of you. A sainthood for Greco no more."

Sixteen

The girl's name was Catarina de Preboste. As Orsini had proposed, she was from the country, from the hills of the Abruzzi, the younger sister of a woman who worked in the kitchens of the Palazzo Farnese. A head shorter than Domenikos, she was a strongly built child of sixteen or seventeen (she herself was uncertain), full of peasant laughter, tender and expressing a gay gentleness for his early embarrassment in her presence.

She was passionate too, and touchingly concerned for his pleasure with her, her intensity seeming to him inspired by natural, animal urges to which she submitted cheerfully, without reserve or inhibition, just one more aspect of life. In her utter artlessness, Catarina was different from both Veronica and Maria.

"Oh," she said, giggling helplessly as she finally saw him unclothed. "You're very big there for so thin a man." Her dark eyes grew wide and bright with mock apprehension. "You frighten me, signore."

Domenikos laughed nervously, trembling with excitement and anticipation. "I'm afraid, Catarina, that I'm going to be very quick, the first time."

She shrugged. "It's all right. You shouldn't have waited so long."

He sat on the edge of the bed, grinning. "That's why I'm in such a hurry."

"Oh, I understand. But couldn't you just look at me first?"

Catarina threw back the thin coverlet to reveal her full young body, her marvelous heavy breasts quivering slightly, tantalizingly, in the winter chill of the room, the dark nipples almost black, the flesh amber in the candlelight, the black-tufted groin a fearful, a forbidding invitation—Eurydice's temptation of Orpheus, he thought. He laid his clean-shaven cheek against it, found its wiry coarseness thrilling, its faintly gamey odor at once repellent and compelling. He sat up.

"Am I not pretty?" she asked, knowing the question to be rhetorical.

"You're absolutely perfect, Catarina."

Languidly, she stretched her strong arms upward and encircled his neck. She smelled of sweat, an aroma usually repellent to the fastidious Domenikos, but one now strangely attractive, enhancing his desire.

To wait a moment longer was unbearable. Almost with ferocity, he fell upon her, bracing himself by grasping her delicious, spongy young breasts. The touch of her flesh had an explosive effect on his. Its profound warmth, its malleability, its willingness, its lack of restraint as she clutched him tightly with arms and legs, set aflame the tinder of his passion. He kissed her long and deeply. Then, suddenly, with a kind of frenzy, he thrust himself against, then into her hot moisture, firm but yielding.

Soon they were quiet, lying side by side, only their hips touching, the fever of the previous moments spent. Domenikos smiled to himself in the half light. Orsini had been right; no sainthood for Il Greco. "You shouldn't have waited so long," Catarina had said. It was a painful truth. The sins of commission were probably no graver than those of omission. He felt relieved, released, restored; there was health in him. Was it possible that God had been mocking him all this time?

The girl interrupted these thoughts. She turned her face toward him, her warm cheek touching his shoulder. "It's too late for me to go back to my sister's room in the palazzo. May I spend the night here, signore?"

Laughing softly, he reached over to her, placing his hand on her belly, toying with her navel. "Of course, Catarina. You didn't think I'd let you leave so soon anyhow, did you?"

"I didn't know."

"You do now."

She gazed wistfully about the bedchamber with its pale shadows dancing in the faltering light. "This must be a very large house. Do you live here all alone?"

"No one else stays here. There's a woman who comes in to clean for me."

"You don't mind it, being by yourself? You don't get lonely?"

"I enjoy it."

She shuddered. "And you're not afraid of thieves in the night, or being robbed or even murdered?"

He laughed and patted her belly, then slid his hand down slowly. "No, I'm not afraid, Catarina. I have nothing here that a robber would want, just a few pictures. Who'd want those?"

"That's silly."

"Why?"

"How would a thief know that before he broke in?"

Domenikos shrugged. "He'd find out soon enough."

"And then he'd be angry and kill you."

"Perhaps. Are *you* afraid, Catarina?"

"Not of thieves. I'm not afraid of any man."

"Really?"

Her laughter was dark. "*I* have something a man wants to steal."

"You've been raped often?"

She considered. "Two times, three times. I don't remember. Maybe more."

Smiling, he grasped her more tightly between the legs. "It sounds as if you enjoyed it."

"No." She sighed. "But you learn to bear what you have to bear, signore. It's God's will."

"You were never hurt?"

She seemed surprised. "Why should I be hurt? I offered no resistance. If it's the will of God, I accept it. I'd much rather be raped than murdered."

He embraced her tightly with both arms. "You're ravishing, Catarina. Where did you learn such wisdom?"

"From my mother, signore, God rest her soul." She crossed herself solemnly.

"She taught you that?"

"No, but when some men raped her, she resisted, and they killed her."

"My God. When did that happen?"

"Three or four years ago."

"You didn't see it happen, I hope."

"I did. In a house with only two rooms, signore, you see everything. I didn't understand then what she was fighting for. It seemed silly to me. It still does. It was no worse than what papa did to her when he was drunk."

"What happened to the men?"

"I don't know. Nothing, I suppose. They were brigands. They lived in the hills above our town. Most of the time they leave the peasants alone. I guess they were just hungry, like you, signore. Poor fellows. Poor mama."

Domenikos took a deep breath and exhaled it forcefully. "You astonish me."

"Why? It's just an Abruzzi story."

"God."

In the ensuing silence, Domenikos conjured up horrific versions of the scene the girl had just evoked in such laconic tones.

"You need a man, signore," she said abruptly, "a man who lives here with you."

Though unfamiliar with the thought patterns of the Italian peasant, Domenikos knew instinctively, from his experience with the natives of Crete, that this was no idle suggestion.

"For protection?" he inquired, all innocence.

"To protect you, yes, and to keep you company. It's bad to live alone. People aren't meant to, unless they're hermits. And see how *they* live, worse than pigs. A man could cook for you, see that you ate properly and regularly." She ran a strong finger over the prominent corrugations of his rib cage. "You don't eat enough. And he could clean for you, and he could run your errands for you."

Domenikos acknowledged to himself the abstract virtues of this suggestion and wondered what specifically she had in mind. "You're thinking of someone in particular, aren't you, Catarina?"

She nodded, smiling hopefully. "My brother Francesco."

"How old is he?"

"My own age, signore. He's my twin. You'll like him. He's fine and strong. He can do anything you need done. And he's pleasant too."

"I'm certain of that, if he's your brother. But does he think the same way you do?"

She was perplexed by the question. "Think?"

"Does he have your wisdom?"

She tittered. "And more besides. Women don't have wisdom, signore. They're not intended to think."

Like Titian's notion of artists, Domenikos thought. "He's in Rome, your brother?"

"And he needs work. Will you see him tomorrow?"

The painter didn't answer at once. He felt vaguely alarmed, fearful lest he permit his delight in Catarina's superb flesh to compromise his privacy, to clutter and complicate his life. Yet it was a modest request. He was committing himself to nothing. Moreover, he was curious about Francesco. What would a male sibling of Catarina be like?

"Yes, tomorrow."

She nuzzled his ear. "You'll not be sorry, signore."

"I'm sure of it."

She extracted herself from his embrace and leaned on an elbow, her round young face turned toward him in the wavering orange light.

"Again, Catarina?" he inquired softly.

She replied very gravely. "If you would like it, I would like it too."

The first thing Domenikos liked about Francesco was that he came to present himself alone. Short and stocky, like Catarina, but with flesh a good deal harder, he had observant, intelligent eyes. A ready, broad smile revealed an even expanse of white teeth. In his movements there was something electric, a purposeful integrity of mind and body, a surprising grace.

After introducing himself, he waited for the painter to speak.

"Catarina tells me you might like to work for me."

"I would."

"Are you known in Rome?"

The boy grinned. "Only by my sisters."

"Then this is your first visit."

"No, signore. I've been here twice before, to visit Antonia. She works for the Cardinal. But this time I came to bring Catarina to you."

Domenikos was embarrassed. "I understand."

Perceiving the artist's consternation, Francesco waved his right hand strongly from side to side. "My working for you has nothing to do with Catarina, signore. If you want her to stay with you, she will, no matter what you decide about me."

"But if I won't employ you, what will you do?"

The boy began to brush the coarse brown fabric of his tunic with his hands. He shrugged. "Look for work somewhere else."

"And if you don't find it?"

"Go back to our village."

"What do you do there?"

"I work with my father and my older brother Filippo. Papa owns a small farm with many sheep and some fine vines. We make a good wine." His pride was touching. Then he sighed. "But when papa dies, the farm will belong to Filippo and his sons." He shook his head firmly. "I shall never marry."

"Why not?"

"To have no property to pass on to your son is a bad thing."

"How is it that you're not studying to be a priest or a monk? Isn't that the usual thing?"

Francesco laughed. "Papa would give nothing to the Church, so the Church would give nothing to me. This is called Christianity."

The boy's anger wasn't hidden by the laughter.

"You read and write, Francesco?"

"My brother does, signore. Papa thought one son who could do that was enough."

"Your father sounds like a hard man. How does he feel about Catarina being with me?"

"It doesn't disturb him. 'One less appetite is always a blessing,' he told us when we left, 'and two would be a papal benediction.' " The boy uttered this monstrous phrase with neither reproach nor self-pity in his voice. As his sister would have said, it was God's will.

"Catarina tells me you can cook and clean and run errands for me."

"I can, signore."

"But if she's staying with me, Francesco, why would I need you?"

The question provoked genuine surprise. "The woman who's sleeping with the master wouldn't do things like that."

Domenikos blushed once again, appreciating at once and even admiring, in an objective way, the niceness of the boy's reasoning.

"Of course not," he murmured. Then, more forcefully, he added,

"Look, Francesco. I'll teach you to read and write. I'll give you your bed and your food and your clothes. And I'll pay you twelve ducats each year, one ducat a month. Do you count?"

The boy laughed. "Anyone who herds sheep must know how to count, signore. We have two hundred sheep. I can count to two hundred."

"My proposal satisfies you, then?"

"It's very generous."

"Not if you work hard."

"I always work hard, signore. When would you like me to begin?"

"Today, if you want. When you bring your things, you can bring Catarina's too."

Francesco giggled. "We both of us have only what we're standing in."

Domenikos reached into the black velvet purse suspended from his belt and extracted some ducats. "Then you'd better get yourselves something, something good and something sturdy to work in."

"But Catarina can make me things, signore. To buy anything but cloth would be wasteful."

Suddenly, the untidiness of the proposed situation recalled itself to Domenikos. He looked earnestly into the boy's eyes. "It doesn't bother *you* that your sister will sleep with me?"

"Should it?"

"And if she becomes pregnant?"

Francesco accepted this possibility with a faint raising of his black eyebrows. "Then we'll have to get rid of the baby. It's happened to us before."

"But not to Catarina."

"No, signore, to my sister Antonia."

"But what must God think of such things, Francesco? It's terrible."

Clearly, the boy found the question absurd. "What has God to do with it, signore? Does He do anything to take care of the babies after they're born?"

The presence of other lives beneath his roof proved an unmitigated pleasure to Domenikos. Not since the earliest days of his marriage had he felt so relaxed, so unreservedly content. Only his failure to obtain an important commission marred his outlook. And that had nothing to do with Catarina and Francesco.

In this frame of mind, he conceived a new rendition of Christ healing the Blind, a theme he considered more than appropriate now, the more so since he intended it as a gift to Orsini, to whom he owed this change of feeling. He thought it amusing that this painting include the features of the librarian, of Catarina, of her brother, and of himself.

As he was completing this little canvas, much more intimate in treatment than his earlier version, Domenikos sensed the nearness of another person, heard a breath catch. He stayed his hand and listened, realizing from the heaviness of each inhalation that it could only be Francesco, who now stood so close that Domenikos could faintly feel the warmth of the air as he exhaled it. For a time, though, the artist offered no indication of his awareness. Then he turned and smiled.

"You need me?"

The expression on the youth's face changed abruptly from fascination to chagrin. Caught totally off his guard, he felt Domenikos' question like a lash. "Forgive me, master. I didn't mean to disturb you."

"But you didn't, Francesco. When I'm painting, it takes a great deal to disturb me."

The boy hadn't heard him. He stared at the painting, eyes bright, strong hands clasped tightly. "It's nearly done, master?"

"Yes."

Francesco nodded, then shook his head, as if caught between comprehension and amazement. "I suddenly know," he whispered, "what it means to be a painter." He blushed. "I watched you for some time."

Domenikos pointed to a figure to the right of the blind man who knelt before Christ. "Do you recognize him?"

The youth leaned forward, but without moving his feet, as if dreading to come too close. He brightened, then seemed awed, like the characters in the painting. "Is that me?"

The painter nodded. "And if you look again, you may see other faces you know."

Francesco was transfixed with delight. Bobbing with excitement, he moved a single step forward, his eyes darting back and forth across the canvas. One by one, he identified the three other portraits. At last he turned away, dazzled. "Oh, master, can I learn to paint? If you taught me, I'd ask for no money at all."

Domenikos was touched, recalling vividly his own emotions on first seeing a Venetian painting in the cathedral of Candia. He was pensive now, holding Francesco's excited eyes with great intensity. "You'd do that?"

"Willingly."

"It's not just a whim?"

"Oh, no."

The painter smiled and touched the youth's powerful forearm. "There's no need for you to give up your money. If Catarina will share the work with you, I'll teach you what I can."

Francesco seemed about to explode. He jumped up and down. He embraced Domenikos, then broke away to dance in tight circles about the floor, returning dizzily to confront him. "Oh, I promise, master, that everything will be done as before. What a wonderful thing. . . ."

As simply and spontaneously as that did Domenikos acquire a pupil.

The painting was finished in early April of 1572. The artist recognized it as the finest thematic work he had ever done, yet realized, trying to examine it as Titian might, that it owed more to his Venetian training than to a conception entirely his own. The master's words consoled him: "It takes time to become wholly yourself, Greco." Sighing, he affixed to the canvas his signature in Greek.

When he presented it for inspection to Orsini, the librarian's pleasure and approval were gratifying. But when informed that it was a gift, the Roman, though grateful, flatly refused to accept it. "This is for the Cardinal, Greco. And I'll be surprised if it doesn't lead to another commission."

As Domenikos was coming to think inevitable, Orsini was correct in his judgment. Within a week, Alessandro Farnese purchased the painting for seventy-five ducats, a respectable sum in the painter's view, and commanded a large canvas of the Purification of the Temple for installation in the Palazzo Farnese.

A Roman lawyer, Lancilotti, was so impressed by the painting that he commissioned a portrait, although he protested heatedly that Domenikos' fee of fifty ducats was outrageous. More than this, Lancilotti insisted that the picture of Christ healing the Blind should be seen by the Pope, with whom, it appeared, he was more than casually conversant—which was more than the urbane Cardinal Farnese could honestly assert.

With Orsini, the Cardinal, and Lancilotti in close attendance, Domenikos made his appearance before the Pope. For a man who cherished the name of "Father of Poverty," there was nothing threadbare about his surroundings. It was true that he dressed simply, but this merely emphasized the richness of all about him.

After Domenikos kissed his ring, His Holiness asked the painter where he had studied. Hardly had he begun to reply when Pius pointed to him accusingly and said, "But you're not Italian." At the same time, he turned angrily to a cardinal of the Curia and protested. "Why is my time being wasted? We must first take care of our own."

Thus Domenikos was dismissed without another word. At first he was bitterly disappointed, then resigned. He realized that as long as the present Pope lived, there was no possibility of his receiving a commission from the Holy See.

What he did not foresee was that within a week of the interview, Pope Pius V was to die. For nearly a fortnight after the death, the city was inundated with rumors as the Sacred College of Cardinals gathered to select his successor. Roman clerics of Domenikos' acquaintance offered up fervent prayers that the new pontiff would be made of softer stuff than the one now mourned. Indeed, given Pius' insistence on catharsis as the only effective means to assure ecclesiastic purification, it would have been difficult (some said impossible) to find his equal among the present range of candidates.

On May 13, the white smoke that denoted a decisive ballot wafted from the window-mounted chimney of the Sistine Chapel. The College had elected Cardinal Ugo Buoncompagni, who designated himself Gregory XIII. The new Pope, though not the zealot his predecessor had been, would prove a pretty strong man, or such was the view in Rome. He was a former legate to Spain, and quite as dedicated to suppressing the Protestant rebellion.

As Domenikos worked on Lancilotti's portrait, he discussed these events with the lawyer. Posing in the black robes affected by those of his calling, Lancilotti was in his middle thirties, with pale olive skin drawn tightly across precise, well-made features. The face, Domenikos thought, seemed almost too refined; it lacked force. The lawyer, for all that, was not without wit.

"I assume you don't find yourself altogether desolate by what's happened, maestro."

The painter responded to the image on his easel and continued painting. "Desolate, avoccato, but utterly reconciled to the will of God."

"Very sage of you. We must hope that the new Holiness will look on your work with greater favor."

Domenikos' laughter was sardonic. "I'm not worrying about that yet. My first concern is how he looks on foreigners. Do you know anything of this?"

Lancilotti brushed his forehead with a small, fragile hand. "Nothing, but if you like I'll inquire from my spies."

"That would be kind." The artist sighed. "But I fear the worst. Still, I think it very odd that a pope should be a xenophobe."

"But surely there are other churchmen who'll offer you the opportunities you want."

"You surprise me, avoccato. You're so well informed about so many things. Don't you realize that in Rome all church art is influenced by the Pope"—he paused, smiling sadly—"or by the Jesuits, which is the same thing? I find that understandable, even proper. What annoys me is that my nationality should have any bearing at all. I didn't come to Rome to have my art scorned by anyone, especially a pope, for the wrong reasons."

Lancilotti stared at the painter with admiration.

"Those are strong words."

"I have strong feelings."

Although he continued to be apprehensive about the attitude of the new Pope toward him and his art, Domenikos soon had other matters to occupy his mind. A letter from Venice arrived just after he applied the final coat of clear varnish to his portrait of Lancilotti. It was from his brother Manusos, informing Domenikos that he had come to Italy with three other Candiots to petition the Consiglio for permission to operate four pirate vessels under the flag and nominal protection of the Serenissima. The proposal seemed a complicated one, involving not only the ships but their equipment, armament, and crews—all to be financed by the Republic, the costs secured by a bond which the four partners were to post.

In exchange for this support, the petitioners promised to turn over to the Consiglio all captured captains and one-fourth of all other prisoners, and undertook to sell the remaining captives at the rate of fifteen to twenty ducats each, depending on their physical condition, prices somewhat below the prevailing market average for able-bodied slaves.

This arrangement, Manusos wrote, had been accepted in principle by the Consiglio. There remained, however, a small but thorny problem, and this was the occasion for the letter. The Venetian authorities insisted that the partners pay for repairs to the ships made necessary by their use.

"I give you my word," he wrote, "that it is a question of great urgency. It would be impossible for us to estimate before the fact how serious, and therefore how dear, the cost of repairs to any ship might be. Nor can we know when they might be necessary. They could be required before a single contact was made with an enemy vessel, and we would be ruined.

"I beg you, brother, to write to your friend Tiziano Vecellio, and ask him to intercede with any members of the Consiglio he knows. We are willing, as an additional concession, to offer the Serenissima one-half of all prisoners for the elimination of this onerous provision about repairs. Help us in this, Menegos, I implore you.

"Call this, if you wish, my wedding present, for I am to be married. The girl is the daughter of one of my partners and sweet enough, really, although mama thinks her ordinary. The truth is he wouldn't join me unless I married her. That should give you some idea of how badly I want *your* aid now."

Domenikos didn't know whether to laugh or cry. He recalled his conversation with Manusos just after the death of their father. So much had occurred in the six years that had elapsed that he had forgotten his brother's naïve eagerness and enthusiasm over a project the painter could think only both hazardous and ridiculous, yet wholly consonant with Manusos' impulsive nature.

Wearily, Domenikos realized he would accede to his brother's request, not because he approved of the plan, which he thought foolhardy beyond belief, but because of his own guilt at his neglect of his family. He had no doubt that he would be doing Manusos a bigger favor by refusing, yet remorse outweighed sense. Never before had his family asked anything of him.

Less than a month after he had written Titian, he learned from him that the Consiglio had acceded to the petition. Though pleased for Manusos, the painter remained apprehensive. However, as Orsini had pointed out, "You can't deny him the privilege of discovering his folly. That's one of man's inalienable rights."

Seventeen

Alessandro Farnese was pleased with Domenikos' painting of the Purification and promised to arrange an audience with Pope Gregory in September, when the Pontiff returned from his retreat at Castel Gandolfo. In the interim, Orsini introduced him to a number of scholarly clerics, most of them Jesuits, who might prove helpful in advancing the painter's cause in Rome. Among these new acquaintances was Don Pedro Chacón, a frail, middle-aged Spaniard who had come to the Eternal City in the entourage of the Archbishop of Seville and remained, at the Pope's personal request, to help in the preparation of a calendar to replace the present inaccurate method of recording the passage of the seasons.

The greatest authority of his time on numismatics and glyptics, Chacón's devotion to coins and gems didn't prevent a wide-ranging knowledge. Nor had his long stay in Rome at all chilled his ardor for his native Toledo, of which he spoke with nostalgic warmth, convinced he would never return.

His appreciation of Domenikos' painting was profound, and on each occasion when they met, he sought to persuade the artist to emigrate to Spain where, he assured him, his talents would find a far greater hospitality than they had so far enjoyed in Rome. And when he learned that his new acquaintance had received some training in architecture and sculpture, he redoubled his efforts to convince him of Spain's need for men of such skill.

The priest's blandishments were flattering and wholly believable. Domenikos remembered Titian's similar suggestions. But he had yet to be certain that his attempt to become *the* Roman painter would be abortive. He clung stubbornly to the belief that he could eventually prevail here, despite his nationality, the more so because of the Cardinal's recent offer to introduce him to the Pope.

Chacón, when he understood that the painter was not immediately to be dissuaded from his intention to remain, graciously volunteered to join his influence with Farnese's when the papal audience took place. He had known Gregory as a legate to Toledo; and though he modestly denied intimacy, Orsini believed him quite as important an ally as Farnese.

The Cardinal made no secret of his differences with the Pope. "We're hardly on the friendliest terms. These low-born men should never have such power. Not, God knows, that *I'd* want to be pope. What a lonely prospect. But I opposed his election. He seemed to me unsuited, and I said so openly. He's not forgotten that."

Though he admired his patron's courage, the painter could only feel that his endorsement would prove a dubious asset. Farnese readily assented to the intercession of Chacón, but his prognosis was grim.

The audience was surprisingly easy to arrange. ("I may lack influence," said the Cardinal, "but I don't lack authority.") It took place at the end of September, when autumn first was making itself felt in Rome. Domenikos prepared his toilet with care, solicitously aided by Catarina and Francesco, neither of whom quite believed that their master, however they admired him, was to proceed from them into the greatest of all Christian presences.

A sergeant of the brilliantly uniformed Swiss Guards escorted the painter, Farnese and Chacón up a long, vaulted staircase into a richly decorated hall where, on a low-mounted throne, sat Christ's own Vicar, a faintly dyspeptic personage of seventy with wary, bulging eyes and a hand that trembled as Domenikos held it briefly to kiss the pontifical ring.

With a desultory gesture, the scarlet-robed Bishop of Rome indicated that the artist should rise. He complied gingerly, moving back a step to permit his companions to render homage.

When this ceremony was completed, the Pope began to speak, his voice dry and monotonous, his face expressionless. "I have seen your work. I like it well enough. What is it you want of me? What do you expect me to do?"

"I *expect* nothing, Holiness. But I would be most grateful if my work were considered when another altarpiece is to be commissioned."

The Pontiff folded his hands in his lap and momentarily closed his eyes, as if to suggest that such petitions bored him beyond the power of words to suggest. "I understand. However, I am not much interested in such things. When a church is to be constructed, I plan to leave to those directly responsible the selection of artists. My esteemed predecessor, I know, concerned himself greatly with art. He thought it of much importance."

Domenikos, feeling at this point that he had nothing to lose, responded candidly. "But surely, Holiness, this *is* your concern, in Rome especially. The decrees of the Councils—"

Gregory was impatient. "Do you imagine that art is all I have to worry about?"

"I quite understand how occupied you are, Holiness. I shall intrude on your time as little as possible."

The Pope looked thoughtfully at the painter. "You are not Italian, are you? Are you Spanish? I like the Spanish. *They* understand my difficulties, and only rarely do they add to them. They seem able to solve their problems for themselves."

"I'm from Crete, Holiness, but I've long been a convert."

A trace of a smile passed over the pontifical features and vanished at once. "I should be grateful for small things. I am not asked, at any rate, to deal with a separated brother."

Cardinal Farnese interrupted. "He's considered by many to be the finest painter in Rome, Holiness."

"So you have already told me, Farnese, and I have no reason to suppose that you lie—in this case."

The sharp tone of this response boded ill. The artist decided to put the matter bluntly. "Is it the fact that I'm not Italian that blocks my way, Holiness?"

The reply was arch. "*Is* your way blocked?"

"It *has* appeared so."

"If that is the case, I am no party to it. But, as I said, these questions of art are of little interest to me. Under previous popes, the natural sciences have been shamefully neglected. I have decided, therefore, that science will receive as much attention as I have time to give." He turned to the Cardinal, his expression sly. "Besides, why should I extend favors to a protégé of yours? I owe you nothing."

It was clear that Farnese overlooked this gratuitous comment with a great effort of will. "Yet art is more appreciated by the people, Holiness. Science is for scholars."

"That is undoubtedly so. But are you suggesting that this is a reason for continuing to pander to the base public tastes? If we give the people everything they demand, we shall soon find ourselves shrouded in ignorance. To me, the sole purpose of ecclesiastical art is to instruct the faithful faithfully."

"You have no concern for beauty, Holiness?"

The Pope's contemptuous smile was answer enough. "I care nothing for the opinions of the aesthetes of the Palazzo Farnese. If a peasant or a laborer can understand the message of a painting, it makes no difference to me whether it be well or poorly made."

At this point, Domenikos swept the great hall with a broad gesture. "And yet, Holiness, you surround yourself with art of the greatest virtue."

"But not of my selection." He cleared his throat and swallowed, bringing his ringed right hand to his breast, as if he felt pain there. "In any event, Maestro Il Greco, I must tell you that I have taken the trouble of looking into your career. Opinion is divided, and I fear that you have failed to impress the Jesuits very favorably. My views, therefore, become rather unimportant, do they not?"

Farnese rose to this occasion, his tone respectful but incisive. "The objection of the Jesuits, Holiness, is that he is foreign. This has nothing to do with the quality of his work. They prefer Italians."

The Pope was not impressed. "So do I. The reason, however, is unimportant to me. If the Jesuits disapprove of your work, or express indifference, you can hardly expect me to subvert them. They seem perfectly satisfied with Zuccaro and Sicciolante—"

Domenikos sighed. "And with Pulzone. Oh, yes, Holiness, those names are all to familiar to me."

"You think them inferior?"

"Timid might be a better word, or perhaps polite."

"Surely you can find nothing wrong in being polite, maestro." He smiled condescendingly. "And timidity, Our Lord tells us, is well rewarded in heaven."

The painter stood his ground. "I believe, Holiness, it's meekness that is so blessed."

"You question my interpretation of the Scriptures?"

"Hardly. But there *is* a difference of meaning."

"But neither timidity nor politeness is a vice."

"Perhaps not, Holiness, but they don't suffice for God."

The Pope was astonished. "You question my understanding of doctrine, as well?" He turned to Farnese, his voice sarcastic. "Is this man in orders?"

"No, Holiness. I beg you to excuse his impetuousness."

Gregory's eyes returned to Domenikos, and now he spoke with all the authority his great office afforded. "We shall not permit our artists to be too venturesome at a time in our history when there are so many dangers."

The painter held the Holy Father's gaze, his own intense and angry. "And if, Holiness, you find that you've misjudged history . . . ?"

"I cannot misjudge history, young man, for the simple reason that I am making it."

Shyly, Don Pedro Chacón emerged from behind the robes of the Cardinal, as a mouse would slip from behind a skirting board. "I think you may err, Holiness, with respect to this man's talents."

"You should stick to your calendar, Don Pedro."

There was silence. Domenikos realized that there was nothing to be gained by saying more. When the Pope spoke again, it was obvious that he was of the same persuasion.

"The audience is ended. I wish you no ill, maestro, in spite of your

impertinences. A pope is a man of God and must therefore be mag-
nanimous. I have delegated these questions of art and architecture to
the Jesuits, and I have no intention of relieving them of their responsibilities unless I have overwhelming cause. You may well be the
greatest painter in Rome. But that fact would not induce me to extend my patronage to you."

He nodded to a guard at the door, who immediately approached
the three men and escorted them from the hall.

Domenikos took leave of the Cardinal and Chacón as they emerged
from the Vatican. There seemed no need to explain his desire to be
alone; he offered none. His body numb, he walked slowly in
the bright fall air, without definite destination, even without a sense
of the direction he was taking, conditions that perfectly reflected his
state of mind. It was a time for thought.

A door had been firmly closed, the most important door. He didn't
seriously doubt that the papal decision had been made before the
audience, nor could he doubt that if the Holy Father's view had been
in the balance before the interview his own "impertinence" would
have tipped the scales against him. He had been impetuous and foolish. Less so than his brother? It was a nice question. People might
think him courageous, willing to risk his whole future out of a passion for the truth. There was *that* about it, of course, but not only that.
To what degree he had been motivated by principle and to what
degree by anger or arrogance or even priggishness seemed peculiarly
relevant just now.

It was plainly a moment for decision. In the heat of his humiliation,
the temptation was almost overwhelming to run, to leave Rome. But
to go where? Spain? He knew no one in Spain. Venice? Enjoy the
comfort and security of Titian's protection? Become Titian's
creature? It would be pleasant but stultifying. It would be an
acknowledgment not merely of failure in Rome—an admission that
was ineluctable—but of complete failure, a surrender of his identity
as a painter, a creative person. A return to Venice would signify
his acceptance of his role as a second-rate artist, an emulator of his old
master.

What had his father said? "I will not stand for your being second-
rate at anything." And then: "I don't want you home thinking of yourself as a failure." Well, there was no question of going home to help
poor Manusos save himself from himself.

Look at reality. Stare it down. He would have a pleasant, remunerative career under the Farnese patronage. He would become Rome's greatest portraitist (he was that already; no one questioned it). He would live out an amiable existence. Catarina would bear him bastards. Francesco would become a useful assistant. He would enlarge an already extensive acquaintance, deepen his intimacy with Orsini, perhaps find others whose friendship was as great.

But—the reality again—he would *not*, would *not,* be Il Greco, Rome's new "Divine One," not so long as the present Pope reigned. And the most wishful thinker could scarcely predict the end of a rule that had just begun.

Polite, timid success might be enough for the Roman painters, but it wasn't enough for him. Yet was this not precisely what he had been pursuing, not consciously, perhaps, but in fact? Wasn't this what he had been asking of the Pope? "Let *me* become a polite, timid leader of Roman art." He had not said so, but his request for consideration bore this implication. He could see that now.

Indeed, he saw more. He saw that the painting he had so far accomplished in Rome was both polite and timid. He had not copied Titian, but he had reflected him. He had made no effort to break the hold his master's example imposed on him, had not even considered it, not even been tempted. He had made no advances in his personal style since his painting of the Adoration of the Shepherds five years before. Improvements in his craft, in the quality of his figures, the application of his colors, yes. But his vision, his art, had remained static. At thirty-one, Il Greco was still not completely formed either as a painter or as a person. But at thirty-seven, Raffaello Sanzio had died, his legacy vast, his identity firmly established since adolescence. It was depressing and inescapably true: he had stood still for five years, let life happen to him, offered no resistance, formed no coherent plan. He had drifted.

Granted. What then? Spain, said Titian. Orsini said there was tranquillity in Spain. Chacón too urged him to go to Spain. Philip II was building the Escorial and would offer him more commissions than he could manage. Yet wasn't it madness, like Manusos' piracy, to strike out for something new just because it was new and unknown?

Spain? It sounded attractive. But now there must be a plan. He must never again permit himself to be borne along by irresponsible circumstance. He must prevail on Chacón to introduce him to Spanish visitors in Rome, those who would soon return. "We need friends wherever we are," said Titian. He would cultivate the Spaniards. He would learn Spanish. He would solicit Philip II's patronage. He would ask Titian and Orsini and Alessandro Farnese for letters of recommendation. He would mount a campaign.

Domenikos stopped walking. Where had his feet taken him? He looked up and laughed aloud, inviting the curious glances of passersby. But laughter was the only possible reaction. He was standing before the great Church of San Giovanni in Laterano, seat of the Bishop of Rome, the Pope's own cathedral.

He entered and prayed for a happy issue out of all his present afflictions.

Eighteen

Domenikos was not long in discovering that a decision made was not a decision put into effect. The flow of life as it had been, as it was, could not be arrested simply by his determination to arrest it or to alter its course. In the wake of the disillusioning audience with the Pope, Cardinal Farnese and Orsini vowed to obtain significant commissions for the artist outside the purview of the Bishop of Rome, from Dominican and Franciscan orders, for example, from the Kingdom of Naples, from Milan.

Their efforts met with just the sort of success the painter most dreaded in his new state of mind. Commissions for small altarpieces were surprisingly numerous, all requiring that he duplicate paintings he had already made and now deplored. Demands for portraits multiplied. Yet it would have been churlish, in view of their devotion, to suggest that he would prefer no orders at all to many that he must now fullfil.

He had not concealed his intention to investigate the opportunities in Spain. Farnese thought him rash, but readily volunteered whatever assistance he could give; he wouldn't dream of standing in Domenikos' way. Orsini was more optimistic. "Spain would suit you, Greco," he said. "I've told you that before. But you mustn't make definite plans to leave until your position there is absolutely assured." Pedro Chacón was delighted and promised to introduce him to any Spaniard of relevant importance who visited Rome. "No matter what the Holy Father says, I needn't devote *all* my time to the calendar," he wryly noted. "I know better than most that a coin has two sides." No less enthusiastic was Titian's reaction. "I shall communicate with His Most Catholic Majesty directly. I am glad that at last you plan to do the reasonable thing," he wrote.

"So far away?" That, the painter supposed sadly, was a maternal reflex. But Cleo consoled herself in the next phrase. "I shall soon have a grandchild to divert my last hours. The girl is plain but honest, and devoted to your brother. Manusos," she reported, "appears satisfied with his exploits on the seas. But as he tells me nothing precise, I can tell you no more than that." Word from the Venetian branch of the family was hardly more specific. "I am making important progress at last," his uncle wrote. "I shall soon be a member of the Council of Forty. We see your brother now and again. He is well and seems pleased with his new venture, but I despair of the wine and oil trade with him. I have established contacts in Ragusa, with your aunt's family. I suppose, since we do not see you anyhow, that Spain is no farther away than Rome. We wish you success."

The tendency of his life to flow in two directions at once was sharply underlined by Catarina. When Domenikos informed her and Francesco of his decision, offering to take them with him or to provide for them if they preferred to remain behind, both expressed the most eager desire to accompany him. Although he recognized that the girl's role of mistress-housekeeper might not be viewed in Spain with the same degree of forbearance it enjoyed in Rome, he couldn't in conscience consider the alternative. If there was not love to link them, there was a joyful and wholly mutual affection; and, on her part, he understood, something like adulation. "You're so good to me," she would say, "so gentle." But soon after 1572 became 1573, she blandly announced a pregnancy.

Domenikos was uncertain of his feelings, a condition he didn't enjoy in this period of almost imperious decisiveness. He welcomed the idea of a son; he even accepted the possibility of a daughter with equanimity. But the arrival of a child precluded the undertaking of the arduous journey to Spain for a long time—the period of her gestation and at least a year after that, until the infant was sufficiently strong to endure the trip. Thus trapped between a present that was endurable though unsatisfactory and a future that appeared promising though uncertain, the painter recalled his father's resignation: "Who am I to fly in the face of nature?" What would be, would be.

It was the afternoon of a February day. Domenikos, now appreciably aided by Francesco, had been painting an Annunciation commissioned by the Cardinal. The work was uninteresting to him, for his mind was filled with other thoughts, with the perversity of events and his own still-muted discontent.

He had promised Don Pedro Chacón that he would go to the Palazzo Farnese to meet yet another visiting Spanish dignitary of some sort. (There had been, over the previous months, a large number—none, alas, of more than casual attraction.) The painter hesitated. It was a temptation to sit by the cheerful fireside and seek diversion in a book.

Abruptly, or so it seemed, for he had paid no attention, a spectacular electrical storm manifested itself, the most violent he could recall since his boyhood days in Candia. It was accompanied by torrents of rain that turned the streets of the city into fast-moving streams. He stood by the window of his studio, while Francesco completed the ritual of work's end, and contemplated the wind-driven rain as it relentlessly fell, splashing on the tiled rooftops.

It would be folly to leave the comfort of his house at such a moment. He smiled to himself. *Because* it was folly, because Don Pedro would excuse him from his promise on such a day, he would go. It amused him to be as perverse as the events that were bearing him along.

Wearing a densely woven cloak of heavy black wool with a rather monastic cowl, he ventured into the downpour. Though only a few squares separated his house from the palace, Domenikos was drenched to the bones by the time he reached his destination, his soft leather boots oozing water as he stepped into the arched entry. An amused page helped him to remove the cloak and joined in his laughter as he sat down on a stone bench to take off his sodden footwear, turning each boot upside down. They were so thoroughly soaked that no purpose could be served by putting them on again. He handed them to the page and in black-stockinged feet walked gingerly across the icy marble floors to the library.

It was hardly surprising, given the weather, to find no one there. Yet if it was unlikely that anyone had come, it was equally implausible that Orsini had gone out. He moved, on tiptoe, through the storm-darkened library to the closed door of the gallery. As he approached, he heard voices. He knocked and entered.

Orsini was in conversation with Chacón and another cleric, the latter taller and markedly younger than the other two, a slender figure with long features whose pale angularity was emphasized by thick, steeply arched brows, a flaring moustache, and a pointed beard.

As the painter made his entrance, the librarian smiled. Then, noting his bootless feet, he burst out laughing. "Oh, Greco, you're a model of devotion. Come and stand on this rug."

Grinning, Domenikos bowed briefly to Chacón and joined the group on the handsome carpet in the center of the small gallery. "Devotion may not be the right word," he said to Orsini. "Madness is closer."

"I quite agree. But since you're here, we'll accept it as devotion and pray you don't die of the madness." He took his friend's arm and turned him toward the stranger. "Greco, this is Don Luis de Castilla. He's an acquaintance of Don Pedro's."

Castilla bowed and offered his hand. He was about the painter's age, a man of elegance and poise. He bowed and smiled; his teeth were excellent, his clear dark eyes bright with gaiety, his grip strong but not overbearing.

"Don Luis," said the eager Chacón, "has come to Rome on a very important mission to the Holy Office."

The Spaniard frowned. "Not important, really. Routine diplomacy." The painter had the impression that behind this mask lay mockery. "I'm learning the attitude of the Holy Father toward literature and the arts, as well as other heresies."

Chacón was obviously puzzled, even vaguely alarmed. "Heresy is not to be joked about, Don Luis."

Castilla gazed calmly at his compatriot. "Was I joking, Don Pedro?"

Domenikos wondered about this man. He resembled no other Spaniard Chacón had introduced. "You're connected with the Inquisition in Spain, Don Luis?"

The responsive expression was of sardonic amusement. "In Spain, maestro, every cleric is connected with the Inquisition."

"That explains its success. I've been told that nowhere else has it been so effective."

The priest bowed. "Our friends abroad are generous. If we've been successful, it's perhaps because we've learned to be selective. We're not confused, if you follow me. The Inquisition is intended to suppress heresies among the people, and in *this* we've met with a gratifying success. But never would we jeopardize the investigations of the true scholar whose aim is to improve man's understanding of God and the Church."

Chacón was astonished. "I doubt that you could find a canonical basis for that statement."

Don Luis laughed softly. "I've discovered that since I came to Rome, Don Pedro." He sighed. "Alas, I fear that my colleagues in Toledo will prove unsympathetic. Our university is a source of great pride. To suppress certain studies would be painful."

"Painful," said Chacón primly, "but necessary. You agree?"

"But of course, Don Pedro. Can you imagine our Archbishop setting himself against the will of the Holy Father?"

Domenikos noted little sincerity in this reply. "But surely you've suppressed undesirable literature wherever you've discovered it."

Castilla regarded him curiously for a moment before responding. "Is that a question?"

The painter laughed. "A rhetorical statement."

"No answer required, then. But I'll answer you nevertheless. Until now, at any rate, we've felt that knowledge should not be repressed until it proves clearly in contravention of holy ordinance." He paused and gazed evenly at Chacón. "I don't believe a notion so firmly established is likely to be dislodged, not in Spain, where Protestant heresies are all but unknown."

Orsini interposed here. "Greco's question was not wholly abstract, Don Luis. He has a library that contains an important number of proscribed volumes."

The newcomer's expression clouded angrily. He clenched his fists as he turned to reply. "How dare you say a thing like that to me, Don Fulvio? You don't know who I am. Suppose I were an *agent provocateur* of the Holy Office. Suppose my reason for being here were precisely to find out what you've just volunteered."

Orsini reddened. Domenikos had never seen his friend so discountenanced. "I simply assumed—"

Castilla relaxed at once. "Forgive me for that outburst. Your assumption was correct. It simply struck me as odd, reckless, perhaps."

The librarian too recovered his poise and smiled. "You're quite right, Don Luis. I was actually making a point that I thought would interest you. My spies described you as 'worldly and broad-minded.' Since Greco is a scholar who's seriously thinking of Spain as his final resting place, it seemed an appropriate observation."

"Scholar," said Domenikos, "seems not quite the right term, Fulvio. The scholar gives his whole life to learning. I think of myself as a dedicated amateur in all but art."

Castilla shrugged. "I think the dedicated amateur just as important as the true scholar. The key is the degree of dedication, isn't it?"

The painter found the question just. "It would be difficult for me to think anything else."

"You're too modest, maestro. Look at Leonardo, at Michelangelo. How much poorer the world would be without their knowledge, not only of art but of other matters. And we must suppose they gained at least a part of this knowledge from books. If you come to Spain with your library, you'll have no trouble, certainly not in Toledo."

Chacón was scandalized. "Then the Inquisition has lost its true meaning. If it can be manipulated to serve personal ends—"

"Not at all, Don Pedro. In Toledo, at any rate, the Inquisition has *found* its true meaning. We've learned how to distinguish between the man who seeks truth and the man whose mind is depraved. I can scarcely think that manipulation."

Orsini was delighted by this exchange. "Who makes these extraordinarily fine distinctions?"

Before Castilla could reply, a cold-voiced Chacón interrupted. "I suspect it would be Don Luis' brother, the dean of Toledo."

"Ah?" said the librarian softly, his eyes bright with pleasure. "Then Toledo is just like Rome. Connections are more important than virtue."

Over the months that followed, Domenikos saw much of Castilla. Acquaintance rapidly developed into friendship. The Spaniard, whose duties were not arduous, spent many hours with the painter. Once he became a familiar of his house, he was not at all disturbed by its "eccentric but efficient domestic arrangements." Francesco, whose opinion of the clergy had been admirably summarized in his first interview with his master, quickly made an exception of Don Luis. "If there had been a priest like you in my village, father, I'd still be going to mass." The ripening Catarina, not so skeptical as her brother, found the frequent presence of a cleric a fair omen for the unborn child.

As Castilla and Domenikos came to know each other better, it was clear that for all that they were worldly, in the sense that they had known life and accepted it as they found it, they were fundamentally aescetic, with little affection of superfluous luxury and none at all for conspicuous display. They were comparably and exceptionally spiritual.

Though Castilla confessed himself no authority on art, he described his brother Diego as a reputable expert. As dean of the chapter in their native Toledo, the elder Castilla was, moreover, a figure who could assure the artist a splendid flow of commissions were he to settle there.

The friends discussed this possibility on many occasions. Domenikos resisted the strong temptation to commit himself definitely to a long stay in Castilla's city only because, as he explained, he had yet to have a reply from Philip II, who had been importuned by all the proponents of the artist. Indeed, only the Spanish ambassador had proved unresponsive, evincing what Don Luis agreed was "an evasive warmth."

It was, their community of spirit aside, undoubtedly their love of literature that drew the two men most strongly together. Unlike Orsini, Castilla was discursive, exploratory. The printed word provided the basis from which lengthy discussions could spring.

If Spain had required a further advocate, no more convincing one could have been discovered. To Spain Domenikos would certainly proceed, and though the delay imposed by Catarina's condition was an inconvenience, Castilla's prolonged stay in Rome made it easily bearable.

The baby was born in October, a splendid jet-eyed girl whom they called Francesca, to the pleasure of her youthful uncle. Unlike the painter's poor Maria, Catarina was a mother who required no assistance. As she had accepted pregnancy without qualm, she assumed maternity with a grace that profoundly moved him. She was disappointed for him that she had not produced a son. "But wait, *caro*, Francesca will be useful to you, and I'll give you a son next time."

In spite of his impatience to leave Rome, Domenikos found life's sweetness mollifying. His revenues from paintings, while less than astronomical, exceeded his expenditures. And the work itself, if uninspiring, was sufficiently varied to prevent him from becoming utterly indifferent. With Francesco an increasing aid, he even found time occasionally to experiment, to make tempera studies of pictures he hoped one day to paint on a larger scale, and to sketch in detail such masterpieces as the Laocöon group in the Campidoglio and Michelangelo's wonders in the Sistine and Pauline chapels.

The infant Francesca was as robust a specimen as her mother and passed into her second year without once having given her parents the slightest cause for alarm. Preparations for departure were begun as 1574 drew to a close. Since no word had been received from King Philip, Domenikos had agreed, with no reluctance whatever, to settle at least for a time in Toledo, where, Castilla's brother had written enthusiastically, "you will find yourself the most welcome of men."

Though further commissions were declined, a number remained to be completed. Travel arrangements for a household now surprisingly encumbered with possessions (Catarina had a childish love of objects) were not easily made. Clearly, the little family would not be on its way before the summer. To leave sooner would invite complications from the elements, especially since the journey would take longer than would ordinarily be the case; Domenikos would have to settle his financial affairs in Venice and decide which of his effects there would accompany them to Spain.

"Plague!"

The sound of this word cried out by shrouded figures from street to street had for centuries evoked panic throughout every city of western Europe. During the fourteenth-century epoch of the Black Death, bubonic and pneumonic plague had carried off something like twenty-five million souls, about a quarter of the Continent's population. A pandemic of such magnitude had never recurred, but minor epidemics were frequent and widespread. One never knew at the outset how long or how virulent the pestilence would prove.

The cause and nature of the disease were unknown. Treatment was nonexistent, survival all but unheard of. The afflicted were instantly hustled into the appalling isolation of what were virtually charnel houses, almost surely to perish in agony and squalor. No one, however high-born, was spared this fate. The house believed to harbor a victim of the plague was usually set afire.

The plague struck Rome in the spring of 1575, barely a month before Domenikos and his little household were to leave. The city shriveled. The streets, usually noisy with people and vehicles, were all but emptied. Even the cats and dogs retreated, as if they too were frightened by the rats that died in their thousands in gutters glutted with ordure. A few scattered men and women, remembering hopefully the legend of an earlier Pope Gregory whose vision foretold the ending of another plague, gathered on the banks of the Tiber, before the Castel Sant'Angelo, looking for a second sign from God that relief was at hand.

Only the churches continued to attract people in any numbers. Only prayer could prevail against this pestilence. Conversations in public were brief and curt. Friends exchanged few words, their faces anxious. They looked at one another and wondered, "Are you next?

Am I next? Shall we ever see each other again?" Like the bubos that typified the disease itself, the city was in a state of suppuration, rotting, festering, dying—helpless and terrorized.

Domenikos couldn't share the anxiety or craven fear that beset most Romans. But, as Orsini complained, he accepted the possibility of death as easily as he did the reality of life. Fear proved nothing. Yet if he was unsympathetic, he was made intensely aware of conditions, for neither Catarina nor Francesco would leave the house. It was the painter who had to do the marketing.

That so many people should give themselves up to a despair so uncontrolled dismayed and oppressed him. The panic of those beneath his roof imposed on him a pressure that was almost palpable.

Happily, there was little painting still to be done, but even this became impossible. With curtains drawn against the incongruously brilliant sunlight, the painter sat brooding alone for long hours in his studio. The plans so carefully made were suddenly made meaningless. At any moment, he or Catarina or Francesco or the baby might catch the dreaded fever and be littered away to expire ignominiously in some putrefying dungeon.

Mostly, in this gloom, Domenikos thought of the past. He recalled with a shiver Don Giulio Clovio's lurid account of his experiences in the wake of the sack of Rome in 1527, when the plague had last visited the city. The tale had seemed improbable. But as the creaking tumbrils rolled past his window, each sound reminded him that another human burden was being transported to a living grave.

It would have been too coincidental that such a moment be interrupted by the arrival of Clovio himself. The appearance of Castilla would have been more welcome. That no one came was not surprising. The painter, reproaching himself for his indolence, had to be contented with a contemplation of emptiness, a void at this moment not even clarified by what he had recently described to his Spanish friend as the light by which he conceived the paintings he would one day make, the light within.

The torpor to which he had submitted was cruelly shattered. First Francesca and then Catarina contracted the plague. Domenikos refused to believe it, would not summon the ponderous cart that would take them from his house. It was not panic that he felt. It was, initially, anguish. And in the crisis of his indecision, a frightened Francesco disclosed his competence.

"There's nothing to be done, master. They have to be taken away."

Numbed, the artist could barely nod his assent. When the masked attendants knocked and entered, marching with measured resoluteness up the stone staircase to present themselves at the door of the bedchamber he and Catarina had shared during their happy years together, he couldn't bring himself to help them bear the swollen bodies out of his house.

When they were gone, Francesco returned to find the painter standing in the center of the room, sobbing.

The youth touched his arm. "Let me give you wine, master."

Domenikos made no sign, but turned and descended the stairs. In the dining room, he seated himself mutely at his customary place and watched as Francesco filled his goblet from a flagon and set it down on the table.

"Drink with me," he muttered, and waited till the second goblet was filled before raising his own. "What are we to drink to, Francesco? Is there anything?"

"The safety of the souls that have left us, master."

The painter slowly shook his head. "Never have there been two purer souls."

"That's true. But Catarina would like a final glass raised in her name." He raised his goblet, but drank from it only when Domenikos has taken a sip of his own. "We must go away soon, master."

The artist nodded. Then, without warning he hurled the wine-filled goblet against the distant wall. "God hates me," he roared. "And I hate God."

He watched with grim pleasure as magenta streaks of wine spread slowly down the pristine whiteness of the wall.

PART IV:

Toledo (1575–1589)

Nineteen

THE journey to Venice was without incident. When Domenikos and Francesco reached the Serenissima, the painter accepted with mixed feelings his father-in-law's invitation to be his guest. Francesco was also offered accommodation, though with the servants. This condition annoyed Domenikos, and he was on the point of disputing it with his host when Francesco intervened. "Don't worry about me, master. It's comfortable, and I'll have plenty to eat and drink."

The bitterness of his last days in Rome had been somewhat dissipated in travel with the resilient youth. It would have been difficult to remain wholly morose in the presence of the gay Francesco, who, as he himself had repeatedly pointed out, had suffered an almost equal loss. "God's will," he would say. "Nothing to do but go on."

Yet Domenikos wouldn't have described his mood, when they reached Venice, as bouyant. Nor did he think his conversation with Mario would cheer him. They talked after dinner, the evening following his arrival. The two men sat in the same salon, on the same couch, where he had met Maria eight years before. This memory caused the artist to shiver with hopeless sorrow. So many sad events had occurred, but so little of meaning had happened; everyone involved had been changed, been maimed or killed by life, yet conditions were substantially as they had been. In the most depressing way, he felt himself right back where he had started. Spain alone loomed brightly.

"Tell me of Maria. Is there any change?"

His father-in-law clasped his fine small hands over a knee

and shook his head. "And barring a miracle, Greco, there'll not be any."

Domenikos could hardly be surprised, except that the pain this response evoked surprised him. After so long, he wondered that he could still feel the separation so deeply.

"But she's comfortable. She's not at all violent, so there's no need to keep her chained."

"Thank God for that, at least."

"Why do you go to Spain?"

The painter explained. Mario listened carefully, his small eyes holding his son-in-law's as if he placed more confidence in facial expressions than in words. When Domenikos concluded, he nodded briskly.

"Then, if you plan so permanent a move, you'll want your things to go with you, yours and Maria's too of course. They belong with you."

"I'll take only the things you want me to have, Mario."

"I'd rather you took everything. We've not used your apartments since you left. It even pains me to think of it. I can't bear to open the door." The man's eyes were moist.

"I understand." Domenikos laid a hand on his shoulder. "I'll ask Francesco to make arrangements for the packing. You need do nothing about it."

"I'd be grateful for that, Greco."

"But I'll take none of Maria's gold, Mario. Use it to keep her comfortable, and when she dies, see that it goes to the nuns who are taking care of her."

"That's good of you."

"I could hardly do less."

"You're staying long?"

"Only as long as I must. We have to arrange transport to Genoa over land, and from there to Barcelona by sea. These things take time."

"You'll see Tiziano tomorrow?"

"I'll certainly try."

Mario sighed. "You'll find he's aged a good deal, but he's no milder."

"It's impossible to imagine Titian mild."

Older and frailer the master surely was, but as Mario had said, he had lost little of his vigor. Orazio had changed more dramatically. He seemed to have become even gentler than before, more inconsequential, his identity as a man quite as lost now in his father's as his art had always been. His greeting was warm and tearful.

"You're welcome, Greco. We've missed you."

Domenikos released himself from Orazio's embrace and bent over to kiss the seated master on both cheeks. "I've thought of you both, much more often than I've written you."

"So Rome didn't suit you." Titian seemed pleased.

"It was even worse than that." He described the tragedy of Catarina and their daughter.

Orazio handed him a glass of wine. "You've had more than your share of pain, my friend. You accept it gracefully."

Domenikos grimaced. "You'd not think so if you'd seen me the night they were taken away." He gave a vivid account of his violent outburst on that occasion. " 'I hate God.' That's what I said. I'm ashamed of myself."

Titian was unimpressed. "Everyone thinks himself singled out for God's anger at one time or another. Who is God that we shouldn't reciprocate in kind?"

The master's son shook his head in pleased deprecation of the old man's blasphemy. "Utterly unreconstructed, as you can see."

The old man snorted. "Orazio seriously thinks it possible to reform me at ninety-eight. Don't worry. I'll die in a state of grace, but I'll go to hell all the same. The company will be more entertaining there than in heaven if the righteous are all as dull as the ones I know."

Domenikos grinned. "Still talking about death, master?"

"Why not? It doesn't get farther away, you know." He paused and became wistful, a mood his pupil had rarely noted in him. "But I *would* like to see my hundredth birthday."

Orazio laughed. "But you don't even know when it is."

Titian brightened. "Perhaps I'm a hundred already. That would be ironic."

"Well, master, I hope you live as long as you're comfortable—"

"And able to work, Greco. That's all that matters to me. It's all that should matter to any artist." He changed the subject. "Did you learn anything in Rome?"

"As a painter or as a man?"

"Both, but as a painter, first. Tell me that."

"That I was making no progress. That I can't paint any longer the kind of picture I *have* been making. That the Italian Jesuits only patronize Italian painters. . . ."

"Well, it's good at least to know what you can't do. It's a first step. What *can* you paint?"

"I'm not sure yet. I'm still thinking about it." Before the old man could interrupt, Domenikos continued with a chuckle. "I know. I know. I shouldn't be thinking. As a matter of fact, that wasn't the word I meant. I've been experimenting, sketching, making studies."

"You'll show them to me?"

"I hoped you'd ask."

"And what did you learn as a man, Greco?"

"That's harder to say, master. I've learned how to get along in the world. I made friends, real friends."

"A large number?"

Domenikos shrugged. "Two, a Roman and a Spaniard."

"You don't exaggerate."

"Two is more than none, master. I don't find it easy to be intimate. The only pain I felt in leaving Rome was that I had to say farewell to Orsini."

"Well," said Titian, "*that* never grows easier. I'm pleased that you've grown up a bit, Greco. What are you now, thirty-four? It's about time."

"I've realized that."

"By the time *you're* ninety-eight, you'll realize that everything I've ever said to you was true."

Orazio, standing behind his father's chair, was delighted. "You see, Greco? The old devil hasn't changed."

Domenikos agreed. "But monuments aren't supposed to change."

"No," the old man growled. "They're supposed to stay in one place and catch pigeon droppings."

"And Spain," said the son. "You've heard nothing from the King?"

"No."

Titian was angered. "Nor have I. Who do these kings think they are? But you're not going so far on pure speculation."

Domenikos explained his friendship with Castilla and his assurances of commissions in Toledo. "It sounds ideal to me, except for the climate. Luis says it's very hard."

The master grunted. "Nothing is ideal. The world always catches up with you, wherever you are. You should know that better than most."

The visitor folded his arms before him and stared at Titian with amusement. "Whatever made you think I was trying to run away from the world?"

"Your letters. You wrote of tranquillity and peace and serenity. If you're not seeking escape, what then?"

"A fair chance to compete. It was hopeless in Rome. And after all, master, it was you who told me that Spain is where the power is, and where the power is, you said, the commission must be also."

The old man opened wide his eyes. "Did I say that? What an intelligent, perceptive old gentleman I am. And these commissions you're promised, are they rich ones?"

"I don't know. But they'll be an improvement on anything I was offered in Rome."

"I have only one reservation about Toledo, Greco. It has to do with the Church. After all, you've had difficulties with two popes already, and now you propose to move to the heart of the Spanish Inquisition. What a fire-eater."

Domenikos laughed. "I've been told that it's always calm in the center of a storm."

"I hope you're right."

Arrangements for the journey to Spain were difficult to negotiate, requiring a period of many more months than Domenikos anticipated. He used this time to paint, happily accepting Titian's suggestion that he make use of his studio with the same freedom he had enjoyed as the master's pupil. The old man expressed no rapture, however, over the painter's new lines of approach to his art. "The technique is fine, Greco, but the rest I don't like. It's more Tintoretto than me. Too dramatic for my taste. But tastes change. You'll arrive. You'll arrive."

He made occasional visits to his aunt and uncle. Anastos had virtually assumed control of the family business, leaving Manusos free to advance his political career, an obsession that appeared no more likely of realization today than sixteen years before. Fortunately, the uncle was blind to the facts and deaf to Marica's persistent denigration of his efforts. Word of the painter's brother continued to be vague.

In the late spring of 1576, the plague came to Venice. Panic reigned here as it had done in Rome. Travel to and from the city was cut off. It might as well have been besieged, and this despite the fact that the epidemic, as it developed, seemed milder than Rome's. Conditions at the end of June were unchanged. Therefore, Titian could not take his customary holiday at Vincenza. He expressed no disappointment over this. "I feel safer in Venice, somehow, with my things and all my friends."

His judgment was mistaken. In the final week of August, he was struck down. He died on the twenty-seventh.

As soon as he heard the news, Domenikos, beyond tears in his grief, hurried to the great house in the Biri Grande. He found Orazio in the master's studio, standing by his father's chair, bewildered.

"I believed he'd never die. Not even when I knew it was plague did I believe it. God knows, there were times enough when I wished him dead. He suffocated me. But working with him, in spite of everything, was enough. And he *was* my father."

"And mine too," said Domenikos softly.

Plague or no, Titian's funeral was celebrated on a scale to be compared in grandeur only with Michelangelo's a dozen years before. Domenikos knew that Venice saw no alternative to such a ceremony. He recalled the master's prediction: there would be great public displays of grief, but in their hearts men like Bassano and Tintoretto and Veronese would hold intimate celebrations of joy. The field was now theirs.

An impressive requiem mass was offered in the splendid church of the Frari, where Titian's remains were to be interred. Afterward, Orazio, Domenikos, and Francesco slipped away to the quiet, familiar church of San Canciano to offer their private prayers for the master's soul and for their own.

Orazio succumbed to the plague only a few weeks later. By then, Domenikos had departed; it was a long time before he heard the news.

A fortnight after Titian's funeral, the painter and Francesco left for Genoa, where they boarded a ship bound for Barcelona. Throughout the long journey, Domenikos tutored his assistant in the Spanish he had himself acquired in Rome. Though scarcely fluent by the time of their arrival in Spain, the youth believed himself capable at least of negotiating elementary but essential transactions.

It was the nights that proved difficult. For as he lay in his hammock, Domenikos was aware less of the hope he cherished than of the sense of loneliness and loss he suffered. Not since the time of his first departure from Venice had he felt constrictions of the chest, the shortness of breath, the physical pain of anxiety. Maria, Catarina, Titian. Their names and faces filled his anguished sleep.

Twenty

The vegetation and configuration of the land impressed Domenikos as he and Francesco made the slow, difficult journey from Barcelona to Madrid. More blasted by the elements than either Italy or Crete, the landscape had a quality of despair and desolation that cried out a grim, bitter welcome. Francesco responded differently. "There's a madness even in being born in a country like this."

Traveling on roads that had been laid down fifteen centuries before by the conquering Romans, Domenikos sought an explanation for his feeling of dark joy. The blighted soil, the sparse, dry vegetation, the empty stream beds gouged from the sullen hillsides seemed uniquely consonant with his nature and temperament, implicit of events as black as had been his own most recent life. The inhabitants they encountered could only belong to the grudging earth from which they scratched their livelihood—creatures of sadness, anger, anxiety, suspicion; creatures too, he felt, of ecstasy and rapture. There was a profound spirituality in the sun-coarsened faces of the black-clothed Spaniards who silently stared at them as they passed, responding politely and timidly to their requests for direction.

It was a hard land, dour and bleak, yet not without a dull, subtle coloration. It was a land of intense shadows, illuminated by visions, by fervor, by faith, by agony and death, Domenikos couldn't yet know these things of Spain, but he felt them, and believed completely in his intuitions. He was certain that at last he had found his home.

The Spain of Philip II was paradoxical. It should have been Europe's richest nation. Imports of gold and silver from the New World should have swelled the coffers of the crown to overflowing. But it wasn't so. Expenditures were immense on foreign wars, on the construction of merchant and naval fleets, on the subjugation of Moriscos in the south. Added to these were the costs of such ostentations as the Escorial and the buildings of Madrid, the newly designated capital. There was a severe inflation which, combined with every-increasing taxes, had brought the country virtually to her knees. In 1576, a large portion of Spain's foreign debt was canceled; she was practically bankrupt.

There were other anomalies. Although considered Europe's most piously Catholic country, Spain had been struggling for nearly a century to rid herself of heresy and nonbelief.

The Moors had inhabited Spain for nine centuries. They had been offered a choice of expulsion or conversion to the Catholic faith. Most had chosen the latter alternative but had in fact remained Moslems, not always because they willed it so. Effective conversion demanded knowledgeable missionaries, familiar with the dialect, who could make the faith intelligible. Few could be found. Thus it was left to the army to convert by force, the Inquisition by terror, a campaign to which most of its energies were devoted.

There was also the Jewish question. Offered the same choice as the Moors, however, the Jews had mostly opted for exile, taking with them their gold and, more significantly, their knowledge of commerce and banking. At a single stroke, Ferdinand and Isabella, hailed as Spain's saviors, founders of the new nation, had deprived the country of the backbone of her middle class.

In pockets throughout the country, and especially in Valencia, there were hardly clusters of Protestants. Near Granada, a sect subscribing to the most heretical aberration of Christianity, Manichaeism, had so far eluded complete suppression.

The Inquisition's persecution of Moriscos and Marranos (converted Moors and Jews) was at least as much political as religious in motivation. The role of the Holy Office was that of unifying force. Accusations were couched in religious terms, but the cause was patent: opposition to the power of the crown was to be eliminated.

Philip's problems weren't confined to Spain. He was quarreling with Portugal. The Reformation had taken a strong grip on the Low Countries and it was evident that external pressure would fail to impose a viable Spanish, and therefore Catholic, rule. In France, the wars of religion represented a constant menace to Spain's northern provinces, a threat aggravated by the possibility that the Protestant Henri de Navarre would accede to the French throne. Relations with Britain were unfriendly. Elizabeth's ships marauded Spanish merchantmen that carried cargoes of treasure from the New World. Her funds aided the Huguenots in France, the rebels in the Low Countries.

The King, administering his manifold responsibilities from the bleak fastnesses of the Escorial, found his authority virtually unquestioned. He controlled the Church through bishops he himself appointed. He could govern his towns through the Cortés, whose membership he supervised and whose powers he sharply limited.

Philip II was no less paradoxical than the land he ruled. Monarch for twenty years, he was both brilliant and obtuse—perceptive of what must be done, ignorant of the way of doing it. He was three times widowed, married now to Anne of Austria. An affectionate father, he had nevertheless countenanced the imprisonment and execution of his son Don Carlos. An ardent Catholic, he didn't hesitate to use the Church as an instrument of purely secular policy, though he was not the only king to do that. He recognized the need for financial stability, yet he succeeded in bankrupting Spain on three occasions. Nor could he doubt that each of these disasters was his own handiwork. The country displayed appalling extremes of poverty and wealth; peasant, merchant, and tradesman alone were subject to national taxation; clergyman and noble were exempt. It was hardly surprising, therefore, that one-fourth of Spain's adult population had some occupational connection with the Church.

Geographically, too, Spain offered dramatic extremes. Much of it was mountainous, the soil poor and arid, governed by a climate violent in its swings from intense cold to scorching, rainless heat. Few regions were significantly arable, yet so fertile were these that their harvests provided more or less adequately for the country's needs.

If the windswept bleakness of the Spanish landscape satisfied some deep longing in Domenikos' soul, the modesty of Madrid (as a great nation's capital) was a disappointment. Since Philip's decision, more than a decade earlier, to transfer the official seat of power from Toledo, little of importance had been done to transform bucolic Madrid into a city worthy of the monarchy. Only the Alcázar, recently completed, bore witness to Philip's grandeur. Other construction was under way, but obviously much time would elapse before Madrid could be favorably compared even with the old Phoenician city of Barcelona. Nor was there evidence of urgency. The King spent little time in Madrid. In 1573, the royal family had moved into the newly completed palace portion of the Escorial. Where the King dwelled, there too resided the court.

Domenikos and Francesco spent only one night in Madrid. On a morning in early February, 1577, they set out on the final stage of their protracted journey, a short and simple passage, with a night's pause midway at Illescas, the traditional stopping place en route to

Toledo, where there was a splendid royal hostelry. By starting the next morning at the earliest daylight hour, they reached the outskirts of Toledo before sunset.

Crowning the summit of a broad butte which was all but encircled by the river Tajo, the walled and ramparted city seemed suspended in the cold, clear air. Its high bluffs descended precipitously to the murky, swift-moving stream, its colors brown, beige, and gold. Two features of the city's profile stood out dramatically among the more modest buildings to be seen—the massive Alcázar with towers at each of its four corners, and the cathedral whose single high-Gothic spire reached above all else toward the fast-darkening sky of late afternoon.

Passing through the Puerta Nueva de Bisagra, they could see the remains of an older portal which was a vestige of Toledo's Moorish fortifications. Always moving upward, they traversed the *Mudéjar* Puerta del Sol and then mounted the steep, narrow, dusty alleys to the principal square of the city, the Zocodover.

The word "forbidding" crossed the painter's mind as he traversed the last few hundred yards. As elsewhere in the Spain he had seen so far, everyone was in black, but here the impression given by pedestrians was different; so many were of the Church—priests, nuns, monks, clerks. Churches, monasteries, convents, seminaries, and hospitals abounded in Toledo. This was doubtless the source of its tranquillity that Castilla had extolled. It wasn't merely tranquil; it was quiet, almost silent. It was the silence, so unexpected in a city, that made it seem forbidding, but not inhospitable. As he had responded instinctively to the Spanish land, so now did he feel the same about Toledo. Its compactness, its hardness of aspect, its frigidity, its austerity, its difference from all he knew, reached out to Domenikos and took possession of him. At weary last, he stood with Francesco in the small, triangular Zocodover. "We're home," he announced triumphantly. Francesco shivered, but said nothing.

A legend held that Toledo was the earth's first city, founded by Father Adam himself. Another had it established by the descendants of Noah. It was certain that Toledo existed before the Roman conquest of the second Christian century. Two hundred years later, the Visigoths made it the capital of their Spanish domain. So it remained until the Moorish invasion of the eighth century, when it became a dependency of the great caliphate of Córdoba.

Toledo remained in Moslem hands until 1085 when the Castilian king Alonso VI recaptured it for Christianity, with the aid of El Cid.

Thereafter for nearly five hundred years, the city figured largely in the development of Catholic Spain, becoming its capital and seat of its principal cardinal. The flamboyant white church and monastery of San Juan de los Reyes were constructed by Ferdinand and Isabella to serve as their final resting place, the royal family's Pantheon.

The onset of Toledo's decline was signaled nearly a half-century before Domenikos' arrival when it became a center of a revolt against Charles V. The rebels were defeated, the city's reputation besmirched. Soon after his accession, Philip II decreed Madrid as capital, primarily because he deplored the proximity of the Spanish Primate.

From the time of this pronouncement in 1560, decline became fall. The Church, its attendant offices, and its university remained. In 1577, Toledo still flourished as a center of manufacture, learning, and religion, Spain's architectural treasure house, but no longer the heart of the nation's political life.

Moorish influences in art and architecture were everywhere to be noted. Even after their defeat, the Moors continued to make their impression on later works, a style eventually called *mudéjar*. The master builders of France also left their mark, especially in the fifteenth-century churches of the city. Frenchness had been imbued with a distinctly Spanish flavor in the building of the great cathedral, a voluted and convoluted, intricate, passionate style that became known as plateresque.

For centuries the city had been renowned for its high-quality silks and woolens. And since the time of the Romans the swords and later the armor of Toledo had been celebrated. Yet Toledo's population was predominantly clerical, and the place retained in large degree its character of holy city, the divine fortress.

The hot Christian spirits of Teresa of Ávila and Juan de la Cruz well typified the city they so often visited. In their complex natures, they combined immense zeal, passion for penitent reform, and pure devotion to God with a superb ability to organize. They were selfless, a condition the established Church regarded with considerable apprehension. As both of these eventual saints learned, their ideas were frequently thought very nearly heretical. It was a measure of the Spanish Holy Office's tolerance of eccentrics that Teresa of Ávila and Juan de la Cruz were more often heckled than cruelly persecuted.

Toledo was worldly as well as holy, partly because of its ancient university, partly because, since the time of the Crusades, the city had been the focus of systematic and effective efforts to ransom captives held at first by the Infidels and now by the Ottomans, a work primarily in the hands of the Trinitarian order. Toledo was the object of tragic pilgrimage; relatives of those imprisoned trekked thousands of miles to elicit aid and/or funds for their loved ones' release. Aid was not confined to adherents of the Church of Rome; many members of the Eastern Orthodox faith came to Toledo for assistance, some of them Greek.

Moriscos were numerous in the city. Moreover, for those whose Catholicism was based on the tradition established during the Moorish occupation, no less than six chapels of the cathedral offered masses in the Mozarabic rite.

Toledo was thus the strangest of conglomerates, committed to the suppression of heresy while tolerant of deviations within the framework of the accepted faith. It was, as Luis de Castilla had assured the painter, a very sophisticated city.

Diego de Castilla occupied quarters in the Palacio Arzobispal in the center of Toledo, opposite the cathedral. It wasn't difficult, the morning after his arrival, for Domenikos to find his way to the Plaza del Ayuntamiento where the Archbishop's Palace stood. But he was amused to find that in his practice of the Spanish tongue he had overlooked much vocabulary that would have served him well in his search for Castilla's apartments in the vast building. Guards and minor clerics whom he consulted appeared to comprehend but dimly his requests for directions.

At last, however, he was ushered into the presence of an elegant cleric, second in importance here only to the Cardinal. The elder Castilla was in his sixties, though he carried his age with ease. Understandably, since they were born of different mothers, he bore little resemblance to his brother. Don Diego was shorter and very thin. He shared with Luis the fine black eyes, the ready, intelligent smile, and a composure that left no doubt of his position and authority.

The room was bare, decorated with two large, indifferently painted pictures and, behind the table at which the dean sat, a modest crucifix. As the painter entered, Don Diego rose nimbly and moved to greet him.

"Do you speak Spanish, maestro?"

"Not well, Don Diego," Domenikos replied.

"Then let's speak Italian."

"It would be easier for me," the artist replied gratefully.

Castilla invited his visitor to take a chair and for some minutes they chatted casually of the long journey from Venice, of Titian's death, of Rome, of Domenikos' first impressions of Spain, of Madrid, of Toledo. The dean impressed the painter with his elaborate politeness and graciousness. Yet there was, he thought, no question of this man becoming his intimate. The difference in age was a factor, but more important was Castilla's reserve, far greater, he judged, than even his own. Don Diego would be his patron, his ally, his Toledan Cardinal Farnese.

"I've detained you too long, maestro," the cleric said at last. "You'll be anxious to see Luis."

"He's in Toledo?"

"You're very fortunate, for you probably don't know that since you last saw him he's been made dean of Cuenca."

"I'm delighted for him, Don Diego, though disappointed for myself since it means I'll see less of him."

"Not that much less." He smiled benignly. "I've no doubt that he'll find reason to visit Toledo quite often, as today, for example, though he's here on an unhappy mission. We're gathering to consider the position we must take in the matter of a priest called Don Juan de la Cruz. He's been creating difficulties among the Barefoot Carmelites."

"I'm afraid I'm not familiar with the topic."

"In Spain, we talk of nothing else, it seems." He raised his gray brows and thoughtfully stroked his short, pointed beard. "It's most distasteful, really. Don Juan is a good, kindly Christian, but a little too enthusiastic. He gets carried away and takes matters in his own hands. We've had to punish him before."

Domenikos tried to imagine what sort of offense a kindly Christian could commit that would involve him with the Inquisition. "Is he a Savonarola, Don Diego?"

The dean tipped his head back slightly and laughed. "Fortunately not. Don Juan isn't violent. As a matter of fact, he's said to be an excellent poet. In Toledo, we have a great appreciation of all the arts."

"So Luis has told me."

"That's why you're so welcome. We need fine artists."

Domenikos grinned. "Not, I trust, so you can punish them."

"Only when they're naughty, maestro."

"I consider myself warned."

The dean stood up and took the painter's arm. "Come. Let me take you to Luis."

They walked through corridors crowded with priests and monks of every order until they reached the great tribunal hall of the palace. Here Domenikos immediately made out the figure of his friend, who was in conversation with several richly gowned dignitaries, one of whom was the Archbishop himself. As they entered, Luis turned and hastened toward him.

"Greco," he exclaimed, warmly embracing the painter. "I was beginning to despair of you."

"You didn't receive my letters?"

"But the last, telling of Titian, made me apprehensive. I thought the plague might have cut you down too."

"Well, Francesco and I survived, thank God. And you survived. You're pleased with Cuenca? Don Diego just told me of your post."

The younger Castilla shrugged. "It's not Toledo, but the demands are light."

Domenikos inclined his head toward the dais of the great room. "Am I taking you from something important?"

"It's important, but I'm rather relieved to have an excuse for not taking part. It's a very sorry business."

"Don Diego told me something about it."

The dean of Toledo broke in. "If you mean to leave, Luis, you'd better go now." He turned to the painter. "We shall see much of each other, Maestro El Greco." He extended a willowy hand.

The sound of the "El" in place of the Italian "Il" surprised Domenikos. He nodded. "I look forward to that, Don Diego."

Luis de Castilla put a hand in the small of his friend's back and propelled him into the corridor.

They emerged from the palace into the cold Plaza del Ayuntamiento, drawing their cloaks more closely about them in defense against the sharp north wind blowing down, unmolested by terrain, from the Sierra de Guadarama which separated New from Old Castile.

Castilla turned his cowled head to the painter and laughed. "I told you the climate was vile."

"If this is typical, you were right."

"There might be snow. You shouldn't complain yet."

Domenikos responded with a shudder. They rounded a corner of the plaza and began to follow what seemed an interminable series of winding, narrow alleys. Most of the buildings were of brick, vaguely reminiscent of the Venetian style. They arrived in a small square and stood before a church under construction.

"Shall we go in?" Luis inquired.

"To escape the cold?"

"I think you'll find it has another appeal too."

Despite the scaffolding, it was possible to make out the design of the interior, which was, to Domenikos, gratifying in its simplicity, with a transept crossing whose small, still-unfinished dome was supported by a plainly molded cornice and Ionic pilasters. The barrel vaulting of the apse was broken by groins that gave access to semicircular windows. It was here that Castilla paused.

"You like it, Greco?"

"It should be handsome when it's finished. But what's its special appeal?"

"For one thing, it has an interesting story. Until a couple of years ago, there was another church here. This one is built with funds left by Doña María da Silva." Luis hesitated. "The name means nothing to you, I know. She was a lady-in-waiting to the empress Isabella, Carlos V's wife. When Doña María's husband died, she retired to a convent here and spent the last forty years of her life with the nuns. She left her whole estate for the building of a new church. It's called Santo Domingo, which I thought might amuse you, since Domingo is the Spanish for your name."

"*That* much Spanish I know."

"Am I boring you?"

"I assume this story has a point."

"I'm just coming to the interesting part. My esteemed brother is executor of her estate. But while Doña María was alive, she and Diego asked Nicolás de Vergara, the cathedral's master of work, to make plans for the new church. She died before they were done and Diego was unhappy with them." Castilla laughed. "Diego takes his responsibilities very seriously."

"Is that unadmirable?"

"It can be exasperating."

"So can you, when you tell a story."

"I'll be brief. Diego secured the services of Juan de Herrera, who designed the Escorial. Herrera made the new plans."

"It's a good piece of work. But what about the altarpieces? Who's doing those?"

Castilla smiled and looked abruptly away to prevent Domenikos from seeing him laugh. "Originally," he began, "the plans were made by Hernando de Ávila. But when I returned from Rome, Diego showed them to me and I told him I was sure you could do a much better design." He paused. "That's the end of the story. If you're interested, I'm sure Diego will give you the commission."

Domenikos was incredulous. "You're not serious."

"Can you think I'd joke about something like this?"

"No."

"Well, then?"

"But what about the other man, Hernando?"

"What about him? Diego paid him for his drawings. That's the end of it."

The painter sighed deeply. "I'm shattered."

Castilla became brisk. "Well, that's settled. You and Diego can work out the details. And don't worry. There's no great rush. As you can see, it will be at least two years before the church is finished. We don't hurry things in Toledo. Is two years enough time?"

"It depends on how ambitious a plan Don Diego has in mind."

"As I understand it, you're to design the whole of the main altar and two side altars—everything: frames, paintings, and sculptures."

Domenikos felt like dancing in his elation. "But are you sure I'm your man, Luis? My paintings, of course, you've seen. But all you know of my sculpture are the little figures I had in Rome. They're just studies, after all. And my architecture? Nothing."

"I saw your sketches."

"What confidence."

"You think it misplaced?"

"Not at all."

"I agree. This seems an ideal commission. It should establish you here in three fields at once."

For a long moment, the painter stared at the great space of the apse that he must fill, then more briefly at the spots on either side of the crossing where the smaller altars would be placed. His eyes returned to his friend, and he smiled. "Thank you, Luis."

"Thank Diego." Castilla took Domenikos' arm. "Let's find Francesco and see what we can do about your living quarters."

Twenty-One

Prior to the departure of the court in 1560, Toledo had been over-crowded. Teresa of Ávila had thought it nearly miraculous to find housing for her nuns. Today, however, accommodations were plentiful. Guided by a clerk of Luis de Castilla's entourage, Domenikos and Francesco spent the next days tramping from house to house and orienting themselves to the city's chaotic medieval plan. The artist chose spacious quarters in a narrow street not far from the parish church of Santo Tomé, near the west wall. As sparsely furnished as his house in Rome, these apartments provided sufficient space for living and for work, though for neither on a grand scale.

Daily, Domenikos was more grateful for Francesco's presence. He saw to the unpacking of chests. He did the rudimentary marketing, bargaining with local merchants in his broken Spanish, immeasurably aided by violent gestures and grotesque expressions that delighted the normally dour tradesmen. He located an apothecary who could supply oils and pigments and discovered sources for canvas and wood for stretchers. He obtained the services of two domestics perhaps twice his young age, whom he supervised as if the reverse were true. Thus was his master free to plan for the Santo Domingo commission.

In the week that followed, Domenikos had several discussions with Don Diego. He was given a free hand in designing framework, sculptures, and painting. By comparison with anything he had previously attempted, the amount of work involved here was enormous. Confident that he could accomplish the paintings without difficulty, he first concentrated on sketches of the framework and sculpture. He sought an elegance that would contrast with the white austerity of the apse. He drew his inspiration from similar works he had studied in Italy. The reredos was to be in gilded wood. The same material, instead of marble, would serve for the statuary as well, the custom in Spain.

For two full months, Domenikos drew and redrew his sketches, adding here, subtracting there, rejecting and replacing details. He interrupted his work only for repeated visits to the church to make measurements and, as the image of his plans became plainer in his mind, to "place it," as he explained to a somewhat perplexed assistant.

"Don't you understand? I can *see* it there," he would say.

Francesco shrugged. "And *I* see only a white wall."

By mid-April Domenikos felt sufficiently satisfied with his designs to present the drawings for Don Diego's approval. The dean studied them for an hour. Sheet after sheet passed through his hands. He pored over each detail, referred back repeatedly to pages he had previously examined, comparing one item with another. Nothing seemed to escape his attention.

At first, Domenikos felt calm and sanguine as he watched the older Castilla peruse the plans. The work was good. He had seen enough of the art displayed in Toledan churches to be sure he was the finest craftsman ever to practice here. Only paintings by foreigners disclosed any distinction. There was no reason for doubt, was there? A wave of contempt suddenly swept over him. Of course there was no reason for doubt. Who did this clergyman think he was? Whom did he imagine he was dealing with? Did Castilla dream that Domenikos Theotokopoulos had traveled thousands of miles to submit himself to the criticism of an amateur, however enlightened? The anger passed as abruptly as it had come. He smiled. What an absurd thing emotion was. If Don Diego had reservations, the painter would make the required changes, and without protest. The time for total self-assertion was not yet.

The dean carefully reassembled the broad leaves of paper in their original order. Only when he had completed this meticulous operation did he lift his bright eyes, his face expressionless. He breathed deeply. "It's going to be a masterpiece, the finest thing Toledo has ever seen," he began in rapid Spanish, then stopped himself. "Forgive me, Maestro El Greco. I forget," he went on, in Italian.

Domenikos protested. "No, Don Diego. Please tell me in Spanish. I am learning better to understand. But perhaps you'll speak a little more slowly."

Castilla nodded, and complied. "It's very beautiful, this design. I can see nothing I would change."

The artist sighed with relief. "I'm happy you find it so, naturally."

Very brisk now, the cleric found difficulty in retarding his speech. "We must draft an agreement." He frowned. "If it were only between ourselves, you understand, I should be happy to dispense with this tiresome formality." He raised both fragile hands, palms upward. "My position is delicate. As executor, I'm the victim of lawyers."

"It's quite all right, Don Diego. I'm familiar with these problems. I sat many times with Titian when his advocate discussed such things."

A clerk was summoned and the details of the initial contract were agreed on. When this was done, the scribe disappeared, and the dean appeared embarrassed. He approached Domenikos and laid a hand on his shoulder.

"May I ask if you're occupied this evening?"

The painter grinned. "I've made no effort as yet to become a social being. There were more important things to consider."

Castilla nodded. "But your face is drawn with fatigue, maestro.

You've been working too hard. I'd like you to join me at a little supper gathering I've been invited to, at the palace of the Conde de Fuensalidas. He presides over a little group of intellectuals, a true academy, that I think you'd enjoy. But tonight is a purely social occasion. I believe there will even be ladies present. You need some pleasant diversion."

"I appreciate your concern, Don Diego, but it's unnecessary. I'm really in the best of health."

"Since the concern is genuine, maestro, you'll forgive me for disputing you. I'm only sorry Luis is away. He'd be more persuasive, and more amusing company."

Domenikos could only deprecate this observation. "It's not that, believe me."

"You'll enjoy making a few acquaintances. You must have been living like a hermit these past weeks. That's all very well for hermits, but not for others. Do join me."

The surroundings were luxurious. His host in his fifties, a man of considerable charm who, after an exchange in a mixture of Spanish and Italian, invited Domenikos to take part in the weekly discussions that were the principal activity of "our academy," twenty or so intellectuals—clerics and nobles. "We need an artist," said Fuensalidas, "and Castilla tells me you're a scholar as well." The painter accepted the count's proposal to attend a future meeting.

Once deserted by Fuensalidas, Domenikos was isolated, finding it difficult to catch names in the hail of swiftly spoken Spanish with which he had been presented by a forgetful Castilla, who, in any case, soon left his side. He contemplated the company. In no obvious way did the guests resemble those he had encountered in Rome or Venice. Their dress was more somber, save for the bright swords carried by the gentlemen or the occasional touches of color in jewelry and headdress worn by the ladies. Though animated in conversation, the Spanish were less given to grandiloquent gestures than Italians, not nearly so inclined to outbursts of anger or hilarity.

A woman passed before him. So swift and effortless was her movement that at first he hardly noticed her. As smoothly as a cloud she entered his range of vision, as if she had always been just beyond the edge of his horizon, awaiting precisely this moment to make her appearance.

She was a few inches shorter than he, her body lithe beneath the black folds of her gown, her profile without angularity, soft but forceful. She held her head high, giving prominence to her jaw and a long, delicately fashioned nose. Above a high forehead rose a mass of black hair that was held in check by a crisp white headdress of transparent lace.

It was in the instant when she turned to stare at him (had he made a gesture?) that Domenikos was blinded by her eyes, wide and long as almonds, a clear gray-blue, the irises ringed with black. Her self-possession was absolute; she showed not a trace of coyness. Her brows were thick, almost meeting over the bridge of her nose. Her generous mouth showed the first indications of a smile (mocking? amiable? he couldn't judge).

As her head turned, she paused easily, like the rest in a bar of music. For a fraction of a second, Domenikos' instincts were confused. Should he approach her? What was the proper thing to do? Did it matter? He bowed. She curtsied with such a grace that the motion took on a kind of stateliness. He made two short, hesitant steps in her direction, and reached for her hand, bringing it awkwardly to his lips. She wore a small ruby ring on her right hand. He straightened and smiled.

"Señorita, I am Domenikos Theotokopoulos."

"But in Toledo you're called Maestro El Greco."

"That is so."

"I've already heard much of you. You're a friend of Don Diego de Castilla." She spoke slowly, holding her hands lightly clasped beneath a small bosom.

"That is exact, señorita. But Don Luis is much my greater friend. I met him in Rome."

Her smile dazzled him. "To have one Castilla for a friend is a very good thing. To be a friend of both is ingenious."

"Because they're so different?"

"Because they're so demanding. They don't make friends easily."

"I recognize my good fortune, señorita . . ."

"Forgive me. I should have presented myself. I am called Doña Jerónima de las Cuevas."

Domenikos bowed once more, more profoundly. "I am enchanted, Doña Jerónima. In a single moment, you've done everything to make me happy. You're beautiful, and you've said something pleasant to me."

She laughed easily. "It would have been easy, even without hearing your accent, to know you're not a Spaniard, señor. Your tongue is Italian in its flattery."

The painter feigned seriousness, and lifted a hand in protest. "I'm not Italian. I'm Cretan. And I speak only the truth."

"What a pity."

"My nationality, or that I'm truthful?"

"The truth. I've lived too long with plain truth to be able to enjoy it." She smiled. "I speak, of course, of plain, *unpleasant* truth."

"It has its advantage, nevertheless. One need never be disabused."

The subject no longer appealed to Doña Jerónima. "You're long in Toledo?"

"Two months, and a bit more."

"You amuse yourself here?"

He laughed. "This is my first moment of diversion since I arrived. I have been working very hard."

"You will remain?"

"For two years at least. I'm making some altarpieces for Santo Domingo."

"So I've been told. That's very fine for you."

"And very important." He shrugged. "And by the end of two years, perhaps I shall have your language correctly."

"You speak it well now."

"But slowly. And sometimes, I fear, the words come out in their Italian order, not the Spanish. I read the language better than I speak it. It's hard to bring words from the eyes to the lips, no?"

She spoke so softly that Domenikos had to lean forward to hear her. "Your lips do you well enough, señor. They need no instruction."

Diego de Castilla reappeared. He glanced at Doña Jerónima, smiled, and graciously took her hand. "I see you've made Maestro El Greco's acquaintance."

She nodded. "Our paths crossed, Don Diego."

"Perhaps," said the dean in a manner the painter thought delphic, "they'll cross again. But come along now, maestro. There are others you must meet."

The remainder of the evening passed pleasantly enough in the company of his host, but was pallid when compared with the delicious moments with Doña Jerónima. In the days that followed, Domenikos found it difficult to devote himself exclusively to the working drawings that were required by the artisans who were to make the altar frames and the sculpture. Her tranquil, slightly mocking features too often clouded more important images. It wasn't merely, he felt, that he needed a woman; he needed her.

Although anxious to know more about her, the artist thought it more discreet to question Luis de Castilla than his brother. The dean of Cuenca returned to Toledo a week after his encounter with Doña Jerónima.

"Who is she?" he asked as soon as he had exchanged greetings with his friend. "Tell me all."

"You admire her?" Luis seemed as determined to be sibylline as Don Diego.

"I may even worship her."

"That's not permitted in Spain, Greco. You'd like to see her again?"

"Unless she's betrothed."

"That, I promise you, she's not." He paused. "I make one stipulation, that you not be precipitate."

Domenikos stared at him. "What do you mean, Luis?"

"Doña Jerónima has a past."

"And I?" the painter inquired softly.

"Hers is different."

"You propose to tell me?"

"Not unless she declines to tell you herself."

"How honorable of you. You amaze me."

"I'm only thinking of you, my friend."

"I'd like to hear a word in her favor instead."

"Almost everything about Doña Jerónima is in her favor."

A few evenings later, Don Luis accompanied the painter to another gathering at Fuensalidas' mansion, expressly to see Doña Jerónima once again. With impatient eyes and a nervous smile, Domenikos returned the greeting of his host and escaped with Castilla from the crowded salon into a smaller reception room, where the object of his eagerness awaited them.

Castilla grinned. "Greco, let me formally introduce Doña Jerónima de las Cuevas.

He kissed her hand. "Señorita, good evening."

"Maestro El Greco. I'm pleased to see you again."

Luis closed the doors of the room, then walked to a chair in a distant corner and sat down. "Forgive me," he murmured. "But as Doña Jerónima knows, I'm obliged to remain." He laughed. "It must be one of the few times when a dean has performed the role of dueña. Please ignore me."

The young woman pointed to a couch. "Shall we sit down, maestro?"

He nodded, numbed. They sat together in silence. He gazed into her calm white face. Her beautiful eyes returned his stare without blinking. Then, unable to control her amusement any longer, she laughed, not loudly, but with a musical ring that was, to the dumb-founded painter, an angelic sound.

"Forgive me. Your expression was so comical." She collected her-self. "I wasn't laughing at *you,* you understand, but at your expression. You looked thunderstruck."

Domenikos nodded, embarrassed. "I couldn't believe in you, in the fact of seeing you again."

"But I'm here at your request. What could be less amazing?"

"So often, señorita, our hopes are beyond the possibility of attain-ment."

"It's unwise to hope for the impossible."

"That's very practical."

"You sound surprised, maestro. You think the Spanish im-practical?"

"They have a reputation . . ."

She shrugged gracefully. "Reputations don't always depend on facts."

"I see I need lessons in understanding your countrymen, if not your language."

"Perhaps," she answered, "that's more exact than you imagine."

He studied her for a moment, his composure fully restored. "Will you explain, señorita?"

"We were speaking of reputations." She hesitated. "Mine is . . . flawed."

Domenikos waited for her to continue, then coughed and looked away. "You need say nothing."

"No, maestro, I must say everything. You have a right to know be-fore . . ." Her voice trailed off.

"Before we become friends?" he inquired gently.

"Yes." She sighed. "It's difficult to know where I should begin." She stopped again, adding hastily, "I'm not a bad woman, you know."

He laughed. "How could I think you were?"

She took a deep breath. "Very well. We are of the poor nobility. My grandfather was one of the *Communeros,* one of the rebels against Carlos V. And when the movement was suppressed, he was deprived of all his lands. So my father, who was his only son, was forced to be-come an officer in the army. His only distinction, God rest his soul, was to be killed in the battle of St. Quentin. My mother receives for this a small pension from the King. So all we have, my mother, my brother and I, is our ancient name and our pride." The fixed smile with which she had recounted this became grim. "And of course we have the distinction of having been associated with a lost cause. My brother is in the army now. He sends mama what he can, but it's not very much."

Domenikos shifted beside her uneasily. "Since you've been so frank, Doña Jerónima, I hope you won't think me impertinent if I ask you how you've been able to exist in such circumstances."

She smiled almost darkly now. "You're wondering why it is that at my age I'm neither married nor in a convent."

Appalled by her directness, the painter retreated from the implications of his question. "No, forgive me. You need say nothing."

"I prefer you hear the truth from me and not the gossip from others."

"I accept you as you are, señorita."

"I insist that you *know* who I am." She leaned back and spoke to the ceiling. "It's very complicated. I was unable to marry because I had no dowry."

Domenikos couldn't conceal his disbelief. "But there must have been men, there must *be* men, who would accept you without a dowry."

"Thank you for the compliment. Yes, I dare say that's so. A man might accept *me*, but my mother wouldn't have accepted *him*. She wanted such great things for me. If I married well, the family's position would improve."

"Your mother was correct in expecting great things of you."

"But marriage *wasn't* to be. Any man who would take me without a dowry would have been a small merchant or an artisan. This mama refused to permit."

"I'm desolate for you, señorita. But as I said, I accept you as you are. No explanation is needed."

"There's more. You must hear me out, maestro. Since a suitable marriage was impossible, mama sent me to a convent when I was sixteen. It's the Spanish way."

"It's the way in Italy too. But it apparently wasn't your way."

"It was a failure from the start. I wasn't intended to be a nun."

"You're too direct."

She smiled. "So my mother says too. But Mother Teresa of Ávila is very direct, for all her mysticism, and she's an abbess."

"I'm mistaken."

"You're mistaken. It was simply that I was a woman. Even though I couldn't marry beneath me, as mama says, I enjoyed the company of men. I *enjoy* their company still."

It was almost unbearable not to reach out and touch the soft arm beside him. "I believe you. And as you must feel, you're attractive to men, to me."

"Yes." She sat up and smiled. "I know."

"If I were free to marry, Doña Jerónima, I'd accept you without a ducat of dowry. Would you accept *me*?"

"I might maestro. I can't say about my mother. But it's an idle question. You're *not* free."

"I'm already married. My wife is in Venice."

Doña Jerónima seemed unperturbed. "But she plans to come to Toledo later on?"

"No, señorita. She's very ill in her mind." He tapped his forehead with a finger. "And she'll never recover." The great dark eyes filled with tears. He looked away. "But Don Luis will have told you all this."

"He mentioned only that you were married. I'm sorry to hear the circumstances. She's very dear to you?"

"She *was*."

"But no longer?"

He sighed. "It's difficult to go on loving a woman I haven't seen in seven years." He considered for a moment. "I suppose what I love is my memory of her."

She nodded. "So, in a tragic way, you and I find ourselves in the same position, more or less."

"So it seems."

"Yet not quite, perhaps. I have more to say. It may amuse you, or disgust you."

"You couldn't disgust me."

"We'll see. When I decided I must leave the convent, only one course seemed open, that I become the mistress of an important man, a cardinal or a great nobleman. It was the only way I could help mama and my brother, by having the protection of someone rich and influential."

So matter-of-fact was this statement that Domenikos, who supposed he should be shocked, found himself agreeing with the logic of the idea. "How old were you then?"

"Eighteen."

"And your mother accepted this?"

"She was unhappy about it, but she's a *Toledana.*"

The painter laughed. "I don't understand. What's different about the women of Toledo?"

"Mama is very devout, maestro, but very intelligent, very practical, very reasonable."

"So she approved."

"She arranged everything. She made discreet inquiries. My uncle was displeased. He thought it would hamper his career at court. But then, it wasn't his affair, was it?"

"You leave me breathless."

"If you interrupt, I can't continue."

From the corner came a frequent rumble of suppressed mirth. Domenikos had forgotten Castilla's presence.

"I assume *he* knows all about this," he said testily.

"Oh, yes. In Toledo, everything is known. It's a small town, really."

He sighed. "I'll say no more. Please go on."

"Well, a marqués was finally found. I was taken to see him." She became unexpectedly demure. "He liked me."

Domenikos shuddered. "It's so cold-blooded, like a Venetian slave market. I can't bear to think about it. Did you like *him?*"

"You're too soft. You've been protected from the realities of life."

"Only from realities like this, señorita."

She touched his arm lightly. "That was presumptuous. Forgive me."

"And I interrupted you again."

"Yes, I liked the marqués well enough, not that it mattered. It was a sort of business arrangement. He was a kind man, old enough to be my father." She folded her hands in her lap, as if to signify the termination of the narrative.

"And then?"

"And then, he kept me. That's all. He was gentle with me, and very generous to mama."

"And now?"

"And now he's dead."

"You were his mistress for a long time?"

"Nine years. He died just a year ago, and I returned to Toledo."

"And you found no other protector?"

"There are few men who'd be interested in a woman of twenty-nine who's been another man's mistress."

"*I'm* interested, Doña Jerónima," he said quietly.

"You'd think of becoming my protector?"

"Your lover."

Her smile was grave, but full of admiration. "I think that's the nicest thing that's ever been said to me. But you must consider it carefully. You'll want to discuss it with Don Luis and Don Diego. And you'll have to see mama. I'll not go against her wishes."

"But you yourself, señorita? Have you no wishes?"

"I wish first to know your mind. You must think carefully. To live with a woman who's not your wife might be a bad thing for your success here."

He nodded. "Perhaps, but even in Toledo a sword like that has two edges. *Not* living with a woman is definitely a bad thing for a man."

"I believe so."

"I have a more important question, Doña Jerónima. Can you love?"

Her candid eyes rested on his, her face just edged with a smile. "I didn't love my marqués, if that's what you're asking."

"It's not. Are you capable of loving?"

The responding smile was soft. "I think so. And you?"

"I loved my wife, as I told you."

"That's as it ought to be."

"But it's not . . ." He hesitated. Was he moving too rapidly, being precipitate? Yet he continued, driven by certainty. "Not what I feel for you, what I think I feel for you."

She was solemn, a bright flush suffusing her white cheeks. "You're confusing love with passion."

"I think not. I've known both feelings."

She frowned, perplexed. "How is it possible, maestro, to imagine you love me after knowing my story?"

Domenikos laughed gently. "Where I was born, Doña Jerónima, we never question the wisdom of the heart."

"Nor in Spain either, but we try to protect ourselves against the heart's follies."

"So you see, there's no need to think my feelings strange, because they're wise, not foolish."

She touched his arm again, this time permitting her hand to press it softly and, briefly, to remain. "But I *must* find it strange, for myself, perhaps, quite as much as for you. I've been wanted, desired, but never truly loved." She smiled sadly. "I suppose I've come to think of myself as unlovable."

"You might feel this because you don't love yourself."

"I respect myself," she responded with some asperity, then sighed. "But I don't love myself."

He reached for her hand, holding it between both of his. "You'll have to accept the fact that you *can* be loved, that I love you."

For the first time her smile was broad. Her lips parted, revealing bright, even teeth. "I should be honored to be loved by you."

"And I don't presume that you'll return my love."

"I might surprise you, in time, maestro," she said, then added musingly, "I might even surprise myself."

Love.

How rarely the thought of love had crossed his mind. He loved Doña Jerónima de las Cuevas. There was no doubt of it. Nor could this emotion be confused with the feelings he had had for Maria or Catarina. Jerónima was a woman, not a child. She required no instruction, no protection from life. She was strong, self-assured, straightforward, perceptive and intelligent, fearless for herself, and beautiful.

No, he reflected as he made his way alone through the dark, nameless alleys to his apartments, she wasn't beautiful by objective standards. She was beautiful to him for some other quality, in her eyes, in her grace, in her calm. Like him, she knew her worth, assessed it neither above nor below its true value. She was honest. He loved that in her. Yet he was unable to deny, as he reached his door, that he loved her too for her sad little tale. The outcast has a fellow feeling for another outcast.

He had slept badly, and was bathed and dressed before Francesco was out of bed. He bit uninterestedly at his bread and cheese, his feelings hardly less turbulent than they had been the night before. When his bleary-eyed assistant, running his fingers languidly through his coarse black hair, entered the sunny room, Domenikos stared at him bleakly. The young man smiled and drowsily rubbed his eyes with his fingertips.

"You're up very early, master."

"You're up late."

Francesco approached the table. Laying his powerful hands on the surface and leaning forward, he balanced his weight between his hands and feet, teetering back and forth. "You had a bad night?"

The painter nodded, then smiled. "But a marvellous evening."

"Yet you couldn't sleep. Did you take much wine? This Spanish wine is much stronger than ours."

"I drank very little."

Francesco broke off a chunk of bread, cut himself a substantial piece of sharp, yellow cheese and sat down across from his master. "A woman, then?"

Domenikos eyed him briefly and nodded. "A woman."

"It's very serious."

"What makes you say that?"

"Your manner. You're very disturbed. It's not like you." He took a bite of the cheese, and mumbled. "You're going to bring her here?"

"I've been thinking of nothing else. Would it bother you?"

The Italian shrugged elaborately, forcing out his heavy lower lip to give himself a rather simian aspect. "Why should I care?"

"I was thinking of Catarina."

"She's dead, master." Francesco crossed himself automatically. "She can't do anything for you now."

"I'd still like your opinion."

"Well, since you ask me, I'd welcome a woman in this house. You work too hard. You need to relax. A woman would be good for you." He paused and smiled boldly. "Is she very beautiful?"

"*I* think so."

"Rich and noble?"

"Noble, but not rich."

Francesco snorted. "What good is it to be noble if you're not rich?"

"There's no good in it."

Between mouthfuls, the Italian pressed his master with eager questions. "You'll bring her here to live, like Catarina?"

"If she'll come."

"Soon?"

"I don't know. I've only seen her twice. Much will have to be arranged."

Francesco pursed his lips. "You move quickly, master, once you've made a decision."

Luis de Castilla received him with affectionate amusement. "You look terrible."

"It's hardly surprising."

"You slept on your proposal?"

"I lay awake on it."

"And?"

"Before that, let me ask you this. How would my having a mistress affect my position? I'll not do this thing in a clandestine way. I'll not cheapen her or my feeling for her."

Castilla burst out laughing. "The best answer I can give is that Diego and I planned this. We don't believe in leaving matters so important to chance."

The painter stared at him, stunned. "And Doña Jerónima co-operated?"

"Ask her. Would she have been so frank, with me in the room, if I wasn't deeply involved?"

"It's grotesque. I've never heard of anything so coldly calculated in my life."

"On whose part?"

"Yours, of course."

"But not Doña Jerónima's?"

"But I can forgive her. She had herself to consider."

"And you think Diego and I weren't considering *you*?"

"You were certainly presumptuous."

"If we hadn't done this, would you have made some sort of arrangement on your own?"

"Probably."

The dean of Cuenca nodded. "With a peasant girl. I don't mean to be cruel, Greco, but if you're to live in Toledo, you want someone who has the poise and experience to receive your guests."

Domenikos shook his head stubbornly. "But the idea of your creating this . . ." He gasped in exasperation. "It's more audacious than any advice Machiavelli ever gave the Medici."

Castilla was delighted. "Yes, we Spaniards are underestimated in that respect. We love intrigue just as much as the Italians." He paused and went on, all plausibility. "It's so simple, Greco. Diego and I are anxious for you to stay here. We think you're driving yourself at too furious a pace." He grinned. "Francesco agrees."

The painter sighed. "Treachery everywhere."

"Well, you can see the logic of it. Your circumstances are peculiar. So are Doña Jerónima's. A suitable arrangement isn't easy. You need a woman. What better possible solution? She's an admirable person, a real lady. Her story is perfectly true."

The painter laughed uneasily. "And you had the nerve to describe Toledo as the Spanish City of God."

"You think our plot ungodly?"

"Don't you?"

"Not a bit. Look at it another way, Greco, not from the lofty Cretan perch you favor. Think of Doña Jerónima. If she finds no one like you, she'll live miserably with her mother until *she* dies, and then she'll have to take the veil."

"I see that."

"And what about yourself? You're a victim of circumstance too. You suit each other. I think it the very opposite of ungodly. You see this in terms of social norms, not human needs."

"But won't other women scorn her?"

Castilla smiled. "Fewer than scorn her now. With you as her protector, she'll gain more respect than she loses."

"And if she bears children? Will they be accepted, as in Rome?"

The Spaniard shrugged. "Diego and I are both bastards. You knew that."

"Yes."

"But you may not know that our father was dean of the chapter, like Diego." He laughed. "Don Juan of Austria is a bastard. These things are accepted because they happen."

Domenikos sighed. "And you told me life in Spain was different."

Twenty-Two

Doña Ana de las Cuevas received Domenikos in a modest but formal drawing room. A well-made woman in her fifties, she was more sharply featured than her daughter. Her face was sad and lined but without evidence of great intelligence or wisdom. The painter bowed and kissed her hand, gestures she acknowledged with a slight inclination of her gray head.

"You're welcome, maestro. Be good enough to seat yourself." She took the chair opposite him and carefully folded her white, toilless hands in her lap. "You have much impressed my daughter."

"Doña Jerónima has much impressed *me*."

In the ensuing brief silence, the woman was gathering her forces for the kind of assault that wasn't entirely to her taste, though she showed no sign of chagrin or embarrassment. She breathed more deeply, clasped her hands more tightly in her lap.

"Is there any reason why I shouldn't speak frankly, maestro?"

"None, Doña Ana. Please do."

She parted her hands, lifting one in a delicate indication of warning. "You mustn't imagine that because we're poor, we're to be ill-treated."

Domenikos frowned. "I'd rather ill-treat myself, señora."

"Both Don Diego and Don Luis have spoken of you in the highest terms. I'm sure that's so." She smiled deprecatingly. "Even matters that appear a trifle sordid may be arranged between well-bred people with a semblance of dignity."

"I agree," said the painter, wondering how long it would take her to come to the point.

Nervously, she clasped and unclasped her fingers, her dark eyes looking up, then down, then up at him once more. "What I mean to inquire is whether or not you can maintain a . . . a liaison. I don't like to pry into matters that aren't strictly my concern. But you see, Doña Jerónima *is* my concern. And I've been told that artists . . ."

The painter grinned at her hesitation and cruelly maintained silence until it was plain that Doña Ana was unable to continue. "That artists are notoriously poor and irresponsible?"

Her nod was one of reluctant assent. "It *is* said."

Domenikos laughed softly. "It's also said that they're emotionally unhinged, promiscuous, irreligious . . ."

She waved these adjectives aside impatiently. "I'm not interested in other defects."

Doña Ana's candor charmed him. "I understand. And I imagine there *are* instances where artists, especially at the beginning of their careers, find themselves in financial difficulties. I'm told that the great Michelangelo was in serious debt at the time of his death. But my own circumstances are happy. My father, God rest his soul, dealt very generously with me. I have a certain independence."

After crossing herself, the woman smiled gravely and folded her hands in a gesture of prayerful thanksgiving. "How splendid to have a generous father." Once again, however, the fists tightened in her lap and her breathing intensified. Her smile became forced. "But a mother must assure herself of everything. Suppose, for whatever reason, you decided to leave Toledo . . ."

"Would I desert your daughter?"

"I'm sure you have no such intention, maestro." Her sigh was worldly and resigned. "But it's been known to happen."

It was Domenikos' turn to breathe deeply. "If we separate, Doña Ana, I can promise you that the decision will be Doña Jerónima's."

He paused. "Let me put it this way. I shall regard her as my wife. I would never feel free to leave her. It's my nature. I'm not frivolous. I have friends who think it a fault, but in this case I hope you'll consider it a virtue."

Doña Ana's smile was complacent. "A virtue, indeed, maestro." She stood up and took a small step toward him. "Then, as far as it can be a matter for a protective mother, I think we may say we've completely understood each other."

He rose to join her in the center of the little salon. "Perfectly, señora."

She moved in the direction of the door; he overtook her and placed a hand on the knob.

"I shall bring her to you," she said. As she reached the door, she paused and look up at him, her expression suddenly apprehensive. "I'm counting on you to treat my daughter gently, maestro."

Domenikos was caught between tears and anger. That this should be said as an afterthought was intolerable. That she should have doubts distressed him. He managed a grim smile. "I hope you can't believe otherwise, Doña Ana."

She studied his face briefly. "No. I can't." She offered him a limp hand, then stood aside as he opened the door for her; he closed it softly as she departed.

He returned to his chair. Fragments of thoughts and images, incoherent and disconnected, raced through his mind. So the thing was settled. It was fantastic. He trembled with joy. This had occurred to him before. But the feeling was different. No woman had ever prompted just *this* sensation. Yet that was logical; he had never been in love before. He had felt passion, compassion, tenderness—but never love. Love, for God's sake. He was in love.

Completely bound up in himself, Domenikos hadn't heard the door open. Jerónima stood silent, her hands placidly at her sides, watching him. Then she laughed softly, whisperingly. He looked up and hastily rose from the chair. Her hair was uncovered now; loose, it fell to just below her shoulders. She wore a severely cut gown of black wool that fitted her closely.

He approached her slowly, almost warily, still stunned by the improbability of events. Her smile was grave.

"Mama says you're a good, kind man, and that I'm to cherish you."

Without comment, Domenikos embraced her gently at first, shyly; then, as he felt the warmth of her small bosom pressing against his chest, he squeezed her to him fiercely. She yielded without complaint or reciprocation. She was all compliance; she was simply letting this thing happen to her.

He released her from the embrace and drew back, looking down at her, dismayed and humiliated, for he felt that in some way he had unintentionally humiliated *her*. "Am I so repugnant to you?"

"No, maestro."

"What is it then?"

She smiled sadly. "Perhaps I'd like you to woo me a little."

"You're being coy. I thought you weren't like that."

"Feminine, yes, but never coy." She shrugged. "Or it may be that I'm reacting to my mother's way of bargaining. What was it you said the other evening about the slave market in Venice?" She shuddered. "It was different with my marqués. He was old. It seemed impersonal. But this. . . . And she has the temerity to speak of dignity."

"If you think about it, Doña Jerónima, it's not nearly so crass and sordid as arranging a marriage contract. There are no documents, no exchange of property."

Her anger persisted. "I know, I know. But it was squalid just the same."

He laid a hand on her shoulder, and with the other tipped her firm chin upward. "If it *was* squalid, it can't touch us. It has nothing to do with us."

Despite his grasp, she forced her head downward and shook it violently, freeing herself. "I feel cheapened. I was standing by the door. I heard every word."

He spoke quietly. "If you heard every word, then you heard me say how I regarded you."

"You were just trying to persuade mama."

The painter felt a certain perverse pleasure in having to coax her, yet was annoyed for the same reason. "If anyone has a right to feel offended, it's I."

"It's not the same for a man."

"What *is?*"

"You're teasing me." She looked up, her expression petulant.

"*You're* teasing *me*," he said without rancor. "Just think about it. You're the bait in a trap the Castillas laid for me. It was a very dangerous game, Doña Jerónima, especially for me. If you *hadn't* been the prize, if I'd found out—I'd have been beside myself. I might have decided to leave Toledo. My whole life might have been destroyed, or at least distorted. When you consider it objectively, I'm the one who should feel humiliated. You knew what was happening. I was in the dark." He paused. "But you *were* the prize, so I've won my dangerous game."

She was desolate. "I'm ashamed for my part in it. The only consolation I can offer is that if I'd found you unattractive that first evening, I wouldn't have approached you."

"I accept those crumbs of flattery gratefully." He turned from her and walked to a window that overlooked a small patio where early roses were beginning to bloom. "But I think you mistaken to feel cheapened by the outcome, given your role in the game."

He felt her at his elbow, looking up at him and smiling, not with warmth but compassion. She touched his arm. "But I'm not angry with *you.*"

"You're just sharing your anger with me?"

"And you're not repugnant to me."

"I'm glad of that. But I told you the other evening that I didn't presume you would ever return my feeling for you."

Her small fingers pressed his forearm tightly. "I don't know what will happen. Give me time."

"All you like."

Still clinging to his arm, she turned from the window and spoke into the room, her voice small and remote. "When would you like me to come to you?"

He chuckled. "Yesterday, the day before yesterday."

"Be serious."

He took her chin once more and peered into her pale eyes. "I *am* serious. I'd like you to come as soon as it's convenient for you."

She held his stare, her eyes severe. Then, suddenly, she uttered her delicious little trill of laughter. "I knew everything between mama and you would go as planned."

"You're not answering."

"But I am. I've been packed since last evening."

His tension was dispelled. He felt himself sagging, as from exhaustion. He took her hand and kissed it gently. "I'll send my Francesco and the two servants this afternoon. Will three be sufficient?"

"I think so, with my Juanita to help. As you must have guessed, I have few possessions."

He kissed her forehead. "Your very little means very much to me."

"May you always feel so."

As she had indicated, Jerónima's belongings were few. Domenikos' two serving women, aided by Francesco and Juanita, a hulking, amiable peasant girl of twenty, had no difficulty transporting them the short distance to the painter's apartments.

Doña Ana's farewell was expectedly formal. Yet she smiled wryly as she saw Domenikos turn from her and take Jerónima's arm, leading her from the doorway.

They walked in silence for a block or so, then he stopped abruptly, and looked down at her. "I don't want to take you directly to my house."

"Whatever you want," she responded indifferently. "But why not?"

"I have another plan."

She laughed. "Is it decent?"

"You've much to learn about me," he replied soberly. "My ideas are always decent."

"It's an education I look forward to," she said, smiling archly.

Their walk through the contorted alleys was apparently aimless. The hours of siesta were ending. One by one, and then in larger groups, black-clothed figures emerged from the forbidding brick façades, bustling in purposeful silence hither and thither, their manner oddly furtive (something Domenikos had come to think uniquely Spanish), each person seemingly isolated from the others. Now and again, individuals would pass them, then pause to look back, curious, intrigued—for Jerónima was known, and the painter was coming to be so.

When they stood before the door of the small Church of Santo Tomé, he looked down at her. "Shall we go in?"

"If you want to. But I warn you, I'll not take communion. I'm no hypocrite. I repent nothing."

"But you regret, don't you?"

She smiled wisely. "You reason like a Jesuit. Oh, I suppose I do regret, in part at least. But not very much. Since I left the convent, it's seemed that I could find no alternatives that were as acceptable to God as they were to me."

"I've had the same feelings," he responded quietly.

"And you take communion?"

"Regularly, and with dispensation from a cardinal."

She laughed. "And you propose to obtain one for me?"

"If you want one."

She reflected for a moment. "I don't know. It's been so long since I felt the need. That's shocking to you, I suppose." She studied his face earnestly. "It would please you, wouldn't it?"

"Yes." He took her slender arm. "So let's go in."

She resisted mildly. "Why now? Why not wait for my dispensation?"

"I want us to be seen together first in God's house, not mine."

She had permitted herself to accompany him to the door of the church. She stooped abruptly and stared at him in astonishment. "You mean that?"

He returned her gaze without a trace of humor. "Of course I do."

"But that must be blasphemy."

He shrugged. "Literally, it probably is. But that's not how I feel it in my heart."

"Is that relevant to the Church?"

"What could be more relevant, Jerónima? In my heart, I'm marrying you. If we can't have the Church's blessing, we can have its presence."

She turned, looked up at him briefly, then buried her face in his chest. "You ought to beat me," she mumbled.

Their love-making continued intermittently through that night and the following day and night. Jerónima was candidly interested in his body and voluptuous in expressing this concern. A pair of skilled, daring explorers, each investigated passionately the world of the other's body—ventures, tentative at first, that grew increasingly audacious as initially intense desire gave way to more refined appetites.

This prolonged first union of their flesh reduced them. They had taken no nourishment and had slept but fitfully, returning again and again to the delights of loving. Yet Domenikos felt a sense of increase. He was fragile, tremulous, ravenously hungry; his eyes were weary, his mouth parched. But he was entire.

He painted her portrait at once. Jerónima was a superb model. "I'm used to being looked at," she said. "It was sometimes the only thing my marqués could do." He posed her with a fur about her shoulders and a translucent white scarf over her black hair, her body angled, her face looking directly forward.

Domenikos felt, even taking into account the possibility of bias toward the sitter, that it was his finest portrait. Jerónima cocked her head to one side, her eyes wide and calm, and examined it critically. Her elusive smile played now and again across her features.

She was very grave. "Why, Menegos, you've made me a real *hidalga*."

"God did that for you, *amada*. I've just shown you as you are."

She insisted that her mother see the painting immediately. Doña Ana was as moved as her rigidity of manner permitted. "It's admirable," she observed; "Jerónima as she is." Prompted by precisely what emotion he was uncertain, Domenikos impulsively offered to paint a portrait of Doña Ana. As he expected, the suggestion was accepted. What surprised him was the warmth of the woman's enthusiasm for it. "Would you?" she exclaimed. "Would you really?" When he commented about this to Jerónima, she expressed no astonishment. "Mama's vanity is her most powerful feeling. If that weren't so, I'd be a married woman." "And I," said the painter, "would be a lonely man."

Diego de Castilla was a regular visitor to the artist's studio. Though he greatly admired the two portraits, he expressed concern for the progress of the Santo Domingo commission. That he accepted Domenikos' reassurances was demonstrated in mid-May, when he proposed another commission, this a painting for the vestry of the cathedral, depicting the rending of Christ's garments.

Domenikos thus found himself plunged suddenly into a frenzy of work. He had more commitments than he and Francesco could reasonably manage. For in addition to the altarpieces for Santo Domingo, he had been receiving, from patrons referred by the brothers Castilla, requests for repetitions of pictures he had made in Rome. For the dean of Toledo, he painted a large Martyrdom of St. Sebastian. Don Diego expressed vast gratitude and promptly gave the painting to the Cathedral of Palencia. "I was dean there before I came to Toledo," he explained without apology. "I owe them something, and its being there will spread your name, Greco."

Far from being fatigued by the unaccustomed demands now placed on him, the artist discovered unexpected sources of energy within himself. He liked to think that Jerónima's presence in his life, in his house, was in a measure responsible for his excitement and joy. He was revolutionized, restored, even optimistic. He had never felt so buoyant.

He accomplished prodigies. He continued to make detailed drawings of the altars and sculpture for Santo Domingo. He made sketches for the study he proposed to submit to members of the cathedral chapter, the vestry painting suggested by Don Diego. Following Don Luis' advise, he painted a number of other subjects. "Make a great variety, Greco, so prospective patrons have some idea of how wide your range is." Two works produced for this purpose that spring were a penitent

Mary Magdalene (with Catarina the model, delighting her brother), and a St. Veronica (his own faithless Veronica the prototype).

The working drawings for Santo Domingo were completed in late June. Domenikos took them at once to the large workshop of Juan Bautista Monegro, a builder-architect whom Diego de Castilla described as Toledo's most reliable. A solidly made figure with angry eyes and a temperament to match, Monegro made but a cursory examination of the plans before assuring the artist that his men could do the work and by the stipulated completion date of March, 1579.

"You'll not object, I hope, if I come around from time to time to see what progress you're making," Domenikos remarked somewhat diffidently.

"You don't think we know our craft?"

"I'm sure you do, maestro. I've seen some of your work in the Cathedral."

Monegro remained disgruntled. He cast a disdainful glance at the plans Domenikos had brought. "You're a painter, aren't you? Why did they ask you to do architecture and sculpture? I could have done a better design for them."

The artist looked with perfect calm at this hot-eyed man. "But they *asked* me. That's the only point that need concern you, maestro. If you prefer, I'll have the work done somewhere else."

The architect became truculent. He grunted. "No, we'll do it. Then we'll know it's at least properly made, won't we?"

His wit stirred him to harsh, joyless laughter.

Domenikos smiled. "*I'll* know it's properly made by supervising every stage of the work. If you follow my drawings we'll have no trouble with each other."

Though vaguely alarmed by Monegro's hostility, Domenikos gave it little thought thereafter. Not for some months would the plans he had submitted result in anything tangible. There remained, moreover, much other work to be done; in particular studies for the eight paintings to be framed by the retables Monegro was constructing and for the picture of the Spoliation of Christ that the chapter was proposing to commission.

At Don Diego's urging, the painter first completed a small tempera version of the Espolio, as they called it here. "Then you can get the canons to commit themselves," their dean observed. "You understand that the decision is a collective one." Domenikos expressed reservations about this plan. "I don't want you to be snapping at my heels from two directions instead of one, Don Diego, in your capacity of dean as well as executor." Castilla assured him that there was no danger of this.

The study of the Espolio was viewed by a group of canons in the middle of July. It was clear to the artist that of this small delegation (Castilla was deliberately absent) only the bursar, Don García de Loysa, had more than a passing interest in the task. The dean had described him as a formidable character, brilliant, hard-headed, and reluctant to part with money, especially the chapter's.

After a prolonged study of the little work, the bursar turned to its author. "Do you mind my asking you, maestro, the basis of your iconography?"

The painter was pleased, for the derivation of the picture was interesting, the question, therefore, perceptive. "Not at all, Don García. The theme is very unusual. When Don Diego suggested it, I had to make a long search of my prints and sketches before I found any versions of it. When I was in Italy, I saw only two pictures of the subject, one by Duccio that was done a long time ago." He stepped to a table near the easel and picked up a small print, a woodcut by Dürer. He handed it to Loysa. "I took a few ideas from this as well."

The cleric studied the Dürer Spoliation, looking up from time to time to compare it with Domenikos' version. "They're hardly alike, maestro."

The artist tapped his forehead with a finger and smiled. "The difference is here, Don García."

Loysa nodded appreciatively. "Just where it should be." His eyes glanced back to the study. "Do I see here some traces of the Byzantine?"

"Perhaps, in the arrangement of the figures." He paused, chuckling. "I hope you don't think them wooden, as they are in the icons."

"Oh, no. As you say, it's the arrangement of the figures." The bursar reached into his purse and produced some golden ducats which he placed in the painter's hand. "This is a token of our intentions, maestro. I confess that I was skeptical when Don Diego suggested that you were our man. He was quite correct. That, I presume, is why *he* is dean."

"Surely not."

Loysa paid no attention to this protest. "A contract will be drawn as soon as possible." He paused and regarded the painter curiously. "You understand about the method in Spain of determining your fee?"

"Not altogether, Don García."

"It's really very fair. You designate an appraiser. The chapter chooses another, and agreement is reached by discussion."

"It sounds potentially very dangerous."

The bursar nodded affably. "It is, maestro, for you."

One evening in early August, Domenikos returned home from a meeting of Fuensalidas' academy. It had been a hot dry day broken only briefly by a storm at noon; within an hour, the streets were dry again, the city's few gardens and cloisters as parched as before. He was tired but not exhausted, exhilarated by the conversation (tonight mostly of the King's persistent demands for gold from the Church and of the possibility of war with Portugal, an eventuality that would serve only to increase Philip's avarice). His work had gone well; soon he would complete the studies for Santo Domingo. But sleep beside Jerónima would be welcome.

She was seated at the table in the dining room, her back to him as he entered, her form illuminated by the light of a single candle. She turned when she heard his step.

"You had a pleasant gathering?"

"Money, war, and two or three poems. Very mixed, but interesting. And you? What did you do?"

"I considered my navel. I'm pregnant."

He sat on the bench at her side and in silence embraced her gently, uncertain of his feelings. "You're certain?" he murmured.

She nodded. "You're angry?"

"No, no. Not angry, *querida*. Apprehensive and delighted, and unsure which emotion I should yield to."

"Apprehensive?"

"For you. I was thinking of Maria."

"But not angry?"

"Why should I be?"

"It binds me to you. Or, rather, it binds *you* to *me*."

"But I'm already bound to you."

"You want a child?"

"Yes. I've said nothing because I was fearful for you. I want a child, a son."

She sighed. "Then I'm pleased. Nothing will happen. You'll see. Why should anything happen? I'm a healthy woman. The only reason I've never been pregnant is that the marqués couldn't make children. So there's nothing to fear."

He looked at her earnestly. "But I'm cursed."

"With me?"

"With myself. I feel myself cursed."

"Superstition."

"Perhaps, but I feel it. Even in the most brilliant light, I see a darkness."

She eased herself from his embrace and took his hands in hers. "Who curses you, *amado?*"

"I can only think of the little Tiziano and Maria and Catarina and Francesca. Four lives on my head. It's the will of God. He's chosen me for pain as well as pleasure, and in equal portions."

She stroked his fingers gently. "Don't worry."

He laughed sardonically. "Oh, I'll worry, and I'll pray. But I'm happy."

She stood up and took the candelabrum from the table, moving in the direction of their bedchamber. She paused to see if he followed her, the light dancing across her tranquil features. She smiled. "All's well, Menegos. Come to bed."

Twenty-Three

Anxiety mixed with jubilation was the painter's reaction to Jerónima's pregnancy. The next day he announced the fact to Francesco and ordered him (more summarily than was necessary, he knew) to see that when Juanita, his mistress' personal domestic, had occasion to leave the house some other servant take her place. He immediately consulted Don Rodrigo de La Fuente, Toledo's leading physician. Domenikos' opinion of medicine as science had not risen appreciably during the decade since Maria's illness began, but La Fuente was at least a passable poet with a first-rate intelligence. If his knowledge of cures was limited by the general state of the art, he was at least endowed with more information than anyone else the artist knew.

"Relax, maestro," La Fuente observed.

"If you tell me everything is in the hands of God, Don Rodrigo, I may strangle you. There must be something a mere man can do for her, to protect her, nurture her, keep her strong and well."

The physician agreed. "See that she eats well, sleeps well, and isn't bedeviled by an overanxious progenitor."

La Fuente amusedly consented to be present at the birth and to give instructions to the household for the arrangement of the chamber in which the delivery would take place. He named a midwife. "Your child will have a birth supervised as carefully as if he were Prince of the Asturias," he assured his alarmed new friend after listening to an account of his disastrous earlier experiences. "Nothing less will do," the artist replied.

In spite of this considerable distraction, Domenikos continued to paint with enthusiasm. Only a few days after Jerónima's disclosure of her condition, he was able to announce to Diego de Castilla that studies for the eight paintings to be installed in Santo Domingo were ready for his inspection. The dean, pleased with these little images, responded by ordering that a final contract be drawn, setting a figure of 1500 ducats for Domenikos' share of the completed work, an amount the artist could only think princely for his first large commission.

Yet during the months of autumn and winter his mistress remained his chief preoccupation. The baby was due no earlier than April, if her calculations were exact. The waiting didn't grow more bearable as the seasons passed. Not even when painting was he able wholly to drive from his mind the impending event. He attended evensong with a regularity the most fanatic religionist would have admired, disregarding the rigors of Toledo's winter climate to offer up fervent prayers for her safety and the good health of his unborn child. Much as he wanted a son, he vowed to feel no regret if the infant were a girl, so long as mother and baby survived and flourished.

Jerónima at first remonstrated with him. "I am not fragile, Menegos. I don't need to be treated as if I were an egg, and I don't want to be." But she gradually understood that her need wasn't the operative factor; his was. His rather frantic concern, if now and then annoying, was deeply moving to her. She finally could believe, as he insisted passionately, that she was loved. She finally could say in the darkness of their bedchamber, "I love you. I'm sure of it now." Though he made no statement in reply to this declaration, Jerónima had no need of light to know that he wept.

Just after Christmas, he received from his brother the news that his mother had died. God was balancing things again. He replied at once, reproaching Manusos for not having written sooner, since the letter spoke of a long illness. "I weep as I write, to think of her in the earth of Fodele beside papa. I weep for myself, for you. I have never known anyone who received all of life with such grace. I think she had ultimate wisdom. She knew her limitations and permitted herself not a moment of self-pity for the boundaries they imposed on her." He expressed delight to learn that his brother was now the father of three daughters. "I could wish," he added, "that you were more specific about the prosperity you say you and Katina and your babies enjoy."

Jerónima's estimate was in error. She began to feel pain in late March, causing Domenikos more consternation than she herself could sense. La Fuente was summoned. The physician, most skeptical, returned with Francesco. A brief examination cleared the doubt from his features. He ordered that the midwife come at once and that the young Italian "take that mad painter to a tavern and get him drunk. Take him anywhere as long as you keep him out of this room."

Domenikos at first refused to leave the house. He certainly wanted nothing to drink at such a moment. Then he had another thought. I'll go to Santo Tomé, Francesco. If anything happens before I come back, you can find me there." Before the altar of a chapel dedicated to St. Francis, the artist knelt in prayer, lighting candle after candle as fear and hope still contended for possession of his spirit.

When he could bear the suspense no longer, he returned home, to find the situation unchanged. "I will have something to drink now, Antonia," he said wearily to his cook, a voluble woman of fifty from a neighboring hamlet. She placed a goblet on the table in the dining room and slowly filled it from a flagon. "There," she said. "Now drink, master. It's no good worrying." The painter agreed. "But how do you stop?" He drank deeply and refilled his cup. He drank steadily for an hour, emptying the large flagon. And then he slept.

Francesco awakened him with difficulty. "Master, master," he said when Domenikos was at last aroused. "The baby is born. You have a son."

This intelligence couldn't be taken in at once. He lifted his head and stared drowsily at the Italian who had lived through so much with him. "A son?" he muttered. "And Doña Jerónima?"

"She's well, master. The doctor has just left. He said to tell you she was fine."

Domenikos stood up and embraced Francesco, laughing maniacally. "By God, my friend, what a wonderful thing." He broke away abruptly and made for the chamber so carefully prepared for this great event. He paused at the door and looked back at the smiling assistant. "A son? You're sure of it?"

Francesco merely nodded.

He entered the room cautiously to find the bustling midwife making preparations to leave. Ignoring her, he stood at the bedside, feeling at once awkward and grateful and relieved and bewildered, staring first at the mother, then at the child beside her. He sat on the edge of the bed and embraced her tenderly. Jerónima's eyes were bright with pleasure, her face drawn.

"It's a son," he murmured, burying his face in her hair.

"You see, Menegos? You should have listened to me all along. There was nothing to worry about."

"Yes," he acknowledged, "but hindsight is always better informed."

The infant was named Jorge Manuel, after the parents' fathers. He was baptized a few days later in the Church of Santo Tomé, with an honored Don Luis de Castilla standing as godfather.

The brown-haired, brown-eyed child prospered during his early months of life. His doting father discovered that concentration on his work now was almost as difficult as it had been throughout Jerónima's pregnancy, so often was he tempted to slip from his studio and peer into the elaborate cradle he had designed for the little Jorge. Domenikos was, however, well enough disciplined not to permit himself this delightful luxury to detract from his work. By the end of July, he was able to show his patron Castilla the completed paintings of the Assumption and the Trinity, the two largest canvases destined for Santo Domingo, and to report that important progress had been made by the sullen Monegro toward the construction of the altarpieces themselves. The dean described himself as thrilled with the paintings. He expressed his rapture in practical terms, offering to pay Domenikos the entire sum agreed on for the finished work.

The artist, whose expenditures on materials had been alarmingly high, consented to payment, but he added a condition. "I'll accept only a thousand ducats, Don Diego."

Castilla was perplexed. "But why, Greco?"

"Call it a gesture of gratitude."

"You've already given me that wonderful painting of St. Sebastian."

"Which you sent off to Palencia." He laughed. "This is a present you can't give away."

"But it's not my money."

"Those are my terms. Consider it a gesture of gratitude to Toledo. For the first time in my life, I'm a completely happy man, and you and Luis are so much responsible."

Don Diego reluctantly assented to the artist's demand, promising to ease his conscience in the matter by donating the difference to the poor of Toledo, of whom, as in all cities, there were too many.

Domenikos had by now begun as well the full-scale rendering of the Espolio for the chapter. Don García de Loysa, ever polite but firm, made occasional calls to the studio to inquire about its progress. With equal courtesy, the painter assured him that all was proceeding well but declined to permit his patron to view the unfinished painting. "You might form the wrong impression," he maintained. Because it was a single picture rather than a series and because it was destined to hang in the cathedral, Domenikos devoted proportionately more time to his creation of the Espolio than to the Santo Domingo commission. It must be a striking thing in itself, not dependent on a retable or elaborate frame to make powerful impact on the beholder. In order to give this work just the qualities of light and shadow it required, he followed the example of Tintoretto, visiting the vestry at different hours of the day, in different seasons, to evaluate the intensities of light admitted by the narrow windows of the chamber.

To one schooled in Italy, Toledo's cathedral was a comparatively modern church, the painter's first intimate exposure to the French and Spanish Gothic styles. He had seen the cathedral of Milan only in passing on his journey from Venice to Genoa.

The principal façade was asymmetrical, featuring a lofty spire and a dome in the early Renaissance manner of the duomo in Florence. The central portals were elaborately carved, adumbrating the ornate decoration of the immense nave. Most striking to Domenikos, because they were unknown in Crete and rare in Italy, were the stained-glass windows which cast wonderful colors on the columns and floor.

The church was rich in painting, most of it Italian, with a number of Spanish pictures that were of interest more as a dismal record of native art than for their aesthetic appeal. Its greatest treasure, quantitatively speaking, was of sculpture, virtually none of which impressed Domenikos, whose taste was influenced by the heroic realism of Michelangelo.

On one of his visits to the vestry, late in an August day, the artist encountered Pompeo Leoni, the Italian sculptor. The two had met occasionally, but their relationship had never become more than casually friendly. Domenikos would have welcomed a closer bond, for he profoundly missed informed discussion about art, especially with someone who spoke Italian, a language in which he still felt more secure. He supposed Luis de Castilla's explanation of the general hostility expressed by Toledan artists was exact. "They're simply jealous of you. And why shouldn't they be? You've been successful since your first day here, and you're better than any of them."

Nevertheless, Domenikos believed Leoni might prove the exception. He was in the service of the King. Thus he could scarcely think the newcomer a serious rival, the more so since his father now worked exclusively for Philip at the Escorial, where he enjoyed the highest esteem.

Pompeo Leoni was approximately Domenikos' age, squarely built, heavily bearded, his manner somewhat bluff. He was contemplating a painting of the Flood, one of three works by Bassano in the cathedral, when he heard the artist's approaching footsteps. He turned and brusquely muttered a greeting. After the briefest of pauses, Domenikos moved to the altar of the vestry. To his surprise, Leoni followed.

"Gloating over the space you're to fill?"

The painter laughed, and explained the reason for his frequent visits. The sculptor listened with genuine interest to Domenikos' account of the method applied by Tintoretto in the Scuola de San Rocco.

"Ingenious," he said. "But at least a painter doesn't have to worry about a third dimension."

"But he does, Leoni. The painter's third dimension is all the more difficult because it's illusory."

The sculptor considered this for a time, plainly impressed. "I'd not thought of that." He paused and looked curiously at Domenikos. "You enjoy Toledo?"

"Very much."

"You plan to stay?"

"Indefinitely. It suits me. And you?"

Leoni shook his head. "I prefer a place that's growing. I'm hoping to receive a large commission from the King as soon as I'm done here."

"What are you working on?"

"A bust of the King and a sarcophagus for the nave here."

"I'd like to see them."

Leoni shrugged, though he was pleased. "I'm going to my studio now. Come along, if you like."

Leoni, the painter knew, had studied for a time with Michelangelo; it was this that had prompted his request quite as much as a desire to know the man better. The two pieces, about three-quarters completed, were a disappointment, products of an excellent craftsman who had neither inspiration nor magic.

Yet he was drawn to the man. Behind a mannered arrogance there was something else. Bitterness? Disappointment? Disillusionment? Did he realize that he would never approach in skill or reputation the achievement of his illustrious father? A new father himself, who recalled Titian's poignant observations about Orazio, Domenikos was moved to pity Leoni. He praised especially the bust of the King.

The sculptor pretended to ruffle the white marble hair. "It's good enough for Philip, anyhow."

They talked for a time of the monarch, whom Leoni both loathed and admired. "You have to admire a king, unless you're his mistress or his valet." When he learned that Domenikos had made no effort to establish contact with the great ruler, he was astounded. "You must be the only artist in Spain who hasn't."

The painter shrugged. "I planned to when I first arrived, but I'm so busy now I've no time for another large commission."

"I know all about it. As a matter of fact, I've just seen what Monegro is doing for you. You're not exactly his friend are you?"

"Hardly."

"That doesn't matter, as long as you have powerful allies. That's why you should think about getting a commission from the King. He pays well, and more than that, he pays when he promises to and he never dickers over price, which is more than you can say for most of these church people."

"I've had no trouble," the painter replied, and described his dealings with Diego de Castilla.

Leoni wasn't impressed. "Just wait, Greco."

Domenikos and the sculptor became friends, though they never enjoyed the intimacy the artist had known with Orsini or now with Luis de Castilla. Leoni was more entertaining than profound. He regaled the painter and Jerónima with anecdotes about Philip II and Carlos V, those concerning the latter told him by his father, who had served the emperor and, for a brief period, been imprisoned by him. He pressed Domenikos to solicit a commission from the court, a suggestion persistently rejected. He did, however, prevail in his request for a portrait, in exchange for which he undertook to make a bust of his new friend.

Leoni arrived, one October morning, for a last sitting. He was breathless and excited. "Have you heard the news? Don Juan of Austria is dead."

The painter wondered what sort of reaction was expected. He could scarcely be more uninterested. "Oh?" he said at last.

"Died of fever at Namur," Leoni went on.

"I'm sorry to hear it."

"You don't see the implications? This is the King's half-brother, an international hero, commander of the fleet at Lepanto, ruler of the Low Countries. And he's dead. You must now paint a picture to commemorate his death."

"For whom?"

"For the King, of course. He despised Don Juan when he was alive, but now that he's dead he'll be treated as a hero. They're to bring his remains back to Spain and place them in the Escorial beside his father."

Domenikos indicated that Leoni should assume his pose. "It seems the least the King can do for a man who served him so well."

Leoni pointed to his temple with a work-coarsened finger. "A thinking man would paint an appropriate picture, Greco. The King would appreciate it."

"I don't paint occasional pictures. Besides, what would be appropriate? Another scene of Lepanto? There must be hundreds."

The sculptor sighed. "If you just did a study of something relevant to Don Juan, it would help to establish you with Philip."

"It's too cynical, Leoni. I don't care about Don Juan."

"Neither does the King. Of course it's cynical. But it's practical."

Domenikos promised to think about it, a vow Leoni correctly interpreted as ending the discussion. The painter, however, did give the subject thought and mentioned it to Jerónima, whose judgment about things Spanish he valued. She agreed with the sculptor that a study for a commemorative picture could do no harm. "You can't be considered the greatest painter in Spain if you do no work for the King." Added to this unanswerable point, heartily concurred in by both Castillas, was the announcement, in the winter of 1579, that King Philip was to make a ten-day state visit to Toledo the following June. Domenikos' highly placed friends guaranteed that the monarch would see his work while he was in the city. It would be, he said, foolish to refuse such an opportunity.

The study was of an allegorical scene based on the Battle of Lepanto, a fantasy that would appeal to a patron reportedly enamored of the work of Hieronymus Bosch. It incorporated portraits of the King, as well as of his brother, and representations of Pius V, the Doge Mocenigo, Cardinal Borromeo and Marcantonio Colonna, all major figures in the great victory over the Turks.

Leoni was emphatic in his praise, not only for the portrait of Philip (based on his own bust), but for the great serpentine mouth of hell. "It really seethes," he exclaimed gleefully. "Philip will find that attractive."

Construction of the Church of Santo Domingo had been delayed. Installation of the altarpieces was postponed until late summer. Domenikos, however, continued to press Monegro during the early months of 1579. Only when the retable was fully assembled could the gilding be done. And only when this occurred could he be certain that the work had been properly accomplished. He was relieved, therefore, to learn, just before his son's first birthday, that the various elements of the principal and side altars had been put together. He hastened to the architect's workshop and found the three works propped at a slight angle against a wall.

He took only a single close look at the central reredos when, enraged, he turned to an artisan standing beside him. "Get Monegro at once, at once."

He then considered the smaller altars, his fists clenched, his throat dry with fury, his eyes wide. He turned once more to see the proprietor strolling casually toward him across the cavernous room. Domenikos rushed to meet him, seizing his arm and propelling him forward.

"You've ruined them, you fool. You've ruined them. They're wider than they should be, all three of them, and at least two feet higher than I instructed."

Monegro nodded, not a bit impressed by the painter's anger. "Yes and no."

"What does that mean?"

"Yes, I changed the sizes. No, I didn't ruin them. In fact, I've improved them. Your proportions were all wrong. They would have looked silly."

Domenikos gasped. "Wrong, for God's sake? Who told you they were wrong?"

"No one," was the sullen reply. "I could see it for myself."

"And you just went ahead and made the changes without a word to anyone?"

"You wouldn't want people to laugh at you."

"I don't want anyone tampering with my designs."

The architect folded his heavy arms over his full chest and grunted. "I *told* you the commission should have been mine. You're no builder." He smiled ominously. "I know people who don't think you're even much of a painter either."

The artist put his hand over his face. What was to be done? He stared hotly at his stolid adversary. "This is most arrogant thing I've ever known, Monegro."

"*You* were arrogant to think you could design this."

"That's your opinion. I'm not even sure the thing will fit when the sculpture is attached."

"It will fit. I've measured."

"We'll see what Don Diego says about this. It would have been simple courtesy to mention it to one of us, you know."

Monegro snorted. "Courtesy is for the nobility." He turned over his gnarled hands and held them before Domenikos' eyes as if they were proud banners. "I'm a craftsman. I know my work, which is more than you can say. Those altars are better than you designed them. You'll see for yourself. And they'll fit, too." He grinned. "If they don't, you can have me scourged in the Zocodover."

"If they don't, Monegro, it would give me a sickening pleasure to scourge you personally." He turned to leave. "Don't do anything more until I've spoken with Don Diego."

The dean of Toledo offered comfort that was cold indeed. He listened with polite interest as Domenikos described Monegro's outrage and agreed that even if the altars fitted properly there was an important principle involved. Admitting the builder had certainly been high-handed, he promised to have a word with him.

The painter's rage was spent but he found himself annoyed by Castilla's bland reaction. "This is a very serious matter, Don Diego."

"It is, Greco. But let me ask you this. You're not going to have to change the sizes of your paintings, are you?"

"No."

"And if we insist that Monegro correct the altars now, we'll have to wait a long time, a year or even two. I have an idea he wouldn't rush the work. . . ."

The painter sighed and nodded. "So we yield?"

"We yield."

He made his way home through the gathering darkness, angry, dismayed, frustrated; his thoughts, like the weather, bleak and windy.

Twenty-Four

The arrival in Toledo of Philip II and his entourage was an occasion for rejoicing. The long procession could be seen approaching the city from a considerable distance, and a large proportion of the population lined the battlements to observe its stately passage across the plain, through the gates and the Zocodover, at last to draw up in ceremonial order in the Plaza del Ayuntamiento.

The King, magnificent in his ritual armor, rode directly behind the banners of the vanguard, his black stallion (or was it, the malicious wondered, a gelding?) prancing hotly. In the square, Philip accepted the fawning welcome of the *alcalde mayor,* of the *regidors,* and finally that of his official host, the Cardinal, Primate of all Spain.

The royal party was quartered in the state apartments of the Alcázar which had been refurbished for the occasion by Herrera, the King's favorite architect. Official and social functions had been planned for each day and evening of the visit. If the schedule was rigidly followed, Diego de Castilla thought it unlikely that Philip would be able to visit Domenikos' studio. Pressure was, however, being applied to important courtiers; he wasn't to lose hope.

The most powerful man in Europe spent the first three days of his June visit according to plan, occupying himself with matters related to the real occasion for his being here—his relations with the Cardinal. He was in Toledo to insist that the Church must contribute more money to the crown. The Cardinal was sympathetic but adamant. The Church had her problems too and was not nearly so rich as the King imagined. A *modus vivendi* might be discovered, however. Further discussion was necessary. Committees must be formed.

Late in the afternoon of the fourth day, a perspiring young clerk from the Palacio Arzobispal made a panting entrance into the painter's studio. Don Diego wanted the master to know that the King was coming to his house within the hour.

Domenikos immediately summoned Francesco. Together they brought the recently completed painting of the Espolio into his studio from an adjacent storeroom and leaned it against a high white wall. On an easel beside it, they set his study for the Allegory of the Holy League.

The painter then hurried to the dining room where Jerónima was amusing herself by carefully mouthing the names of objects in view to the little Jorge, who toddled precariously from chair to bench, falling down and righting himself, gurgling and clutching his ears to the delight of mother and nurse.

"The King *is* coming," he announced, quite breathless. "He'll be here any minute. I've just had a message from Don Diego."

For the first time in his experience with her, Jerónima appeared flustered. "Any minute? My God, I've got to change, and so should you. You're a fright."

Domenikos laughed nervously. "It's all right. I'm in my working clothes."

He returned to his studio and despairingly surveyed the unprepossessing scene. It was certainly no place in which one would normally receive a king. However, there seemed nothing normal in the situation. Nor were changes possible at this late hour. How late it was soon became apparent. A courtier, his style most condescending, loomed grandly in the doorway, a wide-eyed Antonia standing anxiously behind him. The man gazed about the room, his face a study in distaste.

"But surely, you don't expect His Majesty to stand."

Domenikos couldn't restrain his laughter. Then, embarrassed, he hastily apologized. "I'm sorry, sire, but until a few moments ago, I didn't know His Majesty was coming at all."

"Then fetch him a chair, a clean chair, if that's to be found in such a filthy loft."

His contempt so outraged Domenikos that he forgot to control his tongue. "Say 'please,' " he commanded.

The courtier was scandalized. "Do you know whom you're speaking to?"

"A messenger boy."

Scandal gave way to confusion. The young man seemed for a moment to lose the power of speech. In this pause, the painter nodded to an alarmed Francesco, who disappeared in search of a chair.

The courtier's voice returned. "You seem to forget that I'm in no way obliged to be polite to you."

Domenikos laughed. "Nor am I to you, sir."

The assistant, aided by Jerónima and Jorge's nurse, returned to the studio with a leather-upholstered armchair. The young man, evidently satisfied, sniffed and disappeared. In a moment or two, he was back again, standing very erect, his spine crushed against the jamb of the door.

"His Most Catholic Majesty," he pompously intoned, the words resounding in the large studio.

The King, in the modest black he affected for modest occasions, was suddenly standing in the studio. He was smaller than the painter had imagined; yet in his rigid bearing and the tight, cautious little steps he took, he suggested something like regality.

Domenikos knelt awkwardly; genuflections to a king were no daily routine. His mistress had fully regained her aplomb, and seemed unawed by the great presence in her house; she curtsied as gracefully as she had done the evening of her first meeting with the painter.

Philip acknowledged her gesture with a stiff little bow, then turned his eyes to Domenikos. "You are Maestro El Greco?"

"I am, sire."

"And the lady?" He looked at Jerónima with unsmiling interest.

"Doña Jerónima de las Cuevas, sire."

The King reached for her hand and brought it quickly to his almost ashen lips. "Doña Jerónima." He released her fingers and took a small step backward. "Don't I know a connection of yours?"

She nodded. "Perhaps, sire. My brother is in your army."

"I recall the name. And your father was in my service too, wasn't he?"

"He fell at St. Quentin, sire."

Philip's expression divulged no shadow of sympathy or regret. "In our great cause there." He paused. "And yet your grandfather, Doña Jerónima, was my father's enemy, I believe."

Jerónima shook her lovely head. "So the emperor thought, sire, but my grandfather considered himself a friend of Spain."

The monarch permitted himself the slightest breath of a sigh, the smallest glimmer of a smile. "Yes, dear lady. All the *Communeros* held that view, to my father's chagrin . . . and their own." He turned to Domenikos. "You're very fortunate, maestro, in having so beautiful a companion."

The painter bowed his head and smiled. "That's true, sire."

"But I've been led to understand that artists are often fortunate in this way. What is it about them that attracts lovely women?"

Domenikos couldn't make out whether the King was asking the question out of interest or simply to make conversation. "I can't say, sire."

Philip turned to Jerónima, his gray eyebrows rising.

She laughed easily. "Nor can I answer you, sire, in general terms. But in particular, for my own part, it's that El Greco keeps all his anger for his painting and all his gentleness for our son and me." She turned to the nurse, who was holding a squirming Jorge.

The King smiled, something it seemed clear he didn't do often, for the expression was a contortion for the muscles of his face, a travesty. "There was a time when I'd have given a great deal to hear such words about myself from the lips of a lady like you, Doña Jerónima. If they were said to me now, I'd have the woman thrown in irons as a liar." His gaze returned to the artist. "Guard her well, maestro. She must be your most valuable possession."

"It's because she's *not* my possession, sire, that I must guard her well."

"Just so," said Philip pensively. Then it was evident that the social aspect of the interview had come to an end. His face hardened slightly as he went on. "You have important and persuasive friends in Toledo. They've importuned my ministers day and night in your behalf, urging that I see your painting. It seems to me your name is on every tongue. But so far I've only seen your portrait of Pompeo Leoni. It is admirable."

"Thank you, sire."

"Since you're a friend of his, I believe, you'll be interested to learn that I've asked him to come to the Escorial to work there with his father."

"He deserves your patronage, sire. He's a fine sculptor."

The King obviously derived little pleasure from being agreed with. He ignored Domenikos' comment and lifted a slim arm, pointing a languid finger at the Espolio inclined against the wall. "This is a new work?"

"Yes, sire, for the vestry of the cathedral."

"I've heard of it from the Castillas and Don García de Loysa. It's to be placed there soon."

"There's to be an evaluation of it tomorrow, sire."

Philip stood before the painting, his eyes traveling slowly across its surface. Then, courtier at his arm, he settled himself at last in the chair and considered it once more. "It's magnificent and quite appropriate for a vestry. Otherwise I'd have it for myself."

"I could make you a replica, sire."

"No, maestro," he said precisely. "The work I commission must be unique." His eyes returned to the Espolio. "But it's superb. What drama, what excitement." He looked at Domenikos, his expression faintly curious. "It's very daring, very advanced. Your friends didn't prepare me for that in your work."

"They haven't your breadth of experience with art, sire."

The King's expression was suddenly suspicious. "You didn't, I take it, mean to be facetious."

Domenikos was pleased to note that this rather hostile observation failed to alarm him. He responded without haste. "No, sire. I meant it seriously. You must be the world's greatest collector. That's the common opinion."

Philip's faint smile was wry. "Spendthrift, extravagant, say my enemies." He paused. "I *am* acquisitive."

The painter nodded. "When I was a pupil of Titian, sire, I had the honor of helping in a modest way with several paintings you'd commissioned him to make, especially the Martyrdom of St. Lawrence."

"He was a great master." The King grew sad. "I miss his presence in this life."

"I do too, sire. I was in Venice when he died."

"I miss his letters. He was a graceful old liar, full of hopeless promises and the most extravagant and transparent flattery." A frown suddenly corrugated the royal brow. "Didn't he write me about you, maestro?"

"Twice, I think, sire, the last time about four years ago, when I was in Rome."

"I remember." He hesitated, then abruptly changed the subject. "Don Diego tells me you've made a study of a subject connected in some way with my late brother Don Juan."

"It's just a small panel, sire." He signaled to Francesco to bring the easel closer to the King.

Philip examined the picture at length. Domenikos detected the trace of a smile as his eyes rested on the portrait of himself. As he stared into the gaping jaws of hell in the lower right corner, he seemed, for an instant, in a sort of ecstasy.

"What do you call this?"

"It's an allegory, sire, of the Holy League."

"It has power, maestro." He turned his eyes from the painting to the painter. "You're very original. I'd like a full-size rendering of this. How long will it take?" He paused. "You see, I'm very impatient."

"I've much to do, sire. A few months, I should think."

"Good. When it's finished, let me know. Then I want you to bring it to me yourself, to the Escorial. We can discuss another commission and some other plans I have in mind. Since Navarrete died, there's been a vacancy for the post of my master painter." He became wary.

"I promise nothing, you understand. You might not be interested. But I've yet to find the successor for poor El Mudo. He studied for a time with Titian too, you know."

"Maestro Tiziano mentioned him, sire."

"We're always interested in artists, maestro. I must say that your work intrigues me."

With the superfluous aid of his courtier, Philip rose, acknowledged the painter's genuflection and Jerónima's curtsy and quickly disappeared.

Domenikos had looked forward to the evaluation of the Espolio with trepidation. As García de Loysa had explained the process, it seemed reasonable enough; impartial "experts" representing artist and patron made separate appraisals and then, presumably, reached a compromise figure. What disturbed him was that even the most open-minded man must find it impossible to view a work objectively. He complained of this to the Castillas, to Leoni, to Francesco and Jerónima. "What's the difference between a personal opinion and a disinterested judgment where a work of art is concerned?" No one offered an answer that satisfied him.

He requested that Leoni act as one of his appraisers, but the friend firmly refused, sensibly arguing that his relationship with Domenikos precluded even the semblance of objectivity. The sculptor suggested a Toledan colleague, Martínez de Casteñada, and a young painter from Murcia, Baltasar de Castro Cimbrón—both unknown to the artist. The chapter selected Luis de Velasco, a local painter, and Nicolás de Vergara, the cathedral's master of works. The choice of Vergara alarmed Domenikos. The architect resented the fact that he had lost the commission to build the church of Santo Domingo and was a close friend of Hernando de Ávila, whom the artist had replaced as designer of the altarpieces.

Just before the appraisers were to arrive on the morning after the King's visit to his studio, Domenikos himself attempted an objective examination of the painting in an effort to see it as if for the first time. Philip's judgment was correct. It was a work of the first order, dramatic, powerful, original, audacious.

In the center of the picture, an imposing, red-robed Christ was set upon from all sides by assailants who sought to strip Him of His garments. In the immediate foreground, to his left, was the bending figure of Francesco as a peasant, extracting a spike from a log. To the

Savior's right were the three Marys (Veronica, Maria, and Jerónima), who observed Francesco's effort. Directly behind Christ's left elbow stood Luis de Castilla, in armor as St. Longinus, the Roman centurion who was finally made to believe. To the right and left of Jesus was the rabble, and some behind Him whose heads loomed over Him menacingly.

The result of the evaluation would have been amusing to the artist had it concerned someone else's work. Vergara and Velasco, after expressing vast admiration for the picture, declared their view that the chapter should pay 227 ducats. For Domenikos, Martínez and Castro Cimbrón set a figure of 900. So staggering a discrepancy seemed impossible to reconcile. Domenikos angrily demanded a second evaluation. "I'll burn the painting," he informed García de Loysa, "before I'll accept so derisory an amount." The impassive bursar declined to budge from the lower sum. He did, however, consent to the second appraisal, adding two stipulations: that it be made by one mutually acceptable expert and that the figure this man set be binding on both parties.

These terms seemed ridiculous. Yet the artist reluctantly concurred, feeling certain that this new evaluation would result in a substantially higher amount. He was anxious that this annoying issue be settled as quickly as possible.

A month elapsed, however, before an expert was selected. Still following Leoni's advice, Domenikos rejected four candidates before the name of Alejo de Montoya was proposed by the chapter. His credentials seemed odd; he was Toledo's most highly regarded goldsmith. But, as the sculptor pointed out, he had no reason to be envious of a painter. To this the apprehensive artist responded that a goldsmith would undoubtedly deal gingerly with the canons, since he must receive important orders from them. In the end, he assented to Montoya's selection. The affair must be settled.

The goldsmith, no less enthusiastic in his praise than Vergara and Velasco, felt a price of 317 ducats would be fair. When Domenikos protested, reminding him of the sum set by Martínez and Castro Cimbrón, Montoya was unmoved. "You can't expect to obtain the prices here that you'd be paid in Venice or Rome, maestro."

As soon as Montoya had left his studio, the painter descended to the strongroom, below ground level, where his coffers were stored. He counted out two hundred gold ducats, the amount the chapter had so far advanced him for the Espolio, and hastened to the Palacio

Arzobispal, where he sought an immediate interview with García de Loysa.

The bursar received him with polite coolness, expressing but mild surprise when Domenikos placed a velvet purse on the table behind which he was sitting.

"This is all you've paid me, Don García. If this is the way things are done in Toledo, I want no part of it."

Loysa responded blandly, pushing the sack to the artist's side. "You have me at a disadvantage, maestro. Do I gather that Maestro Alejo has made his appraisal?"

"He proposes that the chapter pay only ninety ducats more."

"I think that very generous."

"You know it's a scandal."

"You reject it?"

Domenikos pointed to the purse. "Isn't it plain?"

"Yet you agreed to accept Montoya's price."

"I never dreamt it would be nearly as preposterous as the first."

"You're being very unreasonable. After all, we made the same agreement. If the evaluation had been higher, we'd have had to pay."

"I think myself eminently reasonable, Don Garcia. I'm not asking you to pay more. I'm returning your gold and retaining the picture. It's the finest thing I've ever painted. I'll not see it treated as a joke."

Loysa considered this statement for a time. "There is, I think, one thing you should bear in mind, maestro. We thought it ill advised to bring it up until the matter of price was settled. But since you've taken this new line, I'll tell you now. There are certain elements that will have to be changed in the picture, masterpiece that it may be."

Domenikos sat down heavily in a chair facing the bursar and stared at him, incredulous. "What do you mean?"

"As it stands, it's heretical. It plainly violates the decree of the Councils of Trent. There's not a shred of canonical or scriptural evidence, for example, to justify the presence of the three Marys."

The painter agreed. "But the Scriptures don't say they weren't present, and it's certainly plausible to think them in attendance at such a moment."

Loysa evinced mild amazement. "You're offering to instruct the Church on the implications of Holy Writ?"

"Hardly that. I was explaining my position."

The unruffled bursar smiled. "Then perhaps you'll explain something even more damaging, the fact that almost every person in the painting except for the three Marys and the peasant is either taller or posed at a higher level than Our Lord."

In spite of his anger, Domenikos could only laugh. "You're not suggesting that I've not made Our Lord the dominant figure?"

"I'm discussing the orthodoxy of your inconography. You well know that it's been decreed that Christ shall in no way be shown as inferior to mortals."

"You've completely misunderstood the Espolio as I've conceived it."

Loysa bowed satirically. "I leave aesthetics to Don Diego. Regardless of the value of the painting as art, or in terms of ducats, these defects must be altered."

The painter's expression was grim. "I'll make no changes."

"We shall see."

A brief respite from the annoyances of the prolonged dispute over the Espolio was granted by the consecration, early in September, of the Church of Santo Domingo. Though still indignant over Monegro's gratuitous alterations, Domenikos was pleased that they had not seriously affected the conception and general impression he had intended. The effect was of elegance. Throughout the service, the artist was pleased to note that when Don Diego's attention could be diverted from his role in the mass his eyes flitted to the painting of the resurrection in one of the lateral altars, in which the artist had represented his benefactor as St. Ildefonso.

The Spanish City of God responded to this first of Domenikos' major commissions with an enthusiasm that could only be gratifying to him. Don Antonio de Covarrubias, renowned throughout Europe as a humanist, jurist, theologian, and professor at Toledo's university, accosted the artist at the conclusion of the service and expressed his admiration for the work in the warmest terms. He invited Domenikos to pay him a visit. The *alcalde mayor,* resplendent in his official robes, was equally (if less informedly) impressed. The Conde de Fuensalidas was jubilant. "Just think, Greco. You might have become a member of Moro's academy instead of mine." He pointed to a surly nobleman, the Conde de Moro, who stood impatiently in the crowded aisle, waiting to escape. Moro's academy vied with Fuensalidas' for intellectual supremacy in Toledo.

Relief was, as he had anticipated, only temporary. When Domenikos made it clear to the Castillas that he intended neither to accept Montoya's evaluation nor to accede to Loysa's demand for alterations in the Espolio, an obstinacy they vigorously deplored, they urged him to seek legal advice, a suggestion he followed.

He consulted Dr. Gregorio Angulo, a *regidor* whom he knew well from their meetings in the Palacio Fuensalidas. With sympathy and patience, the clever-eyed, cheerful member of the city's governing council listened to the artist's complaints.

"Are you prepared to reach agreement, Greco, or do you simply want to fight?"

Domenikos found the question surprising at first, then grinned as he understood its implication. "You think my viewpoint belligerent?"

"I think it stupid. Which is more important to you, the money or the painting?"

"The painting."

"Then why not suggest a settlement? You accept the evaluation, but refuse to change the picture."

"What's the alternative, Angulo?"

"A hearing in the Ayuntamiento. The *alcalde* will make the decision." He paused. "And he'll decide for the chapter. In legal terms, you've not much chance, and in practical terms, by which I mean emotional terms, no chance at all."

"Do you think the canons would agree to the compromise you suggest?"

The lawyer chuckled. "No, but every possibility must be explored."

"What do you propose, then?"

"Agree to their terms. Get on with your work."

Domenikos thought for a moment. "No," he said defiantly. "There's an important point involved. I want to fight."

Angulo sighed. "I thought so."

When the day of the hearing came, all concerned in this miserable affair appeared before the mayor in the magnificent Renaissance hall of the city's town hall. One by one, the canons gave their views of the religious lapses depicted in the Espolio, the appraisers their opinions on the painting's monetary value. Alejo de Montoya concluded this phase of the testimony, repeating much of what he had said to Domenikos.

"When I first saw the painting, I thought it the finest I'd ever beheld. I'm of the same opinion still. In fact, if I were to have assessed it at its true value, I'd have been compelled to set so high a price that few persons, perhaps no one at all, could have paid it. However, in

the light of present conditions and in view of the prices normally paid
in Castile for paintings of this size by such great masters as El Greco,
I set the sum of three hundred seventeen ducats. Don García
de Loysa has agreed to this."

The mayor questioned Montoya about the iconography. The
witness refused to be drawn out. Those were matters for theologians,
he said, not goldsmiths.

It was then Domenikos' turn to be heard. Angulo's interrogation
of him was designed to elicit as much sympathy for the painter's view
as was possible, drawing attention to his refusal to accept full payment
for the Santo Domingo commission (so admired by the mayor only
weeks before), to his importance as a cultural figure in the
community, his reputation abroad, his audience ("in your own
house") with the King and the royal patronage that had resulted.

Counsel for the chapter, understandably, took quite another course.
"Would you tell us in precisely what manner you live in Toledo?"

The painter shook his head sharply, his expression less agitated
than his feelings. "I see no reason to answer. The question has no
bearing on the matter at issue. My personal life is of no concern."

There was a rumble of astonishment in the hall, but the advocate
himself appeared unfazed by this direct refusal to respond.

"Do you own property in Toledo?"

"I don't see that this question bears on the case either."

The lawyer turned and looked questioningly at the mayor, who
nodded. "It's germane," he said to Domenikos, "because at present
the painting in question is in your possession, isn't it? And you've already been paid two hundred ducats?"

"Yes, which I attempted to return."

"And isn't it true that you came to Toledo expressly to design that
altarpiece for Santo Domingo?"

This time it was Domenikos who looked hopefully at the magistrate, but received no sign. "My reasons for coming to Toledo have
no bearing."

"But it is a fact, nevertheless, that you've now completed the Santo
Domingo commission."

"I have."

The counsel pressed on. "So wouldn't it be possible for you to
leave the city at any moment you pleased, thus depriving the chapter
of a painting for which you've already been paid a substantial sum?"

"Are you suggesting I'd steal a picture after having tried to return
the amount advanced me for it?"

"I am asking you only if the possibility doesn't exist."

Domenikos smiled. "In theory, it exists. But as a man of honor, I'd of course do nothing of the sort."

"I'm certain of it," was the dry, skeptical response. "Now, about the matter of price."

Domenikos didn't wait for the question. "You've already heard Maestro Alejo. If it were appraised as its true worth, no one could afford it. But the price that's proposed is completely unacceptable to me."

Unperturbed, the lawyer persisted. "Nor is your painting acceptable to the chapter. I cite specifically the presence of the three Marys, which is against Scripture, and the placement of figures at a level higher than that of Our Lord, which is against doctrine. It appears that you've taken intolerable liberties."

The painter couldn't repress his smile. "That's not a question."

"You may reply to it, maestro," said the mayor, not unsympathetically, "as if it *were*."

Domenikos bowed. "With respect to the three Marys, it seemed only logical that they be present, even though it's not mentioned."

The lawyer was owlish. "You ask us to think this a Biblical oversight?"

"Something of the sort."

"And the other matter?"

"This other objection is capricious. Anyone who has seen the painting must agree that I've in no way denigrated Our Lord. He's seen to be surrounded by a throng of ignorant, wily, wilful, wicked men who intend to demean him, yet they cannot. He alone stands out in my painting, absolutely triumphant."

"But without a crown of thorns."

"It's my supposition that this would have been placed on his head immediately afterward."

"You think these objections capricious?"

Domenikos hesitated. How plainly should he speak? He shrugged. If he were doomed, let the record at least show that he had stated his view without equivocation. "I can't of course know that. It does seem to me that these questions of iconography, which were raised only after I'd refused to accept the second appraisal, are intended to distract attention from the central point. How serious they are, only Don García and the other canons can say. This is a painting completely within the accepted traditions of Christian art. I resent any attempt to suggest that I am myself a heretic for having made this picture or that the picture is despicable for reasons that seem at best narrow-minded and at worst insidious."

Hardly had Domenikos returned to the side of an alarmed Jerónima than the *alcalde mayor* delivered his judgment. "I direct that Maestro El Greco accept payment in full of three hundred seventeen gold ducats, and that he make such changes in the painting as the chapter deems necessary." He paused and looked at the artist. "I further direct that he surrender the painting at once."

Domenikos sighed and bowed. There seemed no more to be done.

As he and Angulo followed Jerónima and Francesco into the bright autumn light of the plaza, he turned sadly to his friend. "You did what you could. I wrecked everything. I'm sorry."

To his surprise, the lawyer's response was of disagreement. "I thought so too, Greco. You took so many chances. But don't you see? You won your point. In fact, you won all your points. I was astonished when the mayor didn't press you to answer the questions you declined. And you've certainly established the right of an artist to speak his mind."

"I may have done that, but I lost the case."

Angulo laughed. "Not at all. You won the point you wanted. The mayor ordered you to surrender the painting at once. You understand? Deliver it to the vestry tomorrow, unchanged. That's what the mayor was trying to tell you. Once it's hanging, the canons may feel differently."

The painter's face cleared, and he began to laugh. "By God, of course." He slapped the lawyer on the back and then rushed ahead to embrace Francesco and his mistress.

Twenty-Five

The acclaim that followed the consecration of Santo Domingo was modest compared with the reception accorded the Espolio. Although pleased with this absolute public vindication of his craft and artistic judgment and grimly satisfied to have triumphed over the chapter on the more important points of dispute, Domenikos attributed a great measure of the praise now showered on him to the publicity that had attended the litigation.

There was, nevertheless, genuine and touching warmth in the more personal responses of Antonio de Covarrubias, who described it unequivocally as the finest picture ever painted in Spain, and of Luis de Castilla: "If you paint nothing else so fine, your coming here will have been justified by this." Don Diego embraced the artist, his eyes wet, and said, "Now you're a true son of Spain, Greco."

Perversely, he knew, the comment he most treasured came from García de Loysa, who drew Domenikos from the packed vestry into the sacristy next door. "You said harsh things about me in the Ayuntamiento, maestro. And I deny their accuracy. But I respect your courage, all the more because you showed it in defense of something so fine. It's magnificent, truly. When we have the funds, we shall commission you to make a frame for it, something suitable for so splendid a work." Domenikos expressed gratitude, resisting the temptation to ask if this proposed order would be the object of another lawsuit. He was glad he had been discreet, for in the next breath Loysa added, "I'd like to be your friend."

In the wake of his elation came depression. Jerónima, sensitive as ever to his moods, found nothing remarkable in this. "You've done too much too quickly. You're exhausted. You need rest and change." It wasn't so, he thought. He needed work. The first great projects of his career in Toledo were completed, and there was nothing comparable on the horizon to replace them.

He became increasingly restless, unable to concentrate on the smaller pictures to which he was committed, including the Allegory for the King. Francesco and Jerónima watched him roam the apartments, passing through the dining room in so withdrawn a state that he failed even to notice the little Jorge's delighted cries of greeting to him. Only when the small boy rushed to clutch his leg would he pause and look down to pat his beloved son absently on his curly head. He slept badly, which disturbed his mistress, for she recalled his saying that only twice before in his adult life had his sleep been tormented. Beyond that, he would tell her nothing.

There was, in one sense, little to tell. His mind was perpetually active, churning, visualizing, the thoughts and images numberless; it seemed that in their want of a specific focus, a specific purpose large enough to occupy them fully, his brain and spirit were devouring him. He recognized as clearly as did Jerónima that he must relax and purify his soul. He walked the autumn streets, circumambulated the ramparts, studied the faces, visited the churches, conversed with friends. Only the evenings in the Palacio Fuensalidas could hold his attention;

the discussions were active, the exchanges intelligent. For two or three hours he could be taken out of himself. But Toledo's familiar surroundings did nothing to shake the hallucinated configurations of his mind. He attempted to read, only to find his brain racing feverishly beyond the sense of the printed words into images hardly less fantastic and fearful than those which haunted his nights. He felt himself in the clutches of a force like the fires that swept the dry brush of the Castilian plain, completely out of control. If he failed now to take action, he would be consumed.

It was late in October, however, before he could bring himself to a decision. Remembering Philip's suggestion that there might be a chance of his appointment as master painter at the Escorial, he determined to apply his distracted forces to the completion of the painting the King had commissioned and, as commanded, to deliver it in person. Even if he weren't appointed, the journey itself would perhaps give him the change he required.

Even before the picture was finished, Domenikos wrote the King, inquiring whether it would be convenient for him and Francesco to begin the trip on receipt of a reply. The Italian was pleased with the prospect of a journey not only because he thought it salubrious for his adored master but because Jerónima's Juanita was making no secret of her designs on him. To her mistress she confided her intention to have him as her husband before the onset of Lent.

As soon as the reply was received, the canvas was rolled and carefully wrapped. The two men set out on horseback, trailing a single donkey. The time was poor for traveling. The northwest wind drove relentlessly down from the Sierra de Guadarrama, promising the winter's first snow and stirring the dust of the arid plain. The days were at their shortest; it was black dark before they reached their initial resting place, Illescas.

The discomforts of the trip proved oddly invigorating to the painter. The wind, wildly flailing his face, stirred his mind into recollections long forgotten, reminding him of the sudden autumn and winter gusts that had blasted the Crete of his boyhood. He recalled as well the feelings he had had on first seeing this angry countryside. His impression of welcome at that time had been mostly confirmed. If there remained a feeling of incompleteness, its cause lay more in himself than in Spain. No other land, he recognized once more, could prove so hospitable to his nature.

They paused the second night in Madrid, little changed since their previous visit; there was more construction under way but it still failed to resemble the capital of Europe's greatest power. He felt no temptation to linger. By leaving at daybreak, they reached the outskirts of San Lorenzo el Escorial an hour before dark.

The monastery was a dark, grim wonder of the world, ominous and brooding like a malevolent deity, its cold gray façades unrelievedly baleful, their only ornamention the capitals of pilasters, the towers at each corner, and the great dome of the church.

The chill splendor of the Escorial was intentional. Although its facilities included a palace for the King, its primary purposes were ecclesiastic. Philip had vowed to build a great monastery to the memory of St. Lawrence because it was on that saint's day in 1556 that he had gained an important victory over the French at St. Quentin (where Jerónima's father had met his death). It was to be doubted that the simple St. Lawrence would have been entirely happy with the result. Its magnitude was overwhelming. The design was in the shape of a gridiron, for it was on such an implement that the saint met his martyrdom.

Domenikos and Francesco were met at the imposing ceremonial entrance by a guard who sullenly demanded to know their business, eyeing the rolled canvas suspiciously as if he thought it a weapon. Another soldier was immediately summoned, and they were led to the entrance hall of the palace, where they were instructed to wait. Francesco, though plumper than his master, began to tremble with the cold. He clutched the painting to him as if he hoped to derive warmth from it.

A somber, dour monk in black cape and cowl made an almost silent appearance. "You are Maestro El Greco?"

Domenikos nodded, then pointed to his companion. "This is Francesco de Preboste, my assistant."

"You're expected. Follow me."

He led them through one of the smaller patios to the other side of the vast complex of buildings and courtyards, then up an interior staircase to a long corridor lined on one side with windows, on the other with doors. He flung one open and then another. He entered a small, bleak cell, roughly furnished and unheated. Domenikos and Francesco followed him in.

"Excuse me, brother," said the Italian in his still-imperfect Spanish, "but how is it that we're to stay warm?"

A sly grin flashed briefly across the gaunt, monastic features. "There are no fires. The suffering of the flesh is good for the soul."

"In a palace?" Francesco pursued tactlessly.

"This is a monastery. We do not concern ourselves with physical comforts."

The monk tersely explained that their belongings would be brought to them in due course. They would be summoned for meals and prayers, and the King would see them when it pleased him.

The painter asked if Pompeo Leoni could be informed of their presence. The brother promised to see to it and left.

Three nights and two days elapsed before the visitors received any further official communication. They ate in silence with the monks in a lofty, cold refectory, the fare as spartan as their cells. They were treated correctly, the courtesy as glacial as the temperature.

The original guide at last reappeared and announced that they were wanted. Carrying the now-stretched painting, together they followed the brother through a labyrinth of corridors, rooms, and patios before reaching a large hall of the palace portion of the monastery. Here, at the far end, Philip was seated at a desk. A great fire blazed cheerfully behind him. When the two men were announced, the monk curtly instructed them to approach the royal presence.

Philip looked up and permitted a flicker of pleasure swiftly to cross his cold, gray-white features—like a watery, fugitive sun peering briefly between wintry clouds.

"You're welcome to the Escorial, maestro. Almost any face is welcome that has no connection with Portugal or Flanders or England." He paused. "Or with that Cardinal of yours."

The painter knelt, then arose and smiled. "You're harassed, sire?"

"It's the lot of a king to be harassed." He looked at Francesco, who remained kneeling. "Stand up, man. What's your name?"

The Italian stammered badly in reply, then gingerly backed to a position near the fire, propping the picture against the wall beside him.

Philip sighed. "It would be pleasant to have no enemies, maestro. Have you enemies?"

"A few, sire."

"What do they do to you?"

"Nothing, really. They talk against my art, against the way I live."

"Success has its dangers. It wouldn't be worth pursuing otherwise." He spread his pale, eloquent hands on his knees. "What disturbs me most is having always to wonder if a man I think a friend is in fact an enemy. I don't like being suspicious of anyone. That's why I enjoy living here, alone with my wife and children. And then, when the spring comes, with my flowers and fruit trees. I watch the men finishing my church. There is silence."

"I appreciate the silence too, sire. In Crete, where I was born, there was silence."

"You still have people there?"

"Only a brother, sire."

"He'll be safe for a time still. The Venetians will see to that. It's probably *all* they'll see to," he added with some bitterness. "But you know them better than I."

The painter grinned. "In Crete, we have a poor opinion of them."

"As the Flemish do of us. It's inevitable." The King's eyes shifted to the painting near Francesco. "So this is the picture."

Nodding, Domenikos turned and beckoned to his assistant, who brought the canvas before Philip and set it on the floor, steadying it with both hands at the top. Without rising from his chair, the monarch studied it, then looked up at the painter and nodded sharply. "Excellent, excellent. I was quite right. It's much better in this size. What price do you place on it?"

"No price, sire. I mean it as a gift."

A very small, wry smile marred the royal face. "You wouldn't try to bribe a king, maestro."

"It's not often that one is in a position to give a king something he really wants."

Philip chuckled in response, the first laughter Domenikos had heard from him. "You're a diplomat. I should ask you to give lessons in tact to my Duke of Alba."

"And in exchange, would he teach me the arts of war, sire?"

"There are worse masters."

"Indeed."

"I accept your gift with thanks. It's good of you. What's more, I believe your explanation, though I'd have been happy to pay for it." He paused. "No, that's not true. I'd not be happy. Not even kings part happily with money."

"Don't you find, though, sire, that it's more often that you regret your economies than your extravagances?"

"Precisely. I wanted Titian to paint a series of pictures of the life of St. Lawrence, but the price he named was astronomical. I commissioned only the Martyrdom. I've regretted that economy ever since I learned of his death." He paused. "I have the feeling that my association with you is going to be most extravagant, maestro."

"I could hope for nothing better, sire."

"You're familiar with the story of the martyrdom of St. Mauritius?"

"I am, sire."

"Tell it to me briefly."

Domenikos smiled to himself, presuming that Philip was skeptical of his knowledge of this legend. "It's a tale of the third century, sire. The emperor Maximinian ordered the execution of one-tenth of a whole legion because the men refused to make a sacrifice to the Roman gods before going into battle against the Gauls. When they refused a second time, the legion was decimated again. And on their third refusal, the rest of the men were executed, including St. Mauritius and several other men who were also canonized. I believe it occurred in Switzerland, near the Lake of Geneva."

At the outset of the narrative, the King's expression had been of boredom, like that of a teacher hearing a lesson. Gradually he became admiring. "Why, Greco, your friends in Toledo were correct. You're exceptionally well informed."

"The subject happens to interest me, sire. I've read most of the lives of the saints."

"Martyrdom interests you too?"

"Martyrs interest me."

"There we differ. I suppose what's said about me may be true, that I have a streak of cruelty in my nature. But that's Spanish. How else can you explain my people's love of the bullfight? Do you enjoy those spectacles, maestro?"

"I do not, sire." He laughed, embarrassed. "I've yet to make myself attend one."

"Oh, you must. You can't understand the Spanish until you do. See a bullfight and an auto-da-fé. We thrive on blood and tears and pain."

"A simplification, surely, sire."

"But not untrue." The King's mood changed. "Have you seen my church?"

"We've seen nothing, sire. We awaited your pleasure."

"What officiousness. I apologize."

"It was nothing, sire. As a matter of fact, it was very instructive to live for two days as monks do, an enforced retreat. I found it very purifying."

"I'm pleased to hear it. But you must see my church. Your friend Pompeo Leoni can show it to you." He looked back at the painting of the Allegory again and indicated to Francesco that he could lean it against the wall once more. "It's relevant to the commission I propose. We've recently acquired a precious relic of St. Mauritius, so I thought it suitable that we have a painting of his martyrdom. Does the subject appeal to you, maestro?"

"Greatly, sire."

"Good. Leoni will show the space it's to fill. I shall have a contract drawn. Since it's a large painting, I'm willing to pay you eight hundred ducats. Does that suit you?"

"Eminently, sire," said Domenikos, recalling Leoni's description of the King's probity in matters of money, and his own disastrous experience with the chapter in Toledo.

"Done, then. When it's finished, come to me again and we'll discuss the question of your filling the post of master painter. I'll hold it open until that time." He paused. "I assume it interests you."

Domenikos hesitated before responding. "If you feel, sire, after seeing this painting you've commissioned, that you'll have me, I shall of course obey your command."

The King demurred. "I'll not command you, maestro. I know better than most that artists aren't to be commanded. Let's leave it that we'll both give the idea consideration, but no promises." Without warning, he turned back to his desk. "That will be all."

Twenty-Six

In January of 1580, shortly after Domenikos' return from his mission to the Escorial, the academy of the Conde de Fuensalidas could talk of nothing but the implications of the death of the King of Portugal, whose throne appeared available to anyone strong enough to seize it. There seemed only one serious contender, Philip II, who longed to add the country to his peninsular holdings since it represented the completion of the design conceived by Ferdinand and Isabella.

Spanish occupation of the Portuguese throne was vigorously opposed by Elizabeth of England, Philip's most potent enemy. Her ships continued to harass his merchantmen. Drake's operations in the New World threatened his establishments there. Her funds subvened his enemies in France and Flanders. She supplied munitions to the Moors in Morocco.

Philip moved cautiously in his quest, permitting the other candidates to confound one another's aspirations. It was only in the following summer that the Duke of Alba began a military expedition, so brilliantly executed that the war was over within months. The crown awaited Philip's arrival. He failed, however, to make an immediate appearance because he, like countless of his countrymen, had been struck down by the most serious epidemic of influenza ever to occur in Europe. It continued unabated through the end of 1581, killing the Queen. The King survived, though his recovery was slow and his health thereafter severely impaired. He mounted the Portuguese throne in April, still in mourning for his fourth wife, and remained in Lisbon for two years.

The brief change of scene, combined with Philip's commission and suggestion that he might be asked to become master painter of the Escorial, gave Domenikos a new feeling of hope and vitality which prevailed even over his deep concern for the health of Jerónima and Jorge during the terrible epidemic. No less convinced than before that he was the accursed of God, he resumed his practice of attending evensong each day, praying with fervor that all he loved be spared. His fidelity impressed the parish priest, Andrés Núñez, an elegant cleric from Madrid, who became a familiar of the house.

Though no commission so large as that for Santo Domingo was forthcoming, the painter was so inundated with lesser orders and with the financial arrangements that attended them that he soon found it necessary to confide all business matters to the astute Francesco, who handled them with enthusiasm and skill, leaving his master free to devote himself exclusively to painting.

Requests for portraits, paintings of saints (especially St. Francis), and scenes from the life of Christ poured in from all parts of Castile, New and Old, as the artist's fame, based largely on the continuing popularity of his Espolio, spread.

The Martyrdom of St. Mauritius occupied much of his time in the early months of 1580. Then, inexplicably, his apothecary announced that he was unable to obtain sufficient quantities of dry pigments, particularly ultramarine, a color that predominated in this work for the King. Alarmed that a delay might annoy his royal patron, Domenikos communicated this news at once to the Escorial. In the midst of his plans to overrun Portugal, King Philip took the trouble to instruct the prior of the monastery to aid in the procurement of any colors the maestro required. He even offered to advance the artist money, a proposal Domenikos had learned never to refuse. Moreover, the pigments were soon delivered to him.

The painting was by far the largest Domenikos had ever made, measuring fourteen feet by ten. In the right foreground the great Christian soldier was in conversation with a Roman captain. Behind him, clustered tightly together, were other Romans, one in armor who bore the likeness of Philip II. St. Mauritius himself, who figured twice in the canvas, resembled a bearded Domenikos. In a vignette in the left foreground one of the legionnaires had just been beheaded, and the saint prayed for his soul. Trailing off in a sinuous column were the remaining soldiers, all nude, calmly awaiting their fate.

In the upper left and center was a gloria of angels and cherubs in a superb sky of clouds and intense blue. At the base of the painting, in the center, were a small still life of wild flowers and the stump of a sapling. In the lower right corner, a slim, curling serpent carried in its mouth a slip of paper bearing the artist's signature.

During the two and a half years he devoted himself intermittently to the completion of this work, Domenikos sensed a change not merely in his view of the painting at hand but in his artistic vision as well. Here, for the first time, was evidence of the change—a conception that mixed fantasy and reality, a combination that seemed to him to characterize what he now must think of as his mysticism, his private notion of faith, of God, and his relation to them. He realized how much he risked in so daring an effort, yet Philip had appeared to admire audacity. If he had misjudged the King, all hope for future commissions and the vacant post would be lost.

He appreciated to what degree his Martyrdom of St. Mauritius represented a split from his earlier style only when Luis de Castilla responded to it, shortly after its completion, in the summer of 1582. "If I didn't have your word for it, Greco, I'd not believe it your work."

"You find it that different? You don't like it?"

The dean of Cuenca shook his head. "I'm stunned by it, almost physically bowled over by it. But I don't recognize you in it. What's happened?"

Domenikos attempted to explain this feeling of transformation to which he had gradually submitted in the course of painting the Martyrdom. "Call it a sort of chemistry, or alchemy, the blending of El Greco with Toledo."

"Two passionate austerities joining to form something else?" Castilla smiled. "Yes, I can believe that. But beware, my friend. Don't let this new strangeness get out of your control. It's all very well for your vision, your mysticism, if that's what it is, to guide your hand. But don't let it blind you to the practicalities. You're asking a lot of the King, you know. He commands a painting in an idiom he's familiar with, and you present him with a revolution."

Domenikos sighed. "We can't know the answer to that until he's back from Lisbon."

Jorge Manuel celebrated his fifth birthday in a manner his father deemed peculiarly appropriate. He found himself alone in Domenikos' studio; all others in the household were observing the siesta. He had often watched the painter at his work, and now in his absence the little boy decided to make a picture of his own, devoting himself to an incomplete canvas of the Crucifixion to which he made quite individual additions with brush, palette knife, and chiefly fingers.

Francesco caught him at it. Jorge responded to the Italian's yelp of dismay with a gap-toothed smile of delight, pointing proudly to his accomplishment. "See, Franco? See?"

The noises of this encounter drew Domenikos and Jerónima to the door of the studio. She was as outraged as Francesco. The artist, however, expressed almost as much pleasure at the sight as had Jorge. "Marvelous," he said. "Just as it should be." He turned to his mistress. "You see? You see, *querida*. He means to be a painter like his papa."

The argument that followed was a familiar one. Jerónima had long begged Domenikos to let the boy develop as he chose. The painter had early made the tactical mistake of telling her about his prolonged dispute with his own father in his boyhood, a point she never failed to use against him when, as often occurred, she found him encouraging Jorge to draw with charcoal on the reverse sides of discarded sketches. "You're trying to influence him. Let him be."

Today, however, Domenikos believed he had scored a point. "He did it on his own this time."

Francesco was less than enchanted. "And ruined a painting."

The artist shrugged. "It can be fixed." He knew he was too indulgent with the child. He knew himself misguided. But it seemed certain now that Jerónima would bear him no others. Love for his only heir made him helpless.

His second journey to the Escorial was made in more clem-
a donkey-drawn cart that had been especially altered to accommodate
ent weather. He and Francesco transported the awkward burden in
the long rolled canvas. They arrived in May of 1583, not long after
the King had returned from his stay in Lisbon.

Like the season, their reception this time was warmer. Though
unable at once to see Philip, Domenikos had no difficulty in finding
his friend Leoni, who was full of the progress he and his father had
been making with an immense marble retable for the *capilla mayor*
of the great monastery church, a work the painter found more Italian
than Spanish, more worldly than religious—opinions he confided,
however, only to his assistant.

The sculptor and several of his men assisted in stretching the large
canvas and hanging it unframed in the space it was intended to fill.
Only when it was in place, illuminated by the clear spring sunlight of
the bright church, did Leoni express his conviction. "You're no longer
Titian's man, are you? I see Michelangelo and Tintoretto in it. But
most of all it's yourself, Greco. It's pure wizardry, all motion and mystery."

Though gratified with his friend's response, because it was
informed and not merely the emotional reaction of Toledan amateurs,
the painter declined to let his hopes rise too high. It was the King
alone who would judge. Leoni wasn't Philip's Orsini; he relied on
no one to guide his taste.

Physically, the monarch was much changed; time and influenza,
great responsibilities and bitter grief had taken a terrible toll. His face
was deeply lined, his hair and beard pure white, his dress no longer
so fastidious, his speech thick, his pace slow and painful because
he was suffering from gout.

Yet as he made his appearance in the church, two days after
Domenikos' arrival, he contrived a little smile of welcome as he acknowledged the visitor's genuflection.

"Only you, maestro, could have stolen me from my garden on such
a lovely morning. I'm weary and old and sad. Cheer me up."

"I hope my painting will do that, sire."

"And that is it?" He pointed to the work provisionally installed,
then turned to a courtier, who, without a word, brought a folding
chair. The King sat down heavily and contemplated the work for several minutes.

He turned away at last, and looked up at the artist, who stood beside him. "You had a scriptural quotation in mind for this?" There was nothing in his tone to indicate the nature of his feelings.

"Yes, sire, from St. Matthew. 'Be ye therefore as wise as serpents and as sinless as doves.' "

The King nodded, returning his gaze to the painting. "I thought so. Very much to the point. I've always thought highly of the allusion to the wisdom of serpents. However wicked we think them, they never do anything superfluous or unnecessary." He paused. "I take it that you had the ambiguity of that phrase in mind."

"I did, sire. I find it hard to draw an intelligent distinction between the glory of the martyr and his sheer folly."

"Explain that in terms of this," said the King peremptorily, pointing to the picture without taking his eyes from it.

Domenikos spoke slowly, carefully, almost pensively. "I was thinking, initially, of the emperor, sire. He seems to have regarded the legionnaires as traitors, more than six thousand of them, not because they refused to fight the Gauls, which was why they were there, but because they refused to make sacrifice to pagan gods. We see this as folly, but in the emperor's eyes the decision was wholly justified. You don't have that number of fighting men, the pride of the empire, put to death out of whimsy. Not even Caligula would have been so mad as that. So we have to conclude that he called for the execution because the gods that were spurned were the gods of the state. If they weren't propitiated before a battle, Rome herself might fall."

Philip's smile was small. "Are you suggesting a parallel, an allegory of our present Church, maestro?"

Domenikos recognized the trap, and made no effort to avoid it. "Yes, sire."

"You see the Counter-Reformation movement as folly?"

"Not at all, sire. Quite the reverse."

The King pointed to the representation of himself. "Do I appear here as the foolish Maximinian protecting the interests of the empire?"

"No, sire, as the wise leader protecting the interests of the Church."

Still not looking at the painter, Philip went on. "And you, as I believe, appear not once but twice. Whom do you represent, maestro, the sinless saint or the foolish, misguided heretic?"

"Both, sire."

"Then surely my role is as ambiguous as your own." At last he looked at Domenikos. "I'm disappointed in you. I hoped for something as straightforward in its message as your great Espolio.

You've given me an intellectual paradox. I hoped for a master-piece. . . ."

"I'm sorry to have displeased you, sire, but you're mistaken."

"Kings are never mistaken," Philip snapped.

"About this painting you are. Paradox it may be, not ideal perhaps as part of the 'Bible of the illiterate,' but as art it's my masterpiece."

"Not so fine as your Espolio."

"My last picture is *always* my finest."

The King turned to the group of men behind him. "Leoni, come here."

Domenikos followed his friend's oddly shy progress to Philip's side.

"Tell me, Leoni. Is it a masterpiece, as Maestro El Greco says; his finest painting?"

The sculptor nervously wiped moist hands on his gray smock and shifted his eyes from the King to the picture and back again.

"It's very interesting, sire, but not a masterpiece."

Domenikos gasped.

Philip grunted with grim pleasure.

"Exactly. 'Interesting' is the word. I want more blood."

"And less Greco," said the painter sadly.

Having committed himself to this perfidy, Leoni continued without waiting for Philip's response. "I object to these distorted bodies. They have nothing to do with flesh-and-blood humans."

Domenikos protested, knowing the gesture pointless. "They're not to be seen as flesh-and-blood humans. They're men on the point of being martyred."

Leoni shrugged. "To me, they're grotesque."

The King glanced at the sculptor. "I agree. Whom should I ask to paint it properly?"

Leoni responded with neither hesitation nor evidence of embarrassment. "There's a countryman of mine in Madrid, sire, Romulo Cincinato. He'd do an excellent picture for you."

Philip nodded. "Arrange it."

Leoni bowed and quickly disappeared in the direction of the *capilla mayor*. Uncertain whether he was more distressed by rejection of his painting or by the betrayal by his friend, Domenikos stood silent at the King's side, shaking his head.

"I know what you're feeling, maestro," said Philip softly. "I know what Leoni did to you."

The painter stared at him. "And you let it happen?"

"Do you think it's a king's role to protect the sensibilities of his craftsmen?"

Domenikos shook his head sorrowfully. "No, sire, but I would have thought a king might have concern for the truth."

"The truth, maestro, is what *I* choose to believe."

As had happened before in his life, disaster followed disaster. Not long after his dismal return to Toledo from the Escorial, Domenikos learned that his brother was under house arrest in Candia. Three of the four pirate ships had been captured in quick succession by well-armed Turks; the crew of the remaining vessel understandably refused to make further voyages. The Serenissima compelled Manusos and his partners to forfeit their bond of 20,000 ducats. With his debts increased because of poor trade, he disposed of all holdings in Crete except the family house, but there were creditors remaining. To silence them, the brother borrowed from tax money he had collected. Now it was impossible for him to repay. Until he was able to reimburse the amount embezzled, he would probably remain in custody. "I am not asking you for the money, Menegos," he concluded. "You must believe that. It is more than you could afford. Better that one of us remain solvent, no?"

Domenikos had little difficulty in prevailing on the prior of the Trinitarian monastery to arrange for some money to be transferred to Crete. Manusos was doubtless right in saying he couldn't afford the entire amount, but a few hundred ducats at regular intervals would at least permit his brother to keep his head up. Jerónima was appalled. "But if the authorities won't release him until he's paid what he owes . . . ?" The painter was certain that Manusos would think of some solution. "He's like papa in that, very crafty."

Early the next year, Diego de Castilla succumbed suddenly while performing his evening offices in the chapel of the Palacio Arzobispal. Domenikos was numbed, the more gloomy because his great patron's death seemed part of a pattern of calamity whose end he couldn't foresee. And given his grim certainty that once again God was redressing the balance of joy and pain, he was disinclined to accept this sad event as the last of a chain. To the dean's brother, he said, "Don Diego was my beginning in Toledo. And now my beginning has ended."

Twenty-Seven

Domenikos' direct apprehensions failed to materialize. So, apparently, did his prediction that his brother would somehow extricate himself from his difficulties. The years that followed his disillusioning visit to the Escorial were filled with small commissions that kept him so busy that he found it necessary to do what he had at one point sworn he would never do, take in apprentices and assistants. By 1586 he had no less than eight of them. He ruefully confessed to Castilla that he was no more honest in this respect than Titian, except that he never signed a painting made by his workshop.

Life had assumed a rhythm now. Despite the King's rejection of the painting (in any case, he had been fully paid for it), the artist's reputation continued to grow. Orders now materialized from points even more distant than Castile. Francesco made frequent trips to Seville, where he had established an interesting market for replicas of Domenikos' more popular paintings, especially Crucifixions and portraits of saints, that were exported to Spanish colonies in the New World.

In Toledo, his position was unchallenged. Even those who had been his enemies, Monegro, Hernando de Ávila, Vergara and other artists, now accepted it as almost an article of faith that El Greco was unassailably the greatest painter ever to practice here, something Domenikos himself had known since his arrival nine years before. He wore his laurels gracefully and became, in his terms, almost convivial. He even dared to flout his assumed commitment to the Conde de Fuensalidas by visiting the academy of the Conde de Moro, where he found a somewhat more raffish gathering of playwrights, half-pay soldiers, and writers, including Cervantes, whose readings were, if shocking, very amusing indeed.

The temptation to be complacent, to settle happily for what he now possessed (what no one, save God, could possibly take away from him) was great. And to a degree, he succumbed to it. He grew a beard in the Toledan manner, an affectation that only Jerónima found annoying. "You may impress your grand friends, Menegos, but you scratch my face." He ignored her.

She didn't, however, allow him to ignore her a few months later in the year, when he at last permitted herself to be persuaded by Gracía de Loysa to design and construct a sculptured altar for his Espolio. He told her he was agreeing to the project only out of sentiment; Diego de Castilla would have wanted him to. And then, he confessed, he had a kind of perverse curiosity. Would the chapter treat him as shabbily this time? Doña Jerónima offered resistance to the news that Domenikos intended to employ his own artisans to construct the altarpiece in their home. Too vividly did he still recall his experience with Monegro.

She was outraged. "You're not going to bring a lot of carpenters into the house. With all your painters, there's not enough room as it is."

"Well, then, we'll just have to find something larger, won't we?" he said with tranquillity.

Of the many places they inspected over the next weeks, only one appeared wholly suitable to Domenikos, a considerable section of a palace in the parish of Santo Tomé that stood opposite El Tránsito, a former synagogue. The building belonged to the Marqués de Villena, and the splendidly spacious apartments overlooked the churning Tajo and the ancient Puente de San Martín, views long beloved by the painter, who often crossed this bridge to behold the battlemented city from a distance. The quarters included an immense ground-floor room where carpentry and gilding could be done. The upper levels consisted of a handsome series of reception and living rooms, more than enough to accommodate a growing household and a burgeoning workshop.

Jerónima was torn. She, like Domenikos, was intrigued with the idea of occupying a real palace. "At last we can entertain the way you say Titian did," she said. But she feared it was too grand. "What will people say?"

He had no doubts. He signed a lease in September of 1585; they moved in the next week. As they were going to sleep on their first night in their new home, he turned to Jerónima and sighed contentedly. "After forty-four years, El Greco lives where he belongs. Let's have a great reception."

Perhaps not quite on the scale of Titian's, the gathering impressed those invited as conclusive evidence that El Greco was, if possible, even more important a cultural ornament than they had suspected. In the past, he and Jerónima had entertained well but always on a modest scale, choosing their guests with care so that no one might feel offended by the quality of those invited with him. Their dinners had been planned as carefully as paintings; the food, the drink, and the entertainment had been selected with meticulous consideration.

The great reception to mark their removal to new and more commodious apartments was, as Domenikos said to his mistress, to be a rout. "It's the only way. We'll invite everyone we know. No more compartments for this and that sort of acquaintance. We'll have them all together and see what happens."

In their more constricted way, preparations for the reception were hardly less frantic than those preceding the Feast of Bucintoro. The gardens were completely replanted, the exterior of the palace (including those portions he hadn't leased) was cleaned, the interior repainted, floors scrubbed, paintings hung, furnishings redecorated. With Luis de Castilla's collaboration, cooks were dragooned from the Palacio Arzobispal to prepare a mountainous collation, which included a broad selection of wines and brandies that would, Domenikos knew, cause normal hostilities among his guests either to flare into open war or subside into alcoholic amiability. In the cavernous ground-floor room, soon to be a carpentry and gilding shop, an orchestra played for the stately dances permissible in the Spanish City of God. There, too, a group of itinerant musicians demonstrated the *vihuela* and a more recent instrument, the five-stringed guitar, that was used to accompany vocalists whose repertory included the keening Morisco songs that so reminded the painter of his childhood days.

Host and hostess were apprehensive as early guests arrived; there was an atmosphere of tension in the great house. But music and food and drink prevailed over social distinctions hitherto considered sacrosanct. Merchant, nobleman, cleric, and the ladies who accompanied them, soon fell into the Italiante mood of the festivities. Several bishops were heard to laugh, one at least four times; a retired lady-in-waiting to the late queen was thrice compelled to resist the advances of a handsome canon; Jerónima reported that Tomás de Murcia, Domenikos' valued apothecary, pinched her. Juan Bautista Monegro became so enamored of the buxom Juanita that Francesco, her new husband, threatened "measures." Luis de Castilla at one point joined the painter and expressed dismay. "In a single evening, Greco, you've corrupted an entire city. Toledo will never be the same again. I've just seen Fuensalidas embracing Moro. The only less likely thing I can imagine is the Pope embracing the wraith of Martin Luther."

As early as 1584, Padre Andrés Núñez, parish priest of Santo Tomé, had proposed to Domenikos a painting for the church based on the legend of a miracle that had taken place in 1323. The tale concerned Don Gonzalo Ruiz de Toledo, who had financed the rebuilding of Santo Tomé a few years earlier. When he died, the highest celestial authorities, moved by his benevolence, designated St. Augustine, whose monks served the church, and St. Stephen to make personal appearances at his funeral and with their own hands to lay him to eternal rest.

Don Gonzalo's descendants became the counts of Orgaz. A sixteenth-century count had in his will provided funds, deposited with officials of the village of Orgaz, for the further enrichment of his ancestor's church in Toledo. Only after prolonged and acrimonious litigation had Núñez extracted this large sum from the coffers of Orgaz.

Although Domenikos had made some preliminary sketches during the previous year, he had insisted that Núñez consider the matter carefully. "My prices are high, Andrés. I don't want angry exchanges with my confessor." The priest agreed to bide his time, the more so since the artist had said that in any case he was too busy to give the project his attention for at least a year. The padre resumed his siege a year later to the day. "No one else can do it, Greco. We'd be the laughingstock of Castile if our most famous parishioner refused to honor his own church."

The contract was signed in March. Núñez had already described in the most precise terms what and whom the painting was to depict, but he thought it necessary "in the unlikely event that we should one day find ourselves in disagreement" to restate these details in the document both signed:

"On the canvas there must be painted a procession showing how the vicar and other priests read mass for the interment of Don Gonzalo Ruiz de Toledo, lord of the town of Orgaz, and how St. Stephen and St. Augustine descended to bury the body of this nobleman, the one holding him by the head, and the other by the feet, whilst many people should be represented around it watching, and above all this must appear Heaven opened up in glory." It was further stipulated that the painting, to occupy a chapel, must measure sixteen feet by twelve and have a semicircular top, making it even larger than the abortive Martyrdom of St. Mauritius.

Domenikos added one suggestion that delighted Núñez. "Since we can't know who stood around and watched the burial in 1323, Andrés, I'll portray some of our better-known citizens."

While his numerous assistants made replicas of the paintings for which there seemed a never-ending demand, the artist devoted himself to the altar and frame for his Espolio and, when the designs could be safely passed on to the small team of carpenters and gilders in the room below, to the Orgaz Burial scene.

The altar was ready for installation in February of 1587. Though García de Loysa had assured him that there would be no repetition of the debacle over the Espolio, Domenikos faced the evaluation with trepidation. To his surprise, Esteban Jordán, a sculptor from the distant city of Valladolid, set a figure acceptable to both parties and the work, a classical work reminiscent of the pieces he had done almost a decade before for Santo Domingo, was set in place. Everyone was delighted and relieved. The bursar remitted the sum in full without a word of protest. (Final payment for the Espolio had been delayed for two years.)

The next month, Domenikos completed the painting for Santo Tomé. It couldn't be the imaginative work that the Martyrdom of St. Mauritius had been. Núñez's specifications precluded this. But it could be, and he thought he had made it so, a summary of his life's work, the best of El Greco to date. Here he demonstrated all he had learned from the Italian masters together with innovations he introduced from his beginnings in Candia as a painter of Byzantine panels. But, as ever, there was El Greco the fantasist and mystic, the painter of God.

On the richly brocaded chasubles of silk and gold worn by the two saints were Byzantine-style miniatures. On the robe of St. Stephen, who carried the corpse by the knees, a scene depicted his martyrdom. On the border of the mitred St. Augustine's were images of St. Peter, St. James, the great and St. Catherine of Alexandria. Don Andrés Núñez, almost as sumptuously attired as the saints, appeared at the far right of the canvas as the chaplain who read the lesson.

The most highly regarded of his Toledan friends and acquaintances were portrayed as chief mourners: Antonio de Covarrubias, Rodrigo de La Fuente, the Castillas, Dr. Gregorio Angulo, the *alcalde mayor,* and Cervantes.

There was even a portrait of himself in his fine new beard, standing directly behind St. Stephen. Kneeling in the left foreground was Jorge Manuel, now almost nine, as a black-clothed page. From the boy's pocket obtruded a handkerchief that bore the year of his birth and his father's signature.

The gloria occupied the upper half of the canvas, radiating from the top center where sat the risen Christ in robes of white. He was flanked by saints, apostles, and the Virgin. Descending toward the mortal world was a host of applicants for salvation.

From the moment of its completion, Andrés Núñez came almost every day to contemplate this great painting he had commissioned, each visit the occasion for ever-greater expressions of admiration. "But when shall we have it in the church, Greco? How soon will the evaluation be made?"

"Not until after the Fiesta of Santa Leocadia. You'll not find any competent artist in the whole of Castile to come till then. They're all as involved as I am with the decorations for that."

The priest reluctantly acknowledged the probability of this, for the event was considered the greatest to occur in Toledo in a generation. Relics of the city's patron saint were, in late April, to be returned from the Benedictine abbey of St. Ghislain in Flanders. Memories of the Feast of Bucintoro were once more evoked as Toledans applied themselves to the adornment of the processional route from the old Puente de Alcántara through the heart of the city to a small chapel in the Vega, just beyond the walls on the other side. Domenikos' contribution to this splendid occasion was a great triumphal arch of wood, painted white to simulate marble, that stood in the Zocodover. It was, he reflected, just as well that he had moved to larger quarters, because this construction would have been impossible in his former residence. The piece stood more than forty feet high when fully assembled, with a central arch that was ten feet across, flanked by lesser ones.

So significant was the occasion that the King himself accompanied the relics from Madrid. The festivities lasted three days and nights, and featured banquets for the illustrious, street fairs for the lowly, tournaments for the *hidalgos,* dancing in the plazas, and a bullfight. Only Philip held himself aloof from the more mundane of these celebrations, declining (in public, at any rate) to mix the divine with the profane.

As a principal contributor to the decorations, Domenikos was required to attend the King at a reception given in his honor by the

Archbishop. With Jerónima and Jorge (the boy dancing with excitement in a handsome new tunic and ruffed collar), the artist waited his turn in the great hall of the Alcázar where the court was installed. To his mistress he confessed a certain uneasiness over this first reunion with the monarch since their disastrous interview four years before at the Escorial. It was one thing to be scorned in relative privacy, quite another in the presence of his fellow townspeople.

Philip's health appeared to have improved. His face was still careworn, his walk still impaired by gout, but he was in a happier frame of mind, the painter thought, than he had been the last time they met. Indeed, as he acknowledged the homage of Domenikos and his little family, the King was gracious, deigning even to take Jorge briefly on the royal lap.

"Are you going to follow your father?"

The boy flushed and looked away, babbling for a moment incoherently before he could manage an intelligible response. "I don't know, sire."

"Well, whatever you do, Jorge Manuel, I hope you do it with your father's bravery."

Philip looked up as he permitted the boy to slip hastily from his knees, his eyes resting evenly on Domenikos'. "I've not changed my mind about that painting, maestro, but I'm glad to learn that you flourish here. You and I would never get along. We would quarrel and I'd have to put you in prison for disobedience or disrespect. It was simple charity that prevented me from asking you to be my master painter."

The artist grinned and bowed. "I shall always cherish your mercy, sire." He paused. "Are you satisfied with Cincinato's replacement of my picture? Is it bloody enough?"

The King frowned. "Bloody as a butcher's stall, but very common otherwise." He turned to Jerónima. "I remember your saying to me, Doña Jerónima, that this man reserved his gentleness for you and his anger for his painting. I think I should tell you that he saved some of the anger for his King."

She shook her beautiful head. "I feel sure, sire, that any anger he may have felt, any disappointment, has been dissipated this afternoon."

"He still guards you well, I hope."

Jerónima's pale eyes flitted to Domenikos', her face radiant. "Yes, sire."

Philip looked to the painter once more. "Your arch is admirable, maestro. I join my gratitude for it with His Excellency's." He paused, bobbing his head to Jerónima. "And now I must greet the others."

A week or so after Toledo had recovered from this great religious orgy, two painters who were strangers to the city appraised the Orgaz Burial scene. Both were dazzled, especially impressed with the effect of the chasubles and the general richness of the large canvas. With little deliberation, they set a figure of 1200 ducats. Núñez was beside himself, and flatly refused to accept the evaluation. Domenikos pointed out that the contract demanded his agreement, reminding the priest that four years earlier the King had paid 800 ducats for a work that was smaller.

Don Andrés refused to budge. The painter saw no reason to alter his position. The impasse endured for nearly a year, when a second appraisal was agreed on. As with the first, both parties were to accept the price thus determined. Domenikos, in a burst of exasperated generosity, even permitted the priest to select both evaluators. "But no arguments this time, Andrés, or I'll take the matter before the Ayuntamiento."

In the spring of 1588, the second pair of experts called for a payment of 1600 ducats, declaring the painting to be the most magnificent in all Spain. Núñez was apoplectic, and once again rejected the appraisal. He was, however, now willing to pay the 1200 he had earlier declined.

Domenikos lost his temper. "What a charlatan you are, masquerading before your parishioners as a man of God, a man of honor. Twice you've made a bargain, taken a solemn oath, and twice you've broken your word."

"You can insult me all you please, Greco, but this is just a little parish church. We can't afford sixteen hundred ducats."

The painter laughed darkly. "That's what you said last year about twelve hundred, and now you're willing to pay that. What a liar."

Gregorio Angulo advised Domenikos to settle. "Even if you took it before the Ayuntamiento, Greco, and won, you'd lose. Nothing is to be gained by setting yourself against the church."

"But then you acknowledge the Church's right to play the role of extortionist."

The lawyer shrugged. "That's the reality. If you win in a secular tribunal, you might find yourself dragged before the Inquisition.

Settle, Greco." He placed a hand on the artist's shoulder and shook him slightly. "Settle, but in a pleasant way."

Late in June of 1588, the painter and Núñez agreed to the figure of 1200. The Orgaz Burial painting, magnificently framed, was installed at once. From the moment of its unveiling, the picture was the wonder of Toledo, exceeding in popularity even the Espolio in the cathedral. No one hesitated to acknowledge that El Greco was the greatest painter in the history of Spain.

It was Luis de Castilla who put the matter most succinctly as he stood before the picture in its chapel. "It's your apotheosis, Greco."

PART V:

Toledo, the Last Years
(1588–1614)

Twenty-Eight

IN the summer of 1588, the defeat of the Armada occupied the men who met at the Palacio Fuensalidas. The extent of the defeat was as yet not fully known, nor were its causes plain. But it was clear that Philip's grand design to retard the Reformation by conquering Britain, the principal source of its financial support, had been forever lost.

Domenikos' interest in these discussions was desultory at best. His thoughts were elsewhere, and they were disturbed and disturbing. He wanted to escape, not in the physical sense, not as he had felt after the success of the Espolio in 1579. Rather did his feelings recall those he had had immediately after his disillusioning audience with Pope Gregory so many years before. It was ironic that from acclaim he should derive a sense of despair quite as powerful as the one inspired by failure.

A single word stood out: "apotheosis"—what Castilla had said. Was the Orgaz Burial scene his apotheosis? He meant it to be a synthesis, the end of his beginning, the conclusion of an epoch. If his friend's compliment was more than that, was true, was just, Domenikos was lost.

Yet what could be more absurd on the face of it? He *was* the greatest painter Spain had ever known. He felt no compunction in acknowledging this. It was not the accolade it would have been, for instance, in Italy; Spain had seen as yet few painters even describable as competent, none of them natives. He stood out when compared with dwarfs. This wasn't enough. He must be incomparable, unique for all time, must escape the bounds imposed on other painters.

Escape into what, in what direction? Not so easy to know that. A withdrawal into the unexplored recesses of his spirit, his soul. To seek what? He couldn't name the uniqueness, the quality, the vision; but it was there, somewhere within himself. His painting must get closer to the bone, must rely on intuition, on an inward-looking sight, "the light within" that he had spoken of to Castilla while still in Rome.

This new way of painting had nothing to do with reason and could not be achieved by a rational process. In this, Titian had been right. But Domenikos had been right, too; it was to be found by exploration of the spirit, but through feeling.

He tried to explain to Jerónima. "I want the painting of a saint to *be* the saint, not at all as he appeared to people when he was alive, but in fact as a saint in spirit, truly a holy man, a man of God, *full* of God, imbued with all the elements of his nature that made it possible, inevitable even, for him to become a saint."

Castilla thought this new "interiorness" that the artist was pursuing merely an outgrowth of his mysticism, that he asked more of his materials than they could give. "It's nothing but metaphysics. You mustn't permit religious whimsy to jeopardize your future." Domenikos was unconcerned. For he knew that only by finding a completely new direction, by beginning a new career, by being reborn, could he live with himself, with his great reputation—for only by redoubled effort could he feel success deserved in his own terms. In that sense, what Spain thought of him was, if not unimportant, beside the real point. The real point lay between him and God.

However great his withdrawal, life's realities pursued and found him. Rodrigo de La Fuente, who had delivered Jorge Manuel and cared for the household ever since, died early the following year. Only a few months earlier Domenikos had portrayed him—pale, graying, with a long, humane face and tapering white beard, the intellectual and the *hidalgo*.

From his uncle in Venice, a month after La Fuente's funeral, the painter received word that his brother had successfully petitioned the Consiglio to release him from custody. Only thus could he manage to repay the 3000 ducats still owed to the Serenissima. The rest was silence. How Manusos was living, how he proposed to find so large a sum, was left to his imagination. "Your Maria survives," the uncle tersely wrote, "as do we." He had again failed to be elected to the Council of Forty, but hadn't lost hope.

Domenikos wrote his brother at once. "Come to Toledo, Manusos.

If you let me know your exact situation, I shall arrange with the Trinitarians to pay your debts and provide for your passage directly to Barcelona or Seville." There was no reply.

Almost in secret, the painter explored new approaches to his art. Hitherto accessible to all, he established a rule that when the door of his private studio was closed, he was not to be disturbed except in grave emergency. It wasn't that he had something to conceal; he simply required solitude and silence.

The first formal painting in which his preoccupations revealed themselves was a penitent Mary Magdalene for whom Jerónima served as model.

"But you've made me so harrowed," she protested.

"Bereaved," he responded. "She's alone, deserted, desolate, empty of life, empty of hope, full only of memory and God."

Castilla was disturbed. "You've stripped the picture of everything except Our Lord's skull and the crucifix and the rocks and sky."

The painter shrugged. "What's left is the essential, Luis, St. Mary Magdalene herself, in a reverie of death and remorse."

The dean of Cuenca was skeptical. "And how do you think the abbess who commissioned this will feel?"

Domenikos laughed. "That's the advantage of beginning a new career with an established reputation. The patron doesn't question. A signed El Greco original is more to be treasured than an unsigned replica from his workshop."

"Cynicism from you, Greco? I'm astounded."

"Not cynicism, Luis. The simple truth. I can't possibly fill all the requests I have for paintings by my own hand. If a client wants an original El Greco, he'll accept what I offer him."

Castilla shook his head. "Don't go too far too quickly."

The painter replied almost gaily. "I won't. But you know, I feel young again, like Jorge. It's wonderful."

His appreciation of the market for his work was proved exact. His friends, unaware of the practices of Italian masters, continued to look askance at the growing output of workshop paintings, thinking them in some way forgeries because, emanating from El Greco's studio and scupulously copying El Greco's style, they were called El Greco's work—whether signed by him or not. Adding to the confusion thus created was the fact that he did not always put his signature to pictures exclusively made by him. It was one of his few whimsies. To

COLOR FROM A LIGHT WITHIN   330

Jerónima's query, he replied, "*I'll* know who painted it, and so will God. Who else matters?"

The question of signature arose in a different way in 1591, when the parish priest of Talavera la Vieja, a Castilian village, commissioned a large altarpiece to include three paintings and a large statue. Though he wanted an original El Greco, as everyone did, he paled at the artist's estimate of what such a work would cost and agreed to a workshop production for a price that was a minor fraction of the one first named. The paintings were made entirely by Francesco, who by now could imitate his master's techniques with uncanny skill. When the pictures were completed, the Italian expressed a desire to append his own signature to each.

"They're *not* El Grecos. They're Prebostes," Francesco protested

Domenikos smiled sadly, understandingly. "I know. But if you sign them, they'll not be El Grecos."

"They're *not* El Grecos. They're Prebostes," Francesco protested almost angrily, something so alien to his nature that the artist realized attention must be paid.

"They were commissioned as El Grecos. Would you like to obtain contracts for yourself?"

"Who wants a Preboste?" was the sullen reply. The temper flared briefly once again. "But people *buy* Prebostes, thinking they're El Grecos."

"Never." Domenikos paused. His eyes narrowed. "Unless that's how you sell them in Seville."

Francesco shrugged. "Who cares? Most of them are shipped to the New World anyway. The man there knows they're not original, but I have no control over what he tells the people he sells them to."

"No, of course not." He considered this sturdy, swarthy man who had been with him for nearly twenty years. "Listen, Francho. Would you like it if I told Padre Marques that the paintings are wholly from your hand? It's not the same thing, but at least *he'd* know. And if he's agreeable to your signing them, it's agreeable to me."

The assistant shook his head. "He'll say no, master. I'm sure of it. As I said, who wants a Preboste?"

Francesco was quite right.

The paintings and sculpture for Talavera were completed in the spring of 1592, shortly before Jorge's fourteenth birthday. Thoughts of the boy's future were always near the surface of his father's consciousness, though the ever-alert Jerónima compelled him to maintain silence. Birthdays, however, inevitably brought the subject into the open.

Jorge Manuel was slender, fastidious and handsome. His body was his father's, his features and complexion those of Jerónima. He was responsive and quick to learn, a successful pupil in the monastery school nearby. The abbot thought him a likely candidate for the university if he elected to take orders. He was a loving child, though not especially demonstrative. He was affable and got on easily with everyone he encountered. His manners were good without ever seeming obsequious; his politeness was natural. If he could be faulted in his attitude toward others, it was in this very easiness of relationships. Though he was indiscriminately pleasant to all, he appeared genuinely fond only of his parents, his grandmother, and Francesco. He was popular, but he formed no intimate associations outside the household, accepting as a matter of course many offers of friendship but capable of returning none.

One of the boy's qualities, if not to be called a fault, was alarming to Domenikos. "Nothing interests him," he complained. "When I was fourteen I'd known for three years what I was going to be. Jorge does everything well, but he seems to think about nothing."

Jerónima called, as she had so often done before, for time and patience. "He'll find something one of these days, Menegos. You were the exception, because you opposed your father."

But this time the painter wasn't to be put off. "I think something should be said."

She sighed. "All right. But I want to be here when you discuss it with him. I'll not have you try to persuade him."

"You think I'll be unfair?"

"I think you'd *mean* to be fair."

Domenikos embraced her gently, then stood back and smiled into her eyes. Her features, to him, had not aged a day since their meeting fifteen years before. "I'll do anything you like, *querida*."

The boy was aware as soon as he entered the dining room, on his return from school that evening, that something concerning him was to be brought up. His parents' expressions, despite their smiles of welcome, revealed uneasiness. So he became uneasy, walked hastily across the broad floor to embrace them lightly, then stood at the end of the long table, virtually at attention.

"Sit down, Jorge," said Domenikos, trying to measure the tone of his words with great care. "I want to ask you a serious question."

"Yes, papa?" What had happened? What was happening?

The painter looked apprehensively at his mistress. The question must not seemed loaded. "Have you ever considered your future, what you plan to be?"

Complete bewilderment clouded Jorge's expressive face. He looked from father to mother, eyes wary, hands fairly dancing on the table. He didn't hesitate.

"A painter, like papa?"

Jerónima's face registered no emotion. "Are you asking us?"

Perplexity crossed the boy's pale features. "Is it a game?"

"Not a game," said his father sharply.

"I want to paint, like papa, and build things."

"You realize," said his mother, attempting a persuasion she would have reproached Domenikos for, "that it means your leaving school. You'd not be able to play in the afternoons with your friends."

Jorge grinned. "Most of my friends are leaving school, mama."

"It's what you really want?"

He stared at Jerónima for a little time, trying to guess what answer she expected. "Is there something else you'd like me to do?"

"Have you ever thought of anything else?" asked Domenikos, feeling positively heroic.

"No, papa. Why should I? Most boys do what their fathers do, unless they enter an order or become priests."

The painter laughed. "Priests' sons *have* been known to become priests, like the Castillas."

Jerónima refused to permit the conversation to be diverted. "You're sure of this? You're serious, Jorge?"

"Yes, mama," he replied softly.

She turned to Domenikos, smiling. "Well, there you are. So be it." Her eyes returned to Jorge. "*I'm* not sure, though, that your reasons are the right ones."

The boy left school in June, and in the months that followed he began to learn the rudiments of his craft. He seemed happy in the studio, but whether because he enjoyed being in Domenikos' company or because he had a true vocation was uncertain in Jerónima's mind. He expressed naked delight at the prospect of eventually filling the role of Francesco, who was increasingly absent on the painter's business.

For his part, Domenikos found his son as apt and intelligent as the abbot described him. He was able to follow directions and willing without argument or even question to do precisely as he was told.

Jorge was ravished. By beginning the career he had so thoughtlessly embraced, he had, in effect, become a man.

The transformation of style that the artist was so consciously pursuing and so conscientiously developing during the years that followed the Orgaz Burial scene was evident in all his own work—in the portraits of saints for which he continued to receive commissions, in a picture of St. Louis of France with a page (for which he and Jorge were the models), in several versions of Christ bearing the Cross, and in representations of the Holy Family. In none, however, were the gathering mysteriousness and exaltation of his new approach more patent than in a painting of Christ's Agony in the Garden of Gethsemane.

Its power lay in his conception of this fateful moment when Jesus, visiting with His disciples in the garden after celebrating the feast of Passover, paused in the pallid, ominous moonlit setting and knelt before a rock that was almost theatrical in its artificiality. Here He prayed, while His three disciples slept in an oddly formed cocoon of wind and mist. In the middle distance, centurions, accompanied by Judas Iscariot, were approaching to make their arrest. All the force and drama of the painting came from the colors; drawing, as such, had all but disappeared.

Jorge found the painting strange, a reaction he kept to himself because he thought his father at work an almost fearful personage, someone whom, even after three years of observation, he could hardly recognize as the indulgent, gentle parent of other moments. When he painted, Domenikos was transfigured, translated, ferocious in his concentration, furious if interrupted in his self-absorption as hand and brush darted from palette to canvas with a certainty of purpose that was astonishing to the youth and frightening. Yet when he paused in his work, the good humor returned at once. And when he was instructing his son, the patience and tender solicitude were as evident as ever.

The first of Domenikos' friends to see the finished Agony in the Gaden was the poet-cleric Luis de Argote y Góngora, twenty years his junior, a frequent visitor to the Palacio Fuensalidas, tall, well-dressed, perceptive in argument and passionate in manner. He looked at the painting for only an instant before turning silently away, his expression, it seemed to the painter, one of sharp pain. He walked quickly to the tall, wide window with its splendid river view, and paused there, his hands behind his back, closing and opening his fists.

Without a word, he wheeled about to confront the little canvas once more, as if he disbelieved what he had first beheld. But he didn't move toward it. Again, he turned to gaze from the window.

"What have you *done?*" he inquired at last, his voice husky.

Domenikos was silent. The poet slowly turned to stare at the picture, his eyes moist. "It's a nightmare, Greco. I don't feel that I'm seeing it. I'm dreaming it. It's nothing but emotion, all light and color and shadow and swirling. It's as if I were feeling the scene. It draws me imperiously, but it repels me too, as if the moment were too horrible to be abided and too horrible to be ignored. It terrifies me." He hesitated, looking away. Then, abruptly, he walked to the painting, stopping about a yard away. "It makes me feel as if, for the first time, I truly understand just what the nature, the texture of His agony was. I can *believe,* for the first time, that at so crucial an instant of His life, His disciples could possibly have gone to sleep. Who but Our Lord would have managed to stay awake in so strange a setting?" He frowned, then brightened. "I can't explain why precisely, but it's the most religious painting I've ever seen. It's a religious *experience,* not just the picture of a religious event."

Domenikos was grave. "Painting it was a religious experience, Góngora."

The poet was delighted to have understood his friend's intention. "I'll write you a poem."

And he kept his word. The poem, alas, was less moving than his impromptu eulogy, the words stilted and arcane, mannered and arch.

Twenty-Nine

Far from being repelled by Domenikos' increasingly eccentric manner of painting, his important patrons responded to it with eagerness. It seemed that he had hypnotized them. Or perhaps Góngora's explanation was more exact: the painter had discovered a reserve of emotion, of feeling, to which Castilians could instinctively turn as expressions of their deepest selves. The elegance that had always typified his paintings was not lost, but there was, Góngora said, "this leanness, this abstraction of image, this haunting luminosity" that found in cleric and noblemen alike a "sympathy that borders on idolatry. You've understood Spain."

Whether or not the poet's analysis was correct, Domenikos' fame and popularity increased. His style of painting became more and more emotionally charged, his colors more dramatically deployed, his figures more strangely elongated, the atmosphere of his canvases more eerie, more abstracted, more mysterious, and more mystical. Visions of Michelangelo's Last Judgment were recurrent both in his mind and in his pictures.

More and more, as he entered the years of his fifties, Domenikos felt that only in his reading of Scripture and in his work was he finding God, his conception of God. He continued to observe the obligations imposed by the Church, but they failed to answer his needs. As the demands of the world increased, as his importance as a public figure grew, so did his need to escape. And this he could accomplish only when he painted and read the Bible. When he was creating, he was alone, isolated, and this isolation gradually assumed the character of mystical experience; he and God, together and alone.

Though all of the New Testament was familiar, it was the Book of Revelations that most attracted him, most inspired his quality of vision. He promised himself that someday, when the readiness was there, he would make a picture of the opening of the fifth apocalyptic seal.

Domenikos' frenzied withdrawal into work alarmed his mistress. She feared he was killing himself. Yet, like Jorge, she recognized that only when he was working at the edge of his physical limits was he content. Her fear was that he might unwittingly exceed them, so exhausted was he when he finished work each day.

He insisted, however, as he had done after the Espolio was completed nearly twenty years ago, that he needed more work, not less. And more work he soon found, in abundance. At the end of 1596, Don García de Loysa (soon, it was rumored, to become Archbishop of Toledo) requested him, in his capacity as member of the Council of Castile, to design and construct the altar for the collegiate Church of Nuestra Señora de la Encarnación, recently finished in Madrid. The funds had been provided in the will of Doña María de Aragón, lady-in-waiting to Anne of Austria, Philip's last queen.

Domenikos expressed his doubts. "If the Council controls the funds, Don García, what's the position of the King? Does he know my name has been proposed? I've had trouble with the Council before. In fact, I've had to appoint a lawyer in Madrid to help me collect money that the King officially presides over."

Loysa was surprised. "But I thought you and Philip had come to some sort of understanding, Greco."

"I thought so too. I'd not be so concerned if this were a small commission. But it's enormous, from what you say."

"I'm virtually certain the King approves. It was he who gave Doña María the land the church is built on. But if you're in doubt, why don't you ask him yourself? He's in Madrid."

The painter nodded. "I think I'll do that."

"And if he agrees, may I assume you'll undertake the project?"

Domenikos brushed a hand over his nearly bald head. "Yes. It's only proper that my work be represented in Madrid. And it will give Jorge a chance to see a bit more of the world."

In November the painter and his son set off for the capital. The amiable, rather foppish Jorge was all eagerness; this was his first journey of any distance from Toledo. Domenikos was less enthusiastic; though the prospect of so large a commission attracted him, he would have preferred to be painting.

The city had changed remarkably since his last visit eight years earlier. All the energy hitherto devoted to the completion of the Escorial was now directed to the creation of a capital worthy of Philip's Spain. Everywhere, churches, palaces, monasteries, and public buildings were in various stages. To encourage this development, the King himself was in residence, foregoing the bleak delights of his beloved Escorial.

They established themselves at an inn near the Plaza Mayor, and were ushered into the royal presence only a day after making their request. Philip received them in his bedchamber. He was seated, with his feet supported by a makeshift footrest. His skin was sallow, the flesh wasted, the sharp eyes all but buried by the dry, sagging skin of his eyelids. Like the painter, he was bald.

The visitors genuflected, a gesture the King waved aside with impatience. "Don't *do* that. I've begun to think that the people who show the most tokens of respect are the most dangerous. Antonio Pérez bowed and scraped, and he's one of the worst traitors we've ever known."

"I've of course heard the common talk, sire."

"He's in Pau now, in Béarn, tupping every French countess he can find, no doubt, and telling all my secret plans to subvert the Huguenots." A sigh came as more of a gasp. "It doesn't matter. You're look-ing at a dead man, Greco."

"Surely not, sire."

"A dead man," the King repeated, more softly now. "Have you ever had gout?"

"Fortunately not, sire."

"Well, avoid it if you can. I've had it for years." He groaned as he adjusted the swollen foot. "They say it comes from living too well. But of course, like everything else the doctors tell you, it's a lie." He closed his eyes and rambled garrulously on, his ashen hands repos-ing tranquilly on his chest. "But then, everything's a lie of a kind. When I die, you'll say I ruined Spain. Not you, perhaps, but *they*. They'll say I persecuted the innocent, that I failed to break the power of Britain and to stop the Reformation, that I lost the Low Countries, that I betrayed the Pope." There was another rasping sigh. "Perhaps it's all true. But it's a lie in its implication that I did these things delib-erately. I wanted to preserve Christianity and to glorify God and Spain. Was this monstrous?"

"No, sire. It's wholly admirable. But *if* you've failed, you shouldn't be dismayed."

"I'll receive my reward in paradise?"

"Isn't that what we're to believe?"

"I wonder, maestro. I've often thought of your ambiguous painting of me, and of yourself, especially in recent months when I've been so ill and could contemplate my works. I've tried to see them objectively as God will see them. I've done things that can appear cruel and heart-less when considered in certain lights."

"God will understand, sire."

The old King nodded gravely, just the sad edge of a smile flutter-ing wearily across the gutted face. "But have *I* understood? When I let my son Don Carlos die, was I protecting Spain or myself? He might have been a better king than I. And what's the result? I shall be suc-ceeded by Don Felipe, Philip III you'll call him. He's a boy. Will he be as good a king as Carlos?" The monarch's tired gaze fell on Jorge. "What do you think, boy? Would you plot against your father, threaten his life?"

The youth's face was answer enough. "Under no circumstances, sire—"

Philip cut him short. "You don't know what you're talking about. If he were doing something you thought despicable, you'd betray him in a minute." He gave a little shrug, and shuddered from the pain the movement occasioned him. "It's natural. But in the eyes of God, who's right? Carlos thought it right to plot against me. I thought it right to condemn him. But the fact remains that I killed a future king."

There was a silence. Domenikos at last spoke, softly. "In Crete we have a proverb, sire: Everybody pulls the coverlet over to his own side of the bed."

Philip eyed him inscrutably. "The people of Crete are wise."

The painter chuckled. "If they are, sire, it's defeat that's made them so."

The King croaked harshly. "I shall ponder that apothegm in the serenity of my tomb." He paused. "Now, what can I do for you?"

Domenikos started to explain his mission. The monarch raised his hand.

"I know all about it."

"You approve of my doing it?"

He closed his eyes once again, nodded, and slowly turned his head away. "I still fail to respond to your painting, maestro, but you've become the vogue. Our greatest master, they call you." He looked back, his expression doleful. "Why can't you paint as Titian did, or Bosch? You know, Greco, I'd have made you a duke."

"I'm myself, sire. I have no control over it."

"Nonsense. You're a craftsman. The law says so. You can paint any way you choose."

"I regret to disagree with you, sire, but the choosing has long since gone out of it for me. There was a time when I could paint what was expected of me. Today I paint what I must."

Philip nodded slowly. "I understand that. That's been the rule of *my* life, to do what I must."

Domenikos was never to see the King again. Philip died in September of 1598, two months after being borne by litter to the Escorial, suffering hideously but in silence from the gangrenous wounds of his gout. Two days before his death, he summoned the future Philip III to his bedside and urged him to keep faith with his Church and be just to his subjects. He died as the monks of the great monastery sang orisons in his behalf, having spent his last hours contemplating a painting by Bosch.

It was soon plain that whatever his defects, Philip II had been a king; his son was to be a puppet. Philip III's first major act was to dismiss Rodrigo Vâzquez, his father's principal adviser and confidant and president of the Council of Castile, whom he replaced with Don

Francisco de Sandoval y Rojas, the Marqués of Denia, who would soon be Duke of Lerma. Lerma lost no time in making his influence over the twenty-year-old king sharply felt. His son-in-law, the Conde de Miranda, acceded to the Council presidency and, a year later, his uncle was named Archbishop of Toledo, on the death of Loysa.

The effect of Lerma's policies on Spain remained uncertain. The painter was most apprehensive about the shift in the Council with whose members he must deal in connection with his commission for the Colegio de Doña María de Aragón in Madrid.

The contract called for a single high altar of considerable size to frame three large paintings, the Annunciation for the center to be flanked by the Adoration of the Shepherds and the Baptism of Christ. Not since the original commission for Santo Domingo had Domenikos been asked to produce anything so imposing. Nor was it his only major obligation. In 1597, he had agreed to provide a main altar and two side altars for the recently completed Capilla de San José in Toledo, which involved four paintings.

These two contracts alone would have been sufficient to tax the artist's workshop to capacity. But other commissions remained to be completed. More painters and apprentices were added, more carpenters and gilders. Domenikos hoped, moreover, that Jorge Manuel, after so long a period of intensive training, would prove a useful assistant. But it had become painfully plain that his son, as a painter, had marked limitations.

He complained of this to his mistress. "What's wrong with him, for God's sake? He doesn't understand what he's doing, why he's doing it. He doesn't understand what *I'm* trying to do."

She sighed. "And I imagine it doesn't help much when you lose patience with him."

Domenikos nodded. "He just looks at me as if he were a dying fish, mouth open, eyes wide. He listens to everything I say, and then he answers, 'Yes, papa,' and goes back to doing just what I finished criticizing."

Jerónima showed him no mercy. "I warned you."

"I didn't force him to become a painter. And what's annoying is that he has talent, *querida*. He has the craft, the technique."

"What more do you want?"

"Feeling, genius."

"How many artists have genius, how many people? You're

unique, Menegos." She smiled slyly. "And you're the first to admit it."

The painter ignored this attempt to goad him. "He might be an architect, though. He's a first-rate draftsman."

"Then, in heaven's name, let him be an architect."

"I want him to be a painter."

"Dear God, *amado,* what a stubborn man you are. If he hasn't the fire, or whatever, what's the point?"

"Perhaps if I give him more time."

"You can't have it both ways, you know. If patience will help, don't be impatient. He may develop later."

"Not as a painter."

"Then make the best of a bad job. Make him an architect."

Domenikos sat down at the dining-room table and looked across at her. "That's the only reason I agreed to take the San José commission. With the Collegio in Madrid, it would give Jorge a real opportunity to see how altars are designed and put together."

"Have you talked to him about it?"

"Often."

She eyed him skeptically. "*To* him, not *at* him?"

He sighed. "I don't want to hurt his feelings. I have to paint over almost everything he does except the most routine work. What he paints on his own is so reserved, so held back, emotionally constipated. It's like *him, querida.* It's got no feeling, no passion, no power, no conviction. He makes nothing. He doesn't believe in what he's doing. That's what I'm trying to say. He approaches painting like a dilettante."

"Is he as good as Francesco?"

"Yes."

"He can make satisfactory copies?"

"Very." Domenikos threw his hands in the air. "But that's not good enough for the son of El Greco."

"Then let it be architecture, even if you hurt his feelings. Isn't it much better for *you* to hurt him now than for the world to crush him after you're dead? Think about that. And knowing what you've told me, you've boasted to your friends that in Spain he'll one day be second only to you."

"Yes," he murmured, "I've said that. I boast a little. Why not? Isn't that human?"

"Not if he believes it. What's going to happen when you're not here to protect him from the truth you say you can plainly see? The world will eat him alive. How cruel of you."

"He'll survive. I'll leave him rich."

"Oh, Menegos, is that all you want for Jorge, that he survive?"

"That first of all. It won't be bad. My name will carry him along as an artist or architect."

"You want him to have nothing of his own, just to build a life on his father's gold and his father's reputation?" She turned away, thoroughly disgusted. "How can you say that, you who keep raving about the way Titian crushed *his* son?"

"He'll be happy enough."

"Happy enough?" She laughed bitterly. "You don't even know what 'happy enough' means for yourself."

"But I do," he protested plaintively.

"You're happy enough when you're painting. That's it, isn't it? There's your escape, your euphoria. What a coward. You run from reality when it distresses. You run to your art. You're running from the reality of your own son. And you always have the convenient excuse that you've got no choice, the work must be done." She took a deep breath, her tone becoming ominous. "You're a lucky man. You have two ways of living, El Greco the painter and Menegos the man. You're very careful not to let the two become confused. That other world, the one you let no one penetrate, that's the glorious one for you, and it's the world poor Jorge can never enter for himself."

"But not, God knows, because I want to deny it to him, *amada*. He doesn't know where that world is."

Thirty

A great proportion of the work for the large commissions in Madrid and Toledo was architectural. Thus Domenikos found a tactful excuse for directing Jorge toward this aspect of his craft. The young man recognized, without comment, his father's motives, and accepted them as he accepted life—easily, offering no resistance. As the painter had suspected, his son proved a far more proficient student of architecture than of painting. He worked with devotion and enthusiasm; if not inspired, his contributions to the altarpieces hadn't the otiosity of his painting. In time, Domenikos was convinced, he would be a good designer. The artist was no less disappointed that Jorge was not to be his illustrious successor in painting, but at least he found it possible to resign himself to the reality; he could take Jerónima's advice and make the best of a bad job.

The work for the Capilla de San José was completed in the late spring of 1599, just after Jorge's twenty-first birthday. Of the four paintings, Domenikos prefered the large central portrait of St. Joseph with the boy Christ and the picture of St. Martin and the Beggar (with his son as model for the saint), because in both he had introduced views of Toledo. It had been increasingly in his mind to paint a town-scape, something he had never attempted.

Evaluation was less onerous than he feared. Although the initial appraisal of 3500 ducats was rejected angrily by the custodians of the chapel, a second for 2800 was accepted with surprising grace. The three altarpieces were installed the following December, and received with an acclaim almost as enthusiastic as that accorded the Orgaz Burial scene. Jorge, whose share in the work had been less than he imagined, so discreet had been his father's guidance, tasted success and found it delicious. "It's the greatest day of my life."

This latest acknowledgment of his greatness was less comforting to Domenikos. Jerónima, who thought of herself increasingly as his exegete, accused him of being jaded by so much adulation. "No, querida. It's not that. We made this hastily. My mind was always on the other work, the one for Madrid."

Much more grandiose than the Toledo altarpieces, the single retable for the Colegio de Doña María de Aragón was conceived to be unlike anything ever before seen in Spain. The frames and predella were simple so as not to conflict in any way with the paintings which were to be the source of excitement.

The Adoration of the Shepherds was in a sense the most dazzling of the three pictures, a chiaroscuro work of intense drama. The Baptism recalled the quality of color first revealed in the Agony in the Garden that had so moved Luis de Góngora. But it was to the central painting, the Annunciation, that Domenikos brought all his zeal and fire. He endowed it with a freshness and newness that made it differ almost totally from any rendering of this theme he had previously made.

This first of the great Christian mysteries was painted ethereally, for in its very essence it was an event that had nothing to do with real-

ity as the world understood it. Its message of joy and love and hope
and unexpected fulfillment could be conveyed only in a setting that
bore no intelligible relation to any reality that could be identified by
the beholder as mundane, ordinary, immediately comprehensible.

Only the figure of the Virgin could be described as in any fashion
earthbound, and she barely that. She stood, struck with wonder, as a
tranquil Gabriel, his arms folded before him, his smile the image of
the message he carried, uttered the fateful phrases. Above them was
the brilliantly illuminated dove of the Holy Spirit. A celestial choir
and orchestra dominated the heights of the painting, caught in a whirl
of wind and cloud and light.

"Now," the painter said to Castilla. "Now, I'm beginning to approach my apotheosis, Luis."

Negotiations with the Council of Castile were even more trying
than he had anticipated. The Conde de Miranda, no art lover, showed
reluctance to discuss the matter at all. The Council's major concerns
were too important to be interrupted by so paltry a matter as the estate of a dead noblewoman. Domenikos' lawyer in Madrid was of
little assistance. Against his better judgment, the painter eventually
agreed with Angulo that the retable should be transported to Madrid
and installed in the church. This, perhaps, would induce a settlement.
In July of 1600, he, Jorge, and Francesco supervised the loading of
the delicate elements of this great altarpiece and accompanied them
to the capital where the work was set up at once. Not before the end
of August, however, was an appraisal made, with Francesco alone in
attendance. The sum of 5920 ducats was agreed to by both parties,
but final payment was made only six years later, after prolonged and
bitter litigation.

One reason why Domenikos had agreed to part with the Colegio
retable was that it was cluttering a workshop already overcrowded.
With the prospect of further substantial commissions looming large,
the painter decided that his quarters in the Casa Villena were no
longer adequate. He regretted the necessity of moving from these
apartments that he and Jerónima had occupied for so many years
and elicited from the bailiff of the Marqués de Villena a promise that
if more space became available here, he would be given first refusal.
But the matter was problematical.

It was in a mood of sorrow over his decision to leave the palace
that the artist determined he would paint a view of Toledo that would
include the Casa Villena. He might well have sketched it from mem-

ory, so often had he crossed the Puente de San Martín to mount the opposite bank of the Tajo. Yet he felt this an occasion to be memorialized, a moment whose sadness must be committed to canvas from life, not from recollection.

He followed the familiar course, down the cobbled alleys to the bridge. Here he paused briefly to look up at the glittering white brilliance of San Juan de los Reyes towering over him. He crossed the river and ascended the narrow road as it followed the steep ridge occupied by the hermitage of Nuestra Señora de la Cabeza, which stood directly across from his home.

He was tempted at first to make this his viewpoint, but it would exclude the Puenta da Alcántara and the magnificent medieval Castillo de San Servando. He moved on, past the Alcántara bridge, and stopped at a point a few hundred yards north. Here he began to sketch.

The sky, cloudless when he had left the Casa Villena, grew suddenly stormy, full of the angry turbulence so typical of Toledo's summer weather. First the lightning flashed in the northern distance, followed seconds later by deep, muffled thunder. Then quickly the storm drew nearer, lightning and thunder snapping, whiplike, clawing furiously at the spire of the cathedral. The rain came almost timidly at first, then with all the ferocity of a storm. And it passed. He walked rapidly homeward by the direct route across the city, drenched but contented. His vision was complete. Now he could paint his picture.

It was a miracle of greens and grays and browns beneath a sky that signaled the approaching storm. In no other picture was weather so controlling a factor; the city was bathed in a weird bluish light, a sort of halo. He had beatified his beloved Toledo, transfigured it, made it no longer a city of fact, or *in* fact, but a city of the soul, a city of the imagination—Toledo as he felt it.

The household's removal to new quarters had barely been accomplished before the young King and his new Queen made their long-heralded visit. Philip III rode at the head of a long procession. Just before passing beneath the first arch of the Puente da Alcántara, the *cortège* was halted by the leader of the provincial *Hermandad Vieja*, the "old fraternity" whose prerogative it was to protect the highways from bandits. The cowled rider symbolically covered the monarch's face and hands with a banner, signifying the King's confidence in the

fidelity of this monastic police force and blinding him to any punishment meted out to criminals of the road.

When the flag was removed, the procession crossed the bridge and
entered the city. The King was more brilliantly attired than his father
had ever been. Although he was said to be rigid in his piety, his tastes
were reputedly limited to food and the chase. The face was ruddy and
full—like a pig's, said his enemies. The features of the Queen were
familiar to those who had seen a few Habsburgs: fat, shrewd,
ordinary. Margaret of Austria was a suitable mate for Philip III. Between them, they bespoke a minimum of intelligence with a maximum
of indolence. They were rulers of a kind to which Spain would grow
all too accustomed.

The new Cardinal, the Duke of Lerma's uncle, took seriously his
role of host. There was the usual round of visits to the many
religious and scholarly institutions; there were street fairs and dancing
and a bullfight. But the *pièce de résistance* was provided by the Grand
Inquisitor, Niño de Guevara, who underlined the solemnity of the
occasion by arranging a splendid auto-da-fé in the Zocodover. A
pathetic group of unreconstructed Moriscos was ceremonially handed
over by the Church to the civil authority for suitable punishment.
Those who sat near the new King alleged that his nostrils had quiv-
ered with pleasure as the odor of roasting human flesh wafted across
the square. God and the Faith were well served.

Although Domenikos was already committed to as much work as
he could comfortably manage, even with an enlarged workshop, he
felt he should attempt to be received by Philip III in order to present
Jorge as a candidate for any future architecture the King projected.
His relations with the Palacio Arzobispal, cordial for so many years,
had become chilly during the brief tenure of Archbishop Sandoval y
Rojas, an able administrator by all accounts but, like his nephew, not
a connoisseur of art. An approach to the court seemed improbable
until Castilla pointed out that Niño de Guevara had been a friend
of Don Diego. If Domenikos painted the Inquisitor's portrait, an introduction to the monarch might ensue.

Like Titian in his old age, the painter had long been spared the
necessity of courting favor. Were it not for Jorge's interest, he
wouldn't have considered his friend's suggestion, so accustomed was
he now to his unquestioned position as Spain's greatest artist.

He confronted the project with distaste, a feeling in no way altered
when he was presented to Cardinal Guevara, a hard, humorless, but

intelligent man of sixty who posed with soldierly rigidity, as if prepared at any moment to leap from his chair in response to the call of inquisitorial duty. He might not, as Castilla insisted, be a monster, but he certainly was exceptionally unpleasant. And Domenikos, however much he might have wished otherwise, painted the Cardinal precisely as he was, dour, with sharp eyes wary behind their black spectacles, the ringed hands poised uneasily on the arms of his chair. Yet there was elegance, as always in his portraits.

Guevara was satisfied, expressing his aloof approval when the picture was hung in the great tribunal hall of the Archbishop's Palace. He agreed to arrange an audience with the King before the court left Toledo. For whatever reason, this failed to take place. Domenikos suspected the Cardinal of cynicism, but was, on the whole, more relieved thaan disappointed; reports of Philip's interest in things cultural were discouraging, the more so since their sources were reliable.

Jorge's disillusionment, though bitter, was made less painful soon after the royal couple returned to Madrid. His suit for the hand of Doña Alfonsa de los Morales, the beautiful young daughter of a merchant recently arrived from Valladolid, was successful. To honor the occasion, Domenikos named his son a full partner in all future commissions.

Soon after Jorge's betrothal, Domenikos learned from his aunt Marica that her husband had died after a brief illness, "his dream of election to the Council of Forty unrealized." Of the artist's brother she could report only the most fragmentary information. She understood that he was now assisting in the management of the wine and oil commerce he had formerly owned. She knew nothing of his efforts to repay the debt of 3000 ducats to the Serenissima. Most stunning, however, because he was so unprepared for it, was the information appended as an afterthought: "I assume you have heard from the Mother Superior of her convent, that your poor Maria has died."

He put the letter down with a sigh. Memories assailed him like assassins, jostling him, railing at him, accusing him. He rose from the dining-room table and walked wearily to his studio, closing the door behind him, and leaning against it for a moment afterward, depleted and depressed. He sighed once more, and with what absurdly seemed a great effort, compelled himself to cross the great room to a large mirror hanging on the opposite wall.

He studied the reflection for a time, as if it were a painting. At last, he closed his eyes, reopened them, and looked toward the ceiling. "I'm an old man," he bellowed.

The sound of his voice was restorative. He looked at himself again. The face *was* old. The texture of the flesh was rough and flabby, the beard sketchy, the hair even sketchier. But it was a worldly face. In the dark, deep-set eyes that peered at their own image with such weariness, there was the spirituality that emanated from his paintings. There was sadness, too.

It was in this frame of mind that Domenikos painted the first self-portrait he had made since 1570, just before his departure from Venice.

There was, in the sorrow of the face he saw, a ferocity that startled him. He depicted the features of a man whose concern was for the beauty and the truth that lay beneath the surfaces that most eyes perceived. The eyes looked not through the beholder but beyond him. For these eyes, life itself, reality, held no more surprises; yet in his wordless dialogue with God and in his creativity, that universe of light and color and air, there were surprises at every moment. It was the portrait of a man possessed, obsessed, compelled—a portrait of the artist, old but in fullest possession of his forces.

Jerónima refused to marry him. "Call it superstition. Life has been so good to me for twenty-two years that I'm afraid to change its terms."

She declined even to discuss it further, making him promise never to bring it up again.

Thirty-One

Appropriately, Domenikos began the study for a painting of St. Ildefonso on that holy man's feast day, January 23, 1601. It was a commission for the recently completed church of the Hospital de la Caridad in Illescas and was of more than routine importance because, according to Francesco, the authorities there would soon have the funds with which to finance the high altar, an order of special interest to the painter's new partner, his son; much architecture would be involved.

The picture was warmly received in Illescas, and though a somewhat frustrated Francesco reported no progress in securing the altar commission, he did succeed in prevailing on the administrators of the hospital to order a painting of the Coronation of the Virgin. The shrewd Italian, however, was vaguely disturbed by the attitude he encountered there and strongly advised his master against involvement in a major undertaking for the church in Illescas.

The painter had reason to respect his assistant's counsel. Francesco's genius as a negotiator and collector of his master's debts had been amply proved. Domenikos later conceded that he had shrugged off this warning because Jorge and Doña Alfonsa were to be married after Easter the following year; he wanted the young man's name as a cosignatory of the Illescas contract to give him confidence in his future.

To commemorate their wedding, Domenikos painted portraits of the bride and groom a few weeks before the ceremony. That of Alfonsa was a tender rendering of her lovely, cloudless features, comparable in spirit with his portrait of Jerónima made nearly a quarter of a century earlier. A delicate, shy, affectionate girl, gentle and friendly, she made no demand save that she be loved by those about her, an attention no one found it difficult to give.

He had imagined that a portrait of Jorge would be an easier task, but it wasn't so. The son had definite ideas of how his father should paint him. He insisted on wearing the absurd *lechuguilla,* the lettuce-leaf collar of pleated linen that Philip III had whimsically decreed for all gentlemen. His tunic was black, his cuffs in the style of his ruff. In his left hand he held a small, rectangular palette and several brushes. In the other was a single brush, daintily poised between thumb and index finger.

When Jorge first assumed his pose, Domenikos laughed helplessly. "Do you expect anyone to believe you're a painter, dressed like that? You, especially, who still get more paint on yourself than on the canvas?"

The young man retained his dignity. "That's how I want it, papa."

The incongruity of Jorge's conception of himself made his father's task difficult, and he was unhappy with the result. He painted a fop, a dilettante. If, as Jerónima said, the portrait *was* their son, Domenikos disliked the picture for that very reason. He had been unable to make more of Jorge than God had seen fit to make of him.

The nuptial mass was offered in Santo Tomé, in presence of his painting of the Orgaz Burial. Domenikos wept joyfully as he toasted the young couple at the conclusion of the wedding breakfast. But the memory of his portrait of Jorge, of the misgivings it inspired, made him grim later on, as he walked home from Alfonsa's father's house with his mistress. He prayed silently that God would endow the young artist with genius. He realized, however, that he was praying for a miracle.

The door of his studio was closed this chilly February morning in 1603. The Jesuit Church of San Juan Bautista in Toledo had recently commissioned a large painting of the Crucifixion, a theme he had often treated. For so important a work, however, he would introduce significant modifications. He was concentrating.

There was a knock. Annoyed, he got wearily to his feet and walked slowly across the cluttered studio to the door. He grumbled angrily as he opened it. Before him stood an old man, his features so begrimed that they defied recognition. The old eyes, red and watery, stared at him balefully. The right hand, holding a crude walking stick, trembled violently. The cloak, apparently of good black serge, was now brown with dust and age.

For a long moment, Domenikos contemplated with hostility this pathetic ruin. The other at last wrenched his eroded face into a toothless smile, an expression so obscene that the painter felt his stomach turn. He reached for the purse at his belt and hastily extracted a coin which he held out gingerly.

The intruder made no movement to accept this offering. He shook his shaggy, matted head and began to weep, softly at first, then sobbing bitterly, staggering precariously in Domenikos' direction. The artist reluctantly extended his arms to support the unwelcome stranger and with even greater reluctance led him to a chair, steadying him as he painfully seated himself.

"What is it you want?" he asked irritably. "I'm very occupied just now."

The wretched old man continued to sob, his frame shaking, the hands still trembling. At last, he made a visible effort to control his emotions and looked up at Domenikos, the old eyes still streaming, his throat giving out little rasps of unintelligible sound. He shook his head once again and finally found words—in Greek.

"You don't know me, Menegos?"

The artist paled, was giddy, felt his skin creep. He shivered. He grasped the arm of another chair and sat down heavily, staring at this bedraggled lump of flesh, appalled.

"Manusos?" His voice was soft, high-pitched, hardly recognizable to him. "Manusos?"

The vermin-ridden intruder nodded, his wet eyes glittering ominously. "You didn't know me," he muttered. "You didn't know me."

Domenikos wept. "I wasn't prepared for you, brother. I wasn't prepared for it to be you at my door."

"I'm much changed."

"And in such clothes, Manusos. God in heaven."

The brother drew a filthy sleeve over his broad nose and sniffed vigorously. "Is there a God in heaven?"

The painter stood up and walked as quickly as he was able to the door, where he paused. He looked back at the figure in the chair, incredulous, then loudly summoned his mistress. He returned to his seat and studied what was discernible in his brother's face.

"Oh, God, Manusos," he cried. "What have they been doing to you? What have they done to you?"

Manusos softly rustled his execrable cloak, clutching his arms to his breast. The voice was cracked, the vowels guttural, the sibilants thick, drunken. "Better ask what I've done to myself."

Jerónima, suddenly appearing at the door, took a single step into the room, then stopped abruptly, bringing a hand to her mouth, her face full of alarm. The artist rose and went to her, drawing her over to the tremulous hulk that was Manusos. "This is my brother, *amada*," he said quietly. "But I'm afraid he hasn't any Spanish."

Unbelieving, she looked with fear at the pitiful figure, then glanced back at Domenikos. Her eyes filled with tears and, with a gesture he would always remember, she bent over, as graceful as she had been a generation before, and gently embraced Manusos, holding the grimy, tear-streaked, bearded face between her immaculate hands, smiling compassionately. The old man looked into her clear, pale eyes and once again contorted his features into a dreadful, gummy smile.

"*Gracias*," he mumbled. "I have very little the Spanish," he went on in Italian, "but *grazie*, no, *gracias*."

Jerónima straightened and extended her hand to him. "Come."

Manusos nodded and, with Domenikos' assistance, struggled to his feet.

"Ask one of the men to help him bathe," the artist said. "Then get rid of those clothes and give him one of my gowns and put him to bed. I'll send for the doctor."

Together, they bundled the pathetic old prodigal out of the studio.

Two days later Manusos was sufficiently recovered from his fatigue to converse more or less coherently. The physician reported that apart from the gout he was in reasonably good health; rest and food would restore him quickly.

Domenikos breakfasted with Jerónima, her mother, who had recently joined the household, and with Jorge and his beautiful Alfonsa. He went immediately afterward to his brother's bedchamber and found him propped up with bolster and pillows, gravely contemplating the remains of his meal. He looked up and smiled horribly as Domenikos entered.

He pointed to the tray. "You see? I'm taking nourishment."

"You look better."

Manusos ruefully stroked his face, clean-shaven now. "I feel naked, but better, much better."

"You're safe now. You're home. You'll be all right now."

"I know." Tears came. The old voice was thick. "Thank you."

"No need for that. I told you you'd always be welcome."

"But such a welcome, Menegos. Such kindness, such gentleness for such a sack of old flesh."

"You're my brother."

"My keeper?"

"Of course."

"And you don't mind?"

"How should I mind, in God's name? You'd do the same for me."

"Don't be too good to me, Menegos, or I shan't know how to stop weeping. I'm not used to kindness."

"But what happened? It's been so long since I heard from you or heard anything about you."

Manusos' sigh seemed to Domenikos almost mortal in its depth. "A chronicle of catastrophe. That's been my life for twenty years. Most of it was my own fault, of course. You saw it. You warned me. I was a fool."

"Why did you leave Candia?"

"There was nothing to keep me. My Katina died, a year ago, I think. I don't remember. I've lost the sense of time."

"And your daughters?"

"Two are nuns. The other two are married. They've all left me to die."

"You're exaggerating. Where are the married ones?"

"With their husbands. One is in Venice, the other in Candia."

"In Candia?"

Manusos nodded. "Little Katina. It's worse being left alone by someone who lives near you."

"She never came to see you?"

"Only when she needed something she thought I had." He sighed again. "Oh, I can't reproach her, Menegos. I wasn't much of a father to any of them. And with Katina gone, they wanted nothing more to do with me. I was a scandal, not the kind of man anyone would have reason to be loyal to. Only you were loyal. Your ducats saved my life, literally."

"And your debt?"

Manusos uttered a sound his brother supposed was laughter. "That, ostensibly, is my reason for being here. I obtained the Serenissima's permission to leave Venetian territory so I could come to you and beg three thousand ducats." Before Domenikos could speak, he pressed on eagerly. "Of course, I have no intention of doing anything of the sort. It was the only thing to say. Besides, I don't believe they have any illusions about it. It probably seemed a fair gamble. They knew they'd get nothing from me as things stood."

"But it's a debt of honor."

"Honor, Menegos, is only for those who can afford it. I can't."

Wearily, Domenikos rose and walked to a window. For some minutes he stared into the patio below, where nothing bloomed now; all was barren. Then he turned back.

"I'll see to it. Don't be concerned about it any more."

"I'm not concerned, Menegos. It doesn't matter to me."

"It matters to me," he answered with a softness that failed to conceal the iron of his undertone. "I'm concerned because I want nothing to affect papa's name, in Venice or in Candia. That's important to me."

Manusos shook his head. "You mean you're so rich you can afford to pay debts of honor?"

The painter laughed sharply. "If I were poor, brother, debts of honor would be paid first."

"You'd go hungry for the sake of honor?"

"I think so."

"We're very different, you and I. But of course we always were."

Manusos' strength returned quickly. Seventy-three now, he established himself in the household with the ease of one who, though unaccustomed to luxuries, liked to think them due him. He vacillated between a childish delight in the richness of his new clothes and the quality of the wine normally served at table and a poorly contrived equanimity in his acknowledgment of introductions to the many splendid guests, lay and clerical, who frequented his brother's home.

From Jerónima and Alfonsa he garnered more and more smatterings of Spanish, enough so that it became safe for him to venture into the streets of Toledo. He recounted, as if they had in this hospitable atmosphere become hilarious, his adventures as sponsor of four ill-fated pirate ships. So much older did he seem than Domenikos that Jorge treated him as a grandfather rather than uncle, finding him a figure of fun, a role that Manusos accepted with silent good humor. To spend his last years in comfort, even as court jester, was preferable to the sorry existence he had left in Crete.

He hobbled frequently to the Moorish section of Toledo where most of the transient Greeks found accommodation while they awaited the assistance of the Trinitarians in rescuing their relatives from Ottoman bondage. Occasionally he returned with one of these acquaintances, and, to the entertainment of all, conversations would take place in Greek, whose strange accents provoked laughter throughout the house. Manusos made his brother feel guilty for having so long failed to concern himself with plight of these people. Domenikos gave him gold with which to make himself a missionary to the Greek community, realizing that he could no nothing more effective to restore Manusos' self-respect. The old man distributed this largesse with tact and without pomposity.

"He amazes me," said the painter to Jerónima one day in late spring. "He's so happy, so pleased. He seems to have lost all his bitterness. I couldn't manage that if I were in his position."

"But he's a simple man, Menegos, and you're a complicated one."

In the aging but still-proud Doña Ana, Manusos found someone with whom, in the gathering darkness of fall and winter afternoons, he could sit quietly, now and then exchanging a few phrases that didn't unduly tax the limits of his improving Spanish. She even expressed an interest in learning Greek. For Domenikos and Jerónima it was touching to see them together, he looking much the older though in fact Doña Ana was more than eighty now.

Her repeated boast was that her sole remaining ambition was to live to hold her great-grandchild in her arms. If Alfonsa's casual assertion could be relied on, the infant should be arriving in March. The girl treated her pregnancy as she treated everything that had to do with her person; it was a matter of no great moment. As her term drew nearer, she couldn't understand why her father-in-law insisted that she rest. Gently but firmly, she declined Jerónima's offers of assistance. "I've always done things for myself. I wouldn't be happy otherwise." The thought of Alfonsa unhappy stayed all hands.

A son was born during the last week in March, 1604. Domenikos thought himself more delighted than Jorge, who had another reason for rejoicing. He had just been asked to make plans for the refurbishing of the Casa de Comedias, the theater where Toledo's growing school of poet-playwrights could present their stylized pageants of manners and morals.

Jorge was surprised by his father's jubilation. "I think," he said to Jerónima, "he's happy because Alfonsa survived the ordeal."

"No," she replied, smiling, "he knows his name will endure for another generation."

"It means so much to him?"

She stared at her son hotly, amazed by his obtuseness. "You don't know that? You've spent so many years working beside him. Have you ever asked yourself a single question about him?"

"Many, mama, but not that one."

"His name means a good deal to him, and for that reason, if for no other, it should mean a great deal to you."

He grinned. "I can't even pronounce it in the Greek way."

She sighed and turned away.

The entire family, including poor Manusos, who had to be carried in a chair so painful was his gout, duly trooped to Santo Tomé where, with Dr. Gregorio Angulo standing as godfather, little Gabriel Theotocopoli, as it was spelled in Toledo, was baptized in the shadow of the Orgaz Burial scene which Toledans continued to call El Greco's masterpiece.

Domenikos himself was bored with the painting. As he looked at it now, Angulo joined him, chuckling.

"Admiring your handiwork?"

"No, I was thinking how I'd paint it today. It would be much different." He pointed to the portrait of himself and smiled. "But I was a handsome dog twenty years ago, wasn't I?"

The lawyer shrugged and looked at his own image in the great picture. "So was I." He turned back to the artist. "If for no other reason than that, I'm happy you can't change it."

Domenikos smiled abstractedly. "My last earthbound painting."

In July the painter was informed that larger apartments in the Casa Villena were available. The word seemed a godsend. The small family of a few years before had grown substantially. Moreover, with so much more space, Domenikos could increase the production of copies for which the demand continued to increase. To his bedridden brother, who deplored the idea of renting an establishment of twenty-four rooms, most of them very large, he explained that the augmented overhead would be more than offset by greater revenue.

In early August, the household returned to the beautiful Casa Villena, now occupying all but a few of its rooms. As they had done on the first occasion, they held a reception for all their friends and acquaintances in Toledo. Domenikos, never pleased with the apartments they had taken four years before, felt that he was home again.

This illusion of contentment was dashed in December when Manusos finally succumbed to the agonies and putrefaction of his gout.

"I mourn him," said Domenikos, "but not with my whole heart. The pain was too terrible."

"But you made him as happy as you could," said Jerónima.

He nodded. "It's strange. Even though he disapproved of our moving, he enjoyed it. I told him that with his gout he was just like Philip II. That pleased him. He said, "Well, at least I can die like a king, and in a palace at that.' "

Thirty-Two

The early months of 1605 were tranquil. Work on the large commission for Illescas was nearing completion. Jorge Manuel was delighted with himself. In addition to his major contributions to their altarpieces, the first in which his name loomed as large as his father's, he had finished the decoration of the interior of the Casa de Comedias. His accomplishment so impressed members of the Ayuntamiento that the *alcalde mayor* presented him with a silver fountain.

While Jerónima and Domenikos were spending a week in Cuenca as guests of Castilla, Jorge decided to surprise them by painting a portrait of the family who stayed behind: Doña Ana, Alfonsa, the little Gabriel (just past his first birthday) and the child's nurse. The indulgent father thought it not an especially estimable work—"cramped" he described it to his mistress—but he offered his son gentle congratulations. Soon afterward, he was pleased that he had held his tongue, for Doña Ana, long frail, died in May. Though naturally saddened by this loss, all could agree that she had led a happy life, at least from the time of Jerónima's liaison with her marqués, and had lived to spend a year or so with a great-grandchild.

From January, the main topic of conversation at the Palacio Fuensalidas was the first volume of Cervantes' *Don Quixote*. Led by Gregorio Angulo, who knew the author well and admired him, most of the count's friends found the book a sheer delight. There were, in fact, only two dissenting opinions, that of Fray Hortensio de Paravicino, a young Trinitarian to whom the artist had become greatly attached, and Domenikos himself, who conceded that Cervantes could often be exceedingly entertaining, even painfully funny. But the author struck the fastidious Cretan and the scholarly Spaniard as inept. He lacked a sense of order. He totally ignored all questions of style and polish. They found *Don Quixote* artless.

Writers loomed large in Toledo that year. Lope de Vega, a rakehell poet and playwright, made a spectacular entrance into the city in the company of a charming new wife and a magnificently beautiful mistress, Micaele de Luján. Micaele, an actress married to an actor, had brought along her seven children; the entire progeny generally was believed to have been sired by her present lover. Lope blandly installed his two ladies in separate establishments, a discretion the painter thought amusingly gratuitous. No one, least of all Archbishop Sandoval, raised either a hand or cry against this openly scandalous life. The Church, it seemed, admired Lope's morality plays, and the *regidors* liked his comedies of manners.

Domenikos considered both types of work unbridled and facile (hardly surprising, since the playwright was said to have created several long pieces in less than three days). As with *Don Quixote*, he found himself in a minority of two with Paravicino, the only other defender of classical austerity in the group who discussed the plays at the Fuensalidas meetings. Lope didn't stay long in Toledo. His sudden departure with wife and mistress was especially and most warmly mourned by many creditors. The good Angulo undertook to take care of his debts, for he considered the man a genius. It was at least true, as the kindly lawyer said, that "never has the city been so gay as when Lope was here."

By August, the Illescas work was ready for installation. With Jorge

and Francesco, Domenikos traveled to the town to supervise the placement of altars and paintings. When they were assembled, he expressed
himself as well satisfied. Only to closest friends did he confess that it
wasn't a masterpiece. Yet he had created something never before seen
in Spain, paintings that were proportioned (or disproportioned) to
be viewed from below. He believed that the problems involved had
been satisfactorily resolved. And he was pleased too because so much
of the work, even the painting, was Jorge's. As an architect, the young
man's abilities seemed to his father now beyond dispute. He was proud.

After the three men returned to Toledo, a full week passed without
word from the Illescas authorities. It was only then that Domenikos
recalled Francesco's warning of three years before. For only then did
events begin to unfold that would seem "a chronicle of catastrophe,"
as Manusos had described his later life. The two years that followed
were his Gethsemane.

The first indication that there were to be difficulties that would
make the Espolio dispute appear amiable came late in August. Without a word to the painter, the hospital administrators named a sculptor
and painter from Madrid to appraise the altarpieces. They proposed a
figure of 2200 ducats, a sum, as, Domenikos later testified, that didn't
even cover the cost of materials and labor.

The monetary appraisal wasn't the most demeaning aspect of the
matter. The "experts" criticized the work from an artistic and technical
standpoint, alleging that the principal painting, a large Virgin of Charity, was imperfect because Domenikos had included among the recip-
ients of the Madonna's largesse portraits of Angulo and Jorge, who,
like the others, wore the fashionable *lechuguillas* prescribed by the
King. They demanded that these figures be replaced with something
"more seemly."

Narbona, the painter's advocate in Madrid, who had undertaken the
case, advised the artist against making a personal apperance before
the authorities. He had heard of his daring performance before the
alcalde mayor in 1579. Domenikos' written deposition was hardly tactful, however. After complaining of the secrecy in which the appraisal
had been carried out, "like thieves in the night," and deploring the
derisory price suggested, he went on to defend the portraits. If such
objections were to be taken seriously, the "experts" were criticizing a
tradition in painting that was as long as Christian art itself. He cited
the presence of donors in panels made as early as the thirteenth century. If he were to substitute "more seemly" figures, he would be, in
effect, creating saints, not mere mortals, which would be out of keep-

ing with the theme of the picture. He concluded this statement with a demand for a further appraisal.

The Illescas administrators immediately petitioned the Council of Toledo's Archbishop for relief. To their consternation, Domenikos' request was granted. This time, the Council named two appraisers, neither known to the painter. In September, they evinced no hesitation in arriving at a sum twice that of the first. Reaction from Illescas was instantaneous. The authorities added objections more capricious than the first. They rejected the larger price.

It was well into November before Narbona lodged Domenikos' response to this second diatribe. No more could be accomplished until after Epiphany. At the end of January, the Toledo Council sent two more appraisers who were not only to establish a reasonable fee but were, as well, to answer point by point each of the authorities' complaints. This they accomplished with commendable celerity, siding with Domenikos on every issue, even agreeing that the portraits of Angulo and Jorge were perfectly in keeping with the spirit of the painting in which they appeared. They expressed their conviction that the sum of 4835 ducats would be proper, an increase of more than 400 over the second.

The artist's delight at this news was matched by a correspondingly intense dismay in Illescas. The administrators maintained that the experts were personal friends of the painter, "men who have frequently been guests in his house." Their appraisal, therefore, was not to be given credence. There was no truth in the accusation, but as Domenikos wryly observed to Angulo, "in a case where enormity has become the rule, truth no longer has meaning."

The hospital board refused to pay the new sum and went further: they would send a representative to Madrid "to seek out an artist who can paint a genuinely suitable picture of the Madonna of Charity," a threat that both amused and enraged the painter.

In March, the Toledo Council did an astonishing thing. It ordered that everything of value belonging to the hospital, including treasure and vestments, be seized and impounded until a settlement was reached. The board responded by trying to bring the case to the attention of the Apostolic Nunciature in Madrid, stating that if necessary to prevent "this miscarriage of justice" a delegation would be sent to Rome, to His Holiness himself.

Painting was all that prevented Domenikos from nervous collapse during this period of agony. But not even his work could save him from the next, and wholly unexpected, development. He was sum-

moned to make an appearance before the collector of taxes of the
Royal Council of Castile, to show cause why he shouldn't pay a tax
on the 1000 ducats already advanced by the Illescas authorities.

The position was confused, to say the least. An artist was considered
a craftsman, as Philip II had noted to Domenikos a decade earlier. Any
piece he sold, therefore, was subject to taxation. This accounted for
the custom of artists' pawning their works instead of selling them outright. It was a subterfuge he had always despised, despite the fact that
it was perfectly legal.

Both Angulo and Narbona were convinced that the collector of
taxes was merely responding to pressures applied by the Illescas
authorities, since he was based in that town. It was only a formality.
All the painter had to do was state his intention not to sell the altarpieces to the hospital but to place them in what amounted to perpetual pawn.

Flanked by his lawyers, Domenikos appeared at the appointed hour.
There was much panoply in the great chamber of the Royal Council,
although few of its members were present. He stood at the end of a
long table and proceeded at once to surprise his audience, for he made
it plain from the beginning of his statement that he wasn't going to
make the anticipated defense.

He spoke politely, carefully, slowly, his aging, agile hands flutter-
ing, clenching, splaying, giving added effect to his eloquence.

"In what respect," he began, "does the artist differ from the scholar
or the lawyer or the physician? Is his training not as long and as rigor-
ous? Is the work he does less demanding of spirit and intellect? Is the
work he does not beautiful in and of itself? Does art have a practical
value that makes it comparable, for example, to a chair or a loaf of
bread or a pair of boots?"

He paused to let these rhetorical questions make an impression, then
continued. "In his own way, the artist glorifies God quite as much as
the theologian or the parish priest. He doesn't contribute to our cor-
poreal, but to our spiritual needs. Therefore his work should be regarded not as craft, not as something mechanical, but on a par with
the contribution of scholars and others who practice the liberal arts."

Both Angulo and Narbona were at first alarmed by Domenikos' decision to take such a stand. Why bother, when the alternative was so
simple and straightforward? Yet it seemed to the painter that because
of the anguish and confusion surrounding the Illescas debacle,
he would like to state the position of the artist in society, to make it
clear, once and for all time, that he was in no sense to be compared to

the cobbler and the carpenter, and that he deserved official recognition as an equal in every way of the most respected figures of his time.

His judgment was completely vindicated. The members of the tribunal enthusiastically agreed with him in all respects. From April, 1606, onward, the artist was no longer thought a craftsman. Domenikos made legal history. To have made it in Illescas seemed all the sweeter.

Settlement with the hospital seemed no nearer. The Council in Toledo, still in possession of the treasure, pressed for payment of the 4200 ducats. The board countered with an offer to pay the initial sum of 2200, which the artist naturally refused. By now it was March, 1607. The Council stipulated a final, definitive appraisal, to be binding on both sides. Domenikos opposed this, but permitted Angulo and Narbona to convince him that at this point any settlement was preferable to deadlock.

The moment the names of the experts were made known to him, the painter despaired. For one was Pompeo Leoni, the erstwhile friend who had betrayed him over the Martyrdom of St. Mauritius a quarter-century before. The final sum was set at 2093 ducats. Given the stipulation, Domenikos had no choice but to accept. He had been beaten by those he now called "the monsters of Illescas" who had found in Leoni a perfect foil. To Jerónima he bitterly observed, "Not even Judas Iscariot was given the opportunity to betray Our Lord twice."

But the matter was settled. And he could draw consolation from his victory in the tax matter. He couldn't immediately know that he must pay another and more tragic penalty. Only in the first week of June did this become clear. Francesco announced his intention to return to Italy.

Although the indispensable and beloved assistant attributed his decision entirely to the frustrations of the Illescas dispute, Domenikos was certain that Jorge's having superseded him as second in authority was of at least equal importance. The artist only then acknowledged that his son had treated Francesco tactlessly on more than one occasion, a rudeness the Italian had accepted, as he did so many things, with a shrug. Armed with letters of introduction to Spanish clerics and diplomats in Rome, the companion of more than thirty years took tearful leave of his master, bundling Juanita and his children into a carriage for the journey to Seville.

Domenikos turned away from the sight of the departing family and entered the broad patio of the Casa Villena. He walked alone in the aromatic gardens overlooking the Tajo and the old bridge. He was sixty-six. His breath came shorter than before. It took more brandy to make him dizzy. He was, if possible, even more abstracted, more inward-seeking, more bitter, more determined than ever that the painting of his last years be his supreme work, the image of his soul laid bare. There must be in his art an end to his agony.

Thirty-Three

If the Illescas disaster hadn't broken Domenikos, it had certainly winded and depressed him, notably affecting his capacity to produce. This was embittering; as his physical energies diminished, his ideas proliferated. To conserve his waning powers, he confined himself exclusively to his own work, leaving the management of the workshop to Jorge. This new role, added to the fact that he had just received his first commission as a painter in his own right, did nothing to improve the son's tendencies to arrogance in his treatment of assistants. An almost immediate result was the departure of the best of them, Luis Tristan. Domenikos refused to intervene. Jorge must learn by experience.

Although he was able to divert most commissions to Jorge, there were some he found impossible to refuse to undertake himself. One involved the decoration of a new chapel in the Toledan Church of San Vicente, financed by a bequest of Doña Isabel de Oballe, a *Toledana* who had long ago immigrated to Peru. The funds were administered by the *alcalde mayor*, who himself proposed the work to a reluctant Domenikos.

A second, even harder to turn down, came from Don Pedro Salazar de Mendoza, administrator of the Hospital de San Juan Bautista, an old friend of Covarrubias, a member of Fuensalidas' academy and a frequent guest in the artist's house. Mendoza requested a set of three altarpieces for the great church of his establishment, agreeing that Jorge might design the architecture but insisting that the paintings be by Domenikos.

Under the mounting pressures of work, in moments of reflection, in reading, and most of all in the generosity of friendship that was lavished on him, the painter's morale was gradually restored to its customary level of introverted ebullience during the eighteen months that followed the conclusion of the Illescas fiasco. The frequent and welcome intrusions of the babbling Gabriel reminded him that life would somehow perpetuate itself, that his years, though surely numbered, would leave among his descendants his work as a testament to his love of beauty and of God.

This return of creative vitality expressed itself profoundly in the number and quality of his paintings. He felt that he was soaring. A meaning more personal than ever and thus more difficult to share with friends became a matter of growing concern. Reading helped him more than conversation. In the picaresque novels and arch verse that enjoyed such a vogue in Philip III's Spain he found diversion and distraction. But in response to a desire for a deeper understanding of himself, of his own nature, he returned often in these months to the Book of Revelations and to its extraordinary exegesis in the poetry of Dante.

Fray Hortensio de Paravicino, the brilliant young Trinitarian whom he had first encountered at the Palacio Fuensalidas some years earlier, became the devoted acolyte Domenikos would have preferred to discover in his nonchalant son. Two years younger than Jorge, the vivacious Paravicino, already widely hailed as a preacher and poet, was a familiar of Casa Villena, never more so than during the first months of 1609, when the artist was painting his portrait.

The monk found in this intense, almost grotesque old genius a master whose intellect and articulateness were incomparably superior to any he had come upon. His respect for the painter was at times nearly idolatrous, which annoyed Domenikos, though he managed to abide it in silence, for his enjoyment in Paravicino was great. Never successful in attracting a pupil who could grasp the principles and mechanics of his art, the painter had discovered in this passionate, handsome young man someone capable of understanding, for the most part, the philosophy and spirituality that underlay it. He was therefore to be treasured.

It was Paravicino who pronounced his older friend an apocalyptic painter when Domenikos disclosed his intention at some point soon to make a picture of the Laocöon legend and the Opening of the Fifth Seal, subjects that had been coming closer and closer to the center of his vision in recent months.

His increasing inclination to the purely visionary, the absolutely mystical, was at least partially induced by a desire to flee the Spanish reality, political, social, and economic. Though he had never become the political animal so many of his friends professed themselves, Domenikos could scarcely inhabit their world without realizing that even if conditions didn't seriously affect his own way of living they certainly affected Spain. And he understood too that, late or soon, they would intrude themselves on the lives of Jorge and Alfonsa and, more particularly, of the little Gabriel.

Spain was in decline. There could be no escaping the fact. The first eleven years of Philip III's reign had been, in Manusos' phrase once more, "a chronicle of catastrophe," small catastrophes which, when accumulated, constituted nearly total calamity. The King's utter dependence on the guidance of the Duke of Lerma had produced a deterioration, political and economic, that subjects of Philip II would have thought incredible. The machinery of government had bogged down in a morass of bureaucracy. Instead of reform, authorities superimposed a second government, rule by *junta*.

If Lerma personally wasn't venal by standards then accepted, he revealed a remarkable propensity to choose favorites whose avarice was insatiable. The first was Don Pedro Franqueza, who had counseled in 1601 a sudden shift of the capital from Madrid to Valladolid, thinking thus to spare the King the "deplorable influence" of his grandmother, the dowager empress. And it was he, five years later, who advised a return of the court to Madrid.

Franqueza's policies of taxation and finance emphasized the already marked discrepancies between the treatment of rich and poor, rendering impossible the recreation of a true middle class, an essential to the establishment of a balanced society. In 1607, Franqueza was suddenly exposed. Forced from power, he was compelled to restore a million and a half ducats which he had systematically filched from royal and provincial treasuries.

Don Rodrigo Calderón, his successor, was hardly more able, more foresighted, or more honest a guide. The King failed to see anything amiss in his realm, which was a tribute to Lerma, who kept his indifferent ruler perpetually in the dark. It may not have been much of a deception. Philip III had long been accepted as an indolent monarch whose ignorance was unfathomable.

But the hard realities had their way of encroaching on the inanities and hollow gallantries of the wilfully obtuse court. Abroad, these intrusions were largely confined to the only war in which Spain was still actively and effectively engaged, that with the Low Countries. Any possibility of ultimate victory had perished with Philip II, but the conflict had dragged miserably on. Lerma, exercising for once some intelligence, was finally made to understand that a settlement must be made. Inflation was so grave that a new copper currency, for domestic use only, had been devised to cope with rising prices. It was no longer tolerable that this feckless conflict should continue to drain so large an amount of gold from a nation now truly near absolute bankruptcy.

In April of 1609, a twelve-year truce was signed. Every Spaniard at all conversant with the situation understood that "truce" was tantamount to surrender. There could be no resumption of hostilities because Spain had neither the funds nor the stomach for it. To divert public attention from this recognition of defeat, Lerma created a circus for the populace. On the day of the signing of the armistice, an appalling proclamation was issued: All Moriscos were to be expelled from the country forthwith. This word was mistakenly welcome by a substantial majority of descendants of the Visigoths. Five years would elapse before the last of 300,000 Christianized Moors were driven from their land, but the popularity of the ruling did in part offset the disillusionment of the surrender to the Low Countries.

The departure of the Moriscos merely demonstrated what many had only dimly appreciated earlier, that they had performed functions, principally menial, which few other Spaniards were willing to assume. Nowhere was this more apparent than in Valencia, where the loss of almost 120,000 all but depopulated the farms. Those left behind had rejoiced, but soon discovered that it was impossible to replace these workers. The result was famine—but only for the poor.

The Church, already improbably overstaffed, received more and more applicants and supplicants. Only in the service of the court, the great families, or the Church was survival possible. Except in Toledo and one or two great coastal cities, there was no industry worth mentioning and little commerce. Poverty was aggravated. Food prices, already inflated, soared out of reasonable reach. The rich, clerical, noble, and royal, looked on with an indifference rarely informed by fright.

No single event in his lifetime so stirred and alarmed Domenikos. To anyone who would hear him in the Palacio Fuensalidas, he protested the expulsion decree as both unconscionable and mad. Even those who agreed with him urged discretion.

"I don't care how important you are in Toledo," said the sympathetic Salazar de Mendoza, "you can't risk the antipathy of the court or the Church."

"Why, Pedro, because you see me as a refugee, an alien?"

"Because they can break you. Because most of the money for the commissions you receive comes either from the Church or the Council of Castile."

"I have a special reason for feeling this way. I'm an islander. My people have spent centuries being buffeted between the Turks and the Venetians. We know in our bones what this kind of persecution is like. It has nothing to do with reason. It has to do with fear, a fear that's been shamefully cultivated by Lerma and his creatures. I've seen the Venetians do it in Candia. A tiny grain of fact can be developed until it's made to seem something frightening. The little truth is that the Moriscos remained pretty much among themselves. But Lerma made a magnificent lie out of it by saying that they were plotting the overthrow of the country."

Mendoza was impressed. "*You* frighten *me.*"

"I mean to. But if you're frightened by mere words, Pedro, think of these poor Moriscos, how they must feel. Where will they go? Where can they go? What's to become of them? Who's willing to help them? How will they live? Oh, no, it's monstrous. If you consider it objectively, after all, they're being driven from a country where they've lived for eight centuries. It's not as if they could be called interlopers." He laughed angrily. "It would be easier to make a persuasive case for driving the so-called Spaniards from the land. The monarchy is Austrian. If you think about it, it's the Moors who've formed this country. Look around you. Why, it's only in the thirty-odd years that I've been here that the peasant customs of Castile have changed much from the patterns set by the Moors. Look at what they've done for our music, for our art and architecture, our attitude toward women, toward life in general. If you think about it honestly, Pedro, you'll see that what we call Christianity in Spain is not much more than a veneer. The spirit of this country is Moorish."

Mendoza was astonished. He stepped back and stared at his old friend. "Does this mean that you plan to set yourself in public against the King?"

Domenikos sighed and solemnly shook his bald head. "If I were Spanish, I might. If I were about twenty years younger, I might. But I'm neither, so I can simply implore someone like you, who are at least Spanish if not young, to do something, to make a Christian gesture. This decree stinks of depravity. When the Moors conquered Spain, they were more Christian in their treatment of the Visigoths than we so-called Christians, purified directly from Trent, are being in our treatment of them. It's unspeakable, Pedro. My father used to say that if he were given a choice between being ruled by the Turks or the Venetians, he'd choose the Turks. By their actions, they'd proved their generosity of spirit. All the Venetians could prove was their bestiality. I'm not suggesting that I'd welcome an Ottoman attack of Spain, but I'd not fear it with the kind of apprehension that I've seen on the faces of the Moriscos here in Toledo. The Spaniards are more savage than even the Venetians."

"But you don't dispute the point that the Moriscos do tend to cluster together and that this can be frightening."

Domenikos was unimpressed. "Is it really that? Don't we more or less compel them to cluster together? We don't associate with them, do we? We don't have them in our homes." He grinned sheepishly. "By we, of course, I'm referring to their peers, the Visigothic poor."

Mendoza frowned reflectively. "And whose fault is that?"

"Yours, mine, theirs, everyone's. Does it matter? You can't call it Christian."

"Many things are done in the name . . ."

The painter didn't hear him.

Thirty-Four

First there was indistinguishable sound, perhaps a rustling, the abrasion of cloth against cloth, or a breath taken in quickly, as in surprise. And then there was a trace of light, barely detectable through eyes scarcely opened; and at last, as vision cleared, there was the greater but still subdued illumination of a room. Was it evening? Were the blinds drawn against the brilliance of a noonday sun? He couldn't be certain. He opened his mouth to speak, but found his lips gummy, his palate dry. He tried to shift his position and discovered that his right leg refused to respond to the brain's command. Once more he attempted to speak, licking his lips as a dog licked its chops.

"What's happened to me?" he mumbled, and was astonished by the feebleness of his voice. He twisted his head slightly and found that he was peering up into the anxious, saddened eyes of Jerónima, who sat at his side, holding his chilled hand in both of her warm ones. "What happened?" he repeated dully. "What is it?"

"You've been ill, my poor Menegos. You've been very, very ill."

With a difficulty that frightened him, he brought his free left hand to his brow, then up over the domed, hairless head, feeling at the temple the slow, lethargic beating of his pulse. "Have I received the sacraments?"

She merely nodded. He sighed, uncertain that he wanted an answer to the question he must ask. "And now?"

She smiled wanly, pressing his hand more tightly for an instant. "And now, if you're careful, the doctor thinks you'll stay with us for quite a long time, may it please God."

In the ensuing silence, the stillness unmistakably of a sickroom, he remembered with a sudden, alarming vividness his brother's last days. He noted a fuzziness, a peculiar thickness in his perceptions, as if impulses were being transmitted through an unwonted barrier. He was aware, but his awareness was only partial, circumscribed; he was not entire.

Jerónima bent over and gently kissed the hand he raised. To feel the sweet moisture of her mouth more firmly, he pressed the hand against it as powerfully as he was able. She straightened and gazed at him intently.

"How do you feel?"

He licked his lips again. "Bewildered."

"Have you pain?"

He considered for a moment, then made an effort to shake his head. "I'm uncomfortable." He laid his left hand over his heart. "Like a stomachache in the wrong place. Dull pain, not sharp."

"You must take no chances, *amado*."

He tried to chuckle, but the result was a rasp of expired air. "What chances can I take in bed?"

"No worries, no disturbance, no visitors . . ."

"No books?"

She smiled. "On pleasant subjects only."

"But what happened to me?"

"You had an apoplexy."

Slowly, Domenikos shifted his pale, gaunt head from side to side. "I recall nothing."

"And no wonder," she said grimly. "The doctor says you were that near to death." She pressed her thumb and index finger together. "The whole of Toledo had been praying for you every day since it happened. You have no idea."

His smile was pained. "Praying that I live or die?"

"Ill as you are, I'll not hear a syllable of vanity or false pride."

"Forgive me."

"God has already forgiven you. You're in a state of grace until you have the strength to sin again."

"There's a doleful consolation."

"No blasphemy, either."

"You're going to be very strict with me?"

"As strict as I must."

He sighed again. "When did it happen? I remember nothing."

"What's your last recollection?"

He considered for a time, then spoke, his voice gaining strength as consciousness was gradually restored. "It seems to me I was arguing with Mendoza." He hesitated. "About the expulsion of the Moriscos? Was that it?"

She patted his hand. "That's very good. The doctor said that if you remembered the last thing you were doing, your mind was undamaged."

He stared at the high beamed ceiling. "Poor Pedro. What a way to win an argument."

"He saved your life."

"I'm sure he did."

"You surprised him. He said he'd never seen you so upset."

"I don't remember that."

"You went all red in the face, and then, without warning, you collapsed." She snorted. "And you say you care nothing about politics."

He grinned. "I promise to hold myself aloof from now on."

Her mood abruptly changed, her tone husky. "You talked sometimes while you were so ill. You called for me and for Jorge and Gabriel and Alfonsa. And then you tore the heart right out of me. You called for Francesco. Over and over again, like a litany, you called our names."

Tears welled up, and he tried to lift his head, to touch with his lips the well-loved mouth. She restrained him with tender determination, then leaned over to kiss him lightly.

"I told no secrets, *querida*. All the world knows my needs."

She turned sharply away and sniffed. "All the *world* knows is that El Greco is an artist."

"And you? What did you know?"

"That you had affection for me, loyalty, consideration, in your own way."

"Did you think I'd call for paint, for God's sake? What's the matter with you?" His voice attained as much shrillness as his energy allowed. "Don't you know I love you?"

Not before January of 1610 was Domenikos able to get about the house without the aid of two canes and a servant constantly in attendance. For some months thereafter he depended on a single cane, and though he was only occasionally aware of it, assistance was never far away.

His debility depressed him. He assured the household and the well-wishers who called at the Casa Villena that his career was over. He would never be able to paint again. Few were deceived. And as the year progressed, as he gained strength, he discovered that far from having lost his powers, he had attained a fluency of conception quite new to his work.

He was ecstatic, almost euphoric. He began a large number of canvases, devoting himself briefly now to one, now to another. None pleased him more than a view and plan of Toledo which he intended as a gift of gratitude to Salazar de Mendoza for having, according to Jerónima, saved his life. It was a fantasy, bearing no similarity at all to the landscape he had done years before.

As his strength continued to return, Domenikos worked with a single-minded fury. Alarmed not merely for his health now but for his life, Jerónima again and again attempted to persuade him to slow his pace. Jorge, who failed to comprehend his father's prodigies of creation, pointed out that while he was applying himself to a dozen paintings simultaneously, he appeared to be finishing very few.

"That's all right. If I were to drop dead, you'd be able to complete what I've left undone. I've blocked in the essentials. The point is to make as many beginnings as I can. It's what I need. Can't you understand that?"

Finally, Domenikos' intransigence was tacitly accepted. Cadaverous now, emaciated, but possessed by the conviction that his survival depended on work, he drove himself feverishly, pausing with bitter reluctance for a midday meal but refusing wine because it induced drowsiness. And, incredibly to those who loved him, he seemed to flourish, to gain force, beneath this terrible pressure. What, of them all, only Paravincino knew, was that he had at last embarked upon his painting of the Opening of the Fifth Seal. So awed and frightened was even Domenikos at what he was now creating he could not confide the knowledge of it to anyone within his own family.

The name of Francisco Pacheco was well known to Domenikos. From better-traveled friends, from the still-lamented Francesco de Preboste, and from his agents in Seville, Pacheco's native city, he had heard extravagant praise for this scholar, painter, and teacher of art. At the end of 1610, he received a courteous letter from this man requesting an opportunity to meet "the great El Greco." Pacheco was touring the major cities of Spain, interviewing artists of all descriptions with a view to composing a history of the country's art.

The *Sevillano* came to Toledo early the next year and was received by the painter almost at once. It was soon evident that the two men would find greater areas of disagreement than of accord. For as soon as Domenikos began, in a monotone, a recital of the essential details of his career, describing Candia, Titian, and Rome, Pacheco broke in to inquire if he had known Michelangelo.

"He died before I left Venice."

The visitor sighed. "The father of painting."

The artist snorted. "He was a good man, but he knew nothing about painting."

Pacheco plainly considered this the most outrageous of apostasies. "I can't believe you mean that, maestro."

"But I do, Don Francisco. He was a great sculptor, but no painter." Domenikos pointed with his cane to a picture at the far end of the studio. "I owe him a great deal, nevertheless. Let me show you."

Pacheco, still stunned, assisted the painter across the room. The painting was a representation of the great Laocöon group he had so often sketched in Michelangelo's Campidoglio. Almost finished, the brilliantly illuminated blue-gray bodies of Laocöon and his wretched son seemed to writhe, to coil as did the serpents in their hideous mission of revenge and punishment. Beneath a sky streaked with angry clouds was a view of Toledo and its barren hills beyond.

Shuddering, the guest turned to face the artist, his face tormented. "Your boldness amazes me. You dispute Aristotle's rule that the artist must record objects with fidelity to their form and nature?"

Domenikos laughed. "I no longer paint objects. I paint the spirit, the soul."

"If that's so," said Pacheco with steely politeness, "perhaps you'd be good enough to show me how you do this miracle."

The artist nodded, and moved with difficulty toward a chair that stood before a large canvas of the Immaculate Conception, the principal work for the Oballe Chapel. Groaning, he seated himself and took up his palette and brushes. Breathing heavily, Pacheco stood directly behind him as he began, with characteristic haste, to apply broad streaks of bright yellow to the robes of an angel who dominated the lower third of this celestial scene.

The audacity of his technique was matched by the daring of his colors—the intense green, the brilliant rose, the icy blue, the irrides-

cent white. As he worked, his visitor's breathing increased in rapidity. After perhaps ten minutes, it seemed he would burst if he remained silent.

"And this is really how you paint?"

Domenikos set down the palette and wiped his fingers on a clean
rag. "You don't think I'd pretend, do you, as a bravura gesture?"

"Naturally not. But if you work at such a pace, your production
must be enormous."

With a motion of his hand, Domenikos invited Pacheco to sit down.
"Ah, if I only could. I work in bursts, Don Francisco. I've been at this
picture for almost three years, for example, and I imagine it will be
another year before it's done."

"You find it useful to keep so many paintings in process at one
time?"

"I go back to them, do a bit here and a bit there. It can take years.
My pictures are in a constant state of change. In one sense, I suppose,
they're never really finished. But at a given moment, I'm compelled
to part with them, finished or not."

Pacheco smiled smugly. "I always know when a picture is finished."
He paused. "I can't help thinking your method very disorderly."

"I think it sensible, for myself."

The visitor shook his head. "If I had a pupil who treated his work
as you do yours, I'd dismiss him. I demand that the rules be obeyed,
the pictures be planned and that the plan be followed."

"Those are good rules for children, but they confine the man."

"I've never felt confined, maestro. My rules fit me as easily as my
tunic."

"Then I envy you."

Pacheco looked reprovingly at the Immaculate Conception. "No,
I don't like it. I know a lad in Seville, a pupil of Herrera's named
Velázquez who's only twelve. *He* could do better justice to that scene
than you have."

Domenikos' laughter was soft, but it was edged with anger. "Then
I suggest, Don Francisco, that you hurry back there at once and bring
him under your wing. He's a genius."

The guest smiled complacently. "It's already arranged, maestro.
And let me assure you that I shall never permit him the extravagances
you've shown me today."

"No doubt you'll do your best. But let's imagine that after he es-
capes your wise and orderly protection he chooses to ignore those laws
you think immutable."

"He won't. There's no danger of that. Why should he ignore them? He's not mad."

The painter studied the visitor with an interest that was now wholly hostile. "You think me mad?"

"Governably so, of course, but plainly mad."

Domenikos' hands gripped the arms of his chair until the knuckles went dead white. "Then it appears that we've been wasting each other's time. I have my work to do, and you must want to hasten away, to rediscover the certainties I've shattered."

The artist loudly summoned Jorge, who appeared so quickly that it seemed likely he had been posted just outside the studio door. The son's expression of mingled consternation and delight was confirmation of this suspicion.

"It might be enlightening, Jorge, if you took Don Francisco through the workshop. Show him how we do things." He hesitated, smiling with a sweetness he hoped would seem inquisitorial. "Only after this tour can you fully comprehend to what extent my madness, as you put it, is governed." He looked away. "I bid you good day."

Pacheco followed his guide without a word. Jorge paused at the door and considered his father for an instant, his eyes apprehensive. "Are you all right, papa?"

Domenikos nodded, waving him out of the room with an impatient wave of the hand. But as soon as the door had been softly closed, he leaned heavily back in the chair, giving himself up to a sudden shortness of breath, a heavy pounding of his heart, a sharp little pain, a stab that made him gasp—and then silence, thick, like velvet, black and sumptuous; he slipped into oblivion.

Thirty-Five

Domenikos Theotokopoulos did not die. This second attack devastated the household but it was soon evident that it had not been nearly so severe as the first. On balance, it proved salutary, for the painter at last conceded that he had been attempting too much. He would, after his recovery, curtail his schedule of work, a promise which he appeared inclined, if only for a time, to keep.

Jorge Manuel appeared to have learned much about management

since becoming master of the workshops. Now he presided, with an efficiency that gratified his parents, over a household that numbered well over fifty people. The painter willingly admitted to Jerónima the error of his earlier misgivings about "the boy," as he nevertheless continued to call him. He should, as she had insisted, have had more confidence in him, more faith.

A major test of Jorge's capacities occurred only a few months after Pacheco's disastrous visit. The Queen, Margaret of Austria, died as she was giving birth to her fourth child. The Duke of Lerma proclaimed a period of national mourning. All the great cities committed themselves to orgies of official regret. Masses were intoned around the clock. Bells tolled dolorously throughout the daylight hours.

Toledo's Ayuntamiento decided that an impressive catafalque should be erected in the cathedral. The *alcalde mayor,* a frequent visitor to the Casa Villena because of his connection with the Oballe Chapel commission, pressed Domenikos at least to furnish the design. Jorge could supervise the production.

The old master sat in the salon of his house, a room to which he often repaired now to receive his guests. He shook his bald head slowly, painfully, as if almost unable to make the flesh comply with his wishes. He looked toward the distant window through which he could glimpse, bathed in a remorseless summer sunlight, the burned green hillsides across the Tajo.

"I dislike the principle of the thing, *alcalde.* To have the workshops expend so great an effort on a work that's only temporary. How long will it stay in the cathedral? A year? No more. And yet you want my people to interrupt everything they're doing to rush this object to completion."

The official at once shifted his attack. "It would be a great thing for Jorge, maestro."

A wry smile contracted Domenikos' deeply creased features. "Yes, I see." He turned to his son. "You're the master now."

The young man nodded and turned to the mayor. "How soon would you require this, *alcalde?*"

"As soon as possible, of course."

"Would three weeks be satisfactory?"

Domenikos was aghast. "You're mad. Three weeks? It's not possible."

"I think it is, papa. If the men will work by candlelight, we might do it in even less time."

Eighteen days later, the immense catafalque of painted wood was installed in the nave of the cathedral. With Jerónima and their son, Domenikos made his way along the winding, cobbled streets of his beloved city to behold this *tour de force* in its place of honor.

He stood for several minutes, transfixed, at the end of the nave, tears in his eyes, staring at this monument to the royal consort. He approached it, still supported by son and mistress, then, gazing constantly upward, he circled it slowly. Finally he stopped and turned to the red-eyed, exhausted Jorge, sniffing contemptuously.

"The paint's still wet, for God's sake."

Jerónima laughed. "What a beast you are."

The artist shrugged. "Still, Jorge, it makes a wonderful impression, doesn't it? To have done what you did in so little time . . . well, as I said, I didn't think it possible. I'm proud of you."

The men embraced.

The reception accorded the catafalque was unqualified in its adulation. So moved was Paravincino that he composed a sonnet in its praise, taking care to pay tribute as well to the dead Queen. And yet, within a week of its installation, the great structure was dismantled and his parts returned to the cavernous storage rooms of the Casa Villena. A rueful Jorge explained to his indignant father that the King had ordered an end to the period of official mourning.

Domenikos was incredulous. "In Spain? He dares to be so callous?"

"Well, he was hunting when he heard the news of her death, and he couldn't even be bothered to go to Madrid for her funeral."

"That can't be true of a son of Philip II. I thought he had such a reputation for piety."

Jorge knew no other facts. As usual, however, Castilla was better informed. Rumors had been rife that the Queen had been an intimate party to a plot to overthrow the King. Moreover, the story now current was that the principal conspirator was Lerma's own son. No one yet knew all the facts, but it was clear that Philip was convinced of his wife's complicity. He regarded the great display of mourning not an expression of respect for her but of contempt for him.

Domenikos looked gloomily at his son. "But what a blow for you."

Jorge was philosophical. "We were paid the full fourteen hundred ducats we asked for, papa. And the *alcalde* all but promised me the commission for completing the work on the Ayuntamiento. So it's not a total loss."

The son's appreciation of the situation was correct. Early in the following year he was commissioned to make plans for the construction of the remaining portion of Juan de Herrera's fine town hall.

Although he rejoiced in the reflected glory of Jorge's new-found success as an architect, Domenikos was gloomy on his own account.

"I'm not allowed to work," he complained to Angulo. "That's what's killing me, Gregorio. I'm a dying man. I'm perishing, as plants do in the autumn. The frost of age is creeping over my leaves. Two hours a day. That's all they'll give me in my studio."

The lawyer was amused. "What self-pity. You ought to be ashamed of yourself. You'll be around as long as Titian was, and then, no doubt, you'll be run down in the street by an ass and cart."

"I'm serious, Gregorio. I'm dying."

"You have messages from above?"

"My body and my brain inform me. Every day I can feel more of the force of life seeping from me, one dismal drop after another. It's torture, like standing by helplessly as your house and everything in it burns to the ground." He paused, and Angulo saw that his old friend was indeed serious. "I think I should do something about a burial place."

"In Santo Tomé?"

"No. In Santo Domingo. My altarpieces there are the first work I did in Toledo. I'd like to lie in the place where I began."

"It's unusual, Greco."

"I don't see why. Titian is buried in the Frari, but his parish church was San Canciano."

The lawyer nodded. "Jorge and I will see to it. What do you have in mind?"

"A small chapel, near the transept. I'll make a painting for it."

"We'll arrange it. But stop fretting yourself with such dark thoughts, Greco. You're not dead yet."

"No," the painter said, "but soon." His voice grew almost inaudible. "Soon now."

The year 1612 dragged miserably on for Domenikos. As Jorge's successes multiplied, his own energies continued to ebb. To friends, he repeated his pathetic litany of despair, assuring them that he wasn't much longer for this world.

Only the vibrant Paravicino, now prior of the Trinitarians in

Toledo, seemed able to lift even a corner of the pall. And he had been away for some months, attempting, as he explained on his return, "to overcome the bigotry of the King," whom he had much impressed some years before.

It seemed paradoxical to everyone but Jerónima and the painter himself that the occasion for a revival of his spirits and his urge to paint should be Angulo's announcement just before Christmas that a funerary chapel in Santo Domingo had been placed at his disposal. The transformation was remarkable. As soon as the lawyer departed, Domenikos hastened at his now-retarded pace to his studio and there immediately began, with all the frenzy of the period between his two seizures, to design the painting for his ultimate resting place, an Adoration of the Shepherds, the theme of the first freely painted work he had ever done for Titian more than half a century earlier. The new version, however, would differ from any other he had made, be comparable in intensity, in brilliance of color, in exaggeration of form to convey the sense of upward movement and in luminosity, only with the Immaculate Conception for the Oballe Chapel, now nearly finished.

As 1612 ended, Domenikos recognized in moments of contemplation to what a degree his startling restoration was attributable to his fear that he might not live long enough to complete this picture. As if to defy his grim forebodings, he began attacking several other commissions.

In contrast to the dramatic treatment of the Adoration of the Shepherds was the tranquil, intimate, almost quietist painting of the Visitation, an oblong picture to be mounted on the ceiling of the Oballe Chapel, "as in Illescas," the *alcalde's* contract stipulated. He conceived it in direct contradiction to the formula generally accepted. It was a scene of bewilderment, of lostness. Everything about it suggested mystery, secrecy, and above all, simplicity. For he had chosen to depict the moment after Mary and Elizabeth had spoken, after each woman realized what was happening, a moment of letdown. They ceased to speak. They could only look at each other in stunned, silent astonishment, in awe. What was happening in their wombs was miraculous. In the most intimate possible way, they had been touched by the hand of God.

Thus did Domenikos explain his penultimate painting—to his oldest and dearest friend, Luis de Castilla.

The dean of Cuenca smiled. "Blessed is the name of El Greco."

Paravicino, during a recent visit at court, had so praised Jorge to the spiritually unreconstructed King that Philip III demanded that the young Toledan proceed forthwith into the royal presence.

Domenikos was happy. Jorge would succeed where he himself had failed; he would secure the patronage and protection of the King. To Castilla he said, "You told me that the Orgaz Burial painting was my apotheosis. You were wrong. I knew that. In fact, it seems that I'm to have it in my son. That's how it should be."

But it was not to be. Jorge's mission was a failure. He found the King vapid and whimsical. There was a vague promise that at some future date a project might come up that was suitable for the son of El Greco, but apart from polite admiration of studies for pictures and proposed buildings and sculpture, Philip had been, in terms of definite commissions, very elusive.

Paravicino, though disappointed, remained confident that the auguries were favorable. He was chatting casually with the painter and his son in the spacious salon of the Casa Villena when, inspired by what whim Domenikos never knew, the prior suddenly turned to him and, with an odd urgency in his tone, altered completely the tenor of the conversation.

"When will you show me the Fifth Seal?"

Domenikos reeled. He felt his weight fall heavily back in the couch, as if he had been struck sharply across the face. In the gathering darkness of the December afternoon, he looked at the coffered ceiling, at last speaking thickly.

"It was only this morning that I felt I'd opened it completely." He leaned forward, still giddy, and struggled to his feet. "We'll have to get the servants to bring candles, but I think you'd better see it now."

Paravicino rose quickly to take the master's arm, and protested. "It can wait until there's full light."

The painter stubbornly shook his head, and forced his way forward. "I don't think so," he muttered darkly.

Aided by the monk and a surprised and puzzled Jorge, Domenikos shuffled slowly through the long series of rooms, the broad doorways, the lofty, narrow corridors that separated the salon from his studio. Servants were summoned to bring all the candelabra in the house.

Aware of the oddness of the request, perhaps intuitively stirred by its brusqueness, these domestics in their turn called all the other members of the household to join them—the painters, the carpenters, the gilders, and lastly, Jerónima, Alfonsa, and the nine-year-old Gabriel.

Like lemmings rushing toward the sea, all hastened, not immediately comprehending yet fearful to refuse, toward the master's studio.

Silent, except for the occasional rustle of clothing or scuffing of shoes on the dusty tiled floor, all stood against the row of unfinished paintings that lined a long, distant wall, watching with fascination as the bent figure of Domenikos, flanked by Jorge and Paravicino, stood in the brilliant amber of the candlelight before the picture the prior had asked about.

The painting of the Fifth Seal of the Apocalypse wasn't a very big one. Nor was it brilliant in range of tone or color. Only remotely could its atmosphere compare with that of the Laocöon legend, but there was no evidence of landscape. Indeed, it lacked everything—except people, all nude save for a blue-robed figure in the left foreground. And beyond the strange, straining, tormented souls, there was a sky, muddy and morose, pierced here and there with a light one could only imagine to be apocalyptic. As he stared at this painting in silence, Domenikos perceived that he could press his art no further along the chartless pass he had followed for so long. It was an end.

Without turning back to the picture, but solemnly, as if he were speaking from a pulpit, Paravicino recited the scriptural words here so frighteningly delineated: " 'And when he had opened the fifth seal, I saw under the altar the souls of them that were slain for the word of God, and for the testimony which they held: And they cried with a loud voice, saying, How long, O Lord, holy and true, dost thou not judge and avenge our blood on them that dwell on the earth? And white robes were given unto every one of them; and it was said unto them, that they should rest yet for a little season, until their fellow servants also and their brethren, that should be killed as they were, should be fulfilled.' "

The final phrase hung portentously in the air of the great room. Then all at last was silence. Domenikos detached his right arm from his son's grasp and brought the white sleeve of his linen blouse to his nose. He sniffed.

"It's too bad Castilla isn't here. He'd say that I've not kept to the letter of the text. There's only one white robe in it."

He slowly revolved on the arms of his son and young friend and, in the dancing light of the candles, for the first time saw that the entire household was gathered behind him. He took a single step forward and lifted a tired arm in greeting.

"I thank you from my heart for this gesture of your affection. I hope I shall rest with you yet for a little season." He silenced himself and turned, looking first at the weeping Jorge Manuel, then at this painting he had so fearfully brought near its completion. He smiled. "But I am fulfilled."

It was a very little season. On April 7, 1614, Domenikos Theotokopoulos, at peace with man and God, died in his sleep.